LAND OF TEARS

Park Sangseek

LAND OF TEARS

Park Sangseek

Translated by Inyoung Choi

Homa & Sekey Books
Paramus, New Jersey

FIRST EDITION

Copyright © 2018 by Korea Digital Library Forum
English Translation Copyright © 2018 by Inyoung Choi
This publication was supported by a grant from the Literature Translation Institute
of Korea (LTI Korea).
Published by arrangement with Korea Digital Library Forum

All rights reserved. No part of this book may be reproduced, stored in a retrieval
system, or transmitted in any form, or by any means, electronic, mechanical, photo-
copying, recording or otherwise, without prior permission from the publisher.

Library of Congress Cataloging-in-Publication Data

Names: Pak, Sang-sik, author. | Ch0oe, In-yfong, 1967- translator.
Title: Land of tears / Park Sangseek ; translated by Inyoung Choi.
Description: First edition. | Paramus, New Jersey : Homa & Sekey Books, 2018.
Identifiers: LCCN 2017057680 | ISBN 9781622460496 (pbk.)
Subjects: LCSH: Korea--Fiction.
Classification: LCC PL994.62.S257 A2 2018 | DDC 895.73/5--dc23 LC record
available at https://lccn.loc.gov/2017057680

Published by Homa & Sekey Books
3rd Floor, North Tower
Mack-Cali Center III
140 E. Ridgewood Ave.
Paramus, NJ 07652

Tel: 201-261-8810, 800-870-HOMA
Fax: 201-261-8890
Email: info@homabooks.com
Website: www.homabooks.com

Printed in U.S.A.
1 3 5 7 9 10 8 6 4 2

TABLE OF CONTENTS

Translator's Note

Land of Tears by Park Sangseek is an anthology of short stories about the Korean experience of poverty and mental and physical anguish. The collection is about the period of 1950 to 1962, the time after Liberation from the Japanese and the Korean War. In this anthology of short stories, the author has recreated what he has experienced and witnessed from the first two periods of his life in accordance with his literary point of view.

In the twenty-one stories of the anthology, all the stories except two have to do directly or indirectly with the Korean War. This shows how paramount the War was in shaping the author's literary perspective. In September of 1962, the author left South Korea and embarked on a US military vessel to go study in America. It was on this voyage that he made up his mind to pursue his studies in political science, shifting from literature. The author had undergone Japanese Colonialism, Japanese militarism, the division of his country, domestic political crisis and turmoil, economic impoverishment, the Korean War, and the April Revolution of 1960 in a span of thirty years. The twenty-one stories in *Land of Tears* were for the most part written during this era of turbulence that was the second phase of his life (1952-1962). Undoubtedly, it was the Korean War and the April Revolution that he underwent that led to this decision because from what he had seen and heard during the first phases of his life, he had come to believe that the driving force behind human history is man's desire for power. But he didn't reach this conclusion from in-depth research to support his thesis. It was not until the second phase of his life where he was able to carry out a broader study, coupled with research that he gained conviction of this belief.

In these stories, Park Sangseek poses the following two central questions: What constitutes a human being? How can one discover the basic nature of a person? The author believes that there are two ways in which these two questions can be elucidated. One is to place a person in an extreme condition and observe how he behaves; the other is to place a person in a diametrically opposed extreme situation where he is happy and watch how he acts. In the *Land of Tears* anthology, Park Sangseek has for the most part chosen the former circumstances to examine his thesis by asking: How do people act when they have seized political power? How do they respond when they have come face to face with death? How does a person behave when he is about to die of starvation? What consequences do wars and revolutions bring about? The author endeavors to better understand those fundamental questions of human existence by way of the human actions in the most extreme circumstances, in each of the stories.

The stories depict characters such as a North Korean People's Army soldier, a South Korean Communist Party Partisan member, the wife of a Partisan, the life of an ordinary South Korean person in the midst of hardship during the Korean War, the life of a North Korean refugee, and the anguish of a South Korean intellectual. The common thread running through all these characters is the author's portrayal of the inextinguishable humanity in each one of them. In no sense are these people monstrous or less than human, even in the severest of human circumstances. In fact, the author shows how the most extreme hardship that each of the characters encounters draws out the most exalted nature of being human. Therein lies the literary distinction of *Land of Tears*, which depicts the particularities of the traumatic Korean twentieth-century tragedy; yet, it is about the manifestation of transcendent human nature in the worst possible circumstances.

Song of Devotion

The clouds lined the sky like a silk drape and the deserted mountainous road was filled with the fragrance of the azalea. Lord Sunjeong, Kim Yun-jeong turned around to look at the group of people turning the ridge and after spotting the palanquin with his wife, floating in the air like a lotus leaf, he then relaxed. The white horse he was riding on felt like it was gliding through the blue clouds in the sky. His nose was suddenly overwhelmed by a powerful saline smell that spread from the east. He turned to the official, who had come to receive him from Gangneung, to inquire what the smell was and he responded by twitching his nose and raising his hand toward the east. It was the smell of salt carried in the wind. Kim Yun-jeong was on the way to his new post in Gangneung, a coastal town.

It could be embarrassing for Yun-jeong, of royal lineage, to move to a far, remote place since it could be viewed as an exile, however, apart from worldly affairs or an appointment, he harbored one and only joy and pleasure in his heart. As a member of Hwarangdo, he could not deny wanting to be active part of a unified Seorabeol (capital of the Silla Dynasty), but for his wife, Choga, the ascension to the throne or a high-ranking position was immaterial to him. The several thousand *li* journey he was undertaking along the East Sea did not feel solitary or draining not because it was springtime but from his belief that his wife, who was as lovely as a lotus flower, would soon become joyous. It pained him to reflect on how there was still a distance between his wife and himself after almost a decade of being married. She appeared to be bereft of any desire to have a close relationship in this life, wanting to live in this world all alone. Yun-jeong thought that

1

might be the reason why they were childless but how terrifying if it were from the absence of love for him that caused it. It was a thought he wanted to put out of his mind for good. Was the rumor true that her heart belonged to the servant, Jinul? It didn't look like she could tolerate a mountainous village after living in a bustling place near the palace in Seoul where there was a mob of people all year round, however, if it was her wish to return to Myeongju, her birthplace and spend the rest of her life, amidst the passing seasons and ripening wild berries, then he would oblige gladly. Yun-jeong wanted to find out why his wife, who had been full of laughter and joy, was no longer the woman he once knew. That was why he constantly instructed the junior official to check his wife's mood, while he in the lead got the official from Myeongju to inform him of the village news, stopping every now and then for his wife to enjoy the scenery to her heart's content. He was elated to hear from the junior official that after passing Jukbyeong and Gigok she appeared much lighter-hearted than when she left Seoul, showing pleasure and excitement like an innocent child over the scenery, also asking the people around her their whereabouts. He almost felt like bringing her out of that tight space in the palanquin and put her behind him on his horse.

Yun-jeong was hastening their crossing to have lunch at the next town when the provincial official came to a halt before him and said, "Lady Suro asks to rest here."

"How about if we take a good rest at Imwon where we will arrive shortly…But did she look fatigued?"

Then he added with a concerned voice, "There doesn't seem to be any inn nearby…"

The provincial official pointed at a pub alongside their path. He waited until his wife's palanquin reached him and asked,

"Is it tedious?"

"No. It's just that the blue water and the cliff look as though they've been carved by hand…it is a rather pleasing scenery."

"I see. And indeed, it is. Your description of it is more pleasing."

It was a beautiful sight. He was chagrined that he did not become aware of it first. But then it seemed more charming because his wife discovered it, for he could've just passed through had he been journeying alone. No, it was true the scenery looked beautiful because it had appealed to his enchanting wife.

Lady Suro came out of the palanquin and took gentle steps back along the path they had traveled, viewing the awesome nature-sculpted cliff that adorned the seashore like a wall painting. Her glowing face was so serene and the contour of her face exquisitely soft that the ethereal beauty of the woman would daze anyone.

The dress like a cloud around her rustled as she took one step after the other, barely showing her blue shoes. Everyone stood around speechless, thinking that a Bodhisattva incarnate would have the same look as Lady Suro. She exuded a radiant dignity that seemed beyond the realm of an ordinary person.

"Goodness, look at that azalea." She was smitten with the azalea that she spotted on their way here. A luminous azalea, as in a dream, was swaying in the wind against the backdrop of a blue sky when one bent the neck and looked up at the bluff. Everyone had his eyes fixed on a spot where Lady Suro's finger was pointing.

"Can someone pick it…is it not possible?"

"What a rare proposal…there is not a person who can pick that azalea up there in all of Seorabeol. It is all the more precious treasure since what everyone wants cannot be had by anyone." The junior official from Myeong-ju said, with an askance glance at Yun-jeong.

"That is why I must have it. I want that lovely treasure…Ah…"

Lady Suro trembled in excitement and a fine shiver ran over her face. Yun-jeong rushed to his wife, and as he supported her by her shoulder, he had to give the bluff just one look before he shuddered. How joyous his wife would be if he were to pick that azalea for her? How she would shake if she saw him climbing over the cliff to pluck the flower that no one in Seorabeol was capable of picking. At the moment of getting the azalea from the peak, ah, if she desired the flower even at the price of my life—but I couldn't. I can't let this lovely heavenly maiden tremble with fear. With the azalea in hand, she might fly away, back to the heaven.

Resolutely, Yun-jeong looked around him but he did not find anyone who showed willingness. Instead, they all evaded his eye.

"I wish I hadn't seen that flower. Now I won't take another step unless…"

"I shall offer a thousand *nyang* to anyone."

Yung-jeong wanted to possess her, more than the azalea. He wanted the heavenly maiden more than he wanted to die for her. Though he knew there would be no one who would come forward, he shouted aloud, "Is there no one? I will offer as much as you ask."

Right then, a man with a big cow approached them from behind the pub. He did not appear too old; however, with his white hair and shabby clothes, he seemed at least ten years older than his age. One of his eyes showed only white, making him blind on one side.

He bowed deep and said, "If I may, I will try."

"Who are you? Where are you from?"

"I live in the valley of Imwon."

"You will climb up that cliff? And pluck the flower?"

"How much do you desire?"

"I do not ask for anything."

"You're asking for nothing?"

The old man, Jinul, had been waiting ardently for the journey of Lord Sunjeong to his new appointment. He had the cow graze everyday on the path he and his entourage would pass, not to see Kim Yun-jeong but with the determination to see Mistress Choga, who hadn't been out of his mind even in his dream, and whom he wouldn't forget even after death. It was with the greatest longing to see the woman who was his old master and for whom he had devoted his heart. It scared him to know what motivated him to see her. He could be sure of only one thing and that was, if he couldn't see her then he wouldn't be able to die or let die. The Mistress will not know me. Neither will Lord

4

Sunjeong. He was quite stupefied to see Lord Sunjeong about to heed to the mistress's plea to pluck the flower for her. But he must not bring death upon himself. There isn't another man who is as devoted to the mistress as he. Her life would be so lonesome and scary if she were to live the life of a widow. But…as terrible as it may be…did she ask him to go up the cliff with the intention of killing him because she loves me therefore cannot forget me? No, that can't be. There can't be anyone who does not desire the beautiful royal azalea. There is nothing inappropriate about the mistress who is as lovely as a heavenly maiden to come in possession of a treasure that no one in Seorabeol could lay a hand on. Wouldn't it be glorious for me to die for that? I, too, have tried my utmost to pick that flower that seems to be instilled with a spirit. Jinul's only pleasure in life was raising his cow; he had no other ambition or desire, and that is why he lived the life of a recluse in the village of Imwon. He tied the cow to the rock. The cow mooed at the sight of the sea, sending out an echo to the valley across.

Jinul kept his eyes on the shimmering haze far in the distance for a long time, and then started climbing up the cliff. He was blind in one eye and had a blurry vision in the other. He went up by holding onto a stump and stepping on a jagged rock, then looking for more trunks to grab, groping his way up.

It was springtime when the petals of the cherry and apricot trees would fall profusely in the rear garden of the Yi Beol-chan residence in Seoul. Mistress Choga closed and opened her eyes with her arm around the apricot tree. Jinul, who returned from an errand for his lord, caught her.

"My Mistress, what're you looking at?"

"See over there. The bee is crawling inside the flower with lots of pollen on it. It is just crawling. There is honey made in the flower. Maybe…pluck me a branch."

"If I do that, all the petals will drop. Would you look at yourself? You look like you have on a petal wreath around you."

5

"Jinul, I'm bored to death. Shall we play hide and seek? I will count and you hide. One, two, three."

"My Mistress, the lord might hear you and you will be in trouble. You'll be punished for playing with a servant. Please go inside."

"Stop it. I think I'm going to die of boredom. I will die if I can't talk to other people."

He was deeply regretful of not taking a good look at the Mistress. The stump underneath his foot collapsed and he quickly shifted his foot to another rock. His shirt was wet with sweat already and his back itched. Warm sunshine sparkled above his head. The shimmering shadow of a pine tree whose roots sprouted out from the crevice of a boulder dazed his vision. Inside the paved concave of the rock, there was some kind of grass and a bird landed near it. He heard a sound from what felt like right underneath him but also from a road far down below the clouds.

"Jinul....Ji....nuuuul."

He wasn't sure if it were an actual voice or an echo but he heard it again.

"Jinul, Ji...nul."

It startled him and he almost missed his step. Who could be calling out my name? It can't be the Mistress...It must be my thought spoken aloud, which resounded in the mountains as I recalled the past from when I was a child.

Jinul had trained at swordsmanship in the mountains in order to free his father from false charges. A tiger attacked him when he roared. Why did the echo in the mountain reverberate so much? To avenge his father's enemy, he became a servant and practiced his swordsmanship; however, it was because of baby Choga that he put down his sword. Who had stolen the credit for the meritorious deed at Mobeol Fortress and who had cunningly conspired against his father with wiles and deprived him of his rank, thereby sending him into exile and murdering him? Jinul knew that but for Choga, he had renounced it all, to forget everything. On the night of the Autumn Game Day, he was standing discreetly behind her, who was singing the "Song of Defeat."

"It is me, Jinul. I didn't think there was anyone…"

"The moon can see you. What did you want to tell me?"

"Nothing. I simply wanted to look after you."

"You have really nothing to tell. Not even a story of the moon?"

"On the contrary, my Mistress, there is too much I want to tell but I can't say a word."

"What do you mean! Stop following me around all the time. There are other servants in the house. Go away from here. Don't show me your face. I might be leaving this house for good. Did you think I'd be here forever? I am being sold to another family."

"No…your marriage has been set? My Mistress!"

Choga cried her heart out in Jinul's bosom.

He looked up above, startled at the loud sound that was echoed back in his ear after muttering to himself. Salty blood ran down his face, from his forehead to his lips. The blood, combined with his sweat, dried up on his face. The crimson azalea was lush above his head and cast a shadow against the blue sky. Holding firmly on to the stump with his right hand, he picked the flower with his left hand. He felt a whiff of the fragrance of the flower on his face. He could no longer look down below him now. He held the flower as gingerly as when he was bequeathed the blue dragon sword, a family treasure from his father. He closed his eyes and took a step down.

Kim Yun-jeong was somewhat drunk. Or rather, he was trying to become drunk.

"I know everything. You can deceive the mountain god but not me. You coveted my precious Choga, my wife, servant that you are. You have dishonored the king of Seorabeol who abdicated. I don't want to disgrace the name of Hwarang blood. A man must purge himself of dishonor with a sword. Meet me at Yeona tomorrow midnight."

It wasn't Yun-jeong's intent to get into a sword battle or bring Jinul's life to end; however, he felt it unjust to gain a woman with matchless beauty in the whole kingdom without any arduous effort. How could he win a heavenly maiden like her without a deadly duel? It was unheard of. He wished to be recognized as the winner of a battle against a thousand competitors.

Snow blew with the powerful wind in the field of Yeona. Jinul pulled out his blue dragon sword. The duel of swords commenced in the air.

"Strike."

"Of course. What nonsense that an ignoble lowly servant can behold a beautiful maiden. You have laid your dirty eyes on the heavenly maiden. Thus, I will gouge out your eyes first."

"It was prescient that I used my sword against you. Do you believe your eyes will be safe?"

Yun-jeong fell after being struck on his arm with the sword by Jinul's blue dragon sword. Jinul returned home.

Yun-jeong summoned Jinul.

"I will pluck out your eyes which have Choga's image engraved on them."

"Have you gone mad? How do you intend to remove the visage of the mistress from my heart?"

That night, Yun-jeong stabbed one of Jinul's eyes.

"Ah…ah…" Jinul fell into a deep pit with a groan. The petals of the azalea flew like butterflies and landed on the ground. The rock Jinul rested his foot on loosened and rolled down.

"Jinul. It's me, Choga. I am here for you."

Lady Suro called out his name again and again, with the blood from his mouth smeared on her face as she held him close to her.

The Valley of the Shadow of Death

1. Prologue

Mount Jiri is not the tallest Korean mountain but it is the most renowned for there isn't a person who doesn't know about it. Mount Baekdu, the highest mountain, boasts of many myths about it, but Mount Jiri offers many fairy tales. There is hardly a Korean who, as a child, has not heard of a Mount Jiri hunter. Once upon a time, there were so many tigers that it was famously known as the land of tigers but it has now become a den of partisans for they now are the greatest in number.

There is a saying that once a person has witnessed the peak of Cheonwangbong at Mount Jiri being covered with snow three times, he has become familiar with winter. Nobody knows that on the slope of Cheonwangbong that there is a corpse, its flesh all rotted away with only the prostrate skeleton, freezing and thawing over a number of years. What could be the meaning of this weathered carcass that was tossed on the slope where there are hardly any human tracks? It is now winter and snow must cover the carcass so that even the crows don't know about it.

2. First Speculation

Surely the fate of human beings is like that of the animals; the same fate awaits them both: As one dies, so dies the other. All have the same breath; humans have no advantage over animals. Everything is meaningless. —*Ecclesiastes 3:19*

The jagged mountain ridge was covered with snow. The sleet was turning the sky upside down. The wind felt frozen the moment it wrapped around your body. Four people, blown away by the snowstorm, were going up the snow-covered ridge of a mountain, like a herd of animals. A man dressed in traditional Korean clothes collapsed on the snow. The man next to him, dressed in a People's Army uniform, who was also supporting wounded Yeung-bin, opened his eyes wide amidst the heavy snow. The blood from Yeung-bin's shoulder had seeped through the clothes of the fallen man. It was difficult to tell who was really injured. A woman, who was also attired in a People's Army uniform and carrying two submachine guns, looked at the man in a People's Army uniform, who turned around in great fear to see who was shot this time. Right then, the sound of a carbine rifle pierced through the sleet. Far away in the distant, dark valley a dull humming of an avalanche sent out an echo. The sleet that covered the whole sky collided against the ridge, being crushed. The man in Korean traditional clothes jumped up in panic.

"Hey, Comrade Jeong-jun, the bastards are ruthlessly after us."

The man in a People's Army uniform put Yeung-bin down on the snow-covered ground and began to untie his shoelace. The woman rushed forward and supported Yeung-bin with her shoulder.

"Comrade Park Nan, put your shoes on backward. Otherwise, we'll all perish here."

After he did just that, he went over to her. Park Nan, whose feet did not feel like they belonged to her, let him do what he said and turned to shake Yeung-bin's head forcefully. Instead of altering the position of his shoes, Jeong-jun adjusted the sack he was carrying on his back. Yeung-bin could feel the snow-covered soil that fell from the sack melting on his face.

"Chong-wi, let's take the shortcut by the side path," Jeong-jun said.

Baek Chong-wi got up after helping Park Nan with her shoes and when he noticed Jeong-jun hadn't corrected his shoes, he said with anxiety, "What are you doing? We don't have a second to lose."

"That's an outdated method. We, the partisans, will not resort to something that's not clever."

"So then, what're you going to do?"

"I will keep racing straight and you can take the side path. We have no other choice if we want to bring Comrade Yeung-bin."

"Nope, we can't do that. The only way is to cross this ridge. Let's go!"

"It will take us beyond sunset to climb over this mountain with a wounded man."

"Who's injured? We don't have time. We can't stall a moment here."

Instead of helping Yeung-bin up on his feet, Baek Chong-wi grabbed both submachine guns from Park Nan's back and started walking. The snowflake on Yeung-bin's earflap refused to melt. With a confounded look, Park Nan looked for the face of Jeong-jun as Baek Chong-wi marched on. Instead of a human face, a trace of it, devoid of smell and color, was what was formed in the snow. Jeong-jun vacantly looked down at Yeung-bin, who was being buried in the snow, but turned his face toward Baek Chong-wi when his eyes came in contact with Park Nan's pleading look.

"I am telling you not to go that way. There's no need for you to become an easy target."

"I told you already if the snow gets heavier, it won't leave any trace."

"We don't need that kind of cleverness. We're not descending the mountain but ascending it."

"So what should we do?"

"I am saying we should all move together. We can't abandon our comrade."

"He'll manage."

11

"I don't think so," Baek Chong-wi replied with certainty. He was confident that Park Nan would think more dearly of him than Yeung-bin who was from the same corps as he. When the UN forces severed the People's Army forces, their unit had retreated to Jiri Mountain. Comrade Park Nan was the announcer for the culture section of their brigade. Because both she and Yeung-bin worked in the same propaganda unit, they were inseparable. Since they joined the partisans here, they stayed in hiding, like wild pigs during the day, and pillaged the villages at night.

With his machine gun slung upside down, he was gazing down at the gorge where the village was buried in darkness. He simply wished all this would just end quickly.

"How can we leave behind someone who's still alive?" Jeong-jun's voice rose from below, barely audible as though the voice froze in mid-air. He imagined it as Park Nan's voice.

"When did I say we should abandon him? Stop talking nonsense."

Yeung-bin got up, leaning his shoulder against Park Nan's back. Looking in vain for a spot to hang on to, he shook, tightly grappling the air. They decided to go along with Baek Chong-wi and continue going up the ridge.

Swiftly grabbing Yeung-bin's hand, Jeong-jun said loudly on purpose for Baek Chong-wi to hear, "Please stop playing a risky game here. We should drag him along until he drops dead." Right then, a couple of gunshots was fired into the sky.

"We're being besieged!" Baek Chong-wi screamed fearfully.

"The Black Dog is signaling."

Dragging Yeung-bin's body, Jeong-jun ran up to where Baek Chong-wi was.

"All right, you take the side path as you wished. I am going to climb across," he said, like he was giving an order, as he looked around at Park Nan and told her in an almost whisper. "And you follow him."

He looked at both of them alternately and dashed forward. Baek Chong-wi remained dazed by his order, then briskly turned and ran to

Park Nan. He tapped her on the shoulder twice but all he could grab was a pile of snow. Park Nan's eyes shone amidst the blizzard.

"Let's go with Comrade Jeong-jun's advice and take the side path."

They set off, dragging Yeung-bin's body as though it was an object cut into two pieces. Park Nan preferred to move by holding him but Baek Chong-wi would've rather pulled him. Yeung-bin put weight on both his feet, as though he was running on his own strength. But the tip of his feet raked through the snow as they slid. Occasionally, his feet would bump against a tree trunk underneath the snow, buried like a clam in the sand. Each time, a spasm ran through his body. A stone was dragged along for quite a distance until it fell into a hole. Park Nan's body collided against the trunk of a pine tree. The frozen snow on the branches fell on the ground, like broken pieces of the sky. From right above their head, a wild bird fluttered its wings and flew away in the blizzard. Yeung-bin's hair stood on its end. He felt life burning up from his head to the ground. The two people were exhausted. They found it difficult to untangle their feet, even against a small tree trunk. The two collapsed at the hilltop. The snow reached their knees. Park Nan searched for Yeung-bin's wrist. She couldn't tell whether or not his hand had any warmth, for her hands were almost frozen. She tried desperately to look for the veins. She brought her cheek closer to his nose. There was a slight steam and a smell of flesh. She put his hand down and combed his hair with her fingers. As though she was looking for something, she clutched a fistful of his hair or held a strand with two fingers, examining it at the root, looking at his face very closely.

Baek Chong-wi, who was watching her quietly from behind, said, "Not much we can do?"

His breathing had become harsher. Park Nan's eyes quivered. He looked for the dagger around his waist. He could feel the cold metal all the way to his head. His hand by the dagger, he walked toward Park Nan.

"We don't have time. Get up. Take this gun. I'll drag him by my-self." He took off the submachine gun and handed it to her. Holding the gun in her arms, she stepped back from him, for he felt too revolting to her. Baek Chong-wi groped for his dagger again. He held it by its grip and looked down at Yeung-bin's body for a long time. Then bending Yeung-bin's torso, he helped him sit up. Yeung-bin stretched his hand up in the air and made a motion of urging them to go. Baek Chong-wi pulled out his dagger with force and took a few steps forward. He felt the tip of the dagger against his pants. Park Nan's face shimmered in front of him.

"Ah," Yeung-bin made a strenuous and excruciating sound as he fell over.

"Nan, let's hurry. Let's hurry. We must end it. We have to."

Like a man talking gibberish, Baek Chong-wi jabbered as he walked toward Park Nan.

3.

Dying was nothing... But living was a field of grain blowing in the wind on the side of a hill. Living was a hawk in the sky. —Ernest Hemingway, *For Whom the Bell Tolls*

The sky was as turbulent as a tempestuous sea. A wall of the blizzard, like a huge wave, crashed against the ridge. The snowflakes splashed like foam. It looked like at any moment a heavy snow landslide would bury a whole village ensconced in pitch darkness between the ridges. Sporadic gunshots pierced the sky, leaving a white trail in the air. The night that was crouching in the valley echoed like some specter.

There were four shadows, like a wild boar shot by a hunter, fleeing along the mountain ridge. A mound of snow that covered the ridge rolled over in the blizzard. Another gunshot was fired. One of the two people, who were holding the man from each side, wearing knee breeches, fell down. From right behind them, the woman dressed in a People's Army uniform, who was carrying two submachine guns upside down, dashed forward, her face, panic-stricken. The man who fell with a sack across his back couldn't get himself up for a long time, but then abruptly got on his feet with an amazing alacrity. The woman, in place of the man in Korean attire, dragged the injured along. Blood from the injured man's leg seeped through the snow as his body shook. The sound of the gunshots closed in around them.

"Baek Chong-wi! Let's take the side path," the man in Korean clothes shouted. Snow flooded his mouth as he spoke.

"No, we should continue this way."

"The blizzard is hitting us from the front. At this rate, we'll all be captured any moment."

"The snow will cover our traces."

Then the woman fell. Baek Chong-wi's heart paused with the fear that she might've been shot. He let go of the injured man and raised the woman.

"Nan, have you been shot?" he asked and shook her by the shoulder. Nan's faint smile was visible in the dark. Her face was frozen stiff and only wrinkles indicated a smile that froze around her mouth. The man in Korean clothes took hold of the injured man who fell with his clenched fists in the air. Shaking his almost frozen wrist, he cried out, "Hey Comrade Yeung-bin, stay alert. We're almost there."

His pants were wet with Yeung-bin's blood. Because her hand was completely numb Nan felt his vein but she couldn't tell whether or not he had any warmth left in his body or if his pulse was beating. Furthermore, the blood beating in her heart was too loud for her to tell if what she could sense of his pulse was actually his or hers. Nan brought her cheek closer to Yeung-bin's nose. A breath, smelling like flesh, washed over her cheek.

"Do you want to perish here?" Baek Chong-wi, who was watching her, reproached her with a stern voice. He and the man in Korean clothes began climbing up the slope, dragging the body of Yeung-bin, which was more like a corpse. Yeung-bin's two legs raked through the snow like a hoe in the sand. Like clams that were caught by a hoe, Yeung-bin's feet jammed into a tree trunk or stones in the snow. Why does my body feel so heavy when my mind is quite lucid? Why does my body want to tear away from me? On my left, I have the dependable Baek Chong-wi and to my right is the partisan comrade. But then, where is my dear Nan? Where could she be? Ah, my mind is so clear but my body has vanished! Where is Nan? What is going on, I can't turn my head? It seemed like his bottom half had been sucked into something.

Yeung-bin and Baek Chong-wi were fellow soldiers who worked together in the culture section of a brigade. When the UN severed the boat route from Incheon for the North Korean People's Army, they became as a mouse caught in a trap. It led to chaos when they tried to find a way to escape. They had no choice but to flock to Mount Jiri, and together with the partisans there, they pillaged the villagers in the mountains. Park Nan and Yeung-bin were inseparable, for she was the announcer for the culture section of the brigade, while he was the writer of propaganda.

A rock caught by Yeung-bin's foot dragged along with him for quite a distance until it got buried underneath a pit created by an avalanche. What felt like an electric current ran through Yeung-bin's foot to head.

In order to survive winter, they had all together set out to amass food before the snow mounted. It was reckless to begin with for them to barge into the village without an initial search.

The wild goose flew across the sky, leaving a trail of their cry. Some of it felt like it had been transmitted to his head, and then it began to resonate in his chest when all of a sudden it turned into a sound of an exploding avalanche. The body was crushed, with all its parts torn into pieces. But the spirit felt like it was floating in the space. The sound of the geese was still heard like a whistle. The face of Baek Chong-wi spun before his eyes, then only his nose could be seen; and his eyes were the only thing remaining with the nose and the ear floating around soon thereafter. The sound of the geese was still heard through the space. Baek Chong-wi had difficulty keeping balance as the slightest tree trunk was a disruption and caught his leg. Yeung-bin's legs, messy with blood and snow, looked like a chunk of novel creation. A rock was caught in his leg and something stuck to his flesh; it was excruciatingly painful. Yeung-bin screamed in pain and passed out; without thinking, Baek Chong-wi and the man in Korean clothes slumped down alongside him. The cry of Yeung-bin echoed on all four sides. It seemed as though the sound would never vanish but permeate through all things to resound again. The man in Korean clothes felt Yeung-bin's vein which was still. The three of them, with their spirits dispossessed, looked down at the body of Yeung-bin who was being covered up with snow. Snow turned into ice on their eyebrows. How much time had passed? They came to their senses when a ball of snow fell from a tree branch. Yeung-bin opened his eyes and for the first time he looked at the sky. Right above him, there was a body of a partisan frozen like a snowman.

"Hey, what was your name?"

"It's me, Jeong-jun. Don't you recognize me?"

Nan grabbed him and placed his head on her knee. Yeung-bin did not open his eyes again. Jeong-jun turned around to Baek Chong-wi and shook his head, saying, "There's nothing we can do."

"We must leave him behind," Baek Chong-wi said and inspected Nan's mood. Right then, there was gunshot fired close by.

"I don't want him to suffer anymore."

"So what do you suggest? Isn't it a question of time?"

"Are you sure it's a question of time?"

"What if it is? What can we do about it?"

"Then all the more reason not to let him suffer longer."

"You're saying we should bring about his death?"

"If that's better..."

"I can't do that."

"But it can't be better just to leave him behind."

"Why not?"

"Comrade Baek Chong-wi, you're trying to escape."

"Is that bad?"

"No, it's only natural that you should want to. But I am saying it's not right to abandon Comrade Yeung-bin like this. It'd be all right if we were all going on a death march."

"But it can't be. How could I kill Yeung-bin with my own hands?"

"We're not killing him! If we leave him here, he will end up dying in the end. If our enemy finds him, then they'll kill him."

"We have no time for this. Nan, get up quickly."

Embracing Yeung-bin's head, Nan did not budge.

"It is much more cruel not to do anything."

"Why's that?"

"You want to fool around a bit longer before he has to die."

Nan refused to rise.

"Comrade Park Nan, please go ahead with Baek Chong-wi," said Jeong-jun and shook Yeung-bin who did not show any sign of movement. Jeong-jun grabbed the dagger from inside his breeches. It was frozen stiff and difficult to pull it out of the case. The chilly feel of the case penetrated his stomach. His hand gripping the dagger, he walked toward Yeung-bin.

"Comrade Nan, you get up and I'll help him sit up," he said as he shoved her knees aside. Yeung-bin's eyelashes flickered. Jeong-jun sensed Yeung-bin's face right before his eyes. With his one hand, he pulled the dagger out. He could feel Yeung-bin's heart beating inside of him. His hand, which was holding the dagger, suddenly lost its grip. He closed his eyes and prayed that he would regain the strength in his hand. Right then, he heard a series of gunshots. He heard Baek Chong-wi's rough footsteps and felt his hands forcibly pushing him.

"What're you doing? We'll have to leave him here. Do you want to die here, like a wild pig being chased?"

"Why must we leave him here?"

"I don't know. There is no reason."

"No reason? There is no reason?"

18

Screaming his head off, Jeong-jun fanatically stabbed Yeung-bin's body. He could not rationalize killing him unless he counted on a rebellious emotion outside of him. By getting angry at what Baek Chong-wi said, he was able to kill Yeung-bin. Yeung-bin's last cry agitated everyone mercilessly. Nan grabbed hold of the corpse and cried, making a screeching sound like an animal.

"Baek Chong-wi, take the side path and I'll climb up the slope. Let's confound them."

Jeong-jun was racing up to the mountain, like a wild boar that had been shot, but not fatally. Baek Chong-wi brushed past Nan and swept down the path.

It was arduous for Jeong-jun to have to drag the body of Yeung-bin that was close to a corpse, on top of a heavy load he was carrying already to go up a steep slope. When he felt he could no longer take another step, he let go of Yeung-bin's hand and plopped down. It is truly mysterious how a human being could turn into an object with a single gunshot. He must have seen or sensed something exiting from Yeung-bin's body, like power coming off a mechanical doll. Like a veterinarian examining rotten meat, he frowned and looked absently at Yeung-bin. But strangely, no matter how much he thought he was looking down at a thing, it did not feel like it. He watched Yeung-bin's face quiver and felt like his own face was quivering. It was obviously Yeung-bin's face that was trembling. But why did his face tremble? He needed a witness and looked at Nan and Baek Chong-wi alternately as Yeung-bin let out a moan. Scared out of his wits, he sat up Yeung-bin. If life was something that didn't die but required killing, then why did it need so very long to perish; or if it were something that didn't need killing but simply died of its own accord, then why was it taking so very long to happen? His moaning proves life is ebbing away. And if Yeung-bin is being killed and if that were unavoidable, then shouldn't one help accelerate it? It was clear Yeung-bin was the one moaning but it was the two of them who felt the pain. If feeling the pain of the other was the pain itself, then he, too, was in pain. Yeung-bin was now close to an object but that's not how it felt to him. If what he were holding onto was a boar, he could have gorged on it this instant. But what he was clutching at this moment was a human being. He had a trace of a man.

He was said to have been an officer who never even had to fire a single gunshot but wrote only propaganda. The comrades who worked at X brigade had to flee to our hideout when their retreat route was blocked. Since they had worked together in the same place, he and Nan could not help but be close. But he seemed close to Baek Chong-wi also. In the end, though, as long as Nan was involved, it was inevitable that they clash. Still, Baek Chong-wi could not have intentionally dragged him into town, knowing there was police there. All these thoughts of mine could be my far-fetched imagination. In any case, Yeung-bin wrote the script that Nan broadcast. Nan's voice was quite sonorous and I'd heard her occasionally reciting the poems Yeung-bin wrote. Baek Chong-wi was an incredibly eloquent speaker. Yeung-bin would wash his underwear and give his clean ones to Baek Chong-wi to wear. But that very Yeung-bin is now dying. Until now, I had perceived of him as a concept. The Yeung-bin, being dragged away by me until now, was just his body, and the Yeung-bin I had in my mind was only a concept of him. Isn't it a concept of a person that actually lives in this world? Consequently, as long as I am a human being, even if my body perishes, I, along with Yeung-bin, will forever live in the world. Does death really exist to rob of life or is it that life gets transformed to death? In any event, it is evident that life must suffer pain. Although Yeung-bin is under excruciating pain, all that is so unfair and futile because he will die anyway.

The Journal of a North Korean Soldier

I am going to add some superfluous words to the following trifling journal that I am going to share with you. They will certainly be uncalled for. Instead of how I was able to obtain this journal, but by adding what might seem like an unnecessary explanation, it could serve as what is similar to an illumination or a prompter for a greater stage effect. Or I would be content if my explanation could fall outside of unnecessary words. I was a Private in the Squad 5017. Nine o'clock that night we were given an order to march since a woman captive had disclosed the enemy's hideout. As a gunner on a machine gun squad, I was less concerned about climbing up the mountain in the cold winter night and more worried about having to carry the heavy machine gun. Taking turns with the assistant ammunition carriers, we tracked up the Baekun Mountain. It was a great adventure to climb up the mountain in pitch dark, with the waning pine trees and thickening of the slope with the trunks of other dead trees and thickets, not to mention the snow that was piled up to our ankles, filling our mouths with frost the instant we took a breath. I couldn't help feeling enraged at the treacherous woman ahead of us, regretting why we hadn't just shot her instead of holding her captive. Still, the march of the squadron in a single line along the pathless mountain slope reminded me of the explorers of the South Pole and I couldn't help feeling the thrill akin to the pioneers who raced on wagons across the virgin soil of the newly explored North American continent, hollering "Westward!"

"What is a path? It is where it has been trod, where the thorny bushes have been blazed into a trail."

Could it be compared with the pioneering of a path of life that Lu Xun wrote about? At any event, oblivious to how many hours we've

21

marched, we kept walking to the distant sound of what were our own footsteps in the snow when Private First Class Jang, who was in front of me, turned around and cupping his hands like a trumpet, said:

"We found the enemy!"

I instinctively turned around, delivered the message to the assistant gunner, and fell flat on the ground. All of a sudden, everything came to a standstill as though the Earth had stopped its revolution and all we could hear was the blood pumping in and out of our hearts. It seemed like the order to shoot would never come. The mountain revealed its shape as the dawn began to break. Holding the trigger, I was fretful for no reason.

"Fire!"

I heard the commander's order and the sound from my machine gun all at once. Perhaps it was like the anxiety of a sprinter in a 100-meter dash. I fired everywhere. The bullets exploded like shooting stars before my eyes. The more the red flashes soared in the sky, the darkness, which concealed the blue sky, evaporated into nothingness. It was right then that we saw the woman captive, whom we brought with us, fleeing into the thick bushes to the west. My body was inflamed with excitement from head to toe. I felt the urge for a devastating thrill that surpassed ruthlessness, which was a wartime sentiment. It was a heinous elation. I abruptly turned my machine gun barrel in the woman's direction. At that very moment, she looked like she crumbled and was nowhere visible. Although I knew for certain that there was a cliff at the west end, I did not think she had been shot by our side, for I had undoubtedly heard the repeated shots of a submachine gun, which I had not heard until now.

In any event, when I got to my feet after I heard the ceasefire order, I could already clearly see the shadow of the soldiers searching the hideout. The plan had failed because the place was vacant. The commander immediately gave an order to encircle the area where the roofs looked like mushroom heads in the basin, which was precariously situated down below. We surrounded the houses with straw-thatched

22

roofed houses, which seemed to have sprung up for their inhabitants to eke out a living near the Buddhist temple, and ordered the evacuation of the villagers. After ascertaining the enemy's hiding place, we carried out intensive firing and conducted a scrupulous search. I left my heavy machine gun with another soldier and volunteered to set out. I heard a baby cry when I had arrived at a house with a mud-plastered wall. I, along with two other soldiers, pushed open the A-frame stick gate and pointed our guns.

"Come out!" Private Jang barked.

It was silent. Suddenly we felt shivers and became afraid.

"Come out! Or else we'll fire!" I made a threat by speaking extra loud in order to boost my courage.

"What to do…?" We heard a voice from inside. We all exchanged glances, as if to read our own fear in the other person's face. There was not one of us who looked confident.

When we heard the wailing of a newborn infant, we were sure that coupled with the woman's voice —heard shortly before— that the baby was born just a few hours earlier. We couldn't help being struck dumb at this coincidence. We didn't find out until we talked about it later but all of us were reminded of our own mothers in that dark room. Private Jang entered with a lantern.

Startled, someone asked, "Who is it?" and we heard an incredibly loud gunshot, enough to bring down the house.

"What is it? What is it, Private Jang?" We rushed in and his lamp lit the chest of a North Korean solider who was lying in a pool of blood. Next to him, we saw the body of a woman who was dead. At the same time, we knew instinctively we were in danger and felt the need to do a thorough search of the house. I went out to the yard and ran toward the hut and the outhouse.

Gripping the gun, I repeated to myself, "Come out. Or else I will shoot!" At that moment, what I saw before my eyes was a wooden bowl for fodder. But I viewed it as a human head and I tightened my grip on the trigger. At the time I had felt so threatened that I mistook anything as my enemy. Even if it had been a bowl, I believed it would be safer for me to pull the trigger when I was startled by some movement. It was a person. But the moment I acknowledged it to be a person, I lost all my courage to shoot. I sincerely hoped that it was someone I didn't have to kill. When I discovered that it was not an enemy but an old man, I was greatly relieved. I was unaware at the time that it would also be more fortuitous for the journal I am going to be sharing with you. I took the old man into the room. I do not want to go into any more detail about what happened then. Except that the old man's daughter-in-law was unable to flee because she had just delivered her baby, and the North Korean soldier had entered their house, injured, most likely because he had suffered a gunshot wound in a hideout. With an impulse that I could not for the life of me explain, I felt the urge to rummage through the enemy's blood-clotted chest to discover his identity. Private Jang's bullet had penetrated his heart and near his lower left abdomen where he was probably shot while in hiding, there was a tattered blood stained notebook covered by his crossed fingers. I cannot say it for a fact so I do not want to construe it as his desperate wish to preserve the notebook to his dying moments. It was more probable that he was instinctively using it in an attempt to prevent the blood spurting from his abdomen. It is unfortunate that I cannot share the entire journal because of the blood-saturated parts. As luck would have it, the notebook had a thick strawboard cover, for without which it would not have been possible to read even a page. The last thing I will add is that Park Young was his name and he was a militiaman who graduated from J High School in Pyongyang.

June 29, 1950

I stood up as the Chairman had ordered and I gave my speech: if the young people remained bystanders and were mute about the invasion of North Korea by the South Korean National Army three days before, they would be viewed as being uninterested in the Democratic People's Republic of North Korea; therefore it was imperative that we courageously volunteer to be militiamen. Then I suggested we have a show of hands for the comrades who were in favor. One by one, they raised their hand.

When I spoke out, "Those who agree, speak up," suddenly all the members of the Reading Circle raised their arms. I gave my absolute support to Comrade Yi, who had been instructed by the Comrade Chairman to propose that the Chairman stay behind for the sake of our group. That is how we came to march tonight as soldiers of the People's Army. Before the meeting of the Reading Circle, the Comrade Chairman, Comrade Yi, and I had made an undisclosed arrangement, following an order from the Party, that I make a suggestion with Comrade Yi assisting me. We had to make certain that the decision was apparently of my own volition. When all things proceeded as planned, I, all of a sudden felt sad. To think that I saw my mother and sister for the last time tonight made me feel very lonesome. I wanted to take a little time to visit my home but was not granted permission. The train was to depart Pyongyang Station at ten in the evening. We were going to head to the Front for the Liberation of South Korea that we had dreamt of. I took one more look at the tranquil Freedom Tower that was in the Pyongyang Park and repeated, "Hail to the USSR, Our Grateful Liberator!"

June 30, 1950

At nine a.m., we have arrived at the X zone. We have received our khaki army uniforms and caps. We were now the soldiers of the People's Army.

(I arbitrarily decided to omit about a page...)

Since my family was in the printing business, it was something I was good at. In view of it, I was assigned to the culture division of the brigade. It is a terribly lonely thing to be separated from your school friends. But no matter where one goes, there are bound to be strangers and one simply has to acclimatize to the new environment. At the moment, I am on top of mounds near houses, somewhere. I have become a soldier. I must become a heartless person who is indifferent to the stars that serve no purpose but move one's feelings. Let me close my eyes and hope for a dreamless sleep.

July 1, 1950

It is damp and soggy as though the dew had invaded the night. My head feels achy and heavy. Tonight we might leave Seoul for the southern part of the country. It was liberated on the twenty-eighth of June. Comrade Director left a good first impression on me. As a member of the South Korea Labor Party, he appeared affable and kindly— personality traits which have been extirpated a long time ago.

July 2, 1950

Ah, the hundred *li*[1] march! I was thoroughly exhausted and I couldn't make an entry in my journal last night. But to cross the 38th Parallel Line… How deeply moving! As in a dream, I am standing on the soil of the South. Uijeongbu City! Seoul, which seemed within arm's reach. Still, I am a soldier in a comfortable position who only has to be in the liberated regions. In the afternoon, I did the printing of the propaganda for the people of Uijeongbu City.

July 3, 1950

At last, we arrived in Seoul. Instead of giving a lavish description of my impressions, I must say, I was deeply stirred. Let me cheer to my heart's content. However, just like on the Liberation Day of August 15,

---

[1] A traditional Korean measurement of about 0.4 km.

after experiencing a torrent of powerful emotions, it was also an impetus for a great psychological shift. It is an indisputable "treason" that I am scared to record it in my journal. I am a member of the Labor Party who has been most passionate and loyal. There shall be no diminution of my dedication but rather I shall continue to be loyal to my death to the Party, no, the Republic. But my preconception of Seoul, which was until now a capitalist market and a mass of slums, could not help but crumble before concrete evidence. The brain wants to ferociously fill the void where there was an absence of critical thinking. The functioning of the organ for critical thought, which had been eliminated like an appendix for the past four years, was back in operation. Sadly, it was a conclusion derived from experience and I had to accept it. The general merchandise and linen stores that sold goods indiscriminately, not to mention plentiful books without any restriction, censorship, or constraint—what am I to make of all this outrageous assemblage, of which I stole a quick glance? However, I do not forget that I am a member of the Party. I know it can but be an excuse, like that of a criminal justifying his crime, when we find relief in extolling the marks of the collapse of capitalism. And to pacify my agitation I found myself more and more compelled to enumerate the evidence of decline, as predicted by Marx. The Comrade Head of the Special Services had talked of the USA as a commodity market. That's right. There must be a consumer's market for the excessive production from American imperialism. They have certainly discovered a market that substantiated our expectation. The Comrade Head muttered, "The sons of bitches are devouring Joseon Korea like this." It certainly seemed that way. I tried to negate all my impressions with that one statement. But when I realized what a feeble excuse it was to cover up my weak point, I just wished I didn't see anything. How fortunate are the dimwits who live like slaves....

July 4, 1950

It is now unquestionably summer. The heat from now on will herald the real summertime. A female comrade was introduced to our squad. Jeong Eun-hui is a militiawoman who is a member of the Seoul division of the Labor Party. She will be working as a typist along with me. In other words, she was hired as a female staff member. Any more information about her isn't necessary. I don't need to know more about her for us to work together. I might feel discomfort in having to work with someone like her. That she is pretty makes it all the more difficult. But strictly speaking, I don't like her because she made me think of my sister. The closer we had to work together, the fear that she would remind me of my older sister, whom I forced myself to forget, was what greatly perturbed me. She was an agitator who instigated nostalgia that was absolutely forbidden. Yet I cannot fathom myself in acknowledging the greater reason for disdaining her. I am a strange pervert who can only view her as an object of angst instead of my comrade and a Party member. She is going to become a member of the Republic like myself. Like myself…It was a scary thought but why did I want her to be part of the Rhee Syngman regime? No. I must remember I am a member of the Party.

July 5, 1950

Shall I have to go down to the South again? Before leaving, I wrote to my elder sister.

"Elder Sister, I know you must have been greatly worried about me. I half expected it, but it must have made you even angrier. Not only that, mother would have admonished me. Here, I am in Seoul! It is indeed Seoul! How do I feel about it? In short, it was a tumultuous encounter. As the word connotes a great upheaval of feelings, it would take my hardened emotions a certain amount of time to soften, just like it would have to be spring before the winter ice will melt. What I meant to say is that it would require time for me to put into words what I've seen and heard thus far. By the way, Elder Sister, as I myself have a great interest in dance, I went straight to the Joseon Farmer's Dance Association here in the South. I saw a dance with two farmers carrying a hoe and to my eyes it looked quite inadequate, perhaps because the Association is so new. In any event, I am concerned about sustenance for our family, without me there."

I stopped writing at this point as I lacked the courage to continue for I knew my skepticism and confusion is what would inevitably follow. It was also clear the query about my family's welfare would be censored and the letter would fail to be delivered.

July 6, 1950

Comrade Jeong Eun-hui who resembles my sister, and Comrade Park Nan who worked for Pyongyang Central Broadcasting, and Comrade Ju Gil-sun quickly became close. It must be because the world of women does not suffer from duplicity.

July 7, 1950

The female comrades' faces all looked whitish. They had dabbed powder on their face. They also carried a cosmetic case that I hadn't seen. For some reason, they were constantly looking at a mirror, fixing their hair and were fidgety. Of course, as they are women, they cannot but be indifferent to beauty. Even if a draconian ban forced the women to dedicate their time to a five-year plan for the increased production of garments, instead of embellishing themselves in not so much a glamorous but an elegant manner, it would be impossible for them to do away with human instinct, for it will be like severing them from human labor or organization altogether. What kind of freedom does a country entail where women are deprived of a chance to make themselves look pretty? For whom in Joseon Korea is the increased production for—where posting a flyer with that very slogan on every wall isn't enough and therefore it is even printed on all the cigarette packs? If calling production, "For the Nation," isn't appropriate and if it should be, "For the entire proletariat," then of what use is the "entire proletariat" when it cannot provide nourishment for individual members of the proletariat? The entire proletariat surely must not bear any relation to the people of the Democratic Republic and be but an idol, be it the Great Leader Kim Il Sung or the USSR, changing with the times and the circumstances. Ah…I am now probing into a terrifying truth.

"Are you going to use your face as a weapon in war?" The deputy commander blew up at the women who had to wipe the powder off their face right there and then but still could not give up their urge to look beautiful. Southward again. I shall be setting off shortly.

July 24, 1950

I couldn't write in my journal for a long time. Trekking a thousand *li* in ten days. Have we become beasts that could only be on the move during nighttime? The bombing from the enemy planes has become second nature. It's part of our life. There were many times I was going to throw away this notebook. I am now frightened. I have become afraid of you. That is because around you I could boldly become forgetful of what I need to be most mindful of—that is, my present condition. I become audacious enough to want to become a reactionary. Come to think of it, I am betraying myself. But if I am not going to sense this kind of fear in you, the journal can no longer hold any appeal for me. Perhaps this is the kind of stuff I want to record. So then I want to have a chance to view my life through my feelings for the opposite gender, since until a month ago till now when I have been blindly faithful, devoid of any subjective reasoning or critical thinking. Ah, I am exhausted. It's been a long time since I slept in a house. I shall stop writing. But for the sake of reference, I shall write about the student incident today, which indicates we have arrived in a different Gwangju.

LAND OF TEARS

July 25, 1950

Jeong Eun-hui, is like my elder sister. Why am I calling her by name? Is it because I don't want to regard her as a comrade or a Party member? Or a sister? No. She has long ceased to be like my sister. Eun-hui! That's how I want to address her. Why am I becoming more and more like a moron? For all of us in Joseon Korea, everyone is a comrade. If anyone were to compile a dictionary, it is a given that we add the word, "comrade," as a prefix to all nouns about people. But here I am, I dare want to call someone by her name. That is why I am an imbecile. But what I am to make of a world where an idiot could pretend to be a genius? It is necessary for me to become an imbecile to be able to address Comrade Eun-hui as Eun-hui.

July 22, 1950

I shall add the entry of this day for Eun-hui.
"Where are we?"
"We are at an Eup."
"Which Eup is it?"
"It's called Jeong-eup."[2]
We roared with laughter but the more we laughed, our stomachs shrank and the abdominal muscles kept contracting. Jeong-eup must be close. Then the sound of Comrade Eun-hui dragging her feet behind me had tormented me. I did turn around repeatedly to look at her but could not bring myself to ask her. I finally took courage and grabbed her shoulder to the point of being rude and offered her my left shoulder. Without saying a word, she let me do what I did and leaned against my shoulder and made a tremendous effort to walk. I fixed my

---

[2] This is a play on words. "Eup" means township, but the name of the city (Jeong-eup) has as its suffix, a homonym, of "eup," but with a different meaning.

gaze on the faint color-laden mountain where dawn was breaking so as not to see her ashen pale face.

July 26, 1950

I did a printing of the song exalting the People's Army that was written by a Soviet writer, Kochev, with the opening that goes, "I gaze at the sky…," and printed the declaration with the heading of "To the defeated soldiers." Comrade Park Nan, the newscaster is scheduled to broadcast it tonight. Formalism. That's what it was, always a provocative speech against the enemies in the same pattern with a slightly different tone each time. Could this possibly be a society in which people come first? Or could human beings be just an experimental entity for Marxist theory? We, the people, who must feel honored to have been chosen as an instrument to test Marxist theory, are truly a sorry bunch.

July 27, 1950

I discovered something that astounded me. I didn't know about it till now. Our Great Leader, Kim Il Sung, made a fabricated statement—that the crossing of the national boundary was unavoidable due to the invasion by the South Korean army—to gain sympathy of the world press for our inevitable engagement of arms for self-defense. The disclosure of this information does not mitigate my astonishment. But it did become a cause for my extreme skepticism for my life of the past few years in which I lived in a dreamlike state of mind, along with the thought that countless false facts must've turned into truth. It was afternoon. It looked like Comrade Nam Chong-hui was giving a briefing on the meeting to the Comrade Director and the officers; a little later, he said he was flummoxed earlier in that no one seemed prepared to give a response to unexpected questions from the citizens; he then remained silent for a short while, expecting the Comrade Director to provide an explanation of issues like private property, freedom for businesses, and judicial trials for people. As I was sweating away, working on a mimeograph, I couldn't quite hear the Director's answer but my curiosity was piqued whenever the topic as to the truth of the matter regarding the invasion of the North across the 38th Parallel Line. To summarize, the consensus was that going out of our way to repudiate the allegation of the South concerning the invasion across the 38th Parallel Line would set off more skepticism. I was dumbstruck. Go out of our way to repudiate it? Then did it mean we could endorse it? Did we have in our possession an eraser that could eradicate a fact and create a different truth? We clearly knew it was an invasion by the North. Suddenly I felt an odd skepticism. I made up my mind to clandestinely ask a resident in our area. I invited a couple of people from the vicinity and preached the glory of the People's Republic in an impassioned speech. I spoke indeed from the bottom of my heart. Then I asked how the bastards disseminated the failure of their invasion. Of course, that was the point I was trying to get at. But I viewed their hesitancy as natural and I had to prove to them that I didn't mean any harm as to get them talking. But then a middle-aged man said it was the first time he'd heard such a thing. He took out a newspaper and handed it to me, pointing at a section with a title for the special issue that read, "The Communists Are the Invaders," and underneath the subheading said, "The UN proclaims a Just Verdict." In the past, I would have roared with laughter, calling it a shameless defense. Even now, perhaps. But have I acquired enough of a critical mind not to burst into laughter? I couldn't help feeling frustrated and enraged like I'd been cheated. My mind is becoming more and more disordered. I cannot write anymore.

July 28, 1950

I feel this recurring urge to torment myself to death. It isn't by any means self-contempt or self-denial on my part. It's actually the complete opposite. It is more like that of a meditating or ascetic monk.

Ah… (just like words from a distant land) these words have become archaic—monk, monk in pursuit of truth. They cannot be found in our dictionary. I want to make myself suffer to the point of feeling utter pity. A nation of paradox where self-deception is a prerequisite—the inevitable conclusion of this statement is that the purpose of its existence lies outside of the people. Those who have forgotten to look into themselves are betraying the law of nature and are no less like a puppet controlled by someone else in a show. I don't even want to know who are the Sutradhara of Park Cheom-ji, Hong Dong-ji, the puppets, and Pyo Saeng-won. Just like when the Sutradhara's hidden hand controlling the strings in a puppet show gets exposed, it becomes a farce—the spectators from other countries perhaps have the magnanimity to look the other way for the fiasco during the drama. I got hold of the *Joseon People's Daily* and read that Gwangju had fallen as a result of a people's uprising even before the Liberation. But no other place had collapsed before our arrival. As a Party member, I can say it was a false report or remain mute. Why do I feel such pleasure in exposing our errors? It is because I wish to know. The truth lies in the realm where our wish to know is thwarted.

June 29, 1950

Eun-hui washed my clothes for me. I am committing a scary treason. Thinking about a woman is the same as adultery and changing the word adultery to reactionary would constitute a fine bible for the Party. And "Love for a cause is an exception" is a very appealing clause.

August 1, 1950

"Ignorance is the mother of faith." The maxim by Pope Gregory VII from the Middle Ages is indeed a very relevant saying even today. The object of faith just has to be different. One simply needs to alter

34

one's faith in God to the material world. In other words, faith in Jesus was shifted to faith in Marx. The Bible will gradually be revised.

August 2, 1950

"I saw a bird in the absence of a scarecrow. Preached to two farmers on the distribution of free land." I was barely able to come up with the things I did for the people. I am ashamed of not being able to fill a page. But I'd feel more shame to fabricate lies. I am a dodgy Party member.

August 3, 1950

Just as theorems can be subverted, the same can occur in a revision of the Bible. "Men cannot live on bread alone," and "If one voluntarily is enchained, then he cannot feel the chains; it is only when one rebels against it and wishes to flee that he will suffer"; it simply has to be rephrased to "Men live on bread alone." In this society where my life is rooted, must I voluntarily be chained to the shackles of materialism that Marx has postulated, like the doctrine of original sin? I refuse. It is human nature to rebel against it and to flee as far away as possible. Even if it tightens its grip on you more strongly the more you resist, you must rebel. Then you simply have to die afterward. In a Socialist society, it is only natural that people die. The only exceptions are the puppets who have been changed as a consequence of materialism.

August 5, 1950

Comrade Yi Jun-sik, who was an exemplary soldier, died last night. It was in the middle of a great storm; however, he was summoned to repair a broadcasting antenna. According to female Comrade Park Nan, climbing to the antenna, which was high up along with the rain and wind, was a highly risky venture, especially with thunder and lightning;

therefore a number of comrades wished that he waited till the following day. But it was an order by the Director. That is the reason no one could intervene. He was electrocuted. Besides there was only one male comrade with no lantern or matches, and he kept screaming at the female comrades to go and fix it, behaving like a man who had lost his mind. That's it. The Director ordered that Comrade Yi Jun-sik be buried on the hill where the antenna was. The only regrettable thing is that a useful communication device was destroyed, violating the economic principle of maximum utility. An artillery salute for the dead is against the principle of unnecessary expenditures and was thereby suspended. I, too, might die without being put to good use. But I do not want to become a useful machine. I want to be a human being who perishes.

August 5, 1950. Night

I love her so much I want to kill her. I am lying on the ground where the starlight is shining its abundant light on my heart and I write her name in the sky. Eun-hui! I want to engrave it in our galaxy. With a confined thought the galaxy is but a constellation of countless stars, amidst this mechanism I am yearning for the interiority of the sky. Can one consider materialism as being progressive, for everything is characterized, including human emotion by its number, quantity, mass, size, width, and length, like rice and millet? In a mass of sorrow that is five centimeters in radius, there is twenty-five trillion tears—is there such progressivity? Eun-hui! That's why I begrudge you. The human being has departed from being a human being. I must go to sleep.

August x: In the dictionary, "The process of mechanization is socialism."
August x: Nostalgia
August 12: Admiration
August 13: Sturm und Drang

36

August x: Love
August x: Love
x. x.: Mother, Sister
September 1: Khozhdenie v narod (Going to the People
Movement)
September 2: Foxtail
September 3: Foxtail
September 4: Corpse, Eun-hui, Freedom
September 5: Eun-hui
September 6: Eun-hui

(Comment: It looks like the writer was going through intense confusion. He must have jotted down an impression that came to his mind each day, repressing the turbulent emotion he felt during this time. A single word, instead of a tedious sentence, expresses all the more sincerity.)

September 10, 1950

Eun-hui is leaving me. She will be heading for Mokpo, South Jeolla Province, tonight. Comrade Directors said she'll be back shortly. But a human being cannot be so divided. It is dubious. However, I am ecstatic about something—that Eun-hui didn't seem to want to leave at all.

September 11, 1950

I have not once thought of confessing my love.

September 12, 1950

Is there such a thing as self-dissolution or a self splitting apart? I have not forgotten for a split second that I am a member of the Party.

That's how out and out I am when it comes to being a Communist. But I who mull over the injustice and paradox of Socialism, the inadequacy of physiology, can I settle into this sphere of life? Don't I long for a new model of human nature? Indeed, more than anyone I desperately yearn for it. That is why I am sorrowfully fated to bury my heart in the Marxist Communist experiment of the kolkhoz. And my will for freedom shall be liberated. A new wine needs a new bottle. In the kolkhoz, the scorched and worn out body can disintegrate like a wrecked machine, like a slave. And I must die in accordance with the nature of a red society. That is one's duty. There is no denying what I want to say is, I want to live like a human being. To die fully, after living to the fullest. But I am a passive entity who has to perish. Ah…but I (who cannot die) but want to live instead! Because of Eun-hui!

(Comment: There are no more entries from here on probably because of the September 28 Retreat. It is a pity that there is only one entry after entering the mountain. Actually, there were a few more pages but they are illegible because they were saturated with blood.

January 20, 1951

I am still alive. In some sense, I am infinitely happy about it. I must be a type of person who cannot be free from a kind of splitting of the self. There are times when I don't know myself. Instead of not knowing, I delude myself in seeing myself as another. That is why my life is principled on seeing the brighter side and pleasure oriented. It is inevitable. I have killed people and have felt overwhelming pleasure. And we could lose the war, but still accomplish the purpose of Communism. Because the UN Forces might temporarily become the victor but the people of this land will suffer from famine, destruction, and diseases, and therefore they cannot help but be more communistic in the distant future. Therefore, I emphasized to our Partisan Comrades that we must indiscriminately murder, destroy, and pillage as a shortcut to realizing Communism. Meanwhile, I let someone go. I killed my comrade. And I have put Eun-hui out of my mind. How much more contradictory can my actions be? I don't know. I don't care to know much more. All I know is that I should have long ago been dead. I am going to kill Eun-hui!

(Comment: This was the last entry. But I discovered our female captive from earlier turned out to be Jeong Eun-hui and based on her uncertain behavior when we arrived at the hideout and how she was killed by the enemy's bullet and Park Young's last line, "I am going to kill Eun-hui," I came up with a record of what could have been Park Young's entry for that night. Please pardon me for it is of course, entirely from my own imagination but I had to satiate my unbearable curiosity in this way.

December 3, 1951 (this is the imagined entry...)

In a cowardly manner, I intend to be killed by a higher-ranking soldier's bullet. I am a coward who has deceived himself to the last minute. But I am relieved. In fact, I am content. That is because I was able to kill my Eun-hui. Because she is dead. I thought I could not possess her, ever. I don't know how much tears I shed when she was held captive. But on the other hand, it is fortunate that she was not sent to my cozy hometown. She has every right to live in my hometown. But when I saw her tonight! Ah, what a lovely enemy she was. I killed her. Initially, I had no intention of killing her. But when the face of Eun-hui, who ran up the rock, coincided with the person who was pointing his gun at her, when I knew she was going to come to me, I thought then she was about to commit a mortal sin of abandoning paradise. To stop her from coming back to the kolkhoz ever again, I killed her. It was done with my free will that I so wished for.

The Wife of a Partisan

The rain continued through the spring, and there was not a day with bright sunlight until summer came. The endlessly messy and wet marketplace was even more unbearably soggy these days. It was a place where the mud turned solid after much kneading by people's feet. Irrespective of whether or not it rained or snowed, people were crouching down to stake their posts, tired of the ceaseless rain. They wanted to block off the sun with some kind of an awning.

In the corner was the old man fortuneteller who was known to anyone that frequented the marketplace. In front of a couple of books that were smudged with black marks which he had placed on the ground, the old man dozed off, occasionally waking up to mutter to himself while looking up at the sky, "Looks like there's going to be a market."

Then as though it had slipped his mind, he began to stretch himself. In the middle of a yawn, he lost his balance, for his foot had cramped. There were rows of shanties alongside the creek down to the marketplace. Each shanty was decorated differently for an owner's particular business. In a place that looked like a box, there was just a machine for baking bread; a two-floor restaurant where the ground floor was plastered with a somewhat luxurious patterned wallpaper; a secondhand store filled with all kinds of metal objects for businesses and furniture; a portable bread shop with wheels; and a drug store where multi-colored flags hung loose with red and blue promotional objects....

Among these shanty houses, it wasn't too difficult to find Geumnyeo's bread shop. Her place had a tin roof made with flattened cans

—God knows where she got them—giving it the look of a floral cushion. They were put together in a quite presentable way. On the curtain, made of burlap flour sacks, was written Bread, Substitute Bread. When the burlap curtain fluttered in the wind, the face of Geum-nyeo, who was kneading the dough, appeared then disappeared. Her skinny frame made her appear much taller than she actually was. Her face, which had developed of its own accord from top to bottom only, looked hideously long. Her cheeks were sunken and her mouth protruded like a monkey. There was not a redeeming feature in her dark skinned face without a hint of luster and her ears pointed up like a donkey's, but the reason why she didn't look all that repulsive could have be on account of her eyes and eyebrows. Her relentlessly drawn eye line was thick and black, providing a refreshing air about her; her eyes were not like those of an adult's but contained a spark so that when she lowered her eyes in a vacant gaze, she could actually come off looking quite attractive. But the charm of her face bore no relation to her means of livelihood. The tale of how she came about building her shabby bread shop is loaded with enmity.

Geum-nyeo, who was terribly busy, kicked in irritation whatever got in her way.

"You, little bum!" Suddenly her youngest child screamed and pretended to stop breathing. As she was about to strike him again, she thought it strange that she did not hear anything. Worried, she bent down to take a look. The little boy, who was licking the crumbs off the ground, sensed the shadow over him and looked up to stare right into his mother's face. Right then, he acted as though he has found his breath again and burst into tears.

Shuddering, Geum-nyeo screamed at him, "Drop dead. You think then I'll make you some bread? Wrong! Wrong! How wicked you are, little rascal."

The little boy thought if he pretended to be dead or cry, his mother might proffer him some bread crumbs but his mother was not the type of woman who would be duped by such innocent trickery.

41

There was not a chance. As though she found it more infuriating the more she thought about it, Geum-nyeo kicked again in the direction of the sound of crying. The kick happened to land in the mouth of the boy who yelped like a dog and crumbled to the ground. Without giving him another glance, she thought he would stop crying when he got tired and she put the dough on the wooden board and began slicing. When she finished, she stole a glance at the boy, while checking the flame outside. In the spot where the boy should be asleep, there was no one. She turned her gaze in the direction of the stone bridge, thinking the boy could've crawled to the garbage bin but what she saw was a mob of people who were heading for the marketplace that was already completely set up. Once more, she looked up at the sky to check the weather, then turned to look at the crowd again, noticing how many soldiers there were. All of a sudden, she felt rushed, thinking she would be a fool not to make big bucks today. But when she saw her six-year-old daughter who was half-carrying and half-dragging her younger brother on the ground by the creek, she was enraged.

"This rascal wants to avoid getting the water by carrying her brother," she thought and threw a silent fit.

"Brat! Hey Bong-deok! Bong-deok!" Not caring whether or not there were people around her, Geum-nyeo hollered. Bong-deok, who was plenty scared of her menacing mother who was after her, froze. Right in the middle of anticipating in great fear that her mother would grab her head and mercilessly drag her by the hair, she shouted, jumping up and down, "Look over there, there, on the bridge!"

Then right above her head, along with the smell of the cooked flour, Bong-deok heard her mother's voice, "What the hell, you little cunning rascal!"

"Mommy, there's a newborn baby over there under the big bridge. Someone left it in a container," Bong-deok rambled excitedly. Then when she saw a mob of people swarming to the place, her heart started beating faster. Wanting not to miss out on the action, she tiptoed to grab her mother's sleeve to hasten her.

"Let go, you rascal. Did you leave your honey there? Let's go back."

"Mommy, I saw the baby. It was just born. Jeong-seok helped. The kids got to hold it."

Bong-deok offered all kinds of tales to appeal to her mother but Geum-nyeo was not interested at all. She was just too preoccupied with where all the soldiers were headed, in their raggedy and faded mud-stained uniforms. It was Sunday and a shopping day for the soldiers of the Jeolla Province Army Combat Unit. There was a jumble of people, possibly watching the itinerant medicine man at the boundary of the factory wall. Some thugs put an apple crate before Geum-nyeo's place and did the rounds of switching the three trump cards, being merry.

"What country bumpkin would be fooled?" she snickered but then she thought the boisterousness couldn't harm her business.

The orphans, wearing the faded earth colored clothes from the Peace Orphanage, marched along in a straight line. She wondered why they were taken through the marketplace where their appetites can only be whetted and not satiated, but unbeknownst to Geum-nyeo, that was what the orphans wanted. Each time someone walked past, one could see the seated beggar who was bending over. He was a crippled man who was without his left foot. Holding his foot that was cut off, he kept shaking his ankle up and down. The people turned away, as though viewing his foot, which had become as hard as plaster had completed their chore.

Geum-nyo trembled after seeing him. As though she had seen something she ought not have, she turned around with her eyes shut tight. But it was peculiar that she should feel so disturbed at seeing another cripple since she regarded her own husband, who had also become crippled, like a stranger whenever she saw him through a hole of her shanty. Even now, she could see her husband from a certain distance away.

While baking bread in the iron pot, Geum-nyeo tried to figure out as to why she had been so agitated earlier and looked to where her husband was sitting. Two people were seated like moving statues. The couple, who were leaning against each other, looked like they were husband and wife. With a straw sack wrapped around her, the woman appeared to be exhausted and vacantly stared at her foot that was sticking out under from the sack like it belonged to someone else. As far as Geum-nyeo could tell, it was rare that they were still not up, although it was past noon. The man was always seated upright like a stone Buddha. One of his legs was severed at the ankle and the bones lay bare, which was a revolting sight. It almost looked like someone had axed his foot and left it like that. The blood, mingled with earth, filled the gap but where the flies were swarming, the flesh on the edge wriggled like seaweed. Undoubtedly, there would be maggots underneath but he remained undisturbed. One could see his ribs moving in the direction of his body's motion and his flesh undulated this and that way. It would be apt to say that his bones looked like they were wrapped with earth-colored cloth. His sunken face showed eyes with only the white part remaining and his mouth, with missing lips, were there for the sole purpose of its link to the throat. His hair looked as though it had been chopped with dull scissors, for with erratic bunches of hair it looked like a field after a harvest.

That man was Hyeok-gu, Geum-nyeo's husband. She was not impressed with her husband who made a heroic contribution to the Party. It was the same man who probably thought his two children could live only on their mother's milk. But a human life was not something that could easily be done away with.

When Hyeok-gu was arrested, being charged with evading responsibility for the Haenam Rebellion, what he left for Geum-nyeo were their two children and a house that had burned down to ashes. All that she had was a body that felt like it would crumble any second.

It was she who had to shoulder his crime all by herself when Hyeok-gu went into hiding after instigating the uprising. Although she begrudged and pitied Hyeok-gu, who paid a visit at night like a burglar, she did not feel resentful or afraid once.

Geum-nyeo could remember those days very clearly.

Grabbing her slip, the police had threatened her, "Confess where your husband is or else we're going to mutilate your vagina." He then really pointed the knife very close to her body, not to mention how the column of her house was painted red to deter her neighbors from interacting with her, and admonished her like she was hiding a person inflicted with an epidemic disease, and then made it impossible for her to take one step out of the house. She could not forget it. She was all confused, recalling how she had denied all the accusations, when after all that he ended up getting caught. It wasn't because she wanted to be a faithful wife of a laudable Communist.

Geum-nyeo believed she had to be faithful to her husband, no matter what and being imprisoned couldn't but be a dreadful thing for her. Therefore when Hyeok-gu was released on bail, after not quite completing a year and half of his prison term, she could cry and lament for him although she herself was all skin and bones.

"I am now free…let's leave here once I get my Provincial ID card. They could take me back in since I'm out on bail," Hyeok-gu showed sincere remorse and regret to his family.

She also construed his passionate statement, "Let's move to a bigger town. I must pick up the *jigae*[3] again to make sure my own children don't starve. I want to feed them all the cooked rice they want…and pork to their heart's content," as his desire not to get involved with the Communists again. It was understandable that he should talk this way, for Hyeok-gu had never seen white rice in his life. But he backed up his words and worked like a slave since moving here. He felt dizzy and his legs trembled when he picked up the wooden frame but he didn't care and kept moving.

Then the Korean War broke out. Without being unduly alarmed, he sold melons to the People's Army. Other than that it no longer mattered whether or not he had a Provincial ID card or that he didn't have to hide his name or have others call him out loud, life didn't appear to

---

[3] A traditional Korean A-frame carrier.

be that much different. But suddenly Hyeok-gu departed for his hometown. He couldn't behave like that unless he was possessed or had gone out of his mind. Perhaps he himself didn't know what he was doing.

Geum-nyeo had to resort to selling melons, so as not to have her children starve. Lamenting her fate, she walked miles to sell wood and obtained a small amount of barley, as she found comfort in being an able mother.

I am better than you. It may be admirable to do great things for the country and thereby forget your family; still you are no better off than me, not even providing a single grain to the members of your own kin. Geum-nyeo had to once again struggle laboriously for her pathetic livelihood.

While she had gone to the mountains to get wood, Bong-deok had fallen asleep on the ground, carrying on her back her younger brother who swallowed earth. By the time she returned, his stomach had turned hard and he had stopped breathing. Fifteen days had passed and when there was no news from Hyeok-gu, she became disgusted and enraged at the same time, cursing socialism and what not.

As Hyeok-gu had left like a possessed person, he returned like a mad man. Even after seeing his family who had not eaten for two days, he occupied himself with a resume he wanted to submit to the People's Committee, only to awaken his enervated wife, who didn't have the energy to say even one word, and ask her senseless questions like her age and birthdate; he didn't seem to think that his family could starve in a Socialist country. In fact, thinking it could be a mere possibility for him was a reactionary act. Yet, in actuality, Hyeok-gu could not attend to his family, but not because of his dedicated involvement with the Party, as his wife believed. He was a man who was most definitely possessed by something. Two days after his arrival, he all of a sudden urged his family to leave for their hometown. He told them to just put on their shoes. Instead of being surprised, Geum-nyeo was sickened.

"You son-of-a-bitch, did the Party give you a rice paddy or a lot in a field? Or look after your wife and children?" she wailed and swore never to go back of her own volition to that revolting place where Hyeok-gu wanted to take his family. She screamed and pounded on the floor and Hyeok-gu was at a loss.

"All right then, stay here. It's better. Bong-deok, come on," he said, grabbing the hand of his daughter who had no idea what was going on, as he put her on a bicycle, grinning.

Once more, Hyeok-gu was gone like a mad man. Geum-nyeo had to go back to getting wood from the mountain and selling melons. Then the People's Army retreated. Amidst chaotic confusion, Geum-nyeo couldn't figure out what was right or wrong.

Bong-deok returned home, after walking for three hundred *li* all by herself. Geum-nyeo was so shocked that she broke down and wept before even giving a thought to how Bong-deok was able to come back. She was dressed in the same hemp clothes she wore when she left and seeing her frighteningly sunken eyes and emaciated body, Geum-nyeo cursed the Heavens and wished she could just go out of her mind.

There could be no life energy in those bones. If the bones are said to contain any spirit, then surely it must be a lie. For amidst the skinny ribs, there was only a large food sack left. And Bong-deok's five fingers were digging ferociously into her bosom. Hyeok-gu never returned.

This is what Bong-deok said afterward, "Father was talking to someone on the road then he was gone. And I just kept walking."

After standing motionless for God knows how long, Geum-nyeo came to her senses when a smiling face came into her sight. The vision of Hyeok-gu's face—as he put Bong-deok on the bicycle with a grin—flickered before her eyes then vanished. Beyond the wrinkles of her eyebrows, there were two shadows and one of them was looking into the iron pot.

"Is there…any bread?" She heard a voice ask.

"Yes, of course. How many pieces would you like?" She hurriedly wiped the table, which was originally used as a desk in the elementary school. Shaking the soy sauce bottle, and then putting five pieces of bread on the plate, she glanced at the customer, silently asking him again how much bread he would like. But oddly, the man just stood there.

"Sit down, please, sit down here," she hurriedly invited him. She didn't want to lose a customer. At first sight, he looked like a soldier but then he wasn't wearing a hat and his hair was too long, giving him a look of a laborer, although his body was too thin and fragile. After standing still for a long time, he plopped down on the chair, as though he'd made an important decision.

"Just ten." He held up both his hands, palms open and looked proudly around the place. He snatched the bread and gulped it down as soon as Geum-nyeo placed the steaming dish in front of him. But as his throat wouldn't permit the bread to go down readily, with his mouthful he shut his eyes, opened them again and gulped it down. When he sensed Geum-nyeo's gaze on him, he looked embarrassed. He searched for water, guzzled it, then turned his eyes toward the square opening to the creek and became lost in thought.

Geum-nyeo hunted the corners for Bong-deok. She was relieved not to find her, stealing a glance at the mouth of the customer from under the table. But as she bent down to check the flame for the iron pot, she couldn't help cursing her, "Worthless rascal." She thought it necessary to correct her daughter's behavior and came out of the store to look for her among the merchants. She knew very well that a six-year-old couldn't earn all that much but then again if she were put to work, she could make at least ten *won* a day. The thought aggravated her to no end. She had a good reason to be upset. For no matter how hard she worked, all she could afford was barley or Annam rice.

She turned her gaze toward Hyeok-gu again. When she realized the child next to him was Bong-deok, she became fidgety and disoriented. She had to stop her from going near him. Bong-deok might have already talked to him. The thought of it brought tears to her eyes. How painful it must be for Hyeok-gu to have his daughter acknowledge him

48

as father…but it startled her to think this way and Geum-nyeo cast her eyes on the woman who was lying beside him.

She could have been jealous of the woman next to Hyeok-gu but she rationalized it didn't matter who was by him and therefore there was no reason for her to be irked; nonetheless she couldn't deny the seething emotions she experienced.

As though the woman had read Geum-nyeo's mind, she made great effort to sit up straight with a vacant look at Hyeok-gu, only to give up shortly after.

The woman met Hyeok-gu when the leaves were changing color with the arrival of frost. The retreat for the Communist Army was cut off due to the amphibious landing of the UN Forces in Incheon, which forced them to flee to the mountains. The woman, who was part of the Female Corps Culture Division, had no choice but to enter Mount Weolchul on their way to Mokpo. They merged with the Partisan fighters from the area and taking control of one of the townships, they fought against the South Korean army.

Since she was a member of People's Army and Hyeok-gu was a Partisan fighter, it was virtually impossible for them to encounter each other. It would seem that Hyeok-gu, whose daily work involved building a stone wall around the town and getting ideological education, would be in frequent contact with a woman in the Culture Division, but as it stood those of the People's Army shunned and at the same time were wary of the native Partisan fighters; therefore, it was quite rare that Hyeok-gu would meet them in the house where he was staying. It happened after the stone wall was almost completed and a special ideology education program was scheduled for the South Korean Partisans. The woman couldn't bear to see Hyeok-gu being mercilessly thrashed by a member of the Politics Division who happened to be from North Pyeongan Province as well. What's more, the reason why he was being beat up seemed to be because Hyeok-gu glanced at her. She thought—looking at another person couldn't possibly be a sin—and even if he looked at her much more than the others, the man had no right to rant and rave, citing negligence of education as Hyeok-gu's wrongdoing, and to attack him like a lunatic. The woman did not approve of his punitive action, not because she was secretly enamored with Hyeok-gu or even felt sorry for him, but because of the man's possessory attitude toward her, not to mention his using ideological education as a pretext.

"Comrade Jun-hyeok, did you find a reactionary trait in him?"

"It's worse than that. How could someone who is ignorant about the three atrocities of Capitalism be guilty of one of them?" Fuming, he abruptly turned to Hyeok-gu and again shouted, "Recite the three atrocities of Capitalism. Come on! What are they?"

With a vacant stare, Hyeok-gu ignored him, as though he had no idea why Jun-hyeok was so enraged. He was engrossed in some other thought and didn't feel like responding at all. The woman felt if she didn't do anything, the situation would get worse and to hide Hyeok-gu's expressionless face, she came between him and Jun-hyeok, with an intention of giving the former a discreet sign to answer the man but instead, she unexpectedly blurted out, "Monopoly of the commodity market."

It was not the woman herself but Jun-hyeok who was completely taken aback by her words, and his face became grotesquely contorted. Instead of feeling frightened, the woman was gratified that she had somehow paid him back for all his sly, sleazy, and cunning taunting of her. She also wondered why she wanted to protect Hyeok-gu from him and couldn't figure it out.

When the frost arrived, the South Korean Army launched an all-out attack of the North Koreans, besieging them and blocking their food supply lines; Hyeok-gu and his group could not simply live on ideological education in the midst of an intense threat to their lives but Hyeok-gu remained unmoved by even this kind of peril. Since the responsibility to penetrate the besiegement and scrounge for food daily fell on the native Partisan members, many of them vanished without anyone knowing or died, having their lives terminated when they were abandoned in the mountains as living corpses, shot in the leg. The woman got in the habit of idolizing the heroic deeds of Hyeok-gu.

Since Hyeok-gu was working in the food supply group, she could only see him during the day or at mealtime. For several days, she didn't get a chance to talk to him in private and then stumbled upon him when she ventured into the woods to clandestinely treat an injured member who had been deserted like a boar that was shot. As she walked stealthily through the thickets, she heard something move and was surprised to see a man who was on his last breath. She witnessed Hyeok-gu, tramping on a body near death. The woman was so aghast that she was unable to say anything for a long time. Breathing in deeply, she rushed to him when she saw that the person was dead.

"Comrade, you must know the consequences of your action. I shall report you."

Hyeok-gu's face was impassive. As though he found all things a nuisance, he tracked down the mountain. She was once again dumb-struck. She was thoroughly taken aback by not so much his composure after bringing someone's life to an end, but his complete apathy to her declaration that she would report him.

"Comrade, don't you understand what the Party stands for?"

"I do."

"Then you must know what will happen to you next?"

Hyeok-gu didn't say anything more. To make sure no one was eavesdropping on them, she checked their surroundings and was about to repeat what she had said when she saw his face becoming oddly contorted, saying, "I shall report you also. You must know what results await for those who use valuable medicine on almost decaying corpses…"

At his threat, she was at loss for words. The reason why she had threatened him was to make sure that he wouldn't do it again and in case someone else had been privy to the scene. But she also couldn't help feeling rage at his cruelty with no compunction whatsoever at inflicting death upon someone else. She was afraid as well, at having been found out, going around treating the injured ones. It was when the South Korean army began its pursuit of them that she couldn't help being terrified of Hyeok-gu's state of mind. It was perhaps a personal expression of one's contempt for life that was rooted in despair but he displayed horrific ways of massacring the kidnapped civilians. He made them line up on the grass and with a multi-tipped bamboo spear, he spiked their abdomen and wrenched the victim, which made blood spurt in the air, splattering everyone nearby and the whole area with blood. Hyeok-gu especially went out of his way to do this in the presence of Jun-hyeok, a member of the Political Division, which alarmed her to no end. Having captured some civilian, Jun-hyeok labeled him as a reactionary and gave a hysterical order to have him killed. Without saying a word, Hyeok-gu took a multi-tipped spear and did as he was told.

There was no one who could begin to fathom Hyeok-gu's display of utter brutality, and the woman took it upon herself to throw a hint at Jun-hyeok, "Comrade, looks like you don't suffer from boredom." He had no idea what she truly meant but was simply flattered that she would talk to him.

"Ha, ha, that's right. Our Comrade must be tired of the mountains?" he replied thoughtlessly.

But one day they became completely isolated because of besiegement by the South Korean army and while engaged in a ferocious battle in search of a retreat, countless people died. They had to give up the town of Munpyeong, North Gyeongsang Province and Hyeok-gu ended up killing Jun-hyeok by the self-same method. No one knew found out about it. As he collapsed, trying to avoid Hyeok-gu's multi-tipped spear, Jun-hyeok fired his gun but all the bullets hit the earth. He spewed forth blood as he crumbled to the ground when Hyeok-gu struck him with a multi-tipped spear. But the curse of the dead man must have spread because the bite of Jun-hyeok dug deep into Hyeok-gu's flesh and his left leg began to rot away, as if a poisonous snake bit it. Holding the dead man by his head and jaw, Hyeok-gu tried to force open Jun-hyeok's mouth that was locked on to his thigh but fainted when he could no longer bear the excruciating pain from the poison that spread all through his body. In delirium, he thought he had to keep moving and tried desperately to shake his leg free but when he could not take even one step, he lay flat and instantly fell asleep.

No one knew about this frightening incident but for some reason, Hyeok-gu revealed to Yeo-jeong the details about murdering Jun-hyeok. She was so shocked and confounded that for a while she didn't know what to make of his confession. It was definitely something to celebrate for her own sake and not be horrifically taken aback or saddened, now that a most bothersome man was gone, but she wasn't sure if she could bring herself to understand Hyeok-gu's contradictory state of mind; moreover, she had the prescience that her own life could perhaps be in danger as well. But this incident spurred her to fall madly for Hyeok-gu, while glimpsing into his insane longing for freedom in the midst of understanding the implications of his cruel behavior, and she felt she was responsible for helping him regain his freedom. When Yeo-jeong felt a similar passion for Hyeok-gu, previously akin to what she had thought was genuine love for Seok-hyeong who was also a member of the Culture Division, she found herself feeling enraptured in a way that was hard to describe. She recalled the time when she couldn't identify her emotion that she now recognized as passion and the strong affection she felt toward Hyeok-gu was most definitely founded on concrete grounds—that is, she rediscovered the humanity of Seok-hyeong in Hyeok-gu.

There was nothing else he could do but helplessly stare at his leg that was rotting away. High up in the mountains, the winter was long and the flesh froze and the body could not feel any pain, which was all the better for Hyeok-gu who dragged his leg around. Yeo-jeong gazed at their footprints in the snow as she walked alongside Hyeok-gu on a mountain path. In the smooth slope where there wasn't one imprint of a bird footprint, they cast a single shadow like a tree in the rising sun. Each snowflake was sparkling in rainbow colors against the slant of the slope. The footprints they left behind told a story, as though from a dream, and appeared forlorn like the boars that had passed through.

Looking absently at their footprints, Hyeok-gu said, "We should've left it unspoiled. Let's sit down here. It makes me guilty to step on more snow." Then he blew out some air as though he didn't want her to hear his sigh. In the small pine tree next to them, a spider in the web was quivering in the wind, its body shining in the bright sunlight.

"What's there to eat, hmm? Baby spiders are known to feed on their mother but here I am with a rotting body that is worthless to my children."

Yeo-jeong was at a loss as to what to make of a man who showed empathy for spiders and expressed his appreciation for snow yet didn't hesitate a second in spearing a man to death and then nonchalantly wiping the blood off his blade with the grass. When it occurred to her that Hyeok-gu was deprived of all judgment and no longer knew where to direct his love, Yeo-jeong suddenly became terrified of the Party that had completely reshaped a human being.

"You're the type of person who must live in the village there. You've already lost your right to be a Party member."

"How could I live there?"

"Have you ever longed to be free? To be able to do the kind of work you wish?"

"I don't know. I just did as I was told."

"Don't you have any desire to do something you want and make your own mistakes?"

"I can't....I don't think I can even die freely. For who will want to bury me?"

"We are very unhappy people. But you can escape from being unhappy. There is a way. You need to leave here."

When Yeo-jeong at last uttered the words that had constrained her heart, she became teary.

"I cannot do that. Let me die here."

Yeo-jeong kept persuading Hyeok-gu that he had every right to leave, that he must go away and he argued that she, too, had the right to leave and cajoled her to go with him. Perhaps she had tried to coax him only to come to this. It was difficult to suppress the indescribable joy that was arising from the bottom of her heart and she wished she could beg him right then to take her with him; however, she could not deny that she had already been irretrievably reconstructed by the Party.

When there is snowfall in the mountains, even the boars go hunting in the village and they, too, searched for food in the town and returned, exhausted, when the moon waned. In the morning, they darted around, like a boar that missed being shot at a critical point, sprinkling blood in the snow-covered slope, collapsing in the snowstorm; as the winter passed, there were more days when they could not return from the village. Like a mountain boar, Hyeok-gu, with a gunshot in his leg, ran around in the snow like a mad man, spattering red blood on the white snow. The gunshot wound, which happened to be in the infected rotting section of his body, became a critically severe injury and Hyeok-gu could no longer stand still or even eat. As it would have a deleterious effect on the others just to leave him in the snow, and was too tedious to watch, waiting for him to die, he was ordered by the Party to go down to the village and work on food supply. He had vainly thought that his body was at least a single bullet's worth but to them even one bullet for him seemed like an extravagance, but so as not to lose even a small cog in the wheel, they had sent an almost a walking dead man to get food.

Gazing down at death ascending from the bottom of his leg, he vomited a pool of blood, not knowing where to target the rage he felt. But in effect, it was fury directed at himself. With all his strength he clawed the earth and pushed himself forward to reach for the gun in front of him. In no time, he was dragged by Yeo-jeong, like a log, and they tumbled down the snow.

"Leave me alone."

"No, you must live."

"No, leave me alone. I want to die here by their gun. I want to put their gun to use on me. I know nothing. I was possessed and I just followed orders."

Like a mad woman, she dragged him down the slope.

Suddenly, with a groan, she felt like her body was about to drop into the deep ravine and soon enough she lost her consciousness, like she was falling asleep. But then she also felt like she was still dragging Hyeok-gu's body, yet not being able to move one more step, unaware that he had been shot in his other leg. Perhaps it was inevitable that they should fire at Hyeok-gu who was fleeing, but he wished that they had shot him, not to kill a betrayer or to pay him back for his contribution to the Party, but because his body was worth indeed a bullet. Regardless of whether or not Hyeok-gu's body still contained life, Yeo-jeong struggled to reach the village, as though all that mattered was to get his body away from the Party.

Geun-nyeo stood there, looking out for a long time, so that she didn't realize her customer behind her kept getting up and down, waiting for her to pay him attention. Neither did she hear the kettle about to almost boil over. Suddenly Bong-deok came to her mind and she became all upset again, asking herself where she might be and what trickery she was up to. Then she remembered her customer and turned around to look at a face she couldn't quite recollect. He had long finished eating the bread and was sitting at the table, with his one hand cupping his chin and doodling something with his finger. Sensing Geum-nyeo's gaze, he startled and looked up. Wondering why he was still there when he had finished all his bread, she walked up to him, and asked, "Do you want more bread?"

Rather than being surprised, he briskly got up instead on his feet like a frightened man.

"I am very sorry." He kept apologizing and as though it was very difficult for him to continue, his lips were quivering. Then with a burst of courage, he spoke in an unusually loud voice, "I don't have any money," taking out a fountain pen from his pocket.

Geum-nyeo couldn't believe it.

"Why the hell did you eat my bread then?" she asked harshly. Her eyebrows were wriggling like silkworm and she frowned deeply, trying to suppress her anger. She ran to the corner of her store and brought back a large box. She poured the contents in front of her customer. There were harmonicas, fountain pens, and whatnot.

"Do people think what I have to offer is for free? All the bastards coming here give me these instead of money. Is there anyone who doesn't know about money?"

"I am sorry. In fact…"

"Being sorry isn't going to do anyone any good. Everyone says that when they don't pay. Do you think I am a humanitarian?"

"But…it's a little different for me. And you can get at least hundred *won* for this fountain pen if you sell it."

"A little different? What kind of nonsense is that? If it's worth a hundred *won*, then you go and sell it yourself. I don't want to buy it."

In the middle of her fit, Geum-nyeo scattered the fountain pen and pocket knife in front of the customer who kept clutching and fondling the pen and seemed reluctant to give it to Geum-nyeo, who didn't even want to take it. It looked like he had a deep attachment to the fountain pen.

"Well, you see…"

"I was a captive until a few days ago. I am an anti-Communist prisoner of war…That's why I don't have any money on me."

"An anti-Communist? You mean you were one of the people in the car with a white tape that went through the marketplace the other day?"

"Yes, yes. Those of us, who didn't want to go to North Korea, all fled."

Even though Geum-nyeo was talking down to him, he did not seem affronted and his calm demeanor indicated he was an educated young man, kind of like an elementary school student who was very sorry for what he had done before his reprimanding teacher, a fledgling who had no experience with society and therefore was innocently clueless about how he should behave.

"I don't know. You go and sell it or do what you want."

Realizing that the anti-Communist prisoners of war were people who were against the Communists, Geum-nyeo lost her will to scream any more at him. She couldn't help feeling somewhat empty in her heart. After sending her customer away, she went out to the street to get Bong-deok to follow him. She never let anyone get away without some kind of security, but watching this man walk into the crowd in the marketplace, she felt she could trust him and in some ways, she was even afraid to see him again.

She walked quite a distance in search of Bong-deok. The customer, who failed to sell his fountain pen, came back to the store and was surprised to find it empty. After placing the fountain pen on the shelf that was outside by the plank door, he came in and sat down again. It wasn't that he couldn't sell the fountain pen. It was his only possession and if the pen contained a spirit, surely the warmth of his being must be imbued in it; hence, he couldn't possibly part with the fountain pen in exchange for several pieces of bread. He was lost deep in thought when he heard a rustle and he saw a hand go up and then down. Suddenly he remembered his fountain pen and he rushed out, only to feel faint, like he had bumped his head against the door. Both the beggar who had shoved the fountain pen by her side and the customer who had darted out of the store froze when they recognized each other. The beggar was Yeo-jeong and the customer turned out to be Seok-hyeong.

"So it is possible for Comrade Yeo-jeong to remain here?"

"I don't know what happened either."

"Of course not. After we split, I voluntarily became a captive. And I was released just the other day. I refused to return to North Korea, even though my parents are still living there."

"But now the distance between us is close but is actually farther than ever."

"I know. It is perhaps because you are in the South that I refused to be sent back to the North."

"Who gave you this fountain pen?"

"I have always cherished it because I deemed it as a token of love from you."

This conversation took place after several minutes of long silence between them. Geum-nyeo, who came back to the store dragging Bong-deok, saw the crouching beggar and was appalled. She turned to look at her customer, not knowing what was going on.

It was Bong-deok who said in amazement, "Gee, mother, that's the beggar who dumped her baby under the bridge."

The three people who heard that looked at each other but were equally at a loss for words. Among them, Seok-hyeong's face plainly expressed a myriad of emotions.

Life

It probably happened on January 1, 1951. The snowstorm created a whirlpool and raked the land. The black dust made a mess of the wind that wrapped around whatever it blew against. First Sergeant Herald Goldberg grabbed the compass from his belt. After checking it, he looked up at the sky again. The dust-laden snow enveloped his face like gun smoke. It was impossible to keep his eyes open. After a ferocious battle at the 38th Parallel, the army retreated. The front became a zone of chaos and the defeated soldiers were left helpless. Sergeant Goldberg was sent tumbling by the wind. The spoon, dangling from his backpack, fell and rolled on the hardened ground. It has been four days since he ate anything. Lying flat on the ground, he scratched the earth. It could be that he was on the 38th Parallel line. Earlier, he could've sworn he saw the shadow of a dark house shaped like a boulder. He began to crawl. His body was being sucked into a mud hole. He buried his face in the mud and drank the muddy water. He could reach the house once he crossed the stream. He held his gun close to his chest as he got up. He could see the house more clearly. The dawn cast a shade on the thatched hut and the darkness around it turned gray. Sergeant Goldberg got his gun ready but decided he wouldn't fire. He walked through the yard without a gate and turned on the flashlight as he pushed the kitchen door open. The beam of the flashlight showed the kitchen in its dimness. Like a hunting dog, he checked every corner. The iron rice pot was there. He ran to open the lid. There was only water inside. He put his hand in it and stirred the water. He aimed the flashlight next at the wall. There were bowls on the shelf. But there was nothing in it. Sergeant Goldberg got completely incensed. He kicked the door open to the room and turned on the light. He was startled to spot something white on the floor. He pointed his gun at it but when he saw that it was a woman, his face softened. Next to her, he discovered an infant wrapped in its mother's black skirt. He was surprised once more but when his eyes caught sight of a basket against the wall, his face brightened up. He pointed the flashlight at the woman's face again. She looked deathly pale but was not dead. She opened her eyes at the strong light, horrified. Sergeant Goldberg's glance traveled from her face to her breasts, then to her feet, stopping at the dried up blood on the floor. Along with an unbearable dizziness, he felt a strong sexual urge and collapsed on the woman's chest. His hands that grabbed her sleeves freed themselves instantly. His hands crawled on the floor to reach the basket. He gorged on the rice. A very faint cry of a baby was heard briefly. He crawled back to the kitchen and gulped down the water in the pot. The flashlight was lying on the ground with a circular light around it. The power of the flashlight had diminished because morning had arrived. He felt like smoking. But he did not have anything to light the cigarette. The soft light from the flashlight made him feel the melting snow. His eyes automatically closed and his lower stomach felt hot. All of a sudden, he smelled the blood and his belly turned over. The cry of the baby sounded like the flute of the Chinese army. Again, the woman's groaning unnerved him. He wished she'd just disappear forever. He grabbed the baby and pushed it onto the woman's chest. The startled woman bared the white of her eyes and fainted. Sergeant Goldberg put the baby on the mother's bosom but her flat breasts could not support the baby who rolled down. He glared at the woman's swollen breasts and pulled her body toward him with great force. The woman opened her eyes again but her eyes were not moving. He brought his muddy face closer to her and smiled. But then chills ran through his body as he gazed at the dying woman. A light flashed before him then. The sunlight entered through the window. At that moment, someone cried, "Hands up," aiming a gun at him but the muzzles of both men were pointed at each other simultaneously, not allowing anyone to shoot first. The enemy was exhausted. His eyes lacked sparkle. Sergeant Goldberg's gun shook as terrifying hatred spread through his body like poison. His enemy was wounded. Their final moment would be determined by one's will. Dark blood was running down from the enemy's side. His face, devoid of any vitality, was trembling. He, too, was a defeated soldier. I simply need to wait until the will of my enemy is completely extinguished from his face. But the enemy, who was standing before a woman of his country, could not be bereft of hatred. He has hatred but I possess the willpower. His clenched mouth will forever be shut. Suddenly though, 'Filthy, Yankee pig, sex fiend, American SOB," came out of his mouth with foam around it. Sergeant Goldberg understood the word America. What if I were British or French? What're you going to do about it? The flashlight on the floor lost all its power of brightness in the morning sunlight. The woman, with her swelled up breast bare, lay stiff and lifeless while the infant with its mouth open appeared asleep and not moving. It was a question of who could bear this tension longer. The enemy was young. I, too, should be attending Springfield University. The enemy is wearing a tarnished brown army uniform with an epaulet of T-shape that hung heavily on the shoulder. His top, shoved under the leather belt is full of mud. He is not even wearing a helmet. His face looked like he's about to cry, especially with his dark eyebrows. In addition, a story could be told from his dusty eyes. He could even see a mole next to his nose. And his parched lips. How much longer did they have to keep on with this silent confrontation? The midday sun must be going down. The shade of the tree was casting the shadow of the leaves in front of the window. It was warm for a winter day. The earth graves by the stream must be melting for one could hear the sound of it from here. Goldberg felt composed. He thought he would love to smoke a cigarette now. His eyes can see through his enemy's eyes. He could sense the story of his enemy's heart from his eyes. Do you have any matches… Goldberg asks with a look in his eyes. His enemy seems to answer—I can't smoke. In spite of himself, his eyes fall on the woman's breast. The enemy's eyes, too, are affixed on it. A pearly milk spills from her breasts and flows down between the mounds. They feel her palpitating heart. She is alive! She'll die if we don't do anything. The words came out of his mouth and it startled the enemy. A cold something passed through his whole body and Goldberg felt an insane urge to scream and fire away. This tension will only disappear with one of them dead. Who will die? All of a sudden, he feels sad. If only they could talk to each other about it all, then they could both live. His stomach is terribly upset from the rice he ate last night. If only he could defecate, he'd feel better. How great if he could share these thoughts with his enemy? Ah, this tension, the silence is making their solitary hostility unbearable. Goldberg glared at the gun sight with rage. It was aiming at the enemy's eyes. Speak! You dummy. He urgently needs to defecate. The eyes of the enemy seen through the gun sight are quivering. His body is shaking lightly. His whole face is shaking. His enemy can no longer stand it. Goldberg excreted in his pants. His enemy's face contorted a little and a sliver of smile passed briefly across his lips. Goldberg felt a huge relief as he felt a cold sweat run down his back. As evening approached again, the shadow of the rafter covered the front gate and the light from the flashlight shone once more. His enemy will not live through the night. The same goes for the woman. The infant will live for several days more. His gunshot wound was rotting away.

The enemy's body was now losing its balance completely. Goldberg wanted to tell the full story. Ah, if I were to talk about my beloved Daphne de Olivier, this is what I would tell him.

"…Herald! I can't bear it. Or else, I will just die. I cried my heart out last night, looking at your picture. Ah…our very own world! The night of the ball. Herald, I can't write anymore. I put flowers in your room again last night. I was too shy to go into your bedroom. Your mother teased me so much…and she played the wedding song you chose on the piano. But I read in the paper that the army has retreated again from Pyeongyang. Where could your battle be now? Korea! Ah, I can't write anymore. Sending you kisses over the Pacific Ocean from afar."

Goldberg glared to the point of being dizzy.

"God damn it. I can't stand it. Shoot!" He screamed. The darkness concealed the face of his enemy. The light of the flashlight was fading except for the circle around the woman's face. He could sense only the eyes and the muzzle of his enemy in the dark. For some reason, Goldberg wanted this moment to last forever. His enemy was before him. He felt secure, like he had a guard. His enemy who seemed like he was going to collapse from exhaustion was leaning against the wall and moaning. Before he knew it, he had fallen asleep. He awoke, startled to hear someone talk in his dream to find out it was his enemy who was groaning and snoring at the same time. The flashlight had gone out and from afar, he could hear the sound of a cry, as in a dream. The front line was far away from here. For some reason, he was not afraid at all. He wanted to stretch his legs out. He had an insane urge to smoke. He put his hand in his pocket and grabbed the cigarette. He didn't want to wake up his enemy. He carefully and quietly took out a cigarette. The smell of it was strong. He undid the wrap and chewed it in his mouth. He knew he could now somehow stand it. His mouth was completely dry. He fell asleep with the loose cigarette in his mouth. When he awoke, frightened out of his wits and aimed the gun, his enemy, like a guard, was opposite him, leaning against the wall, giving him a vacant look. Why don't you shoot? Goldberg screamed quietly, glaring at his enemy whose light was diminishing from his eyes. As they glared at each other, an inexplicable smile crossed Goldberg's face.

"I surrender. Please treat me if you have any medication," his enemy seemed to be saying.

"I have it. Do you have any bread?" Goldberg whispered in English.

"Yes. Save me quickly."

"But this woman needs medication, also." Goldberg spoke a little louder and pointed at the woman.

His enemy was startled and said something after glaring at him but Goldberg could not understand him. Neither could understand the other. Goldberg tapped the emergency kit on his waist a number of times. His enemy suddenly looked disappointed and his eyes welled up with tears. Goldberg couldn't stand it any longer. Ah, the frustration of it! At the moment when he felt unless one of them were to die, they could not be freed from this tension, he screamed, ah, and fell forward. The enemy's tearful eyes shone like a startled deer then he aimed at the floor and fired. After the dust cleared from the room and as Goldberg pointed the gun at the enemy and was about to pull the trigger, his enemy fell flat on his gun on the floor. Intermixed with his groan was the blood gushing out in front of him. His enemy had shot the woman to release the tension. Goldberg became frightened all of a sudden. He could not feel the silent communion between them anymore. The smell of his enemy that bespoke of humanity had disappeared. How they had quietly conversed about the most intimate things. A whole day of sharing their stories, with a gun aimed at each other. But the enemy had fallen of his own. He swiftly opened the medical kit and took out the cotton gauze and the styptic. He uncovered the enemy's side. A clump of blood and his cloth froze on his flesh. Where did he enemy get the strength to endure for so long? His will to live burned with the fuel of hatred. With profuse sweat, Goldberg was gazing down at the ruin of life that had undergone their devastating confrontation. His enemy had a gentle smile on his face and his mouth was open, as if he would tell him a private story in a moment. He looked down at the woman, who was lit in white in the morning sunlight. And her infant. And like a mad man, he ran out the door with a scream. Where should I go? Goldberg now realized he couldn't stand being alone. His enemy was still alive. He ran back into the room and straightened his enemy's body up and shouted—save me. The day was getting dark again.

He held his enemy on his side and like a mad man, he ran through the field. The snowstorm became a whirlpool that ravaged the land. The wind jumbled up with the black dust enveloped his body. First, Sergeant Goldberg turned his enemy's shoulders around and embraced him tightly.

Death in the Cathedral

This story is inspired by T.S. Eliot's *Murder in the Cathedral*.

The people's government retreated in the direction of the northern mountain ranges from where the offensive was coming down, after leaving the tread marks of the tanks on the asphalt, abandoning the nearly dead bodies under the railroad, away from the sea, having dug a pit on the highlands, passing the fields not yet harvested, and seeing the changed signboards of all the organizations. It was strange that the people's regime was retreating to the north where the free republic was launching its offense. The sun was burning the street where not a sign of a person was visible and the evening breeze laden with salt was still blowing from the sea.

The two guerrilla fighters, with a submachine gun slung upside down across their shoulders, were inspecting the street on their bikes. The city was waiting in deadly stillness for the change of government. They were slowly pedaling along the red brick wall of the empty lot where there used to be barracks. The phrase, "Hurray to a Most Courageous and Outstanding People's Army," was painted huge and in white on the brick wall. They turned the corner where it was written, "Army," and entered the path to the public hospital. The shadow of the plane trees lined on both sides of the road shook a little against the sea wind that blew from time to time.

They pedaled past the white slogan on the hospital cement wall that read, "The Great Leader Stalin Who Liberated the People of a Weak Nation." There was not a person in sight. They were now riding past the tall prison wall.

PARK SANGSEEK

Upon catching a sight of flyers pasted on the gate in front of the prison across the creek, they both headed in that direction. They got off their bikes and while pulling it by hand, they read the flyer, "Park Heon-yeung killed himself. Long Live the Republic of South Korea." The prison gate was tightly shut. They got on their bikes again. Right then, they saw a sign of a person. They pedaled more forcibly. They saw a person entering the gate of the Catholic Church with evergreen trees. The shadow of the bell tower descended on them with the sun in the backdrop. The person was entering the gate in the shape of a lotus flower. They rode straight from the gate through the garden to the steps leading up to the entrance. They exchanged a look with each other and walked side by side. Dragging their bikes with one hand only, they took off their hats and fixed their hair.

They stood in the middle of the garden and looked at the entrance for a long time, wondering why they had come there. There wasn't the slightest movement in the garden. They too remained immobile like the trees. They heard footsteps from inside but no one came out. The two looked at each other. One of them straightened his gun and gave a sign to the other that he was going in.

The partisan who remained outside parked his bike in the middle of the cement road and plopped down at the bottom of the steps. He absent-mindedly looked around at the trees. From somewhere there was the sound of a jet. He stole a glance at the door. There was brilliant sunlight in the garden, however there was still no movement whatso-ever. As though tired of viewing the garden, he dropped his head and closed eyes.

He tried to think of something but there wasn't anything that came to his mind. He looked at the garden again for it was right before his eyes and he had no choice but to do that. But he quickly got bored. He then cast his eyes on his clothes. There was no insignia or anything but just five tin buttons showing two ears of rice facing each other. There was nothing more to look at. He began fiddling with the buttons. There was no sense of texture and his hands became all sweaty. He got

68

tired of this, too. He turned his gun around and caressed the round bullet case. He detached it from the gun and put it on his palm, trying to guess its weight. But he wasn't thinking about exactly how much it would weigh. He wasn't thinking about anything. He became tired of it, too. He pounded his fist against the butt. He looked up at the sky, in impatience. There were no clouds. Or color. There was nothing. It was just white. He felt the urge to look at something again. He rolled up his left sleeve and peeked at the compass he had around his wrist, like a watch. A white needle was quivering against the black background. He put his left arm on his knee and scrutinized it. But it wasn't like he wanted to know the direction.

He must have already forgotten about his comrade. The sun was setting. The needle in the compass stood out more. He could tell from the compass that it was near dusk. He could sense disorder inside the church. It sounded like a groan or a scream. He merely sat and listened. Sweat rolled down to his eyebrow. He took out a handkerchief and wiped his eyebrows then looked up at the sky. It was crimson and the church was dark crimson while the garden was yellow.

He heard unruly footsteps and there was a sudden burst of gunshots. The bell rang in the tower. He rushed in. The jet could be heard once the sound of the shooting ceased. The gunshots had left the church interior replete with the smell of gunpowder. His eyes burned yellow. He stood there for a long time. With the gun thrown on the floor, his comrade took a few steps forward, holding his right arm with his left hand. He turned his eyes to where his friend was glaring. There were two bodies before them, that of a priest in a black robe and another person. He began walking toward them, aiming the gun. The Host was visible on the altar. Suddenly, their bodies along with the Host shook. The entire church was shaking. The high glass window shattered. Before they knew it, they were prostrate on the floor. The plane circled above them and when it reached a certain height, it dropped at a terrifying velocity. Their consciousness was swept into roaring of the jet that soared high. The rocket bombs, which dropped here and there, shook the ground. The sky roared with the sounds of the jet. It sounded like several thousand of them, not one. It was a moment of blank oblivion when the plane descended with a metallic screech.

The rocket bombs exploded, demolishing the ground. They crawled to the altar by way of underneath the chairs. The remaining sunshine was still inside the church. When the guerrilla fighter, who came in later, reached the podium, it seemed like the whole church was suddenly lifted in the air then dropped, and the rear wall of the altar crumbled as the bomb exploded in the air. He fainted before the podium. The dust was cleared inside and evening seeped through the broken window. The fragmented dark blue sky hung inside the church. The guerrilla fighter, who came in first, looked for his comrade. But he couldn't move. He felt his leg and then fainted again. His legs were sore and ached terribly. He could feel blood spilling from his side.

Saint Mary or other sacred icons were invisible to his eyes. Only a fragment of the dark crimson sky, and no other reflection, were imprinted on his eyes. The sound of the plane had vanished into the sky afar, leaving a piercing noise as a remnant of it.

The bodies of the priest and another person and the partisan who came in first were spread in the middle of the floor. The one who came in later had dropped next to the broken statue of a sacred icon, his head and face all bloody. The altar and the podium were shattered to pieces. The statue of Saint Mary and the consecrated candle were lying on the floor and to one's amazement, a submachine gun was ensconced in Saint Mary's bosom. The gray sky was drawn like a drape on the rear wall of the altar that was no longer there, and the orange curtain was fluttering on the high mosaic window. Dusk fell on the body of the priest who had died from being struck on the leg and stomach by the shell fragments, with his innards showing. He had died twice. The breeze from the sea moved into the church and hardened the blood flowing from the corpses.

70

The guerrilla fighter opened his eyes as he felt the breeze on his forehead. A shadow approached him. A woman carrying a candlestick was walking toward the corpse. His arm ached terribly when he saw her. His eyes felt too stinging for him to look at the candlestick. A little girl was tagging alongside the woman. She examined the bodies with trepidation. It was difficult to identify them, for the clothes were torn to pieces and the faces were all bloody. The guerrilla fighter fainted once more when he saw the light. She searched around like a mad woman.

When she got to the altar where the Host and the guerilla fighter who came in later had fallen, she took a closer look. Her face froze. The child found the statue of Saint Mary underneath the altar and tugged her mother for attention. In great fear, his mother stepped back. The child held the marble hand. The mother came back to where the body of the priest was and took alternate looks at the three corpses. The light from the candlestick created countless forms inside the dim church.

The guerrilla fighter regained his consciousness upon sensing a powerful light on him. He opened his eyes and looked at the woman. She stepped back nervously when she spotted a bayonet that was not on him but out of its case with half its blade gleaming. The dagger was bleeding like it had stabbed a lump of blood. Her eyes glued to the dagger, the woman took back steps to the corpse lying beside the priest. The child dropped the hand of Saint Mary and ran to the body. The woman was suddenly jolted to her senses and began inspecting the body. When her foot tripped over the shoe on the body, she dropped the candlestick and collapsed, hugging the corpse. The child shook the body but she only got blood on her hand. The woman, with an ashen face, gazed at the head that looked like a lump of blood. Her face slowly turned hateful. She turned to look at the bayonet.

The guerilla fighter tried to move his left arm. It wouldn't move. He couldn't even tell which arm was wounded. He tried to turn his body. His lower abdomen pained him greatly. He lay flat on his lower back on the plank floor and looked for something he could use as support. By pressing down and pushing, his body edged back. There was no wall but a row of chairs behind him. He leaned his back against the chair and sat aslant. His mouth was dry and his left arm ached unbearably. He rolled up his sleeve and looked for the wound. He saw a deep bite mark in the dim light. He looked at the body the woman held.

It was a bite by that corpse. The corpse clutched his sleeve and begged for his life. He had no intention of killing them. But then that corpse was asking for his life. He simply wanted to find out who and why they were here. But they just kept imploring him for their lives. They held on to his clothes and wouldn't let him go. He tried to free himself. If only they hadn't grabbed him, he would've simply left but they wouldn't let go of his sleeve. He got scared. He became afraid of them.

He saw that the woman's eyes were on his bayonet. His thoughts continued.

He had entered the church with his gun slung upside down. There were two people talking before the podium. He approached them. They kept on talking, not knowing he had walked in. The priest in a black robe was nodding. The other person appeared to be in confession. They felt strange to him.

He took out a handkerchief and tied it around his arm. The woman's eye was still on his dagger and it was somehow difficult for him to bear it. He unfastened the belt that held the dagger and shoved it aside. There was no sensation below his abdomen. He was terribly thirsty. He looked back behind the altar where the sky was visible. The sky was already turning dark blue. He wished it would pour rain. If only it would rain on his face.

He got angry when that corpse clutched his bayonet from his side and wouldn't release it. He ended up pulling out the dagger and stabbing the corpse's hand. The corpse's hand was bleeding but still he wouldn't let go. He clawed his arm with his bleeding hand. He couldn't help it but stab the corpse's chest with the dagger. The corpse bit his arm even after being stabbed. Suddenly he became frightened. He thought he would be killed. And he fired indiscriminately at the priest who had his hands clasped as in prayer and pleading.

The child was trembling, buried under her mother's dress. She was thinking of the Virgin Mary's hand that she had tossed earlier. But she was so frightened she couldn't take a step away from her mother. The woman's eye was now on the gun that was in front of him. She wasn't looking at him at all. He could feel the cold sweat on his head. He wished it would stream down to his lips to quench his thirst. The venomous pain in his arm ran through his bones.

That corpse died after unleashing poison onto me. What is now more worthless than firewood bit me. That corpse has poisoned my flesh. It wants to take me along. How revolting. His nature as beastly as a wild animal. A filthy bastard. To drag me down as well.

His abdomen, struck by a shell, felt numb. He wasn't sure if it was even there. The woman looking down at his gun seemed pitiful. Did she want to shoot me? Or did she revile that gun? He thought she should pull the trigger if she so wished. A sharp contour of the woman's face was revealed in the light. She would probably remain seated for hours. His eyes were fatigued. His whole body felt chilly, as though he'd been electrocuted. He suddenly felt the urge to kill the woman. He wished to destroy everything around him. If it were an object, he would crush it, and if it were a person, he would stab him to death. The face of the woman appeared beautiful to a dying person. How could I die alone, leaving behind a face like that? The candle had burned half way already. He wanted to put out the candle. Being able to see was no less than a severe punishment for him at this moment. The brightness was like the eye of an evil spirit. He couldn't possibly die in such a bright and cozy place like this, gazing at the beautiful face of the woman.

He tried to sit straight but dropped down instantly. His limp body was drooped over the chair like a formless hat. He asked the woman to put out the candle by raising his arm. But the woman did not understand him. He gave up and closed his eyes. The sweat dried up near his eyebrows. He was thirsty. He opened his mouth to suck the night air. He wet his lips with his tongue. The venomous pain in his left arm had somewhat lessened but his wound was swelling up. The blood had clotted in his lower abdomen. I am dying now. That was all that he could think of. His consciousness was barely hanging at the tip of his nerve, like dew on a grass. He suddenly opened his eyes as he felt a shadow weighing down on his chest. Like a faint dream, he could see the woman touching his dagger. Then he fainted.

The woman came closer to the bayonet to pick it up. The belt came up with it. She hesitated for a while, as she wasn't sure whether she should release the belt from the dagger or pull the dagger out of the belt, and then decided to take the dagger out of the case by its handle. The bloody dagger was stuck and wouldn't budge. She pulled it with more force. It remained immovable. She then stepped on the case to pull it out. Although half of the blade stuck out of the case, she couldn't get it out. Cold sweat formed on her forehead. She was trembling, holding the handle. She was now panting. Obsession took over. As she attempted to push the dagger back into the case, her hand wrapped around the handle slipped and glided against the blade. Blood spewed from her palm. She wiped the blood on her dress and with her other hand, she shook it relentlessly.

The woman's puffing brought him to his senses. She was glaring at him with a scary look. It was not a murderous gaze but a terrified look. It was unclear whether or not she was going to kill him or herself while he had fainted, however her intent was revealed. He tried to show a smile on his face that was stiff with dried up sweat. He wasn't sure if it showed.

The woman seemed more and more terrified. The candle was still lit and formed countless shadows on the ceiling. The night was so still that they could barely sense they were breathing. Something had to come to an end. It was going to end. The moment was not for the beginning of something but be it good or bad, it was necessary. The time of waiting was insanely frustrating. It was like being in a sunken submarine deep under the ocean. He wished his consciousness would quickly leave his poisoned dying body for his body could not endure it any longer. Yet, he wasn't thinking of how nice it would be to die swiftly.

He let out an abrupt scream to clear his consciousness and tried to stand up but plopped down. The petrified woman ran to him. She collapsed when she saw the face of the fallen guerilla fighter with his eyes open and sobbed. The child awoke and looked for his mother. She looked all around her. She burst into tears when she found her. Still crying, she crawled toward his mother. The tip of her finger reached the hand of the Virgin Mary. All the shimmering shadows of the objects in the church shriveled away.

The shadows on the curtain swayed above them. The torso of the sacred icon and the shadow from the guerilla fighter who came in later flickered on the window, and then disappeared. The shadow of the chair and the candlestick were undulating on the black robe of the priest. The head of Christ with a halo was broken in half and rolled on the floor. Light had vanished inside the church and an illumination from the sky was shining on them. The sound of a jet came from somewhere. Was it coming from the windows that resonated with it from the airplanes? For it seemed to be coming from inside. It was circling above the church ground. The rocket bomb exploded. No matter where it was dropped, a rocket bomb always felt like it exploded in one's heart. The sky was ablaze. A firebomb had exploded. The sound of something tossed from the ground and the ascending jet in the sky and the falling rocket bomb filled the air with a great sound, however, no human voice was heard. Suddenly the church looked like it was surging in space, then the ceiling from the bell tower tumbled down and crashed on the church.

He had the illusion of political authority being shattered by the bomb. Ideology was self-destructing alongside the religion inside this church. The child had fainted in her mother's bosom. The day was brightening with the rising crimson sun. The sky was now light but not from the firebomb. The sun was rising. But there was only an afterglow of the sun and darkness still pervaded the church.

The woman startled as she was about to nestle her child. She found herself behind the guerilla fighter with her head buried in his back. She clutched her child and moved to the back. He flagged his arms, asking for water. The woman got up and ran to the entrance to get water for him. The sound of the jets boomed as it descended, and after a deadly moment of silence, the entrance was shattered after it was struck with a direct hit.

The jets disappeared one by one, and there was a sound of a cannon near the sea. Over the corpses where the bricks, metal window frame, and a mound of earth scattered with dust, fragments of paper, and pieces of rags poured down, while broken glass, from the mosaic window shaken loose from the cannonball blast, fell on the guerilla fighter.

The aftereffect of the jets remained in the church like the mist in the valley. The guerilla fighter groped for the woman's corpse with his remaining hand. The arm that had been bitten by the corpse was digging into the ground in search of the woman. There was a circle with about a twenty-centimeter radius around his hand with its inside completely cleared.

Two soldiers with carbine rifles upside down were pedaling their bikes side by side on a patrol of the street. Facing the church with its collapsed bell tower, they were riding slowly through the power vacuum of this regime. The mountain ranges soared in silent anticipation of an open invasion beginning tomorrow. The coal tar of the asphalt road had been pitifully ruptured in the shell explosion last night. Their buttocks on the bike seats hurt immeasurably and their skin was raw from the carbine rifle that mercilessly drummed against their back. They got off their bikes. There wasn't even a mouse on the street. The area around the church had been completely demolished. It was a region with a concentration of lumber mill and ice factories. There was petroleum spilled here and there, broken desks with documents strew about, burned pieces of cloth on the street with flyers from a printing store, and pieces of newspaper were flying around. They entered the church. The gate had vanished in the explosion. Inside the church they saw a fluttering People's Army uniform, covered face of a dead body, a dead woman with a pale face and not a single visible wound lying facing the sky, a broken half head of a sacred figure laid face down, and a statue of Saint Mary with all the limbs gone but her face miraculously intact in the spot where the altar should be. The soldier gently kicked the face of the Virgin Mary. They heard a rumble of a jet from somewhere. They both looked up at the sky. But there was nothing. Not even a cloud. Where ideology had swept past, not even a blade of glass remained. The political power had mounted death as it thrust its way in and left behind deaths as it relinquished them.

The Blazing Thorn

There the angel of the Lord appeared to him in flames of fire from within a bush. Moses saw that though the bush was on fire it did not burn up. —Exodus 3:2

The moonlight falling on the sea waves that were scraping the sandy beach unveiled a rainbow. The beadlike foam that dissolved under the moonlight dispersed the fog-like clouds in the air. The milky moon shadow flickered over the white sand. A corpse was being pulled and pushed somewhere in the middle of the sandy beach. The moonlight shone on the dark body that faced the sky. The dead body opened its eyes when it felt the moon shadow. What entered the hollowness of his consciousness was not the chilly sensation of the sea or the whiteness of the sand but the weeping of a soul. The waves rolled into its consciousness. The sound of a jet exploded somewhere in the consciousness. The sound of a submachine gun crashed against the bone, overlapped with the people's scream. The universe was filled with sound.

He clawed his way forward on the sand but gave up in exhaustion. His right arm hurt like it was being sliced by a knife. His wrist, which was tied with an electric cord, was bloodstained. He stretched his left arm and started crawling again. The cord that was still around his left wrist was digging into his flesh. He bit on the cord. Just a tiny movement of the cord gave a shock to all his nerves. He looked at the village afar concealed amidst the shrubs. With a greater resolve, he thrust his body forward. I must get to that house. Then I can live. But I can't move anymore. The wave slid underneath his tummy and sucked the sand away from him. He looked up at the sky, with a heavy breath. The moonlight that shone on his face was pitiless. There is no one who can save me. I am alone. I am all by myself in this universe. He began losing consciousness again and a dull milky shade took over it.

The silhouette of the moon quivers then dissolves into the dark sky as it surrenders to the silver powdered light. A dark stain spreads over the waned side. The moon recovers its contour and before long, a half moon becomes visible. A blue glimmer is disseminated from the edge of the moon, glowing then vanishing. It is as refined as the line of a celadon piece. For about three minutes, the inner curve of the crescent moon loses its outline. Shortly, the moon transforms itself to a white curve and is spinning in the sky.

He opened his eyes when he felt something dark and heavy weighing down on him. Instinctively, he swung his arms. Instead of sand, his hand came in touch with the hard floor. He looked around him but couldn't make anything out in the darkness, except for the smell of a person that stunned his nose. I made it here. All the way to this house by myself. He lay on his back, facing the ceiling. The dark wall on both sides felt like they were closing in on him. His heart was pumping so hard that he thought it would burst. The ceiling descended on him like an evil spirit. With his eyes closed, he tried to ward it off by flagging his arms. But his hands that were on the floor would not budge.

Some time passed. There was light. He opened his eyes at the onset of darkness and saw the moonlight seeping in through the door. He felt incredibly thirsty and was astonished to discover a bowl right by the threshold of the door. By some miracle, there was a steaming bowl of porridge. He ate it ravenously.

His mind became more and more lucid. He was lying down and listening to the sound of the sea. He felt an urge to smoke. With that thought in mind, he couldn't bear not being able to do it. The salty sea wind blew through the window.

It was at sunset. The water bubbles tossed by the seagulls flying aslant over the horizon, scattered like white bead. The sun, like a gigantic balloon, dropped to the horizon. The partisans boarded fifty of them onto the boat and sailed toward the sun. They were tied with a cord by a group of six. On their back was a yellow fabric with a shooting target. The partisans tossed them into the sea in the direction of the sun, firing indiscriminately at the gigantic sun. The seagulls, too, soared toward the blazing sun. The partisans were firing away in frenzy.

He had fallen asleep. He awoke suddenly at the sound of the door opening. It was someone's footsteps that walked up to the wooden floor. A flashlight showered light onto his face. His eyes could only make out the hand that held the flashlight. Was it a hand from a dream or reality? Was it a hand? Or not a hand? The partisan tied his hand in the back with an electric cord.

The two shadows passed the mountain shade and came out to the asphalt road. On both sides of the road, the shadows from the building, mixed in with the other two, were in motion. At last, they arrived at the plaza. The prison guard stand cast a shadow deep into their heart. He abruptly raised his head. The moonlight was shining on the plaza like a searchlight. The two shadows came to a sudden halt. The final cry of a person reached the sky and bounced back as an echo, extending between the heaven and the plaza like some spirit. Who were the killer and the dead between the bamboo spear and the club? With his eyes closed, he crawled back like he wanted to flee. The thick hand of a partisan grappled his shoulder. Was he asking me to look at this slaughterhouse of men? To be the witness of the execution? Ah, this regime was massacring men. It was committing an act beneficial to the enemy.

Licking the glob of blood spilling down from the head, the man dies with his eyes open. Another man, with a spear through his chest, rushes toward his attacker and drops dead, fists in the air. After a terrifying convulsion, a body, with its white brain bared, crawls to death.

Is that how this man is going to put me to death? He is going to bring me to that prison ground. He wanted to get away from here quickly. The partisan pushed his back. They walked along the prison wall. He must leave here right away. But the brick wall kept following them.

They arrived at some Catholic church. The shadow of the bell tower overwhelmed him. The moon glided toward the tower. The clouds passed by the edge of the moon. Like a flower, the moon blossomed. The passing of time that took a flower to bloom fully. The moon was a blazing clump of chilly heat, having just undergone a lunar eclipse. The moon, with its contour still blue, radiated translucent rainbow light.

He could not stand still. The moonlight was too potent for him. He felt dizzy and nauseated. He needed to vomit. They entered the church gate that was shaped like a lotus flower. He smelled the human flesh. Several dozen people were packed in the dark hall. The door was locked after they entered. It became darker inside, with only a lit candle on the altar. Not even the moonlight seeped through the mosaic window. A single candle was too weak to light the entire hall. When his eyes got accustomed to the darkness, the shape of each person came into view. Whose sinners were they? Were they God's sinners? Or were they no one's sinner? He looked at the altar. Christ on the cross was still bleeding. It was ablaze above his thorny crown. Was his Passion not yet over?

The partisan had him walk ahead to the podium. Several dozen eyes were glued to his back. The partisan put him under the podium and walked up to the altar by himself. He shut his eyes. Everything wheeled around him when he opened his eyes. Nothing remained still. All things were spinning with him in the center. All of sudden, it became silent. He could hear time passing through his consciousness.

Time passed, enveloping him. Right then, everything seemed to come to a stop and he heard someone call out his name from the podium.

He opened his eyes and looked. With the painting of Christ in the background, a small and skinny man was looking down at him. When he looked at the man, he said in a sharp but low voice, "Yi, look at me."

Who could be calling out to him? Was this what's called "God's mercy"? Or the blessing of Saint Mary? He calmed himself and looked up at him again. It was someone he had never seen, even in a dream. Who could that be? Is he my friend? Perhaps. Or my relative? Could be. But it could be none of the aforementioned. But should I have recognized him? Who on earth could he be? I must find out who he is. He looked at the man in frustration. Ah, he's smiling at me. He must be someone I know very well. Let me talk to him. Say anything. As he is about to say something, the man at the podium spoke, so as to stop him from talking first.

"Don't you know me?" he asked and not waiting for him to reply, he rummaged through the papers in front of him. Licking his parched lips, Yi spoke, "Ah, you're..." but couldn't continue.

The man at the podium looked askance at Yi, while still perusing the papers.

"You're wrong, Yi. You don't know me. How could the owner recognize his worker?"

Yi felt like his whole body was aflame.

"Worker?" he replied inadvertently.

"Yes. I'm a proletariat and you're a bourgeoisie

I'm Kim, your acquaintance. We went to college together. But that's all and it holds no meaning here."

With a smile, Kim said in the same low and quiet tone as earlier, "Yi, it may grieve you but there's nothing that can be done. A single man is powerless."

His sonorous and eloquent speech resonated through the hall.

In a fit of rage, Yi cried out like he was spitting fire.

"That's right. Your Republic will kill me twice. You have drowned me to death the first time and now you will burn me to death. Your Republic resorts to the same method used by past dictators."

"Past dictators?" Kim repeated the words then burst into laughter.

"Were there ever dictators? Nope. If there were, then they should be living still. For only those who live forever can become dictators."

He then raised his arm to point at the painting of Christ and said with a somber expression, "Look over there. There's a dictator, albeit pitiful."

"So does your Republic want to become a dictatorship?"

"Yes, Yi is right. We want to become a dictator. A dictator permanently rules over those who don't work. A dictator executes judgment here on earth. And the acts of a dictator are forever legitimate."

He felt a hateful urge to spit on Kim's face.

"I have been a witness to your judgment and I will be an eternal witness."

"You're in a frenzy now. It isn't like I don't understand you. In fact, my sympathy to you. Earlier, you were desperately trying to figure out who I was. For what reason? Because you were glad to see me? No. Not at all. You were hoping I would perhaps save you...that was the reason. And since your expectations have been crushed, you're throwing a fit. We'll yet see who is right or wrong."

He held his breath.

Right then, the gate opened and a partisan dragged in two convicts, with their hands tied in the back. He brought them to the podium. Kim recorded their names in the registrar and he entered first after pointing at the vestry. Yi was taken with them.

There was inside a table and couple of chairs strewn about. The partisan, who dragged him in there, sat on the edge of the chair and then gave the seat to Kim, who pointed at the chair next to him and told Yi to sit.

But he remained standing while looking at the other two people. There weren't enough chairs to seat all three. Kim sensed it.

"So you're protesting. But you've misunderstood. I asked you to sit down because you'll be the last to be judged. We'll just go by the document." He said and turned to the other two indifferently. One of them was wearing a priest's robe and the other was a stalwart young man. Kim looked at them for a long time. Overpowered by Kim's gaze, the young man slumped down. Kim then wickedly turned his eye to the priest but he refused to sit.

"Fine. A silent protest, it is. Then answer standing up. Do you know why we summoned you here?"

"Because I'm a priest."

"You're free to have a religion. You are a sinner. To have a religion is not sin."

"Everyone is a sinner before God," the priest replied with calmness.

"We're God. We're here to judge you."

Kim threw a quick glance at the young man and said, "It's been disclosed that you made a contact with the enemy."

"I've done no such thing."

"Even though the young man here confessed?" Kim said, looking at them alternately. The young man dropped his head, to avoid his eyes.

"It's a lie."

"An unrepentant sinner will not acknowledge his sin."

Kim turned his attention to the partisan who seated the priest on one of the chairs. Then he aimed his gun against the priest's forehead.

"We do not carry out torture. That is a sadistic act done by past dictators who wished to be legitimized by their traitors. How pitiful they are. Death is the most somber thing in life. No one can tell a lie before death. Thus, we bring the betrayers to confront death."

With his eyes closed, the priest did not budge. In the same clear consistent voice, Kim prodded, "Answer quickly."

But the priest remained still. The partisan fired the gun at the priest's chest. He fell with a scream. Ten eyes remained fixed on the black robe of the priest for a long time.

When the smell of the gunpowder dissipated, the gazes that were affixed on the back of the priest began to scatter.

"Was it right?" Kim asked the young man as though nothing happened. With an ashen face, he glared at Kim and attacked him like a

84

madman. When he realized he couldn't move his hands freely, he clutched the priest's robe and collapsed in tears.

Blue flame discharged before Yi's eyes. Several hundred, thousands, tens of thousands of sparks surged with ferocity. They set the universe ablaze. He focused his eye on one thing. Several thousand sparks all became one. The candle was burning on the desk before his eyes.

"You killed the priest." He screamed like he wanted to extinguish the horrific rage inside of him with this one statement.

"We didn't kill him. We eliminated him. How can a man kill a human?"

How terrifying. He shot him to death before my eyes, yet he's saying he didn't kill him.

"That's cowardly. You're saying nonsense to legitimate your action. It's a lie. A deception. Treason."

His hands were shaking and he couldn't continue as he ran out of breath.

Kim, who was not perturbed in the least, said in an icy voice, "Why? We eliminated him because he was not a citizen of the Republic. Even if he were left alive, he couldn't survive in the Republic. Like a fish that can't live on land…"

"That's why. You killed him."

Kim prevented him from rising by holding his hand up.

"I'm not finished talking. You say I killed the priest…" he said and pointed at him. "But he never existed in this world. He has never lived in the Republic. He is thoroughly extinguished. We will remove his speech, art, soul, and religion completely. What will end is not just his life. His whole entity will be eradicated. We don't exterminate his body but his soul. We can send him to heaven or hell."

"And you view yourself as a human being?"

"Who's asking? Are you a human being?"

A man worse than a beast is asking me if I am a human being.

"You're worse than a beast."

"Do you think men are better than a beast? I am saddened by how I am not as good as a beast."

"Do you mean to annihilate men? Human beings will never die. Look. The priest has died but his spirit will live on."

"And where does it live?"

"It lives in my heart. It exists in your eyes."

"All right. Give me a proof of how men are better than a beast. Show me how great men are." Kim said then looked through the papers on the desk for a long time. In an extremely formal voice, he said, "Yi, we're looking for your family. Can't you tell us where they are?"

"I don't know. That is your job."

Kim looked at the partisan who pointed the gun at Yi's forehead. All his nerves were sucked into the muzzle of the cold metal gun. Had his body turned into nothingness? His consciousness deprived of its physical body was gazing at him. In the valley of his consciousness, he was swinging his arms and screaming. The echoes resonated through the valley. There was only one person screaming, however, several thousand words echoed back to him.

I will show them where. I'll find it. Somewhere, somewhere, it's there. Where? They're there where they are. Somewhere, somewhere, it's there. It's there, there, somewhere.

The moonlight was falling on the grapes. He was dragging the partisan like a shadow. It was difficult to take a step forward, for it felt like something was grabbing him from the back. He was pulling his shadow like a torture device. His shadow for now could only be a severe punishment for him. Wasn't being alive an original sin? He could hear the footsteps of the partisan in his consciousness. From afar the cannonball blasted like a thunder. Several dozen bikes were racing in a line. From the north, there was an explosion that shook the earth and red flames surged to the sky. The People's Army exploded the powder keg, as it retreated. A platoon of the People's Army, with a machine gun slung over their shoulders and a rifle on their side, went past them, led by a military dog that was as tall and lean as a deer.

He raised his head and took a deep breath. The moon was locked in his eyes. The light from the stars felt cool on his head. All of a sudden, the universe fell headlong and created in him an illusion like he was walking on the sky, looking up at the earth. Ah, how dizzying. He couldn't walk straight. He took a step forward with his right foot, and then took another step with the right foot. He tried to take a step with left foot but it was his right foot that came forward. Ah, I can't seem to walk. Which one is my right foot? Which is the right side? They entered a grandiose building that looked like a royal palace. There was no light in the room and it was dead quiet. A frog leapt into a pond with lush foliage. The shadow of the eaves, which looked like a lotus flower facing the sky, quivered on the water.

"Call out the names." Kim said, untying the cord in his back. He wasn't sure how he had got there. He couldn't answer. He didn't know where his family was. He had brought them to this point in his unconsciousness.

"Speak." Kim pressed him again. Whose name was I supposed to call out? My wife? Or my father? There was no way they would be home. They had been deceived by his words.

"You're not mocking us, are you? For there can't be anyone playing around with death." Kim said and made a hand gesture to the partisan. The partisan turned on the flashlight and entered the place. When did I tell them that they were here? Search. You won't find them in hundred years.

Yi was looking at the bright room with the moonlight. What if his father and wife were still there? What would he do? They couldn't possibly be here, they couldn't possibly be here, he kept repeating to himself in a prayer-like way when all three doors to the room that were closed, opened one by one, and his wife dressed in a white mourning clothes came out to the wooden hall. She burst into tears upon seeing him. You poor angel. Don't shed tears. This is a dream. A dream. Then his father wearing a white hanbok, traditional Korean clothes, appeared. His whole body shook, with cold shivers running through him.

"He was solemn before death." Kim said and handed him a gun. His face showed a terrible spasm. With bloodshot eyes, he glared at the partisan, who gazed back at him strengthening his grip on the rifle. Kim shoved his gun against his back.

"We don't kill people. There's one bullet in my gun and you're going to shoot the people in front of you."

Ah, he's told to kill his wife and his father himself. To choose one to kill. It is horrifying. A horrifying test.

"Are you testing me?" he screamed.

"Not at all. You will be testing yourself."

Kim put the muzzle very close to his back. His mind turned once more into nothingness. Cold sweat ran down his neck to his spine, down to his calf.

He couldn't see or feel anything. Except the universe was filled with sound. The sound of the waves colliding against the sun and scattering. The sound of several thousand seagulls fluttering their wings in the air. The mourning sound of the soul. The sound of the gun. He dropped his gun at the sound of a bullet being fired. His father and wife, looking scared, stood before his consciousness, enveloped in the smoke of the gunpowder. Their eyes were crystal clear. He could hear Kim's voice, like water flowing underneath a thin layer of ice.

"You haven't made your choice yet. You probably want to kill them all at once. Even better if the three of you could die together. That's how cruel you are. You don't want your wife to live while you die because you don't want anyone to steal someone whom you love more than anyone. But that's not what we wish for. We want to do away with only one person." Kim picked up the gun that fell on the floor and handed it back to him with a new bullet. He looked in front of him. Like a skull, the partisan did not have any eyes but just two holes. He could no longer bear his father's icy and venomous eyes or his wife's tearful eyes. He could not cope with the suffocating tension any longer. Something had to end. O Heaven, just collapse on me. He closed his eyes then opened them again. His wife's imploring eyes. He heard Kim's voice from the back. Shoot quickly. Now. He pulled the trigger like a mad man. I don't want to see you. I don't want to see you. I don't want to look into your eyes. I don't want to look at your eyes.

He fell down, unconscious.

The violet dream effervesced in the early morning sky which became fogged. The eastern sky turned crimson like a blossoming flower and colored his consciousness pink. Night fluttered away from the sky and the clouds glowed in red. His consciousness was saturated with the sunlight.

They were walking but he didn't know where. His body lost balance every time his foot tripped over a rock. He dropped his eyes to the ground. He saw some kind of an object. The shadow cast over his hazy consciousness was lifted. It wasn't an object but a human corpse, a woman dressed in white. A child was crying on her back. They walked past them. His consciousness became delirious again. He felt dizzy. He felt nauseated once more. I need to throw up. The woman's body was no longer before him but instead a bell tower of a Catholic church oppressed his heart. His wife's corpse could not be there. She could not be carrying a child on her back. But she must be dead for certain. And the woman, too, was dead. Everyone was dying. He thought they were walking too fast for him. I must follow them. Follow them. I must follow them to eternity. Even the underworld is connected to this world, so I must follow them there. But they're walking too fast. I can't walk anymore. There's a tree by the side of the road. I must take a rest, then keep going. Ah, but I have no legs. My legs have vanished. He collapsed by the tree.

What is shaking me so hard? When he opened his eyes, the partisan was tying him to a cross. He became terribly startled and looked around him. The early morning wind was cooling the sweat on his forehead. Several dozen people were standing around the churchyard and looking at him. He heard the digging of the ground and the nailing on the cross. The partisan tied both his hands and his waist to the cross with a cord. He couldn't move his body at all. He calmed himself and was astonished to see what was in front of him. His father was tied to a cross, just like him. The penetrating eyes of his father gleamed in the gray morning light. He couldn't look straight at his father. He was scared of the look in his eyes. He tried to turn his head but his neck wouldn't move for it was tied around with a cord. He couldn't bear the situation. Was there anything more excruciating than having to withstand something unbearable? He screamed at Heaven. But it was his voice that echoed and he was still tied to the cross. The cross of the church soared behind his father like a backdrop. Kim came out of the church at last and approached him. There were three partisans with guns, following him. The crowd, who was watching, became very loud. Kim walked toward the middle of where his father and he were standing and looked into the space absently for a long time. Perhaps because it was early morning, he looked thinner and bereft of energy. Yi closed his eyes. Do as you wish. Tear me to pieces if that's what you want. Or burn me to death if that's your wish.

"People," Kim's lucid voice rang out chilly in the early morning air, "This man here killed his wife and failed to kill his father because he ran out of bullets." He pointed at Yi.

The crowd became more rowdy. They weren't shouting loud but it was certain that they were incited. All of a sudden, stones were thrown at him. A number of them couldn't control their rage and assaulted him with rocks. Clotted blood ran down from his head and blinded him. A rock flew over his head. But what was going on? His consciousness was clearer than ever. The blood streamed into his consciousness. The clearer his consciousness was, the greater the pain; and the greater the pain, the clearer his consciousness became.

"People, calm yourself down. The trial is not over yet. He will be punished in accordance with your verdict." Kim restrained them and continued, "What do you do with a person who killed his parent?"

The crowd replied in unison that he should be put to death.

"What do you do with a person who did not kill his parents or siblings?"

90

The crowd answered unanimously that he should be executed. What were they saying? Was there a misunderstanding? Have they lost their mind after experiencing the lunar eclipse? They were all yelling for his death.

"People, anyone who hasn't killed one's parents, step forward and kill that man."

The hitherto unruly crowd remained still. There was no one who came forward.

"There is no one? Has everyone here killed one's parent?"

It was frightening. It was the first time Yi, who had until now remained composed, showed his fury. Grinding his teeth in a rage, he snatched the gun from the partisan.

"I'm the only one. I'm the only man who can kill him."

He sprang out to him like a mad man. He stood before the cross and shouted, glaring at Yi.

"Look! We shall see how great human beings are."

As soon as he said it, he began firing fanatically. Blood spewed out from his father's whole body. Blood streamed down from his eyes, nose and ears. Was the blood going to turn into a river? Was rain going to create a river? Ah, the river. His father's scream will pierce the soul and drip like blood. A river flowed in his consciousness.

"Look! You great conservatives. You killed your wife and let your father live. Did a parent weigh more on your scale of ethics? Is that your kind of ethics? Is that the great spirit of men?"

Kim looked at him with a gun in his hand. Yi spat out globs and globs of blood at Kim's face. He was throwing up a clump of life, a filthy clump of life, a clump of his original sin.

"Spit. Spit as much as you want."

Tears as thick as blood were streaming down Kim's face. Tears thicker than blood were running down his cheeks.

Behold. Take a look at the great outcome of killing your wife. How thrilled you must be to find out the murder you committed has no reward. You call yourself a human being? You, who are worse than a beast? Are you a human being? Do you view yourself as a human being? Are you a better human being than me who's worse than a beast? You did nothing but tremble when your priest was dying. You killed your own wife. Even a beast wouldn't do that. And can you still claim human beings are great?

That's right. Even if I died at your hands here, human beings will never perish. Ah, but I couldn't show you a proof of why they wouldn't perish, whereas you have only shown me how human beings are worse than a beast. That goes to show how human beings are great.

Kim ran to Yi's father's corpse and took off his clothes that were shredded by the bullet.

Behold. Take a look at this pitiful guise of a great human being, a body that's hung like dog meat. Lucid eyes that could see through your heart. Is that a man? I do not know. Ask God.

He bit his tongue and drew his last breath on the cross. Tears thicker than blood were dried up on his face. But strangely, his face radiated an inexpressively peaceful aura in the morning light.

The eastern sky was darker red than ever. A red sunlight shone on the wings of the baby sparrows. There was not even a motion of a leaf in the plaza, which was sunk in a terrifying silence after the regime had retreated. There was the sound of the cannonball from the sea that sounded like a turning over of power. Anyone walking past the church would see three crosses that faced the cross of the church. On one of them hung Yi who died after biting on his angst, the second one was his father who died with his eyes open after much ordeal, and the last one was Kim's who so desperately wanted to witness the greatness of human beings. Kim's body was burned black. Above his disheveled hair, like a bush of thorn, the crimson morning sun rose.

The Mermaid

The sun sank then again soared. Then it went down once more. The horizon floated above the eyes. The sky burned crimson. Mansubadi could not open his eyes. The shadow of the forest and the cliff behind his back grew bigger and bigger in the shape of a goblin's claws. The shadow he was standing on surged from beneath his feet and looked like a dancing fire goblin. Mansubadi held up his hammer and pounding it in the space he screamed, "It's the same fire that burned the oar." He kept saying it over and over. It was an islet of an archipelago that stayed forgotten. It's been a month since a soldier from the People's Army landed on the island and burned all the oars. It's been about twenty days since Mansubadi caught a sight of the barleycorn. Until just a few months ago, he had relished receiving the monthly allocation. The lighthouse keeper was a government employee, and without monthly rations of petroleum, rice, and newspaper brought by a motorboat, the island could not survive. It was strange that there wasn't a replacement after how things had changed, and the women who went out to exchange barley twice a month spread the false rumor that a war was inevitable with all the turbulence in the world, gossiping every night to their husbands about the groundless turn of events, which in turn instilled fear in the men as well. But the truth of the matter was that their impoverished life was made worse from the lack of excitement, and stories were concocted for the people to laugh and cry and be shocked, and then again, new stories were invented after they got tired of the old; that was how things went. But it didn't appear to be an altogether false rumor, for there was a time when they got struck with a bolt of lightning, so to speak. While the Japanese army across the ocean was digging underground by the shore, the U.S. jets had split the lighthouse into two. The damage lasted until the present and an oil lamp was lit instead to guide the passing steamers, however, the islanders made a great fuss about it, saying how the soaring white thing could rob them of their lives, questioning how they could expect anyone to leave them alone with such a conspicuous structure from a thousand *li* away, and cursed it as not only off-putting but terribly threatening. Furthermore, the old men viewed it as a foreboding sign, whereas the naughty young men made disparaging comments, describing it as a male organ erected upside down. Yet they knew very well the monthly ration of oil, paper, and rice Mansubadi got was on account of it, and they would stop talking about it as an unfortunate object, paying it instant due respect. Then there were women who disrespected him, saying that Mansubadi wouldn't give them a kernel of grain had he not been single. But it was just baseless talk by women who liked to gossip. Mansubadi didn't mind giving it out, all except for the newspaper. It was a definite luxury for him, considering how the men couldn't roll a single cigarette or use it as kindling in urgent circumstances. He couldn't tell them he was saving it for toilet paper since the islanders had no concept of using paper as such, and they were sure to be disappointed with him if he didn't give it to them. At the same time, he felt he had become at least a useful person to them, for he too was fed up with their deprived day-to-day life. He enjoyed very much reading the serialized story in the back section of the newspaper.

He had just finished reading the part in the famous East Asian historical novel, *Three Kingdoms* where Guanyu was going to aid Yubi and about to confront Jojo, and he was waiting to read the next segment when the news of the war circulated again and to validate it, the motor boat stopped coming and the People's Army soldiers arrived at the island. They searched for the few drops of remaining oil in the lighthouse and to prevent the people from contacting their enemy, they took away all the oars and set them on fire with the oil, while telling them to store the boat for later use. Panic-stricken, everyone, including the old and the young, tearfully pleaded with the soldiers but their heartless response was that they couldn't help it, for who could give them a guarantee that there would be no contact with the enemy warship. The islanders begged for their oars back, for what else could they live on but raw fish on their island, however, the soldiers just kept saying, they couldn't help it, over and over, before leaving.

Mansubadi, with the cool sweat sliding down his back, awoke at the remote sound he heard in his sleep. "I am starved," thinking how unjust it was, he got up quickly to get ready to work with the stone. As he hammered, he thought again, "What's the use? What's the use of a millstone? A tool container? Or a smoothing stone? I have no strength and there is no hope..."

"Elder, Elder."

He turned around to see who was calling him so urgently. It was the woman he knew from the island.

"What? What is it? Speak."

"It's here."

"What is?"

Instead of finding out from her what had arrived, Mansubadi was running down to the sand. He heard something from behind him but it was buried in the sound of the waves.

"What could be here?" Mansubadi hoped that whatever it was, it had come bringing food for them.

"The People's Army is here." The woman, who frantically followed him, collapsed at his feet, and sobbed, clutching his ankles. When he heard it was the People's Army, he came to a halt and did not move. The sandy shore revealed its white layer in the sunset. Mansubadi fell on the sand that reached up to his ankle and lay sprawled. Their footsteps were shown all the way to the clusters of rocks under the cliff. Until just last year, it was a place where they enjoyed a sand bath and on Thanksgiving day, the young men and women engaged in the all night "welcoming the moon" ceremony whereas they swam and did a group circle dance on June 15 of by the lunar calendar, turning the sandy beach into a wild playground. After a swim, lying under the sand made the world a place without worries, making one's heart beat faster while keeping still for the sake of the many kinds of crabs that darted to and fro. But where have all the waterfowls gone, that adroitly avoided the water with their airy trot, amazingly evading the water, and then to be startled by the abrupt waves that rushed in, to skid away only to return to the sand right away?

It seemed like only yesterday that the woman crouched next to him would cover his chest and hands with the sand for he had a sand bath, and to check if it hadn't been all a dream, he turned to look at her. The woman, who was digging a hole, felt his gaze and made a sign that she knew what he was asking. With a voice that didn't conceal astonishment, she said quickly "A warship passed by," then she quickly changed the topic.

"What's the use of carving all that stone?"

"To trade them for rice outside. Why?"

"You need a boat, don't you?"

"That's right."

He needed a boat to transport all the millstones and smoothing stones. It seemed so hopeless that he didn't say anything.

Mansubadi did not want to do anything with his overflowing energy. Since sea fishing was not possible in Wadal or Yongso, the men went around the tiny island as though on a pilgrimage, and caught smaller fish like gopher, goby, or greening in the shallow waters, while the woman got busy searching through all the available rocks and the mud flat for anything that wasn't poisonous to eat, leaving the rocks all bare, and as a final resort they dived underwater to try their luck with abalone or conch, but in vain probably because of high tide. Although they had to live on seaweed or algae, as long as the sea did not vanish, they could find something to subsist; however, not being a fish or crab, they couldn't just live on raw fish or grass, for the islanders were becoming weaker by day with their complexion turning dark.

Mansubadi saw the woman quickly capturing the little crab and chewing on it. He swiftly got up, swearing to himself.

"They aren't gone yet, right? I will sail their boat and get some rice from the land."

The woman's eyes opened wide at the mention of rice, and she got up too, as though to accompany him.

He held up his hand and said, "You go home and get my two fishing reels with multiple hooks and any kind of meat you can find. Where did they anchor the boat?"

"On the edge of Moshi. And they went up to the lighthouse."

"I'll have to hurry. You go get them quickly."

Mansubadi became impatient once he made up his mind. All of a sudden, he got hungry as well. He had earlier checked the fishing reel and saw only a baby blowfish, which vexed him and he smashed it against the rock. It made him more furious to see its white belly blowing in the wind, and he was about to land a kick but restrained himself for fear of being heard by the People's Army soldiers. Instead, he took off his top and crawled into the sea. The water felt somewhat cold against his body for it was September already. He pulled the seaweed from the mud, and after haphazardly rinsing it in the water to get the mud off, he ate it ravenously. The woman was running toward him as he walked up to the rock. She stepped back when she saw he had no clothes on. Feeling awkward, he quickly picked up his clothes to put on, and hurried to the edge of Moshi.

"Looks like the soldiers will take off soon. Meat's all eaten. I could only bring a bunch of pigweed. It's the twenty-third day, isn't it? There can't be much water." The woman walked beside him and busily explained.

Mansubadi listened half-heartedly then asked nervously, "Meat's all gone? Eaten raw?"

"There's no fire. So you can't make soup. The ember has gone out at Ba-wu's place, too."

His heart sank at the news of no more fire, and he was more determined to sail on the boat to get some food quickly.

It was a big fishing boat that was anchored on the edge of Moshi. He wasn't sure about handling such a big boat but since there was an easterly wind, he decided to go ahead. Oblivious to what the woman was telling him, he hastily untied the rope and hoisted the sail so that he could take off before the soldiers showed up. If he raised the sail only halfway, it would be much easier to steer. But the rust from the water made it difficult for the sail to go up smoothly. He was less apprehensive about being caught and more anxious about not being able to sail the boat as quickly as possible. I am like a mouse in their trap. If only nothing would happen until I returned. He regarded himself as a mouse before a cat but the thought of the desperate mouse attacking the cat did not dawn on him. He was only obsessed with the urgency of getting food from the sea and coming back as soon as he could. When the sail caught the wind, the boat found its balance and it began to glide over the water. He then looked toward the island that looked like a dark prostrate whale, the seawater that crashed against it looking like water spewed out by the whale. The sea wind blowing against his face reeked of salt. He stopped his desperate rowing and let out a long sigh, looking up at the night sky. He felt hot at the groin and had a hard time controlling the impulse to beat up anyone or anything. He raised the front sail only and put aside the oars, taking over the key. It had been so long since he took the oar that he almost burst into tears with gladness. He kept caressing it, holding it tightly, and giving it a loving gaze. His hand that held the key forgot he was headed for land and instead steered toward the sea. "What happened to Guanyu? Will the motorboat never come again? Have the People's Army taken over the land? Will he receive the newspaper ever again? What will be the final outcome for Guanyu?" He wanted to know. These were the questions that popped on his mind and as he retraced the story from the beginning; he was laughing, getting mad, then chuckling again, thinking he was now just like the hero Guanyu in the famous novel, which pleased him. As he passed Yongso, he pulled the helm off, unrigged the sail, and anchored the boat to catch some fish. It was incredibly strenuous for him to do everything by himself on such a big boat, which would usually carry a dozen men on it. There wasn't anyone with a large fishing boat like this on Gama Island, however, there were some who were able to get a couple dozen sacks of anchovies from the net they set up, whereas the seaweed was scarce because of bad conditions; meanwhile, the clams were abundant and half a dozen people could dig up anywhere from forty to fifty sacks on days when the tide was low, which they would bring to land to sell or trade for barley, shoes, or matches. Those were the means by which they avoided an impoverished life, by the people who were poor but not greedy for big money.

A flock of birds, which he couldn't identify, flew away in a circle. Their cries stirred his auditory sense. In the winter, it was quite a sight to behold the flock of savagely clamorous seagulls moving about.

It was a pity to use the pigweed as bait but he had no other choice since shrimp or fried food could not be had. He set up a single fishing reel. It was unlikely that most fish would be looking for food at nighttime, maybe except for the eel; so after the customary prayer of spitting for a good catch, he went ahead. If it had been during the day, he could've instantly caught a large quantity of gleaming kingfish. How he would love to see the happy faces of the islanders with the fish he was going to bring them.

The dark cloud in the sky that was moving fast looked suspicious, and sure enough, there was a strong wind that started to blow. The boat that normally wouldn't budge was swaying because of the waves. He became panicky and decided to hurry to the shore. He quickly raised the fishing reel to discover, to his relief, a few eels and octopuses. But he couldn't hoist the sail by himself. The wind was too strong and something terrible could happen if he went amiss. If only someone would help him raise the sail, it would be all right.

"Darned sail, do what you want." Exhausted, he clung to the rope, inhaling and exhaling deeply to even his breath. The boat was rocking mercilessly. The waves crashing against the side of the boat splashed his face. He remembered how thirsty he was and licked the water running down his face. It tasted salty. It was saltier because it was blended with his sweat. He wondered if he should just wait until the wind dissipated, however, if he were to linger too long, all could go amiss and he tightened his grip on the rope. He had no strength in his belly and decided to eat some pigweed in the back of the boat, wishing he had some bean paste sauce to go with it. He regretted throwing away the blowfish and not bringing it with him, and then remembered how the woman's father had died from eating the poisonous fish. He tried once more to hoist the sail but gave up. He threw the unwound rope in the water, and decided to return with the sail down. When the day broke, he was greatly relieved to at least know his whereabouts. He let out a dumbfounded chuckle when he found out that the land was within sight. The boom had fallen away in the wind and the sail collapsed on him, crushing his shoulder, and tearing his shirt.

For fear of being found out by the People's Army soldiers stationed there, he avoided the wharf and attempted to dock at the remote side of a mountain. But there was no rope. His heart sank, as there seemed to be no solution. How was he going to anchor the boat? He thought about it until the sun was above his head and came up with the idea of untying all the thread from the fishing reels to use as string but a big boat like this was difficult to be tied down with it. The wave could instantly release the boat. He started rowing again in search of a better place to dock. Mansubadi cursed the men who came on a boat as big as this when a smaller sailboat would not have been so troublesome. He somehow barely managed to dock the boat by a big rock and placed the foothold over the rock, fastening the boat with the little remaining rope, and then putting the rock on it.

The world had gone berserk on land and it was next to impossible to obtain any food. And he had come with no money to boot. After much desperate imploring, he got a little bit of flour, a basket of potatoes, and a tiny amount of rice that he carried back to the boat close to nighttime. What's more, he had to walk several dozen *li* into town to seek out a few relatively better off households, for the houses near the dock were too scared of garnering attention. He told them that everyone was near starvation and the people offered food, with someone they knew on Gama Island in mind. It was much better that he arrived at night; meanwhile, it was unbelievable that no one had discovered the boat and more amazingly, the boat had not been pushed out to the water. With the fading of the rising tide, the boat was not hampered by the rock underneath and had a smooth sail back toward Gama Island. It was smooth because nothing dangerous happened.

The sail was flapping wildly against the powerful headwind and he had to steer the helm with all his might to adjust to the wind. He couldn't let go of his grip on the helm for a second. He shrugged his shoulder with much pride, thinking that Guanyu couldn't be as good a sailor as he. He wanted to give the rice to the woman; however, as it was better to boil the barley porridge with albeit the slightest amount of rice, he mixed all the rice with barley.

Yet his spirit was dampened when he thought of how many people could be satiated with the food he procured; however, he decided to put it out of his mind until later—praying that they wouldn't all turn into a beast, eating raw flesh of the animals all the time, defecating dark feces. With the box of matches he got, he vowed he would get the ember again. When the boat got near the island, he heard gunshots. Mansubadi suddenly realized he had completely forgotten about the People's Army soldiers. His body shook with rage, knowing the islanders were being massacred, and he wanted to go and slaughter them all and be killed. Hanging onto the mast, he screamed until he became utterly exhausted, "There's now no need for the rice or barely."

He remained motionless after gazing at the lighthouse soaring at the top of a rock. A People's Army soldier struck him from behind with the gunstock. Another sprang at him with a spear toward his belly. Mansubadi quickly gripped the spear and stabbed him instead. The cry of the islanders rang in his ear as loud as the waves.

The sun rose and sank. The horizon became bloated and floated above the eye. The crimson sun was ablaze. Suddenly it dropped from above at a frightening speed. It kept plummeting. The round sun exploded on all four sides. Mansubadi could not open his eyes. The lighthouse behind him became larger and larger, bringing a bloody shadow of what looked like a live animal. The shadow he was standing on vanished underneath his feet.

While the sun spun, the red spikes of sunshine flew like arrows toward his face. Mansubadi could see nothing.

The Wings of Icarus

The gunfire from the coastal patrol craft of the Royal Armed Forces struck the sentry post of the police station that was now the interim headquarters of the Rebel Army. The Royal Armed Forces, which had accurately measured the range, concentrated its naval bombardment on the Rebel Army headquarters. The remnants of the army rushed out like a swarm of bees through the window with the glass all broken to pieces. The police forces, under the attack of interlocking fire, traversed Mount Aeria and camped out at the city to reorganize their offense. The tumultuous gun smoke from the Royal Armed Forces side soared above the horizon and quietly invaded the streets of Basra, accompanied by night.

The commanding voice of the police forces leader could be heard from time to time through the sound of gunfire and bombs. Abdel Aref, the commander of the Rebel Army, spun around the submachine gun on a leather belt slung around his shoulder on his back and gazed at the sea from the entrance. His bloodshot eyes, which seemed to indicate how his life was being spent, were suffused with much more intense shadow. From the sea, the wave of "ideology" was rushing in with the roaring of guns.

The machine gun blast of the police forces set off the siren bell, followed by a hail of gunfire that pierced the hollowness of the heart. But he remained still. Suddenly, there was dead silence. He felt like he was going to suffocate. Firing blindly at his enemies, he rushed out. There was the soul-piercing metallic sound of the bullet that deviated from its trajectory after missing the pillar, the wailing of his comrade, and walking on thin line between life and death, as his limbs collapsed after being shot. A sudden agony, which felt like all his nerves were sliced by a knife, made him grip his right shoulder with his left hand that became profusely covered with crimson blood. On the sight of blood, he fled to the back and ran like a wild animal that has been shot. He was running, like his life depended on it, through the fish market where there wasn't a hint of smell remaining in the northeast direction. The people had lost all will and strength to take a side and caged in their homes, they were waiting for the replacement of this desperate leader, as a prostitute does a customer.

He reached the field. The chilly sea wind, laden with salt, collided against his sweaty forehead. He ran to the mountain, past the muddy slope without a single tree to the valley, thick with young pine trees. He kept tripping over rocks and fell down when his leg was caught by a tree trunk. He could not get himself up. He must not be captured. But he could not move. With the submachine gun at his bosom, he lost consciousness but his left hand was scratching the ground to the point of bleeding.

With their royal army badges still attached, the 4th Brigade Rebel Army of the occupation forces of the Basra District were lined up in their military training ground to welcome their new leader at the head-quarters of the eastern zone. Soon after, the officer on duty, Saref, the second lieutenant, guided Aref and his twelve guerilla fighters from the entrance to the reviewing stand. The Commander of Basra region, Colonel Mohammed Shaab, ordered the entire army to "Attention!" and stomped toward the guerilla leader. Aref, who wore a soiled blue uniform with his shaggy mustache reaching his earlobes, was of medium height and appeared upright. With a broad grin, he tightly embraced Colonel Shaab, who appeared exceedingly nervous and let himself be held, not missing a chance to scrutinize all twelve guerilla fighters. A faint spasm passed on his face and the sparkle from his eyes vanished. Did these men represent the leadership of our revolution? Did I engage in this revolution for them? With mixed feelings, he led Aref to the reviewing stand and introduced him to the members of the army.

"Comrades. I am glad to be here. We shall build a new nation." This was all Aref had to say in his greeting. After the inspection, Aref, his brother Sharef, the second lieutenant, and Colonel Shaab, went into the commander's quarter and held a secret meeting. Aref insisted on the invasion of Kuwait, whereas Shaab held firm on the advancing into the capital and Sharef demurred. Shaab rose with indignation and directed the men's gaze toward the map on the wall.

In a loud voice, he said menacingly, "Do you know why the 'Karani' rebellion failed?"

Aref did not waver a bit and baring his overly white teeth in the midst of his coarse beard, he said in a formidably forceful voice, "Surely you must know. It was because of the capitalist nature of the revolution."

"No, that is not true. It's because they resorted to a roundabout tactic. Instead of taking over the capital, they chose to attack the Ana region," Shaab explained in a sonorous voice.

"This is an internal strife, not a war. We shall rebuild the country."

"An internal strife is also a war for its nature of a battle. From a strategic perspective, I maintain that we advance to the capital."

Aref's face turned tense as he cut Shaab short. "I am not a strategist but a revolutionary."

"What's the difference?"

"I'm not here to give you a lecture on that. We need supplies. Men and guns."

Aref got up as though he had nothing more to say.

Shaab also rose by reflex and glared at him. "Who commanded it? Is it an order from high up?" He appeared less rebellious and more anticipatory. Aref was taken aback and with a funny expression, he looked at Shaab for a long time.

"It is my order," he said curtly and walked out of the room.

Shaab seemed more surprised than Aref and fixed his gaze on the direction of the door. His expression held somewhat of awe. Sharef stood at attention and was looking at Colonel Shaab's star on his epaulet.

The Rebel Army train arrived in Kuwait City at 9 A.M. Except for a few minutes of gun battle in the police station; Kuwait was seized with hardly any bloodshed. The Rebel Army set up their interim commanding headquarters at the police station and held their second tri-party meeting. Once more, Shaab insisted on advancing to the capital whereas Aref held firm on maintenance of the forces and Sharef remained undecided. In response to Shaab's radical stance that unless they took advantage of the turmoil of the government army and moved forward to the capital, the revolution would fail, Aref asserted that they wait and see, for the people would be compelled to revolt after being inspired by the revolution. Shaab attacked Aref as a dreamer who was ignorant about reality and Aref retaliated by calling Shaab a belligerent soldier who did not understand the true meaning of the revolution. Shaab retorted it was the soldiers that started the revolution; Shaab replied that it would be the guerrillas who would complete it. Shaab contended the party would set the guidelines for the revolution and Aref claimed he would be doing that.

"And why is that?" Shaab asked.

"Because this is my revolution," Aref answered.

"That is different from what First Lieutenant Sharef told me. He said the revolution started at the command of the party and it is for that reason I also took part."

"Now's not time to discuss such matter."

Thus, the meeting came to an end. Aref grabbed the automatic rifle on the table and walked out of the room. The gaze of Shaab and Sharef happened to cross. Shaab asked himself, is it true what he said? Sharef answered in silence: I am not sure. Shaab asked again, Did you not tell me that there would be a nationwide uprising with the party's order? And that the North would send supplies to the South? Sharef responded in silence: That is what my brother said. Their silent conference, too, came to an end. Right away, Aref declared the organization of the Revolutionary Committee and announced as the first decree of the Committee the three committee members and the chief leaders.

The Revolutionary Committee Chair: Abdel Aref
   Deputy Chair: Mohammed Shaab
   Member: Abdel Sharef
The Revolutionary Army Commander in chief: Abdel Aref
   Deputy Commander in chief: Mohammed Shaab
Basra District Commander: Abdel Sharef

Right after announcing the organization of the Revolutionary Committee, Aref drove a jeep around the Kuwait City and directed the residents to orally elect a representative, and then orally elect the head of all the representatives. At 5 P.M., all the administrative organization of the Kuwait City was completed. At the same time, he sent Sharef to establish a similar structure in Basra. At 6 P.M., the second proclamation of the Revolutionary Committee, the temporary constitution that consisted of thirty clauses, was announced; this was followed by putting up a hastily created flag, of all red with a white sun in the center, on the rooftop of the police station, now their headquarters, when a scout delivered an urgent message: the police militia was advancing by train from the capital. Aref ordered Shaab to remain at the headquarters and headed for the station with his associates.

He made the Rebel Army wait in ambush alongside the field by the railroad where the first signal was. All around, it was too still for the impending political collision that would go down in history. The insects in the grass, which were gnawing on the silence of the night that the ear picked up, were soon overpowered by the sound of rolling wheels on the rails. Did an "ideology" pay a visit in October, like a season? Or did it approach like night? At present, the "ideology" was on the train and coming closer to him, stifling his heart. The train was coming nearer and nearer, over the rail where the luminous light of the stars shone brightly. At last, the train like a huge monster was before his eyes. It slowed down on the bridge. At that moment, the firing of the long-barreled rifles resounded, like a signal in the air. The sniper had shot the conductor. Massive firing followed. The train had come to a complete halt. It had stopped right before a landmine. The police militia was much more reckless than Aref had expected.

He instinctively swished around his automatic rifle and fired blindly at the dark wriggling shadows in the freight car. An orderly lying flat in front of him rose and was about to throw a grenade when he fell over on the grass with a groan. Before he knew it, he found himself falling. Where did the sound of life seeping away from the soul come from?

A chilly evening wind was hardening the flow of life. It swept over the river of consciousness, too. The countless stars on the surface of the river quivered like petals. Like Icarus flailing in the sea when he fell after losing his wings, he too was floundering in that river. The star petals dispersed and vanished. He tussled to grip something above the water. He barely managed to grab a twig. He shook it with all his strength. The maple leaves that were darker than the color of the clotted blood fell down on his river of consciousness. And on his face.

He was thirsty. He opened his lips, which were covered with a white film from dehydration and looked for water but he could only get the salty sweat from his forehead that made him more unbearably thirsty. He got himself up with the greatest effort and looked around his surrounding; then he staggered his way up. His left arm was dropping like a bird that was shot in the wing. There is a cave over the mountaintop. There will be water, too. He had to go to the cave. He must. There is water. There was only water in his consciousness. The occasional sound of the wind against the pine trees sounded like the flow of water. It surged into his soul then left. But his soul was saturated not with water but perspiration.

There was no path in the mountain. But the thought of water with bright light became one. And like a mad man, he trudged up his line of thought. The opening of the cave was hollow like the skull's eye. He rushed toward the entrance as though he was being sucked in but froze suddenly. The opening of the cave remained motionless like a monster's eye. He opened his eyes wide. The eyes that shone brightly in the starlight gradually turned into the decayed eyes of corpses. The eyes of the countless corpses, whose death he was responsible for, were before his eyes. Eyes without eyeballs, bloodshot eyes, imploring eyes, abhorring eyes. Once more, he fainted and collapsed.

On the second day, the Revolution Committee held a special conference to declare their third proclamation, martial law, and to discuss the purging of the reactionary constituents. Once again, Aref and Shaab clashed in terms of how the trial should be carried out. Shaab emphasized the importance of a people's trial and Aref averred a military trial was more appropriate under martial law. Sharef, again, remained silent.

In a gesture that indicated he would not give in this time, Shaab stood up and shouted, "That goes against our ideology of Socialism. It violates its fundamental principle."

"That is dogma and not ideology. When a political idea is adapted by a nation then it becomes ideology. Our ideology is promulgated, albeit provisionally, in the Revolution charter. And this charter delegates judicial power to the Revolution Committee. Therefore, it can't be said that a military trial infringes on the ideology of the Revolution, for it is a legitimate course of action authorized by the charter."

"I am neither a theorist of law nor a politician. I participated in this revolution in order to build a socialist nation. I am not here to fight for you."

"Socialism does not build a nation per se. It's the nation that will choose socialism. The ideology is not the absolute goal rather the nation is. We are here to create anew a nation, which is the purpose of our Revolution Committee."

Shaab was astounded and looked Aref as though he was seeing something out of this world. Suddenly, Aref appeared like a terrifying beast to him.

"In that case, I shall not take part in the revolution."

Aref got up abruptly and roared, "Shut up! Do you think you can come and go as you wish? Don't you realize the revolution is about building a new nation? And that is what I am here for."

It was suffocating for Shaab to witness Aref's anger.

With a wrathful look, Aref turned to Sharef and declared, "One abstention, one for and one against, thus as authorized by the Committee, I, as the Chair, reject Comrade Shaab's proposal."

The purges happened immediately. It was not easy to identify the people's "social bent" since no list of reactionaries was readily at hand. Under the pretense of a celebratory commemorative event for the revolution, everyone was ordered to gather at the city plaza. For the first round of purges, it started with ferreting out police and their families. They were given the choice of turning themselves in. But no one surrendered. The captive police were brought out and ordered to seek them out. They could only pick out a few. Then the entire crowd was made to voluntarily search them out and if they couldn't identify more than a hundred, they themselves would be subject to a purge. This fueled their human instinct. The number of reactionaries reached over a hundred instantaneously. When the crackdown was complete, the people had to learn "song of rebellion" while the summary trial took place.

The military trial that determined life or death went on; meanwhile, with the lead singer, a beautiful girl who looked about seventeen or eighteen, the people sang along. The trial ended at the thirteenth round of singing the song. About a hundred people who were judged to be the police and their family members were executed before the people.

The relatives of the dead were ordered to bury the corpses.

In the afternoon, the purging continued with the public office workers and pro-government people. When the purging in Kuwait City ended at 5 P.M., they headed for the Basra district where Sharef was in charge. Aref and Shaab, who sat side by side in the jeep, did not exchange a word all the way there. As though he had encountered a mythical monster, Shaab fixed his gaze on Aref, his mind bereft of any spirit.

They immediately embarked on the trial of the reactionaries on arriving in Basra. Sharef had already hunted them down. When the trial was near the end, they received a message that the government army was approaching Basra. They suspended the trial and made a swift move. They lay in ambush at the canyon and raided the government army that made an advance against them in trucks, killing them all. They returned to resume the purge. After the trial was over, Aref had the same girl teach the "People's Song of Rebellion" to the convicted. Sharef protested what was the use of teaching a song to the people who would soon die. It was the first time that Sharef overtly expressed his disapproval of his brother. In contrast, Shaab was no longer showing his dissent about any matter. Sharef seemed angry in a strange manner. Aref claimed it was important for the people to understand the meaning of the people's revolution before they died. Sharef protested as if that were possible with a song. Aref responded that even if it were impossible, it was the best possible method in the short span of time given. Sharef argued, what was the point of their converting. Aref argued back, what did he think was the purpose of converting those condemned to death. Sharef responded, then they should be given a chance to find out about their conversion with a last word. Aref mulled it over and promised to give them a chance for a final word, time permitting. As though it was pointless to say anything, Sharef shut his mouth as before.

Early the next morning, the executions took place in the public cemetery. Since there was a little time, people were able to express their final thoughts. The girl, who taught them to sing, recorded them in a notebook. Sharef was gazing down at the lovely hand of the girl who was the daughter of a well-known leftist activist, executed on charges of spying. Sharef's gaze was not befitting of a man who was an integral player of the revolution. The first page was left blank, as was the second page. The third page was about an inheritance of wealth. The fourth page again remained blank. The fifth page was about the distribution of wealth and the sixth and seventh pages, about the debt. The eighth page was blank. The ninth page was about the inheritance of wealth as were the tenth and eleventh pages. The hand that was about to fill the twelfth page suddenly trembled. Sharef looked up at the condemned who was quietly gazing at the girl. Even though she sensed his gaze on her, she remained motionless and just looked at the name in the notebook as if it displayed the face of the man. The condemned stood there for a long time with a look of much longing in his eyes then asked Sharef in a resolute voice if he could ask the girl to sing. Sharef asked her in silence if she knew him. It was then the girl looked straight at the condemned and said, "Yes, he was our music teacher."

Sharef said, yes if that were his last wish. With her eyes toward the ground, the girl stood before her former teacher. Her teacher asked her to sing a hymn. Her song, which sounded like weeping of a soul, captivated Sharef's heart. She became one with the song. When she was on the last verse, Aref came. He became enraged on hearing the girl singing and instantly put a stop to it, banning the last word as well saying there was no time. Sharef demanded Aref allow the girl to finish the song and permit the final words of the condemned. Aref rebuffed him and instead ordered him to do away with the girl who sang an anti-revolution song. This infuriated his brother.

"Have you gone mad? What do you plan to cultivate on earth if you annihilate just about everyone?"

"I will cultivate the proletariat."

112

Sharef's mouth was irresolutely shut again. A terrifying disagreement passed between them as they glared at each other in silence. Shortly thereafter, Aref gave an order for the execution of the condemned and to arrest the girl. Sharef blocked her and turned to his brother in rage. Right then, the guns fired at the condemned behind them echoed through the air. Sharef began to scream like a man who had lost his mind.

"Either you are insane or you're not human."

His words resounded like an echo amidst the clamorous gunshots. Yes, I am insane. It may appear to you that I am insane. But I am not insane. I am at present building a nation. I want to show everyone that a nation is a Leviathan. Or rather, I would like to see it for myself first. The explosive sound of the guns continued in the back.

The sound of the guns below the mountain exploded continually. Aref regained consciousness at the sound of it. When it came to a stop, a tracer, with its blue tail, vanished into the dawning grey morning sky. From all around, the roar of the people was heard. The villagers were climbing up the mountain, besieging it like an assailant. Their roar was getting louder at the same pace as the dawn that was becoming lighter. Frantically, he bolted into the cave. His eyes, reflecting the sunlight, were blazing. The advance party cried out to him from below the cave to come out with his arms up. Instinctively, he tightened his grip on the rifle and released the safety catch. When there was no response, guns were fired all at once. Still, he remained motionless. The early morning sky that had reached the crimson sun was now melting with orange light. But a much more powerful life was ebbing away from Aref's eyes. He was glaring into space in the midst of silence that was gnawing at life. Right at that moment when he thought he saw the shadow of a man, he pulled the trigger and screamed, "I'll shoot unless you step back."

It was then he felt a spasm of sharp pain on his left shoulder and he fell forward on the grass, with the rifle in his arms. When the firing stopped, the bell from the church by the mountain could be heard. The police militia carried Aref on a stretcher down the mountain. Upon hearing the news of Aref's arrest, the people swarmed around the stretcher. When it passed through the village, the crowd got bigger and bigger. When the police prevented the people from dragging Aref down from the stretcher, they began to throw rocks, twigs, or whatever they could get their hands on. When they reached the city, the persistent crowd succeeded in taking the stretcher from the police. They gave a triumphant roar and pulled down Aref to drag him through the street after tying his feet with a rope. At the tip of Aref's consciousness, his life was dangling like the last drop of dew. As his body was being dragged, this bubble of life quivered like it would drop any second. The early morning sky reflected on the river of his consciousness was too beautiful for words. But this sky was washed away by the fury of the crowd, like the flood. Am I dead? Or alive? A man who wanted to become god but ended up as a beast. A snake who fell to the ground when he tried to ascend to the heaven to become a dragon. What I am now? A man? Or a beast?

At last, the crowd brought Aref to the cemetery where the Rebel Army had purged the reactionaries. They erected a cross on the wall and tied him to it. They demanded that the police execute him before the people and hang his decapitated head for everyone to see. The police explained that a trial in accordance with legal procedure was necessary, and thus implored the crowd to return Aref to them for the time being. The crowd responded by surrounding the cross, fearing that the police would take him from them, and viciously contended that if the police failed to meet their demand, they themselves would stone Aref to death. Those among the police who lost their family members concurred with the crowd. Suddenly someone fired a gun in the middle of a row between the police and the crowd. A policeman who had lost his wife shot Aref. The crowd roared with glee and ceased their protest. The police, triggered by the crowd's cheer, fired maniacally. The mud-colored clothes of Aref were shredded to pieces. The blood, like the tears of the soul, ran down his chest that was bared in the morning sky.

That is correct. It is unrequited resentment and not remorse. A pang of grievance for not creating a new nation. It is not I, but the nation that is now dying here. The sound of the guns lingered in the air like sorrowful protest.

On Day Three, the Revolution Committee announced the fourth proclamation in the morning, and carried out the distribution of land. When the three men were having a late lunch, an aide entered and reported that their subordinates were raping women. Aref stopped eating and took a glance at the people around him then ordered an immediate arrest of the rapists. He then kicked the door and left hurriedly. Shaab looked over at Sharef who was lost in thought. Aref called off the plan to visit the Kuwait district after lunch and instead summoned a meeting for the military trial of the accused. Sharef proposed that they condone the men, in consideration of their hard work for the revolution and the turbulent political state of the country, whereas Shaab suggested that they punish only the severe cases but not necessarily demote or give them a prison sentence. But Aref adhered emphatically to executing them, saying it was the principle of military law to put to death those who have raped while on duty. However, neither Sharef nor Shaab gave in this time. When the representative system disagreed, a trial became impossible; Aref declared that he would pursue an independent trial.

"That is tyranny!" Shaab shouted.

"What is? Isn't a nation itself tyranny? To negate tyranny is synonymous with the negation of a nation. There isn't a country where people can rule the nation as they wish. The reason why a nation looks after its people is not because that is its duty but as a charity." That was Aref's poor rationale.

"I am not a theoretician of politics. I am a man of the military. As a superior, I cannot kill my subordinates who have risked their lives alongside me. As the commander of the 4th Brigade, I demand the release of my subordinates. "

"Stop your reactionary speech. Have you forgotten that you are only the Deputy Commander of the Rebel Army, Comrade Shaab? If you wish to revert to the position of Commander of the 4th Brigade, then it can be done. But as Chief Commander of the Revolution Army I shall then arrest you."

When he finished talking, Aref ordered the aide to bring in the accused. Shaab turned to Sharef who was quiet and said loudly, "If you go ahead and punish all the rapists then Comrade Sharef should not be left out."

Aref was utterly taken aback and glared at Sharef who raised his head and embraced his brother's stare. Is it true? Yes, it is. Their eyes asked and answered.

"Who was it?" Aref asked not Sharef but Shaab instead.

"That woman."

At the mention of the woman, Sharef who became agitated explained not to Aref but to Shaab, "It's true that I slept with her. But it wasn't rape."

Aref gave him an enraged look and commanded, "You son-of-a-bitch. Get out of here, this instant."

"As an attorney, I believe, Comrade Aref will not acknowledge an exception." Shaab provoked Aref, who ordered him to get out.

"I will not be part of a group of bandits," Shaab replied calmly and exited the room. Aref who watched him leave told Sharef in a low voice, "Guard him."

Sharef left the room without saying anything. Five of the ten men accused were executed as a warning before the entire army. Night arrived. The office of the police chief, which was now being used as the headquarters of the Basra district, was lit with a lamp. Aref was going back and forth, stepping on his elongated shadow. With his arms crossed and lost deep in thought, it suddenly dawned on him that the room was too bright and he turned to look out the window and saw a

116

full moon above his head. The blue shaded moonlight felt tearfully sorrowful. He stood still for a long time under the moonlight. The full moon always reminded him of something. He was told it was on a night of full moon that his father, a peasant, stabbed to death the farm owner who tormented the villagers. His father denied killing him until the end but was executed. It was then Aref decided to become an attorney. He left for Cairo and attended a college of law while working his way through school. It was also then he became Marxist. He had been severely tortured and imprisoned after his conviction of assassinating a key political figure. He saw and heard firsthand countless atrocities that the nation committed. How great the nation was!

He heard the knock from behind him. After a moment of calming his mind, he turned around and said, "Enter."

Shaab came in, looking grave.

"Did you call me?"

Aref increased the flame of the lamp as though he wanted to expel the moonlight.

"And for what?"

"You are asked to resign your post as a member and Deputy Commander of the Revolution Committee, and do it before the subordinates."

Shaab did not show any surprise, as if he already knew and instead with a contemptuous smile asked, "What is the reason?"

"It is a conspiracy I was keenly interested in. But I didn't have the courage. But hearing you, Comrade Aref, speak makes me want to undertake it if it isn't too late."

A look of mixed feelings swept across Aref's face.

Shaab continued, "Why would you make a discreet suggestion as such if I were indeed involved in an anti-revolution scheme?"

There was a gun in Shaab's hand as he took steps closer toward Aref, who did not flinch. Shaab pointed the gun at him and releasing the safety, he cried, "But I did not do anything like that."

117

At last, Aref spoke as he looked at the gleaming tip of the gun, "What you're doing now is an anti-revolution act."

As soon as Aref said it, Shaab felt the guns on his back and he simultaneously dropped the gun in his hand because of their forceful blow. All at once, five gun muzzles were pointed at his neck. They belonged to the guerrillas. Shaab froze, and then looked around him. From his back, Sharef approached Aref who proclaimed, "Relieve Mohammed Shaab of all positions, and Abdel Sharef shall be appointed as the successor. From this point on, the Revolution Committee will be dissolved and Abdel Sharef will take over the duty of Deputy Commander of the Rebel Army."

It sounded like he was reading a prepared speech. Aref then turned to his brother and said, "Imprison Mohammed Shaab and keep a close guard. He will be turned over for a military trial tomorrow."

Aref who was sleeping in the night duty room was jolted out of sleep, like a man who was having a nightmare, when someone violently shook his shoulders. After a hasty military salute, his aide reported, "Mohammed Shaab has escaped with his twenty subordinates."

At first, Aref did not believe his ears. To ascertain what he'd heard once more, he asked, "What?"

It was definite that Shaab had fled with his subordinates. He got up on his feet and picking up his gun, he rushed to the prison that was left wide open. Sharef and a number of his men were talking noisily in front of the place.

With blazing eyes, he glared at them and screamed, "Go after them immediately. If you don't arrest them, you'll all be punished."

The men dispersed like a flock of birds that had heard the sound of gunshot. Sharef had his hands in his pockets and just stared up at the ceiling, infuriating Aref who roared, "I told you to keep a tight guard but how can a door be left wide open?"

His brother remained quiet.

"You let them escape."

Sharef still did not say anything. In great wrath, Aref ordered his aide to have him arrested. At a loss as to what to do, his aide did not move.

"Arrest him, I said!" Aref screamed with bloodshot eyes.

Right then, Sharef shoved aside the aide, who was going to handcuff him, and took a step closer to Aref.

"The revolution has failed—from the time when you decided to kill that girl. To repeat, from when you began to annihilate the rights of man." His voice was unusually calm in light of the tension all around him.

"What? The revolution has failed? It has not. It has not failed! You're impeding it. You're interfering with the revolution and I will not forgive anyone who impedes it." Like a mad man, Aref shouted and uncontrollably thrashed Sharef's head with the gunstock. Standing straight up, Sharef bellowed like a dying animal.

"A revolution is meaningful when it is devoid of man."

Blood from his temple streamed down his face. Aref saw the blood and like a vampire, he attacked Sharef, striking him mercilessly on the face, head, or anywhere with his gun. Sharef vomited blood and collapsed. Aref held him up and wailed, shaking Sharef's shoulders, "I will wait to see how great man can be!"

Tears thicker than blood poured from his eyes at the sight of Sharef's eyes that had turned over and showed only white. He tossed the body of his brother after vacantly glaring at his face whose life ebbed away.

"Behold this man! Behold this man!"

His eyes, which were staring at space, showed the reflection of the crimson morning sky.

"Behold this man!"

Underneath Aref's feet tied to the cross, there was this note. The morning sun, which had just risen, created a red halo around the shaggy head of Aref that looked like a thorny crown.

Let's find out how great humanity is! Aref was dead but his voice was still resonant through the surrounding of the cross.

Note: This is a story that takes place in an imaginary place in the Middle East. The names of people and places may coincide with those of a specific country but are not meant to be the same.

Thicker Than Blood

Part 1

All kinds of sounds—fired in no specific direction—seeped through the sticky sea wind of the early morning gloaming and faded away. He opened his eyes and looked at the Romanesque window formed like a lion's head that was silently fluttering amidst the morning mist. His hand, as though it was ascertaining some premonition, groped for the ivory tuner of the Harry Crafter radio by his bedside.

"The Rebel Army has toppled the Nguyen Dinh Tuan dictator ship and established a new government. The ten million citizens of Annan must support and trust the Revolutionary Government. Hail to the great leader of the Revolution! Hail to the National Security Forces, the Capital Defense Corps, and the Marine Corps!"

Startled, he sat up on the bed. His hand, which fumbled for a cigarette, indicated the turmoil in his heart. The glass cigarette case, which was engraved inside with "comradeship" in Annanese, glowed with luster as though to emphasize the meaning of the word. President Nguyen Dinh Tuan had personally presented it to him, the head of the diplomatic corps the night before at the commemorative reception for the Fifteenth Year Anniversary of the Independence of the Annan Republic.

The official residence of the government general, which in a nutshell represented the power of the oppressor nation, its artistic tradition, and its false compassion for the colonized people, was appropriate as the symbol of the president's charismatic authority and political leadership. The main hall of the guesthouse was filled with key figures and the diplomatic envoy, and the cocktail glasses in their hands made him almost think they were all making a toast to him. Who among them could have foreseen the revolution that took place overnight?

Suddenly, a loud clamor of the trolley and the armored vehicles was heard while the explosions from the tank gun rounds and mortar shells made the windows shake uncontrollably. Still in his pajamas, he went to the window and looked out. The embassy was where one could get a direct view of the Lion Palace and the central government. It was dawn, and he gazed at the Lion Palace Plaza about to become the hub of the revolution, while drafting in his mind the full text he was going to send to his government.

"The malignant dictatorship of the last ten years disguised as democracy has invaded the very basis of people's lives and gotten to the stage of threatening their lives. The Rebel Army has risen to annihilate the root of the corruption and the cause of the exploitative politics that surpass Western Colonialism in its severity and brutality, in order to establish a true democracy where liberty and equality will be guaranteed. Our rebellion is a declaration of the right to live and a testimony to justice. Hail to the Rebel Army! Hail to the Annan Republic!"

He got dressed, memorizing the last phrase of the announcement. As though he wanted to find out through past examples how a diplomat in the nation one was assigned should conduct himself at a historical moment such as this, he glanced at the bookcase in the corner of the room. He must see the light of what happened. It should not be the light reflected from the revolution but the light emanating from it. He took out a notebook and wrote a memo. What is the reason for not turning the revolutionary leader into a heroic figure? What do the two philosophical concepts, "declaration of life" and "testimony of justice," really signify? What set it apart is that there is no precedent to be found in the past revolutions. As he was about to reach for the phone, the attaché of communication walked in, as though he had read his mind. In the vicinity, a projectile exploded. His body shook and trembled like he'd been electrified. He lit a cigarette with his shaking hand and tried to find in the attaché's look a clue for his confusion. His face dissolved in the intensity of his thought. The sporadic gunshots penetrated the magma of thought pouring out. His face was white like the blank paper that demanded a statement.

But it was only through the sound of the radio that the revolution controlled the extraterritorial jurisdiction. In addition, it was possible that people were in contact with the government by way of the radio. It was uncertain what the source of the sound really meant.

"Should we notify the government?" he said, and walked up to him like he wanted to extract a decision from the attaché. But the decision that was required was not so much whether or not to telegraph but the content of the telegram.

At that moment, the radio enforced the decision on them by broadcasting the declaration. The two men froze.

"The revolutionary government has announced the first following declaration."

First Declaration

-All military troops must continue to carry out their given duty at their post.
-Leaving or slowing down work is absolutely prohibited.
-All ports and airports will be temporarily shut down.
-All acts of violence and vengeance are prohibited.

Those who violate the above acts will be subject to arrest, imprisonment, and severe punishment without a warrant from the court.

Nguyen Dinh An, Chairman of the Revolution Committee

All of a sudden, his throat felt parched, as if all the water in his body had been dried up. The revolution was unmasking itself. Did An, who was the son and the Director of the National Security, take over the government through the urgent expedient of "revolution"?

The two men left the room, with the radio still on, repeating the news. Although it was only a ten-minute drive from the residence to the embassy, they were worried that they might by impeded by traffic, for they had to go by way of the Lion Palace, which was where the central government complex was. They relied on their diplomatic license plate and the flag of the Republic of South Korea, next to the headlight, as a mark of their extraterritoriality and raced at 60 mph. As though the morning sunshine had transformed into sound, a loud clamor resounded from the National Security armored cars and the trolleys of the capital defense corps. All the vehicles on the street were carrying the fervor of the revolution. The trolleys all seemed to head for the Lion Palace where new history was being written. Across the window, the two men looked at this no man's land where two regimes were in confrontation. The driver turned on the radio. A crumpling sound of paper was heard from the sheet his left hand pressed down.

It was a program for the fifteenth anniversary of Independence. I must have been a little tipsy. Why did An, who was standing like a shadow next to his father, glare at me with such a tense look, during my congratulatory message mixed in with a semi-joke to the wife of the President? What could I have done even if it were a slip of the tongue on my part, as I held the hand of a thirty-something year-old American wife of the President who had the charm of a maiden and ripe woman? The beauty of a woman can easily turn a man into a fool.

"Doesn't it feel like a wedding ceremony, Madame Nguyen?" I asked in English

"Merci bien," she had replied, blushing, looking tender and timid at the same time.

Come to think of it, An, the son, with the fatigued look of a man in constant mental struggle, appeared last night like some nihilist from Imperial Russia, while the aged President in a sleek black tie and suit, was receiving guests with more spirit than a young man, and appeared as self-confident as a corporate tycoon who had just registered the entire nation of Annan as his own.

Standing right near him, he gave a slight smile as he caught the sight of An dismissively exchanging his cocktail glass for a new one and muttered to himself, "Would've been more appropriate to say it's the birthday of the President." It sounded like he was purposely sneering and he couldn't help saying something to alleviate the situation.

"You like to drink? What is your favorite?"

"I prefer the impression the name of the liquor gives off, rather than the taste itself. On festive occasions, I like Ballantine's but tonight I prefer Pirate."

Could An have wanted to announce the harbinger to the revolution with an allegory like that one?

Back in the office, he wired a telegram to his government.

"Recipient- The Minister of Foreign Ministry
Subject- Annan Coup d'état

1. A Coup d'état took place around 6:00 am on the tenth.
It is difficult to obtain accurate information because of the battle on the street; however, according to the government broadcasting that was taken over by the revolutionary forces, Nguyen Dinh An, son of the incumbent president and the Director of National Security, seems to be the leading figure. The main forces of the revolution are the majority of the National Security, part of the Marine Corps, and the Defense Corps of the Capital City.
2. As of yet, it is difficult to characterize the political stance of the Revolutionary Forces but based on the declaration and miscellaneous evidences of the Revolutionary Committee, the purpose appears to be to topple the one-man dictatorship of President Nyuyen and therefore is unrelated to Communism. The official position of the Revolutionary government has yet to be announced.

3. The Revolutionary Army has besieged the Lion Palace and is in battle with the Presidential Guards. The movement of the Army at the national border is being scrutinized but no information is available. All transportation and communication in the city have been suspended.

The Ambassador to Annan

He raised his arm to beckon Lee, the attaché, who was on his way to deliver it to the telegram office, as he suddenly was reminded of the missing word, "the people" but changed his mind. He was astonished at himself for not having any information about the people. As though he was searching for a concrete entity called people, he looked down at the street from his office window. Down there, there was only a whirlpool of action called a revolution but rage that should be the basis of this action was missing. Did the people deem the turmoil as a domestic strife of a dictator's family? Or like him, are they scrutinizing the situation from their window? Or perhaps they haven't in their wildest imagination thought they could triumph over the present situation? Have they been deprived of a measure of comparison as to what it is that could free themselves from? This will no longer exist the moment it is taken away from them. There are two occasions when the people will ultimately rebel. One is when they are starved to death and the other is when the meaning of life has been stolen from them—because if you can't eat then you will perish but your soul will also die if you can't think.

With these thoughts in mind, he turned his gaze toward the Lion Palace. The white granite architecture looked withered under the sizzling sun. All of a sudden, he felt terribly hot. He turned on the small fan that looked like a blossoming white chrysanthemum on his desk. In contrast to the ancient French baroque office, the fan was strikingly modern. The music on the radio stopped abruptly and a declaration was being announced. It was the voice of An. He turned off the fan to pay closer attention.

126

"This revolution is to free the people from their slavish lives. This revolution is to annihilate the dictator and his followers, who have robbed the people of freedom that they regained. The nation is not the private property of mercenary politicians. The people are the nation. My fellow ten million citizens! We have not brought about this revolution to take control of authority. We have merely destroyed the shackles of the dictator's stronghold to reclaim your sovereign rights and freedom. We urge you to flee from that stronghold for your freedom. The government until now did not represent the people of Anan; hence, it should be viewed as a private organization. People! To prove that I will not be the same kind of dictator, I will make the following three promises.

First, all political prisoners who have been imprisoned since the liberation, except for the Communists, will be released.

Second, the Revolutionary Committee will represent the government only until the new government is established by the national assembly in the general election that will take place within six months; moreover, the Revolutionary Committee members will not take up any important position in the new government or run for candidacy in the assembly.

Third, no organization or agency will be set up that will harass the people."

He felt a chilly sensation, as though sweat on his forehead had suddenly evaporated as well as a sense of liberation, like immediately after passing the most crucial point during a fast. Drowsiness followed the resignation. No human voice has ever knocked on his soul as beautifully as this before. What was the power behind this impact? It was a moment of his lifelong search coming to the fore. Right then, Park, the third secretary, came in with a newspaper supplement. His trembling fingers holding the paper showed the state of his mind. The meaning of the revolution was overflowing in each letter of the newspaper, which until yesterday was too rapt in deifying Nguyen, the President, but was now scorched black by the ferocious flame of the revolution.

"Coup d'état at Dawn Today"
"Lion Palace Besieged by the Revolutionary Army"
"The President and Government Officials Imprisoned at Lion Palace."

Nguyen Dinh An, Director of National Security, paid an early visit to the President. While he was waiting, he walked apprehensively back and forth in the lounge. Contradictory emotions of resolve and fear were intermingled on his face. At last, the President made his appearance looking sleepy and irritable.

"There will be an uprising by the people today," the son blurted out.

"What? An uprising by the people?" the father repeated with a smile at his son, as though the very idea was endearing to him.

"Yes, the rebellion will take place nationwide."

"The police will take care of it."

"Father, I wouldn't have come to you this early if the police could stop it. The force will be greater than I can handle."

"What force?"

"The fury of the people and the military force."

"Did the military betray us?"

"The Capital Defense Corps, the 1st Armored Division, and the Marine are all involved in it. I'd like to propose that the National Security Council be called to seek a measure."

"All right."

The meeting between father and son ended here. Thirty minutes later, a National Security Council meeting was held in the secret conference room of the Lion Palace. It was an emergency meeting for discussion about the security of nation, with the President and his cabinet members, the Minister of National Defense, the Chief of Staff, the

Ministers of Foreign Affair and Domestic Affairs, the Director of National Security, and the Chairman of the National Assembly.

In complete contrast to his earlier statement, Nguyen Dinh An announced the following declaration.

"The people's rebellion is an outcome of fate. It is now not possible to put a stop to it for it is too late. The only way we can thwart it is to get rid of the cause of it. So, I propose the following."

He paused at this point and looked at the President. He seemed to be asking the father to save him from having to speak further.

The President glared at his son with rage, and then examined the people present, one by one. His gaze stopped at the Chairman of the National Assembly, whose eyes twitched as though they were shocked by the President's stare. Supporting himself on the table, he rose from his seat.

"If it is resignation of the President you have in mind, then that is absolutely out of the question. To deny the constitutionally elected national government head is a reckless anarchist atrocity that is equal to negating the Republic of Annan. All actions on a national level must be executed in accordance with the legitimate constitutional proceedings. That is because democratic creeds are constructed in accordance with the constitutional law. Moreover, the President Nguyen was elected with an absolute majority of the votes in the general election this year..."

The Director of National Security abruptly sprang to his feet, preventing the Chairman of the National Assembly from continuing.

"Mr. Chairman! We are not here to discuss law. A drum can make a beat when you hit it with a drumstick but when that drum is old and decayed, and then one must strip off the leather from it. What is a constitution? And law? It is but like the leather on a drum. What is wrong with tearing off with a knife called revolution the drum leather that is aged and decayed? The people are here to serve as drummers and not to safeguard it. A nation is but like the concept of a drum and the government is an entity that realizes this idea. The people have never once been able to beat on the drum themselves. In the ancient times, it was the monarchy then the colonialists in the modern age and now the president in our times who has monopolized this drum. The history of Annan has really been about the search for the lost drum."

The President brusquely got up, to the extent his almost all white hair became disheveled. He cried out, "Are you an instigator of the rebellion or a suppressor?" He was too agitated to go on. Panting, he glared at the men and at last declared, "Arrest the Director of the National Security for mutiny and thoroughly investigate him and those linked to him. All three branches of the military must be on full alert."

As soon as he said it, two undercover National Security policemen barged in. But it was unclear whose order they were going to obey. At the moment when the pendulum of the huge wall clock in the conference room was about to make the first strike for seven o'clock, the trolley with the Capital Defense Corps was slowly but surely making its way toward the Lion Palace,

Even before he had finished reading the supplement, he was put on alert not by the gunshots but the shouting of the people. The cry of the people instilled with a kind of despair and rage, which had been mounting for thousands of years, was dissolved in that roar. If the most humane thing were most meaningful to humans, then wouldn't this fury be it? The reason why a person has an epitaph engraved on his grave is an evidence of his rage that is still there. The reason why it took Nguyen Dinh An's call for the people to come out to the streets for the destruction of the stronghold where their sovereignty and freedom were imprisoned was because their rage had been frozen solid in a tightly sealed structure for too long and necessitated a fuse to melt it.

He gazed out the window and analyzed the constituents of the masses. Most of them were students. When you're starved for justice more than bread, it is only natural that the intelligentsia should be in the forefront. Because justice is a raison d'être and reason for death as well. But since it is so human, perhaps it can be only obtained amidst the thick blood flowing from the heart shot by a gun. Because humans are essentially tragic beings.

He told Park, the third secretary to draft the complete text.

"1. The Rebels have taken over the state broadcasting, National Security Bureau, Public Communications, and other public facilities while having completely besieged the government buildings.

Q. 1. Until noon, it was questionable whether or not the rebellion was a success but with the participation of the citizens of the capital, it has reached a pivotal stage. The corruption, oppression, and injustice of the past fifteen years are being done away with by the furor of the people and the plaza before the Lion Palace is inundated with the waves of people and their call for justice. The fortress of dictatorship is being toppled by the fury of the masses and their hope for justice."

His heart was throbbing as he read the draft. Whose thought was it? It was very impertinent of Park to have written in such a way as if he had read his mind. But he could no longer claim to be impartial. As though he would like Park to take the initiative of erasing it himself, he stopped short of writing anything and instead, handed the text back to him with a forced smile. There is nothing more cowardly than to shirk the responsibility of having to make an important decision and shift it to another person, especially when that decision is a very difficult one that the other person is not in a position to do anything about it. But then he passed over the right to decision by saying curtly, "Those who studied the humanities are dangerous."

He did not think Park's expression was feigned or exaggerated. It's just that he believed an official document should not read like that.

All of a sudden he wanted to observe the revolution as an ordinary person and not a diplomat who represented the government of a certain nation. A formidable entity called the government was hindering him from having an impartial stance on the situation. As though to free himself from that sentiment, he turned his gaze toward the window. The masses were climbing on top of the trollies and armored ve-

hicles, shouting with joy. The cars carrying them were racing maniacally. But a voice that sounded closer than the shouts of joy came out
of the radio behind him.

"The Revolutionary Committee demands that the President resign before the public. All the cabinet members have already officially
resigned. If the President willingly makes his appearance before the
Revolutionary Committee, his safety will be absolutely guaranteed. We
will do our best to avoid bloodshed but if the President continues to
reject the Committee's demand, then it will be our last resort.

The Commander-in-chief, the Capital Defense Corps
Chan Banh Banh, Colonel, Annan Army

He discerned the conflicted mind of Nguyen Dinh An and his
ethical dilemma in the message by Colonel Chan. Although he left his
first wife to get remarried to his present wife, An was the President's
only bloodline. Perhaps the Oedipal anguish was the basis of the Revolutionary force's intent on taking over the government in a lawful way.
Surely, he must know the revolution can no longer serve when it sub-
jugates itself to law that is only an accessory of politics?

The clouds from the squall dissipated and evening arrived with the
wind from the Saigon Bay. While watching the raindrops on the window that manifested the scenes outside in all different ways, he could
hear the inner signal of the revolution going into decline.

The presidential guards who were positioned in the Lion Palace
began firing at the masses indiscriminately. The cries of the people instantly turned into a scream. But what was going on then? The trolley
with the Rebel Army, which should have protected the people, began
to all retreat. Like chicks looking for the safety of a hen's wings, the
screaming people all crowded to the trolley. The trolley that made a
sound, like a beetle with its neck twisted, spun around and around the
plaza. The firing by the guard intensified. Where the people had scattered, there were corpses strewn about like trash. The masses, which

had momentarily lost their mind at the reckless firing, gradually organized themselves. They picked up whatever they could lay their hands on and threw them at the Lion Palace, including the shoes that came off dead people. They took over the Rebel Army's trolley and drove toward the Palace at full speed, only to be crushed against the granite fence. They stole the guns of the Rebel Army. They fired away as they ran to the enormous gate, only to collapse and die. The furious turbulent waves collided relentlessly and retreated, leaving behind the corpses before the Lion Palace. The masses toppled the huge statue of President Tuan in the center of the plaza and they marched toward the Palace, pushing the statue along. The guards focused on direct firing. Everyone fell flat on the ground, relying on the statue as a shield. Then they rose again.

A truck with a still bleeding corpse tied to its bumper sped past the embassy. The people on the truck were wailing and bellowing. The masses who saw the corpse shouted and were shoved toward the plaza. The American correspondent, dressed in an Aloha shirt, was all flushed like a spectator and shook his head in the crowd. He was carrying a camera box on his shoulder and holding a notebook in his hand. Like a person who had come out to purchase tragedy at the plaza, he was marking the price of what was happening. The camera lens could be all bloodshot to capture all the several hundred dollar scenes. The agony of a nation was being commodified on film.

The rebel trolley retreated at a full speed, as though it was being chased by something. The people, with empty hands and naked fists, were the only ones left at the plaza. The presidential guards fired at them even more ferociously. The masses dispersed like a flock of sparrows. A student, shot on his forehead and blood covering his face, ran, supported on both sides by two beggars of his age, past the embassy. Their faces looked enraged. The student lifted his face toward the sky and blew on the blood running down his face. A young man, shot on his arm, was also running, out of breath with a stone gripped in his hand. The people raided the National Security patrol car and raced

PARK SANGSEEK

around uncontrollably. A person who barely managed to hold on to the back of the car fell on the ground and rolled over. He got up again and ran after the car. A clamor from the exhaust pipe let out a thick smoke and the car stopped. The driver did not bother to restart the engine and jumped out. Everyone else all leaped out and began running. Only the corpses remained in the car. The headlights were on with the broken glass from the gunshots that did not quite extinguish the light. The car was dripping with blood seeping from the corpses.

There was no longer anyone at the plaza. It was completely empty. Only the corpses, shoes, rocks, clubs, and paper were strewn about. The evening sun did not shine on the clothes of the corpses. The shadow covered them instead. The anarchist stillness overflowed in resplendence. The radio, which he was listening to, suddenly came to stop. He turned his head with the thought that he was until now listening to the national anthem of Annan. The room suddenly became frighteningly quiet. Feeling a peculiar chill, he stood in front of the radio. Right then, a voice, which seemed like it jumped right out of the radio, was heard on the radio. It was the same language but a completely different message.

"People of Annan, please remain calm. The villainous rebel forces have been overthrown. The most courageous Defense Corps of the National Border are after the insurgents. We are going to mop up every one of them. The President and the First Lady are safe and sound. The President will personally comfort the people of Annan in a short while."

The announcement from the radio was then buried in the sound of a racing car and machine gun shots. The line of trucks loaded with the soldiers was moving toward the Lion Palace. In the vehicles originally from the USA, which seemed to have been put together only a few days ago after their disembarkation, the soldiers with their American helmets, who had been trained in the American military style, were being transported to the palace without knowing why. For a reason none other than being assigned to a border region by chance, he had, unbeknownst to him, become a faithful supporter of the President

134

Nguyen's government. He now had not the faintest idea of what was the function of a so-called government. Leaning against the U.S. made rifle, he was presently lost in thought. His thoughts, like his body, were shaking. But one obsessive thought refused to leave his mind. Why do career politicians devise a government, that is more like a social organization, and harass the people? And why do they place a foreign made rifle in my care and harangue me to shoot the people? The leader of a cult will cheat women but at least comfort their souls as compensation. But the leader of a government will not only manage our whole lives but also ill-treat our souls. Those corpses strewn about in the plaza had even their souls robbed for the purpose of politics. I want to die at my own hands because I want to claim my own soul. That the Lion Palace purports to be my country is truly deplorable. One's country is something that has the most cherished place in your heart and is not defined by a granite structure. The reason why we love our country more than god is that it is something that belongs to us. His right finger is groping down from the handguard to the trigger. But his head failed to comprehend the action of his hand. His head was overloaded with thoughts and did not catch the betrayal of his finger. The treachery of his finger expelled all his thoughts for good with a single bullet. He keeled over, with the rifle. His thoughts gleamed in the eyes of his fellow soldier, who was looking down at his dead body with astonishment. The thought was not his, but rather, he was subject to it.

It seemed as though the border garrison was heading toward the Lion Palace in order to witness the death of the Cabinet members whose bodies were tied to the stakes on the grass. The soldiers could not help a bitter smile at the thought of seeing the ministers in person only after their death.

The ten corpses representing the ten "fortresses" of the central government were tied to the post, looking far removed from the glory of their heydays. These men, who had been executed just an hour ago on the charge of treason, became the great political leaders who had been massacred by the traitors. Political death must share contradictory values.

While the soldiers untied the corpses from the posts and carried them to the ambulance, others looked for the ringleader who could be tied to the stake. It was a simple reason why the stake was not removed; however, the purpose of it was noteworthy for two different kinds of deaths.

He was examining the draft of a telegram to be wired to his country while reading about the death of the Cabinet members in the supplement. He reflected on the text while gazing at the telephone that looked like a stuffed black cat, and then he abruptly thought of making a request to the government for the safety of the diplomats in Annan. As he was about to grab the receiver, the phone rang with a loud clamor. He was startled out of his wits but quickly corrected his expression before Park, the third secretary, who was standing in front of his desk. He briskly picked up the phone.

"Is this the Embassy of the Republic of South Korea?"

"Yes, it is.

"This is the head of the Office of the Protocol of Annan."

"Go on."

"I would like to speak with the Ambassador."

"This is he."

"Oh, I see. It must've been a great shock. First, I'd like to ask how you are."

"Everyone is safe. But I am curious about other embassies."

"Rest assured. The government of Annan will see to the safety of all foreign organizations. If you'd like, we are prepared to dispatch the security corps to each diplomatic organ?"

"We welcome it but I suggest you ask other embassies individually."

That was the diplomatic dialogue in a nutshell. But he couldn't shake off the feeling that he had forgotten to mention something very important to the head of Protocol. Moreover, their conversation was lacking in any kind of political stance. There was sweat on his forehead and he reflected on why the conversation was trying for him. To tell the truth, he was most reluctant to say in their talk what was the most important.

Was he afraid of what could be the outcome of, "Congratulations on the successful crackdown of the rebels"? A single phrase like that one could bring about an outcome as serious as the severance of diplomatic relations. But he did not refrain from saying it for a diplomatic reason. It was also not because he thought it wasn't yet over. Before he knew it, he abhorred the Nguyen government.

Part 2

With a sense of vengeance, he picked up the phone receiver. He felt compelled to talk to someone. His hand was dialing the French Embassy—as though he wanted to protest against the Colonial ruler that it formerly was. Evening was already dimming the numbers on the phone.

The room felt as ominous, as when there is the ringing of a misdirected phone call in a public office after the closing hour. He wanted to get over his rage about something by talking to the chief of a foreign embassy.

The national anthem of Annan was floating over the radio but rage filled him up to his neck. Right then, the national anthem stopped suddenly and an announcement was heard, mixed in with other noises.

"The rebellion has been crushed completely. The government urges Nguyen Dinh An to turn himself in. The insurgents have all been arrested. The government is aware that Nguyen Dinh An was forcibly involved in the uprising at the gun muzzle of the rebel leader. If he willingly makes an appearance, then we hereby declare all his crimes will be overlooked."

The calculation of a father was transparent in the name of the government. He felt nauseated over the sugarcoated political anguish taking precedence over an ethical one.

He turned his head toward the window, as though he wanted to disperse the thoughts that were suffocating him. Had the plaza absorbed the chaos of the day like a blotting paper? It was frighteningly still and dark. Outside the window, the mayflies were fluttering away, breaking the silence. The soul of a dead person appeared to be gleaming. The sound of the radio again broke the brief tranquility of his mind.

"Anyone who has seen Nguyen Dinh An or knows his whereabouts should report at once to the government. One million *piastre* will be rewarded to the one who arrests him."

The father had become so impatient that he was ready to capture the suspect with a scarcity value. His throat stung, as if after swallowing a diarrhea pill with the sugar coating all melted in the mouth. He found himself unconsciously pressing the white button on the corner next to his desk. He could not endure the tension all by himself. He heard the bell ring in the adjacent room. Right then, he heard loud footsteps and the mahogany door facing him opened. With his finger still on the button, he was looking at Nguyen Dinh An, who appeared before him like an apparition. He gazed at him vacantly, as though he was a friend who showed up all of a sudden after his disappearance and being out of touch for a long time. Suddenly, his mind went blank. He withdrew his hand from the button and tried to regain calm. Nguyen was standing precariously, supported by his aide. His mouth was shut tight like he would never speak again; his dark and despondent face was pallid like someone who had been close to death but miraculously resurrected and his left shoulder was drooping like the wing of a wild animal that had been shot; and his blue uniform was stained with dried blood. An stood in silence for as long a time, as if he needed to explicate the reason for his coming here. As though the aide was acting on his behalf, he seated An in the guest's armchair. Amidst the tension among them, they were unaware of the diplomatic issue of protecting a political prisoner in the country of residence. The problem that existed in the form of a body and soul was right before his very eyes.

He thought he had to resort to an action to pacify his tumultuous mind. He silently pointed at An's injury by getting the attention of Park, the third secretary, who took his order as an excuse to bolt out of the room. An's aide stepped forward and gave him a military salute. He had guns on both sides of his combat uniform and the leather belt of grenades crossed his chest on the left and right.

"We request political asylum from the government of the Republic of Korea."

His conduct was imbued with the confidence of a diplomat engaged in a diplomatic negotiation. He could only be overpowered by the aide who was suppressing the urgency of the matter with a terrifying calm.

"They will soon find us. We demand speedy action."

An's aide took closer steps toward him, as though to reduce their mental distance and to block an unwanted response. He thought he had to make a decision of some sort. To help himself with the decision, he gazed at An, who was almost lying in the armchair with his back leaning against the armrest. An was imposing a decision upon him. Their eyes crossed with the aide between them. An's face was bereft of any expression. If there was, then it was the cool air of despondency. As power had retreated from the plaza, the expression had vanished from his face. Was it the political power and not life itself that had sustained his voice? He thought of the voice that still lingered from the radio transmission. Numerous historical cases of political asylum would be intertwined amongst the strands of that voice.

Right then, Park came in with the first aid treatment. But he was not doing anything. Suddenly he felt angry. It seemed like everyone mandated that he make the decision. He felt as though the decision was incarcerating him. Was there any way of freeing himself from it?

An's drained face—from the pain of injury—filled his vision. But An's wound called for action, irrespective of the decision he had to make.

"Mr. Park, what're you doing?"

It was a question that he was asking himself, rather. As soon as he heard that, An's aide snatched the first-aid kit and began to treat An's left arm. The national anthem of Annan, which was played repetitiously on the radio, was then swallowed up by the sound of the speaker from outside. All turned their ears toward that direction.

"The National Security Corps is aware that Nguyen Dinh An and his aide are in hiding somewhere in the city. All citizens are asked to actively cooperate and help arrest them. Those who are hiding them or know their hideout but fail to report it to the government will be subject to severe punishment."

To seemingly augment the announcement, a powerful searchlight penetrated through the window and like lightning, illuminated the room. The four men remained stiff like clay plaster. The inevitable circumstances called for a decision. His eyes crossed once more with An's, which frightened him. He quickly looked the other way. But he felt the gaze of An's aide on him and he closed his eyes. The bright searchlight penetrated his closed eyes. The army march song echoed from the radio. The earlier announcement was being repeated on the speaker outside the window. His head rang and he felt giddy and nauseated. But it wasn't nausea or dizziness. He simply felt suffocated and couldn't bear it.

His mind became more lucid when he closed his eyes. He perused his bookcase, as if he were searching for the political asylum case studies.

There is the case of Victor Haya De La Tore, who was the anti-government conspirator of Peru. He requested political asylum at the Embassy of Columbia in Lima. What did the Ambassador of Columbia do with him?

But what has he got to do with me? Here is An's deathly face and he is bleeding. This blood does not belong to him only. It is the magma of human anguish. Is this blood in vain?

He shouted at Park with a voice so solemn that it could vanquish the sound of the radio and the speaker.

Park looked at him, completely taken aback. He saw that Park's lips were quivering. He shouted once more, to chase away other thoughts.

Without saying anything, Park went to his desk. His typing on the typewriter was heard amidst the sound of the radio and the speaker. An's aide slowly approached him with his hands on his side. It was akin to a movement of a puma, precise and noiseless. A peculiar flash of light beamed from his eyes. Was it the light of despair? With each step he took, the weight of desperation overwhelmed his mind. He remained motionless and stood where he was. An's aide pulled out a grenade from the leather belt hung across his chest.

"Please convey our message to your government. I am delivering this request on behalf of the Revolutionary Government."

He could only be appalled by the precision of how the aide chose the grenade instead of pulling out his gun. His mind suddenly became as cool as ice.

"I am disappointed at your barbaric action. You have not chosen to come here to threaten the Republic of Korea. I would like to believe that you came here specifically with the same rationality that compelled you to draw the grenade and not your gun. You must be aware that although I am in the precarious proximity of being threatened but the government of the Republic of Korea exists outside the domain of your threat."

Then the national anthem stopped playing on the radio and there was an announcement.

"The rebellion was brought about by a number of malcontents in the military and Nguyen Dinh An, Director of National Security, was found out to have been involved involuntarily by their threats. The despicable insurgents intended to take advantage of the Chief's special status and his popularity with the public. Thus, the President declared the leading insurgents will be subject to strict judgment in the near future, whereas Director Nguyen will retain all of his prior positions."

He searched for a reaction in Nguyen's face whose eyes shone in a peculiar way. He lacked the peace of mind to let them know he was not so childish as to believe the President. An's eyes turned dim again.

The door opened abruptly and Lee, the attaché, came with a document and handed it to him quietly. He went and sat at his desk with it. His hand, which reached for the glasses in his inner pocket, was somewhat brusque.

"The Foreign Minister of the Republic of Annan pays respect to the Ambassador of the Republic of Korea while conveying deepest apology for the disturbance that took place on April 19, 1961, in the capital.

The disruption was stirred by a small number of malcontents who have solely their self-interests at heart and is completely separate from the consensus of the public. Thus there should be no damage incurred whatsoever on the long-standing amity between our nations.

Be informed that Director of National Security, Nguyen Dinh An, who is the leader of the rebellion, is presently hiding somewhere in the city; and in case of infiltration into your embassy, please immediately notify the Foreign Ministry.

Once more, the Foreign Minister of the Republic of Annan pays his highest respect to the Ambassador of the Republic of Korea."

It was from an unfathomable rage rather than excitement that his hand holding the full report was trembling. He threw it back to Lee, the attaché, and yelled out to Park.

"Bring me the full text."

He caught the aide's eyes and thought he had to offer him some kind of an affirmation.

"It's a notice asking to report your whereabouts."

An's aide grabbed his hand, with the grenade still in his hand. His action stunned him. He could not endure the physical pressure that he made up his mind as to whose side he was on. The hand that grasped him felt afire.

"We have faith in your judgment."

But is he prodding me about the next step after my decision that he is already sure of? Did my behavior before his armed threat reveal a clue to how I would act? He took a step back as to distance himself from them; however, An's aide came one step closer to him and obstructed his way. An unavoidable something had befallen him.

Park handed him the full text. Without reading it, he gave it to the aide, who perused it with his bloodshot eyes.

"The leader of the Revolution, Nguyen Dinh An, Director of National Security, and Chan Banh Banh, his aide, have asked our government for political asylum at 20:00. They are presently in hiding at the embassy. A swift order from the government is requested."

The aide shoved the text in front of him and badgered him, "Provide evidence to persuade the position of the Revolutionary Government." His rational statement triggered him to regain reason.

"I am in a position where I can only evaluate the situation based on its outcome."

"Are you saying the outcome does not favor us?"

"Unfortunately, I do not think I can take your side."

"Mr. Ambassador, you're reluctant to get down to the fundamentals of the problem."

As though he did not have the patience for such an idle conversation, An's aide made fists with his hands and scanned inside. An was lying unconscious on the sofa. Tension in the room severed the dialogue.

He seized this moment to wire the telegram to his country. Feeling contemptuous of his cowardly act, he reflected on the meaning of the telegram. It was in a language bereft of any soul.

Suddenly fatigue took over him to the point of dizziness. He went over to his desk and plopped down. On his left wrist that was clutching the desk, his Omega watch showed the hour and minute hands over-lapping on twelve. He felt delirious from the fatigue that took over his whole body.

He leaned his head against the back of the chair and closed his eyes. It is obvious that I became overly excited about something. And I know what that is. But I am scared to confront it face to face. I am in subjugation to something. There is a human factor that forbids me from leaving the orbit. There is fatigue from the taut tension between the pressure from the radio waves that pulls perpetually and my cen-tripetal force.

The radio is playing slow and relaxing folk music, as though to mock this sterile circumstance. The radio is now the only sound that connects this room with the outside world. He had fallen asleep amidst the thought that he would like to simply collapse for he couldn't bear the present situation. But it was more like he had passed out. Between them, how powerful was the whirlpool of ideology that gushed and invaded each other's mind? From time to time, their moaning was heard like water crushing against the bank.

He woke up, feeling suffocated, to see the attaché in front of him with a telegram. Tuan's aide and he both rushed to it.

Reply to AW. 0419
Quickly provide responses to the following.
1. Did the revolution fail?
2. What kind of state is the fugitive in?
After a careful consideration of the above two, resort to action based on the U.S. State Department's directive which denied the right of asylum in the 1924 Peru Rebellion.

Foreign Minister

Although it was what he had expected, he could not help the tur-moil in his heart on receiving the telegram. Was this the pillar that had until now sustained him? Did he really believe blood could circulate in something as cold and lucid as an icicle? Did he not know that this icicle would melt the moment blood could flow? He lost all courage to keep on deceiving himself with the pretext of his government.

Moreover, revolution was in too close a proximity to him.

"Mr. Ambassador, we believe in you."

The grenade was no longer in the aide's hand.

"That you believe in me and your being helped has as little relevance as in your believing in a dog preventing thieves."

"You are in a position to help us, Mr. Ambassador. Must I instruct you to use your country?"

"When it is my country that is opposed to helping you?"

"You yourself know better that whether or not your government allows or forbids help is irrelevant."

"Do you think of yourselves so worthy that I would betray my country?"

"We are here before you, irrespective of value judgments. Here before your eyes is bleeding justice on the brink of death."

He has seen through my Achilles' heel. He could no longer carry on the dialogue, for An's aide was too dangerously close to him. Moreover, this sultry air, mingled with the heat of his breath, was enough to melt the pillar that was sustaining him. He realized he could no longer hold on to an abstract idea. The bond to his country connected only through the radio waves could not be as desperately earnest as the body in front of him covered with blood. He could feel the suffering of An, who was groaning in an unconscious state. His face, like an image from the past, which appeared even whiter from the bright fluorescent light, pierced his heart. Was there a reason for two nations to collide because of a being who was close to a corpse? As he was gazing at the body of Nguyen like a territory of a country, his aide clutched his hand like a great opportunity.

He implored, "Mr. Ambassador, you must save him. If I had ten thousand lives, I'd give them all up for this honorable man. His life represents the lives of all Annanese people. If he can only live, it will signify that a basic human value cannot perish. As long as he is alive, our revolution will make a comeback."

His English was inadequate but precise. He felt dazed like he had been struck hard on his forehead. The meaning of his words transcended his expression. The layers were being peeled off his fundamental nature. There was nothing he couldn't do in this state.

"What exactly can I do to help you?"

The aide could not help himself from revealing his joy and launched his final and decisive blow.

"Please do not trample on our intent in purposely seeking out Mr. Ambassador. We have come to you, as a human being, and not the Republic of Korea you represent."

He was getting irritable and irascible at the same time. And it wasn't so much at An's aide but at himself. What was the reason for getting vexed about his not viewing him as someone who was negotiable? Was he annoyed for not feeling his country was first in his heart? Was he, unbeknownst to him, abhorring his inclination to partake in the revolution? But then why was he feeling so much contempt for this irritation and abomination?

"Mr. Ambassador, the foreign embassies are targeted for investigation; except it is certain that they haven't been able to figure out specifically our hideout. The following is my plan."

The aide leaned over the table with both his arms, like a solider explaining combat strategy with a map.

"First, you must inform your government that the revolution is ongoing. It is a tactic to delay them on the decision of allowing political asylum.

Next, first thing in the morning, we ask you to bring us to the battleship at Saigon Harbor that is on a friendly visit. We will disguise ourselves so as not to be discovered.

Next…"

146

The aide could not finish his sentence and just gazed at him. His forlorn face looked like he was on the verge of tears and he could not bear looking at him.

However, the reason why he turned to face Park was not just that he could not stand face to face with the aide.

"Mr. Park."

His face, fraught with fear and anxiety, was starting to resemble the aide's. His trembling heart manifested itself at the tip of his fingers holding onto the Korean typewriter.

"Type what I say."

He closed his eyes and focused on the mind's eye. The Foreign Minister will receive this report and then go to the Presidential Residence.

"In my opinion, the Revolution in Annan has not come to an end. The Revolution is a manifestation of the people's rage over a one-man dictatorship and not an action taken by a single political organization or social class to take over power. The following is the evidence.

1. The main component of the revolution is not a specific group. This is proved by the fact that the National Security Corps and the uncorrupted military are a combined force.
2. The Revolution received the absolute support of the people. In short, it is uprising of the people who counted on the valor and the arms of the National Security Corps and the military.
3. That Nguyen Dinh An, the son of the President, who has received the heroic support and respect of the people, is the leader of the Revolution. Furthermore, that he stipulated ethics which precedes the national interest proves the pure motive of his action and his greatness.

The reason why the National Border Security Corps did not partake in the revolution is that its high-ranking officers are the followers of President Nguyen. Because of the President's adroit military concil-iation policy, they are corrupt to the point of being paralyzed and are incapable of understanding the courage and noble actions of the Rev-olutionary Army. This goes to show the great effort on President Ngu-yen's part to maintain his dictatorship by winning the military's sup-port and also proves that his strategy was effective."

Suddenly he couldn't think of the next statement. He felt anxious. He opened the cigarette case with a mother-of-pearl inlay that was on his desk. "Arirang" cigarettes prompted a memory of his country.

The Foreign Minister will provide a briefing about the Annan Up-rising to the President. The minister will initially be overpowered by this all too sharp analysis of the situation while the President will at first be confounded by the news that is quite different from that of the foreign press and too subjective for a government report. He might even be annoyed. But he wanted neither impression to happen. He had to make them understand and thereby persuade.

The President will probe into the implied meaning in his observa-tion that the revolution was not yet over.

"What then is the conclusion? What happened to the rebels who are hiding in our embassy?"

He squashed the cigarette he was going to light and looked Ngu-yen Dina An's way. The President is too impatient.

"The rebel leader should not be turned in. I hereby request that political asylum be granted to them."

He closed his eyes and waited for the President's next reaction. He could almost see his irritation turning into rage.

"What is the reason?"

The Foreign Minister will become flustered, like a parent before his misbehaving child's principal.

What is the reason? His eyelashes quivered. Come and look. Come sit down here and take a look at him. Furthermore, if he demands a reason even after that, then he can readily come up with one in any textbook on international law.

148

"First, the Revolution is ongoing,

Second, he has formally requested political asylum.

And such a measure is in accordance with the directive of the US State Department that allows temporary shelter for a political criminal who has urgently fled under life-threatening circumstances."

But the President wants to know which side is more advantageous to us. His picture on the wall behind him was glaring at him.

"Raison d'état."

But now was not the time for a diplomatic issue; nor was it a political venue. He wanted to be in control of this minor extraterritoriality that God provided.

Through the curtain, the time that passed was revealed. By now, his words must be coming out in code through the receiver at the Foreign Ministry.

Time does not wait for the instruction from his government. Everything depended on his decision. Right then, the sound of several cars came to a stop outside. He drew the curtain to take a peek. Park, who was looking his way, looked petrified.

Instinctively, the aide and he rose on their feet. A sedan escorted by two white patrol cars was crouching like a cat at the porch.

"It's the General's car." The bell rang as Park opened the door and exited. Tension oppressed his thoughts and suffocated him. Lee, looking nervous, seemed to be castigating him.

"Lee, to the garage."

But the aide's action was quicker than his thought. How should he construe the man who threw An on his back and swiftly left the room? Nguyen's aide was walking ahead with formidable force, trampling on his tension, and dragging with him his thoughts. It felt like his words and actions were being hauled like a rag.

As though Lee, the attaché, too was being pulled, followed the aide out of the room. With his eyes closed, he inhaled deeply. Could he shield An from the intruders? His face stiffened as he waited for the intruder.

The sound of the footsteps stopped as the door opened. He opened his eyes. A soldier in an officer's uniform was standing next to Park.

"I am the aide to Major General Bu Banh Mao, the Martial Law Commander. The Commander seeks an urgent meeting with Mr. Ambassador," said the aide, with a salute. His English was quite inadequate and he didn't seem to want their dialogue to continue. But his brusque and somewhat rude demeanor appeared nearly physiological.

"It is unfortunate that you should pay a visit during work hours without prior notice."

He glared at the aide, putting on a solemn face. The aide instinctively became stiff. It is a sign of person with an unrefined temperament who has not learned to disguise his feelings. He had no desire to talk to that kind of person.

"We didn't have a chance to contact you because of the urgent nature of the situation."

He didn't dare prolong the conversation with such a man. But he needed more time.

"May I ask what the urgency is about?"

"The Commander will let you know himself."

The reason why the aide didn't get sucked into his tactic of stalling was not that he has seen through him; rather, it was because he wanted to carry out the original plan of a surprise visit. In that case, he would confront the commander.

"Then please tell him to enter."

Major General Bu Banh Mao, who seemed to have been listening from outside, appeared from behind his aide. His combat uniform looked uncomely on his chubby figure. The aide executed a military salute as the two men sat across the reception table. Park, too, briskly left the room.

He looked straight at the Major General and silently demanded the other to speak first. All he was going to do was listen.

"We would like your cooperation in arresting the rebel leader."

150

Instead of an answer, he again looked straight at the Major General. He tried to glean from his expression whether or not he already knew their hideout here, for there was no clue to be found in his words.

"With Mr. Ambassador's cooperation, it will be easier to arrest him."

It was clear he knew about it. So as not to lose calm, he crossed his fingers. The Major General was scrutinizing his every movement. But he did not want to give him the slightest hint. The Major General goaded him once more, with what he said. Was he trying to ascertain a sign or demand a concession?

"We hope that the amity between our nations will not be damaged from the disturbance."

He was talking as though the friendly relation between their countries was impaired. But he could not decide whether or not he was asking him not to incur any more damage to an already marred relationship or to avoid doing anything to possibly harm it.

"We would appreciate it if you could immediately inform us in case of the rebel's infiltration."

He spoke like a seasoned diplomat. Yet, he sounded like he was parroting a prepared text, thereby indicating there was a prior discussion with the top officials before coming here and not from speaking in a foreign language.

The Major General did not wait to hear his reply and got up. But it was a very calculated move on his part to give a casual look around the room before he walked out. Was he indeed able to sense the anguish and the deep-seated torment that filled the room?

He waited in the middle of the room and waited for the sound of the engine to fade away. It was apparent they were about to carry out their plan. The day was breaking—outside the window. He hurriedly ran out of the room.

The sedan was already exiting the gate. He hastily jumped into the car. It was a simple act but his determination was more resolute than crossing the border of an enemy country. The darkness still permeated

151

inside of the car, however, the contour of the aide, who had changed into the attaché's clothes and sitting at the steering wheel, was all too white. Then, he was startled by An, who was leaning against one corner, covered with a white sofa sheet. He felt as faint as an apparition.

…What would the masses, who tried to stand up for themselves with An as their pillar, think if they were to see him now? He turned away and looked out the window. The blurriness of the scenery outside must be from the arising sorrow in his heart. The pain that tautened his whole body was a grief that was thicker than blood. The sedan was a territory of its own right. He sensed a kind of heart-rending destiny in An.

When their car reached the path that led to the harbor, he could tell a white patrol car was following them. Instinctively, he turned to An's aide, who was glaring at the rear view mirror, showing his own somber face.

The white needle of the speedometer was quivering between sixty-five to seventy kilometers per hour. There were now two patrol cars. From afar, they were following their car, forming an arc. The patrol cars turned on the sirens and drove to the front of their car, like a figure skater encircling the ice. But their car did not stop. When the patrol car slowed down, the aide kicked the door he had already left open and threw a grenade at lightning speed. There was an explosion and the car on the left came to a halt.

An opened his eyes at the sound of the explosion. His eyes turned toward the window.

The glow in his eyes looked like it would flicker for eternity…what was he gazing at?

They were coming after them. The aide motioned for him to come to the steering wheel. He rushed to the driver's seat. The pocket on his top attire tore as it got caught in the aide's duty belt and at the same time another grenade exploded.

The car was now going at seventy kilometers per hour. The patrol car got closer the more they accelerated. It was so close they could identify the man sitting upright. The speedometer needle was hesitant to go over seventy kilometers. But the closeness between the two cars made it possible. The rear view mirror was shaking. The aide's face contorted in the mirror.

The struggle for distance now ended. Gunshots were fired from both patrol cars, all at once. Compelled by the gunshots, the aide grabbed the gun and smashed the window with it.

An who was sitting up in the back seat did not move. Without even a twitching of an eyebrow, the world was no longer reflected in his eyes.

The tire of the car punctured. But the car was racing uncontrollably. It arrived at the First Harbor. It could go no further and there was no need.

The car came to a standstill after crashing against the concrete column with a flag of a foreign merchant ship company. The aide pushed the door open with his body and fired his gun like a mad man. He had ceased to be a human being. He passed out, holding the steering wheel. He regained consciousness when the salty sea wind almost dried up the sweat on his forehead.

His mind awakened, paradoxically, by the stillness around him. He looked in front of him. An was gazing at him in silence. He looked amazingly peaceful and about to say something. But blood was spewing from his chest. He didn't realize blood was also streaming down his forehead. He wanted to be where he could gaze at An forever.

An's silence made being alive at this moment meaningless. If this were what death was about, he would like to die a million times. From the Korean naval vessel anchored at the First Harbor, there was a trumpet call for morning assembly. Tears thicker than blood streamed down his face.

The Martial Law Commander was walking toward the dead aide, fallen in front of the concrete column, with a grenade in his hand.

The Shack

The shacks looking like toy houses stood on two legs in the stream alongside the market avenue. From afar, they looked like rectangular matchboxes standing obliquely, and did not appear so unsightly as to defame the face of the avenue that was a boisterous part of the town frequented by shoppers. There was a photo studio painted with the outlandish blue and red colors, a box-like shop with nothing but a baking machine, a two-story eatery with a luxuriously colorful wallpapered room on the ground level, a moveable bakery made possible by attaching wheels to the bottom of a junkshop that sold all kinds of hardware and furniture, a store with multi-colored flags advertising pills; it was not difficult to find Bok-nyeo's bread shop among them, for hers had a tin roof that looked like a patched cushion. She had flattened several dozen cans, that only god knew where she got them and transformed them into a decent roof. On the drape made from the flour sack, "Bread" was written large and underneath it, and in smaller crude writing, "Instead of Steamed Bread." When this drape fluttered in the wind, the face of Bok-nyeo, who was kneading the dough, became visible. Her skinny frame made her look much taller than she was. Her overgrown face was too long, to the point of looking ugly. She had sunken cheeks with a protruding mouth like a monkey. There was nothing attractive about her face with the dark, dry complexion and long, donkey-like ears; however, her eyes and eyebrows were the redeeming features of her visage. Her straight and thick eyebrows looked comely and her shiny eyes were unbelievably captivating, and she could even possibly look beautiful by casting down her eyes and making them bleary. Her life was so hard up that she most likely didn't have time to look in the mirror and tidy up her face. Before she managed to build this shanty, she had to go from under the stone bridge to a shelter cave that the Japanese had left behind but only after getting into vicious quarrels with the refugees from the North; thus, unless she had money, she would be out in the open, gazing at the night sky.

Bok-nyeo was annoyed with something that kept tapping her foot.

"You little brat, stop bothering me when I am busy like hell," she said and gave a hard kick. Her youngest child pretended she was on her last breath. Her mother remained indifferent and kept on kneading. But then when she was too quiet, Bok-nyeo became suspicious and bent down and was about to spill out a litany of curses when her eyes crossed with the grandfather, who was glaring at her from the open shack. She instead turned her head.

The old man, who was looking at her from the rear room narrow like a coffin, was as good as a corpse. If it weren't for his disapproval of hitting the child, she would've kicked the little idiot; however, she had to control her anger before her father-in-law. The child who was hurriedly licking the dough crumbs at her feet, as though she was being chased by someone, felt the shadow on her head and looked up to see her mother. It was then she burst into tears, like she had just regained her breath. Bok-nyeo shuddered and cursed again, "Just drop dead. Do you think you can get dough out of me? You're wrong, wrong. Sneaky little mouse."

Bok-nyeo was not a mother who could be duped by her child who feigned near death for dough crumbs. There was not a chance. Vexed, she gave a hard kick in the direction of where her daughter was crouched. Her foot happened to kick her open jaw and she yelped like a dog and rolled over on the ground. Her deaf father-in-law was clueless about what had happened. He shook his head and crawled to where his grandchild was, thinking how heartless of Bok-nyeo to do nothing about it. It was undeniably sad for him to see her get enraged and throw a fit over such a trivial matter. But then, given how she had to support

155

all alone her two children and a good-for-nothing old man, it was understandable that her personality could only turn coarse. He thought his son must surely be dead, for there had been no news from him in the two years since he was conscripted into the army, however, he still harbored hope as they hadn't been notified of his death, and clung to the newspaper he couldn't read when the release of captives was announced. Life could not be so meaninglessly futile, he thought and decided his son was alive somewhere. His belief—that his son was not only alive but would live a long life—was reinforced whenever he thought of how his son had defied many risks of death, traveling on foot all the way from Gando to their hometown in North Korea, and then crossing the 38th Parallel line to the South.

Bok-nyeo, who was going to make fire, did not want to see her father-in-law crawl out, and came outside looking but didn't find the child where she thought she could've slouched down and fallen asleep. She turned to look at the stone bridge where the garbage bin was, and saw a mob of people moving toward the marketplace. They didn't appear to be merchants. She was panic-stricken when she remembered the talk of tearing down the shacks. She convinced herself it wasn't going to happen and to find out what her neighbors had to say, she walked along the stream where she ran into her six-year-old daughter, who was more like dragging her youngest child on her back. It infuriated her to see how the little urchin was trying to evade getting water with the excuse of taking care of her sibling. She thought if she could be fooled like that, she would change her last name.

"Bong-sun, you little bitch, Bong-sun." She was screaming her head off, regardless of the people around her. But in effect she was venting her anger at her innocent daughter over the rumor. Bong-sun halted her steps and stood with her back toward her mother in anticipation of her browbeating.

"Look over there. By the bridge."

"Shut up, you bitch." Bong-sun heard her mother from above her head with a whiff of flour smell.

"Mother, they're tearing down the houses. Near the big bridge. With a truck,"

Bong-sun said tearfully. She was clutching her mother's clothes and shaking with fear the mob might destroy their house next. Bok-nyeo, who could hardly move, barely managed to get herself back to her place. But the sound of her adjacent house being demolished felt akin to her own ribs breaking. The rumbling of the truck stopped before her house and a thick rope around the shacks pulled by the truck made them topple like a row of matchboxes. She sat motionless amidst the pile of planks but when she heard the roof contract and fall on her like in a dream, she rushed outside. She ran after the truck that was driving away but she fell backward. Her ears buzzed with the loud noise all around her, but a clear voice made her jump to her feet.

"Mom, grandfather…"

She hurried into the house and dragged out the old man, who was lying like he was sleeping, between where the tin roof and the plank floor were piled.

With their shacks gone, there wasn't a place they could go. When evening arrived, they could but sleep out in the open or curl up underneath the eaves of someone's house. A group of older men, known to have some say in it, were sitting around, talking loudly about submitting a petition to city hall or waiting a little longer, and the panic of the neighbors did not show a sign of diminishing but grew stronger by night. There was an occasional song mixed in with the wailing, making it sound like a fox cry that was echoed in the mountain valley. Bok-nyeo was sitting on top of the wooden debris, listening to the uneven sound of her father-in-law's breathing. Next to her, Bong-sun, who had fallen asleep with the youngest still on her back, kept pulling the wrap from her grandfather for cover against the chilly wind. When she came to reflect on how they had traveled from Gando to be in their home country, and crossed the 38th Parallel line to boot, this hardship was really nothing to her, not to mention, how it felt unreal she managed not to have her family of four from starving after her husband joined the army. Furthermore, because she was proud to have built the shack amidst it all, it gave her indescribable pain to see it destroyed overnight. All that her husband left with her were his deaf-mute father and their two daughters with not a single possession since they brought nothing with them. There were some who advised her to marry herself to any able man but she didn't think there'd be anyone who would be willing to support her children as well. Not that it didn't occur to her to leave them in their grandfather's care and run away when things got unbearable but that was something she could never bring herself to do, hence she was left to simply survive. Come to think of it, a family, who lived a few houses down, lived off their daughter whose husband died in the battle on their wedding day. She thought it incredulous how they were so shameless as to eat the food the young woman obtained for all of them. But then, she wasn't sure if she herself wouldn't leech off some man if she did not have children of her own. It was because her countenance was not pretty enough, however, if she, too, were born with a straight nose and shapely mouth, why wouldn't she be wooed like her neighbor? Moreover, if she were that attractive, would she just wait around? Such were her thoughts, which stopped her from being condemnatory toward Samson's family. But there was actually a man who came to her of his own accord. The old man fortuneteller, Beon-kwe, who never missed being at the open market, was Bok-nyeo's regular customer, buying bread from her for lunch all the time. He would sometimes tell her to move in with him. She would then test him with a smile, "Will you take my children?"

"The children are who I really want to be with," he would say in all earnestness but then Bok-nyeo would demur and change the topic. As if he were proving his words, the old man Beon-kwe never missed a chance to hold and rub his cheek against her youngest child, who was always playing by herself near her grandfather while Bok-nyeo was working, as well as taking Bong-sun to buy her a snack and sending her back with cigarettes for the grandfather. She was working all day on her feet. This was the reason why she made such an angry fuss about

Bong-sun not growing fast enough to help her out, for all they could manage to buy and eat were some meager amount of Annam rice or barley turnip kimchi. And all she could do for her ailing father-in-law was to fidget helplessly, and not even dream about getting him any medicine. The sick old man, in turn, crawled out of the house unbeknownst to his daughter-in-law, and crouching under the stone bridge, he would beg for generosity from the passing merchants with a sympathetic message written on a piece of paper in front of him. But as he was not blind like some or someone who could speak, he wished at a time like this he were sightless instead, rather than being crippled in a useless way. Bok-nyeo, who also didn't want to see him all grubby, would admonish him by saying he was letting himself become more ill and force him back to the rear room of their shack. Her eyes welled up with tears as she recollected how pained he was at seeing their place demolished. How terribly painful it must've been for him to hold onto the floor of the collapsing house and resist taking even a single step. If he couldn't have the luxury of being buried in a coffin, then he perhaps would rather have died amidst the debris of planks. Sitting on a pile of wood, Bok-nyeo could see the passing stars across the sky over her father in-law's face. The stars had passed in the same way a while back when they were crossing the Tumen River and spending the night in the shrubs by the road. They had then counted the stars as they waited for the night to pass, however, she couldn't get over how cold they felt tonight, thereby making it difficult for her to gaze at the sky. The dew dampened her clothes, and although she was exhausted, she couldn't go to sleep. How was she going to bake bread tomorrow morning? Surely, she thought, they wouldn't kick them out from here, and she was determined somehow she would survive the winter at this very spot. Someone is bound to drive a hard bargain with the city. But false hope was dangerous, for they did indeed destroy the shacks. Were they meant to freeze to death this winter? Yet, there was nothing they could do. Did they want her old father-in-law to just die, abandoned at the stream? Could she cajole the old man, Beon-kwe, to loan her some money? Or what if she moved in with him—like he wanted? Bok-nyeo fell asleep while talking to the stars in the sky, with thoughts that were neither a loud dream nor wishful thinking.

"Can you believe this? There she is, sleeping with a man in a crumbling shack until the sun is high up …indifferent to what other people might think—that filthy woman must love money. How very disgusting."

"Let her be. I wish I could be like her."

Bok-nyeo's neighbor, a woman, told her, as she was lighting fire for the big rice pot by the stream. It was about the young woman from Sam-son's family, who was found out sleeping with a man in someone's shack. Bok-nyeo reacted by saying what was there to reproach the woman for doing what she pleased, and asked if she weren't envious of the money the young woman would get for it. Bok-nyeo cast a sneering glance at the shack for a second, after continuing how her neighbor could regard the young woman as filthy and revolting after seeing Bok-nyeo with nothing to eat but barely boiled food with pieces of wood from the demolished shack for lack of firewood, adding how she must not be desperately hungry yet. Her father-in-law, lying on his stomach as though dead before the shack that had been torn down, appeared headlong like a wrapped bundle, seen from down below. According to the neighbors, a petition had been submitted to tear down the shacks after winter, with a rumor that the area over the bridge was safe, giving some comfort to Bok-nyeo; she'd also heard that since a committee member or the mayor was coming for inspection there had to be good news, yet the sight of collapsed shack took away all her hope. Moreover, she wasn't sure how she'd survive the winter when no houses would be allowed on her side. The cold weather could wait but where was she going to sell bread, and worse yet, find a place for her father-in-law to rest? It was always the old man Beon-kwe that she thought of as the last resort. She was about to start the fire to bake bread with the prepared dough when she saw her father in-law's back trembling almost unnoticeably. She ran over to him and tore off the blanket that covered him. She shook his body but there was just a blank look in his eyes. She had constantly wished for him to just drop dead to make her life easier, however, when it appeared to happen, it frightened her to no end. If he chose a time like this to die, he was committing a big sin, she thought.

She saw Sam-son's family moving with a cart filled with their belongings. She felt like shouting at them that she was not envious, for she had the old man, Beon-kwe, who promised to get her a place and support her.

Right then, the residents of the shacks crowded around someone who was either the mayor or a council member who stood there, looking at the people inside as though they were a commodity he had come to bargain for. The people were standing in a line like in a welcome committee, some trembling, as if they were begging for their life.

Bok-nyeo's father-in-law kicked the blanket with a strength that astonished her, and crawled out to where the crowd was, and was dragged away, clinging to the bottom part of the person standing in the front. She ran after them and pulled his hand away from the person, however, her father-in-law's body had turned hard already. The crowd mobbed up against her and shouted. Bok-nyeo felt dizzy with all the legs around her looking like some barrier. She thought they would attack her at any moment.

She had been well-aware of how her father-in-law, albeit deaf-mute, had also stayed awake all night, as worried as she was about their situation, and his kindly heart that never showed anger with her children whom he doted on, and whose poop and pee he cleaned after. But Bok-nyeo did not have the leisure to reflect on this now. To bury him, she had to get hold of a wooden box right away and she needed money for it. She lamented how a dead man could still be a nuisance. What's more, she had no food for dinner and had to get barley so as not to starve. She could get a porter to bury the old man, however, it dawned on her that there remained only her and the two children here on earth, and they were left with nothing to live on. The fact that they could eat together when he was still alive provided enough solace, not to mention his affectionate gaze toward her youngest, which had filled her heart with abundance.

In the evening, the old man Beon-Kwe suddenly paid a visit. He was astonished to hear the news of her father-in-law's death.

"What a great pity," he said after a long pause. Bok-nyeo was much taken aback with his grief, for she had not expected it. It wasn't until dark that the old man Beon-kwe brought a porter to take the corpse to the field. On the way back, he gave a long sigh and said, "How the old man implored me…"

When Bok-nyeo's father-in-law found out that his son had died, he came to the old man Beon-kwe and asked him to write on a piece of paper how he'd asked to have Bok-nyeo taken care of by him. The old man Beon-kwe asked to be excused for broaching the subject so soon after her father-in-law passed away but since she had no immediate place to stay and not a grain of barley to eat, he suggested that she move to his place for now to stay during the winter, and consider building a shack again at the same place. While Bok-nyeo remained quiet, like she would before her father-in-law, she decided that was what she would do.

The townspeople took their petition to city hall. Bok-nyeo wanted to leap with joy when she heard living underneath the bridge for the winter was going to be allowed, but she almost at the same time burst into tears over her collapsed shack.

She had nothing to bring but herself and the old man Beon-kwe carried her youngest child on his back while Bong-sun tagged along behind on their way to his place. It reminded her of the time when her family crossed the 38th Parallel line.

"We'll build a new shack right here next year," Bok-nyeo said, caressing the wooden piece from the fallen shack.

The old man Beon-kwe replied with a smile, "Of course."

162

Debt

Every morning Eok-seok left the house like a person who had to attend to an important matter, only to find himself standing before that house all afternoon with a vacant look. The house belonged to Myeong-hun, the son of the master for whom he used to work as a servant.

While it would've been early morning when the dew had yet to dry in the country, the sunshine on his back was already sizzling and the winter work clothes he wore became dampened with sweat. Eok-seok felt the urgency to talk to Myeong-hun, to recoup enough money to get him at least some clothes. He made resolute plans, practicing what he would say to him; yet his train of thought was thwarted when he saw a group of orphans from Peace Orphanage, and just as if he awoke from a sweet dream, he could not help but feel empty. When he was conscripted into the militia in place of Myeong-hun at the order of his master, he did so voluntarily. But before long, when he came back, having lost his right eye and one side of his face scarred, he was guilt-ridden and shamefaced. Being crippled, it was painful for him to be amongst people and also uncomfortable to endure his younger brother, Wuk, who was probably going around begging; for that reason, he was not inclined to go back to his hometown, even though he was barely surviving on the streets here. But then after he had unexpectedly run into Wuk at the orphanage, it did enter his mind that he'd be better off, returning to his hometown, like Myeong-hun said, with his younger brother, to lay low and somehow scrape out a living. When he reflected on how Wuk could've ended up in a place like this, it was clear how he must've been treated at the new master's house without his older brother. Furthermore, it anguished him that Wuk traveled all of three hundred *li* to get here and Eok-seok was once more reminded of what Myeong-hun had said—that he should also find himself a bride for the sake of his brother, remembering vividly the conversation he had with Wuk when he saw him the first time.

"How did you get here?"

"I wanted to see you. All the neighbors are going to see their kin. Neok-son's mom even prepared some rice cake."

"You got away because you didn't want to work? You should just be blindly obedient unless you want to be a beggar."

"No, I didn't."

Wuk didn't say anything more and Eok-seok's heart sank as he imagined how badly abused he must've been for him to seek him out. He also thought angrily all that Myeong-hun said were lies to cajole him while he could empathize with Wuk who came looking for him barefooted. He went into the side alley so as not to see his brother and waited for a long time until the group of orphans passed by. He made a resolve to see Myeong-hun, no matter what, and ask at least for a tiny room from him. Although his heart was set on getting his brother out of the orphanage, his guilty conscience—that he couldn't even keep himself well and alive— stalled him. His busy mind hastened his steps but he kept being diverted by the clothes that hung like beef on the window.

"Soldier Myeong-hun, Soldier Eok-seok."

Eok-seok, drenched in sweat, was barely holding himself together amidst the mob of people, pushing past each other in the crowded street when he heard an unrecognizable voice calling out his name. But he didn't bother to turn around, except he collided against a group of people in front of him, making him stand still.

"You don't think I know you?" A man leaped out of the group and stood before him.

"Ah, it's you! So how're you faring?"

"Can't imagine what keeps you so busy. As for us, this is what I do." With the wooden apple boxes sideways, he was showing a trick with a couple of cards, alternating them from box to box. Eok-seok was always glad to see a soldier from the same platoon; however, he was also enraged to see he had to eke out a living, playing tricks on people. But on this day Eok-seok felt envious of the man with the war medal on his chest, who was bellowing with sweat running down his face. As he exited the busy street, he didn't want to hold it against him for wishing he himself could live like that. It wasn't as though he hadn't heard that so-and-so had joined the Wounded Soldiers' Disabled Veterans' Association and was going around selling pencils, while another person was making a good living but he didn't want to become part of such an organization. Moreover, if he were to see his old soldier friends, he was afraid he would break down.

Would Myeong-hun be home? When he arrived at his house, he with a vacant look, stopped before the plank fence, coming up with an excuse that he may still not be up; thereby justifying his turning back. He had always taken hurried steps to this place but was never audacious enough to go in; perhaps what made him aghast was how he had come of his own volition. Once more, he decided he was pleased that Myeong-hun was not home. Still he was reluctant just to leave, so he stayed, looking at a loss as to what to do. Myeong-hun who came out with a brush in his mouth darted quickly back in when he caught a glimpse of Eok-seok who was relieved but couldn't at the same time get over the urge to run away.

As though he had gotten dressed in a rush, Myeong-hun was adjusting his shirt collar even as he was putting on his shoes and asked, with his buttocks facing Eok-seok,

"Did you eat?"

Eok-seok struggled to find the right words with Myeong-hun swaggering beside him in silence.

"I'm sorry that you haven't eaten yet." Suddenly, it dawned on him that Myeong-hun might have missed his breakfast. Eok-seok face flared when he felt Myeong-hun's glance fall on the marred side of his face. Thinking he might perhaps feel bad about it, Eok-seok even felt grateful to him.

"You haven't eaten, have you? So how are you going to live?"

"I'm told to join some kind of an association."

"An association? You mean, the Wounded Soldiers' Disabled Veterans' Association?"

Eok-seok was surprised with himself for blurting it out for the first time and worried that he might have done something wrong, for Myeong-hun didn't appear too pleased at the mention of an association.

"Why would you join something like that?"

Myeong-hun was displeased because he was well aware of what he had done to Eok-seok. It wasn't like Myeong-hun didn't know it was a sin to have Eok-seok conscripted in his place for no justifiable reason. Granted it was something he could no longer do anything about, he still felt a sense of duty that he should be at least responsible for Eok-seok's livelihood. That was indeed his intention; however, he wasn't sure what Eok-seok, who was now crippled, would do if push came to shove, and if he indeed joined the Wounded Soldiers' Disabled Veterans' Association, there was no guarantee that he wouldn't threaten him with the help of others and it disturbed him. He at last was conscionable to realize he had coerced someone to sacrifice his life for him.

Myeong-hun, who felt embarrassed to be with Eok-seok, walked a little ahead of him; hence, it was difficult Eok-seok to start a conversation. Myeong-hun took him to a restaurant and while eating beef stew, he pondered about a way to get rid of Eok-seok from his life.

"They're recruiting veterans these days, I hear?"

"What? Veterans, you say?"

"Yes, they're signing up those with not too serious an injury. Or they're volunteering."

"I think it's volunteering."

"You'd be eligible."

"I'm not sure."

Myeong-hun was sounding him out, hoping Eok-seok would go into the army again. Eok-seok thought he could tell him all that was in his mind but face to face, he was at a loss for word.

"I should get married, before I starve to death," was what came out of his mouth. Myeong-hun, who had other things on his mind, of course, was not quite listening.

"That's why I told you to come back to town—and I'll even look for a bride for you."

Eok-seok became more anxious with his immaterial response. He must not know that Wuk is at an orphanage, Eok-seok thought and wanted to come clean with him, but he was once more stuck for words.

"Truth to be told, I feel terrible on account of you. I didn't say it but I'm ashamed to see you. I feel like killing myself. Find a way and I'll help you live."

Eok-seok was so touched by his words that he almost forgot why he was there. But he realized his desperate situation could not be taken care of simply by his heart being stirred and he mustered courage to take advantage of this opportunity.

"Eh—I need a room to stay," he barely managed to say it and despised himself for it. He felt like a despicable fool for pressuring Myeong-hun with some kind of authority.

"I am much indebted to you. So how much do you need? I want to pay off my debt once and for all."

Eok-seok couldn't say anything more, for he was overwhelmed by what Myeong-hun said. He wasn't sure exactly what Myeong-hun meant by debt but he could make a vague guess.

As he walked away timidly, he was fretting about the piece of beef from lunch that he saved, and how it was dampening the newspaper with which it was covered. He hurried to get it to Wuk. The orphanage was located on the main street across from the movie house and he felt awkward, standing there by himself.

A pungent smell and dust was all he could sense when he peeked at the long corridor that led to the inside of the orphanage. He thought his brother might still be gone on the outing from this morning and was about to leave when a pebble struck him as he heard a giggle. He hastened to exit the door when he saw a child running toward him and behind him was a group of laughing children, mobbing up against him. Among them was the spotted face of Wuk, who was laughing, showing his yellow teeth until he discovered his older brother. He came running to him and tugged his sleeve.

"He's crazy."

"What's so funny about it?"

"His brother is at Geoje Island. He was captured as a prisoner of war."

Afraid his brother's shriveled up stomach could sense the smell of the beef soup he ate, Eok-seok could not bring himself to give him the beef wrapped in the newspaper he had saved for Wuk.

"It's best not to give this to him, for it will only invite worms to his stomach," he thought and turned around to leave. But then he didn't want his visit to be for naught and scrutinized his brother from head to toe, holding back from saying anything. If he were to speak, the smell of the meat might become more obvious. Meanwhile, Wuk kept looking at his mouth as though he could tell Eok-seok had eaten beef. As he left, he worried about where he could spend another night, while chewing over the meaning of the debt that Myeong-hun had referred to, and reaching the conclusion that he'd never see him again even if he had to make it by doing menial labor. But it wasn't like he'd given it a try. Unlike before, his body shook and he felt dizzy carrying even a small trunk. Not only that, people turned away from him on the streets; worse yet, there was no one with whom he could talk to. Hence he had no choice but to crash somewhere on the street when dusk fell or seek out his veteran friends. If he had to sleep on the street, he would prefer it to be in front of the movie house where he can have a view of where his brother was, however, it happened to be the main-street and he had to content himself just looking at the wooden window of the room where Wuk would be sleeping. When the curfew arrived, he left to go sleep under the stone bridge or the open market lot.

Eok-seok pondered about it all day when he heard that the veterans were being recruited again and decided in the end that he'd join the military once more. It broke his heart to have to leave Wuk behind; however, such a sentiment for him was a luxury, as he himself would have liked to enter an orphanage if he were not over the age limit, for he was nothing but a beggar on the street.

Dressed in his winter uniform, he was on his way to the recruitment office when someone grabbed his back.

"Hey Eok-seok."

It was clearly the voice of Myeong-hun; however, he didn't want to stop to turn around, as he was dragged by his clothes.

"Don't you know me? It's Myeong-hun. What's with you?"

Eok-seok didn't feel like showing his face to Myeong-hun, so as not to get back at him to show his displeasure. Neither was he happy with Myeong-hun who had been loath to show any gladness upon seeing him on a street like this before but who now went out of his way to call him out. Myeong-hun, who was breathless as they walked alongside each other, swallowed hard, as though he was bracing himself to say something. Eok-seok hastened his steps, barely suppressing the urge to close his ears in case he mentioned the debt again.

"Here, take this. I feel like I'm indebted to you, although I'm not asking you to forget about it completely—but please don't behave like a creditor."

Eok-seok refused the bundle of money Myeong-hun tried to shove his way.

"I wish I could take it but there is no work for me to do. I'm joining the military again," he said and looked straight at Myeong-hun's face for the first time.

But Eok-seok was rejected because of his poor eyesight. For the first time he felt sad about his face and eyes. It was driving him insane that he couldn't join something everyone else seemed to have no problem with, and then he got worried about how he'd survive from this point on. He wandered around aimlessly, only to find himself before the fence of Myeong-hun's house. He stood there absently as before and before long, it was evening and got dark. He remained immobile, as though he would stay there endlessly. When Myeong-hun's returned home and saw Eok-seok there, he turned pale and froze. Myeong-hun all of a sudden appeared like one of the countless Chinese men Eok-seok had shot to death on the battlefield.

"So what if I kill another one of them? I'll just dump him onto the pile of corpses." The thought comforted him. The dim street somehow felt like a battlefield to him and he felt like grabbing a gun and firing a shot at him. Eok-seok repressed the desire to scream at him and leaped at him instead.

"You son of a bitch! I'm going to kill you! Hands up!"

"What's the matter? Are you really going to do it?" said Myeong-hun, and took a step back, glaring at Eok-seok, who was startled by his own voice. He took two steps back and reached for a dagger at his side. When he realized there was nothing to grab, he seized Myeong-hun by his collar. But when he felt no resistance from him, he released him and looked searchingly for a place to sleep, then suddenly turned in the direction of the orphanage.

As though he'd been waiting, Wuk leaped out from the dark and called out with an urgency in his voice.

"Older brother!"

"What're you doing here? Why did you leave the orphanage?"

Wuk didn't answer but turned his eye toward the orphanage, then back at his brother.

"You escaped? You little brat, do you want to starve to death?"

After admonishing him, Eok-seok forced Wuk to go back. He stood there, frozen, and furiously glaring at the gate.

The Medal

It wasn't until evening that the old man Wu arrived at the bus station. Wu felt relived like he had come back home. He was in ecstasy over how the king (he still believed some sovereign ruled the country) had graciously sent him an automobile, and it was only after he was dropped off at the big field by the station that he became his normal self. The station, inundated with mobs of people, felt like a barren field to him. The old man Wu barely managed to get to a corner with a long plank bench, after squeezing himself through lines of people in the waiting room. He looked around to look for a place to sit; however, there seemed to be a tug-of-war of buttocks for a seat. He gave up and holding a small bundle to his chest, he set to observe people. But he soon realized others were watching him. As he couldn't understand why, he blushed and mulled it over. Where the king was at, the people all looked impeccably impressive, whereas those sitting around at the station, they were pretty much dressed like him; so then, why were they glaring at him? He wondered if it had to with his clothes, and looked alternately at them and himself. When the medal grabbed his attention, he all of a sudden felt lighthearted and cheerful. He even felt like pointing at it for everyone to see.

Above the old man's left chest hung loose the Eunseung Tae-geuk Medal awarded to him by the government. The light on the ceiling of the waiting room seemed to illuminate solely his medal. His jacket was tight for his hefty torso. The contour of his face was uneven, as if it had been squashed by something. But his sharp and intelligent eyes, thick lips, and droopy earlobes assured he would not live a penniless life. His glossy sunburned face was full of wrinkles that were dust-ridden. He was wearing a custom-ordered cotton overcoat, with new silk under-pants. They were prepared overnight; hence, the fit was not so good with sloppy stitching. His shoes seem to have been borrowed as well, for they looked quite awkward on him. Flat long shoes did not go over too well with the old man's hanbok, the traditional Korean clothes. In the bundle, which he held with great care, was a helmet with a picture of a tiger and a chrysographed document.

"Old man, let me carry that for you. It looks heavy."

The old man Wu looked all around when he heard a familiar dialect that cheered him up. An old woman, who appeared to be his wife's age, flirted with him, showing a mouthful of teeth. She was sitting right at his feet. The old man Wu was delighted to have met someone who was from his hometown. It did not dawn on him that the bus he was waiting to take at the station was bound for his town, and hence there'd be people from there.

"Thank you for your kindness."

He was almost absently going to hand the bundle to her but changed his mind.

"Don't worry, it's not heavy," he explained.

"Is it an important thing?" The old woman asked, as though she'd known him for a long time. Wu rather liked it and squatted beside her.

"It's not like that...but it used to belong to my son..." He dropped his head, with tears in his eyes.

"Goodness, I shouldn't have asked."

The old man liked it that she was sympathetic and felt like he wouldn't mind telling her anything. He tapped the helmet like a watermelon he was testing to see if it was ripe and said with a forced smile.

"It's a helmet my son used."

"Oh my! He died in the war!"

The people close by, with their expressionless faces, in no time turned to look at them. Right then, he saw a veteran without an arm going around with some books, importuning people to buy one and

172

someone, who was sitting not too far away from the old woman, discreetly got up. He deliberated whether he should go over there to sit down but another person took the seat. He was troubled to see how most normal looking people avoided the armless veteran. When the veteran passed by after throwing a glance at him, he was a little saddened. He beckoned the man, who was already in the distance.

"Hey, let me have one."

He searched through his clothes but then remembered that he had stashed the money he received from the King in the bundle. He took out a hundred-*hwan* bill and asked the veteran if that was enough. The veteran replied he needed one more. Suddenly, the old man Wu regretted it. But when he saw the multi-colored insignia on the veteran's chest, he thought of his son who might have become crippled like this man if he had not died, and nothing could stop him.

He vacantly looked at the book, of which he had no idea what it was about, except that he guessed it must be a good book. He wrapped it in the bundle, concluding he would use it to do the walls with it at home.

The old woman, who was looking at the helmet, asked with fear in her voice, "Look here, does everyone die when they go into military?"

"My son did. He was my only child."

"Goodness, it's unbelievable. I just came back from visiting my son. What will I do if he dies?"

"Not all soldiers die. It's just one's fate."

The old woman seemed to be comforted and expressed concern for the old man.

"Geez, geez, how terrible. How did he die?"

"I don't know. They didn't even find his body. They told me, my son took control of a large fortress. He killed all the Commies by himself. That's what it says on this big paper here. It says he's been given this award for this and that."

As though she finally comprehended, the old woman clucked her tongue with awe.

"I see, I see. That's what the medal is for."

Putting on a suddenly cheerful face, she asked with an expectation, "They don't award you a medal unless you are killed?"

"Why not? Where is your son?"

"I went to see my son at the front to talk about his marriage but it was hard for him to get time off. My son is very popular in our neighborhood because he's strong and a good worker."

The old man Wu's heart ached at the thought of his son who died a bachelor. To get it off his mind, he broached another topic.

"Old woman, I got to hold the hand of the Sovereign," he said in a whisper, as if he were revealing a secret.

"The Sovereign? You mean, the King?" She was in disbelief. The old man pondered about how he could make her understand. He retraced how he got to meet him.

Six months after he was notified his son had died in a battle, a soldier and the head of his village paid him a visit and told him he would go to Seoul and meet the President. As the President in the olden days would be equivalent to the king, it sounded outrageous that a mere sailor like himself could meet him. But it turned out to be true. He sat on seat covered with a white sheet he could not have imagined, and the minute he got off at the station, he was carried on a chair with a back support to the palace. The Sovereign himself pinned this gold object on his chest and even held his hand. Yes, he clearly held his hand. He recalled vividly how awe-struck he was. What was even more moving was that the Sovereign praised his son and said it was a pity he could not be present. It felt like he was dreaming. The old man wanted to take off the medal and bring it with him wrapped in the bundle. But the Sovereign had pinned it himself and he was too overwhelmed to touch it.

"The Sovereign, eh, I remember now, he's called the President. He gave me money and a ticket to return home." He proudly took out the train ticket he had put in a pouch.

The old woman rubbed the ticket and asked, "Then why did you come back so soon? The train doesn't leave until dawn."

"Because I had no place to sleep. I thought I'd spend the night here."

"And you have money! How thrifty."

The old man all of a sudden felt hungry. He looked around to see if he could get food and spotted a small store in the corner of the station. He rose to his feet with his bundle at his bosom. He bought two packs of cookies and stashed them in the bundle; then he got a soft bun for the old woman for she appeared to have bad teeth.

The old woman looked uncomfortable when he offered her the bun for she declined it, saying she'd already eaten. A dirty palm stretched out between them as they were eating the bun. Startled, they turned around to see a crippled man without legs. He had on his chest the same badge as the veteran. Once more, the old man felt as though he were his son. If my son hadn't died, he thought, he would've become handicapped like him. The thought disturbed him. He gave him his entire portion of the bread that he had on his knee. The veteran was at first taken aback by the old man's generosity, and was hesitant to take it.

The old man feigned a smile and said, "Take it, take it."

When he realized it was a genuine offer, the veteran snatched it. It put him in a good mood, and as he ate he said jokingly, "What an affectionate couple, hmm," which put them in an awkward mood.

The old man thought it over then realized that the old woman indeed resembled his wife a lot. That was the reason why he took a liking to her at first sight. He was glad the veteran helped him see that.

"Where did you fight in the war, mister?"

"At the eastern front."

"Ah, that's where my son was. He wrote it in a letter. Maybe you know my son, Wu Eok-man?"

"Hardly. It'd be difficult to know anyone, out of so many soldiers."

"I only wish to know how my son died. This helmet of his is the only thing they gave me; can you believe it? They didn't even find his body."

The old man caressed the helmet, like it was his son, and blew his nose with his other hand. The veteran finished eating the bun but would not leave. He squatted next to the old man and looked at the medal covetously. The old man thought he must've received a better medal than the one he got, for the veteran had lost both his legs.

"Yours is better?"

The veteran gave the old man a blank look. His long dusty face seemed to have been flattened from the side with his deeply sunken eyes. His overly thick fingers, which looked like they belonged to someone else, were constantly crawling all over like a living snake. His army uniform pants were tied like a sack at the lower half of his body with thick rubber tires attached to the sole of his feet. It gave the old man shivers to think that the flesh was still alive and wriggling. He must not be wearing an under layer of clothes, for his chin was trembling.

The old woman got up and offered her seat.

"It's all the same to me. Please ask the mister to sit down instead," the old man said with a grateful heart and was moved how she so resembled his wife. The veteran said he couldn't sit down and insisted the old man do so. Finally, the old woman sat down apologetically after the two men implored her. A cold draft swept past them in the station where the repair work wasn't quite complete.

The two black legs of the clock that hung at center of the station wall were frozen stiff on the number, twelve. It looked like a cicada that failed to go under the earth and died on a tree. The boisterous crowd had mostly gone its way and only the people who were waiting for the early morning bus and the beggars remained in the station, and were dozing away. A fragment of a newspaper flew around like a bat and got stuck to someone's face, fluttering if not getting caught in a window where half the glass was missing. There were also people already lined up to buy tickets for the morning bus. They were dozing, seated in the line.

There was more room as people left. The old man and the old woman could now sit together. But neither of them could fall asleep. They were yawning but they couldn't sleep, for their hearts felt turbulent. The veteran squatting before her felt like a son to her. It was as though her own son had returned with his legs chopped off.

The old man heaved a sigh, thinking how great it would be if the man were his son, if only his son could've have come back alive. Then he suddenly felt resentful toward the Sovereign for neglecting a person like him. "If my son had been in that situation, would he have been dismissed too? How could that be? Did he receive a medal like mine?"

Seeing that the veteran was awake, he asked, "Didn't you get any money from the Sovereign?"

"There are things like the Wounded Soldiers' Disabled Veterans' Association and the convalescent center but I felt too antsy."

"What's that?"

"They are places that help soldiers injured in the war."

"So you prefer being a beggar?"

"Going around begging on a train feels better."

The old man was rather astounded that a man who had lost lower half of his body could be so affable. The old man really wanted to know how his son had died.

"But does everyone die in the war?"

"Not everyone, but many do in an unjust way."

"How do they die?"

"I became this way after June 25 and the tank made it much worse."

At the mention of a tank, the old man thought it must be responsible for his son's death and with a resolve to smash it, as if it were before his very eyes, he asked,

"The 'tanko,' he must be a Commie?"

"A tank is a combat vehicle."

The old man envisioned the moment of his son's death. How he must've bled to death after being shot. How horrifically if must've hurt when he was shot in the chest, for even a finger bleeding from a thorn was painful. The wounded veteran must know how it hurt since he had been shot.

The old man couldn't bear not knowing how painful a gunshot was. If it didn't kill him, he, too, would like to be shot and share his son's suffering.

"How much does it hurt, to get shot?"

"Don't even talk about it. What's the use of knowing?"

The old man was so very grateful to the veteran, who responded faithfully to all his questions but refrained from talking about the gunshot wounds, knowing how much pain it would cause him. The more he thought about it, the more moved he was. He calculated the money he received from the Sovereign. Out of ten thousand *hwan* he received for travel expenses, he already spent a thousand *hwan*. In order to carry out a shamanistic purging ritual for his son back home, he chose not to sleep at an inn and refrained from buying anything for his wife; perhaps he could share some with the veteran. He stroked the knot of his bundle but decided to wait until tomorrow morning since he might not accept it. He was sure a man with such a gentle heart might decline the money.

The old woman next to them had fallen asleep. The veteran kept yawning, and then dropped his head. The wind became icier. Thinking his day will be easier if he slept a little, the old man was about to lie on his side, using his bundle as a pillow when his eyes caught the scrunched veteran, who looked very cold. There was no certainty that he would not freeze to death. He gazed at him for a long time and took off his overcoat. He was hesitant for a while as to what to do about the medal on it. He had planned to arrive home, wearing it on his chest— removing it and putting it in his bundle to take it out in the morning would be fine—except that the Sovereign had himself pinned it on him. He didn't particularly want to lend his coat with the medal on it to another person, albeit briefly, but he wasn't leaving it in a thief's hand or out of his view. So why bother to take the medal off? It would be the act of a small-minded man who mistrusted everyone.

When he saw the veteran shivering in his sleep, the old man thought no more and quickly put the overcoat around his shoulder. He felt comforted as he rested his head on his son's helmet. He was about to fall asleep when he decided to take one more look at the medal. He turned his gaze toward the flashing yellow medal right before his eye. But the more he looked at it, the more it appeared fitting for the veteran, as though it belonged to him from the beginning.

"What's the point of giving a medal to a dead person? Who can show it to anyone? It should be given to someone like that veteran. Aigo, Eok-man, my son!" He fell asleep with what sounded like a lament or gibberish.

Eok-man is twisting in pain—he says his head hurts. In his sleep, the old man was using his son's head as pillow. Eok-man is wearing a helmet with a tiger on it. He is firing the gun mercilessly as he is racing through the blizzard, unaware he is gushing blood that is spilling on the snow. Aigo, Eok-man, you're bleeding. Then before he knew it, his body vanished from the helmet. He saw the same helmet swinging, like a scarecrow, from a post in the snow. However, it wasn't Eok-man but the veteran. He is wearing a white overcoat and walking on the sea. The old man pursues him on a boat. The waves surged and the overcoat quickly turned into a billow and lashed against the boat.

The old man's eyes popped open with the sensation of disturbance all around him. He turned toward where the veteran should be and was thunderstruck. He felt like the whole world would collapse on him. The veteran was nowhere to be seen, and only his overcoat was sprawled on the floor. He hurriedly picked it up and felt the front part of it, only to flop down on the floor. He couldn't breathe and was nearly choking. It wasn't this bad when he received the news of his son's death because it wasn't as abrupt or as immediate. To lose the medal, which was like an emblem of his son's spirit, was same as losing everything that had to with him. He sat benumbed for a long while, and then suddenly he ran around like a mad man, screaming,

"My son vanished! My medal is gone!"

The early morning bus tickets were now being sold, and the line that had been in disarray at night was crowding to all the different spots. The clock in the middle of the station seemed to have awakened from its winter sleep and showed the larger leg on twelve and the smaller one on five. All the passengers with their life packed in a trunk, baggage, or a bundle, were lining up.

The old man hastily returned to where his bundle was and looked around the surroundings again, wishing that he might've perhaps returned the medal in the interim. His bundle with the helmet remained where he had sat and the old woman was sleeping all curled up, unaware that the ticket counter was now open. Judging by how a gentle soul could've stolen his thing, in total disregard for his feelings, he thought the old woman could also be an ageless cunning fox in a human form. But when he scrutinized the face of the sleeping, clueless old woman, he found himself calming down and felt how childish it was for him to behave in an unreasonable manner earlier. What was he going to do with the medal, with his son gone? Should he sell it for money? The heavens must've read his thought that it was more becoming on the veteran, and instructed him to take it.

The old man saw a whistling man in black uniform and the crowd swarming in this and that direction. He remembered that the old woman was going to take the early bus. He shook her awake and sent her to the ticket booth. As he stood by the line to board the bus, he wasn't sure whether or not he should tell the man in black but decided against it. He was afraid he might be slapped instead. He might be told he deserved to be put in jail for losing the medal awarded to him by the Sovereign.

The old man moved to the back of the line to board the bus to wait for the old woman. He clutched the helmet to his bosom. He felt the warmth of his son whom he used to hold in his arms when he was a child. When it occurred to him that the veteran might not come out alive from jail if he had reported him, he thought he did the right thing by not telling the man in black. He even wished the veteran would become his son, imagining that if his son hadn't died, he would have been crippled like him.

It wasn't until nearly everyone had entered that the old woman came rushing in. She heaved a long sigh, indicating how panic-stricken she was about missing the bus. When her eyes ran down to the old man's chest, she gave him an astonished look.

The old man gave a smile.

"Where is the medal?"

"I wrapped it in the bundle," said the old man and felt his eyes swelling up. He stroked the helmet, and mumbled, "Here he is, my son."

The fog covered his vision of the dawn.

The Legend of Lake Rotorua

A bizarre and hitherto unprecedented war broke out in Korea. In the beginning, it was questionable if it was indeed a war. The Communist North Korean army bulldozed their way to the far end of Busan in their Soviet tanks. The refugees fled like pitiful animals. The Nakdong River became the last foothold of the Republic of Korea. If it fell, then the foundation of the country would be swept away, as in a flood. The people, who remained on the stolen land, were on the throes of death and those who fled to Busan were in a chaotic state. History has never before witnessed such a tragedy. Gu Rin's family was unable to flee and was left helpless. His wife was pregnant. His family would be deemed as a landowner according to the Communists, but Gu Rin's brother, Gyu, had been a freedom fighter in the past and they thought somehow that would help them avoid misfortune. Gu Rin's older brother, Gyu, had to support Gu Rin's wife. As though they'd been waiting for the precise time, the P-51 Mustangs bombed the railroads and the bridge when the trains passed. The B-29 bombers flew in a formation across the sky and trailed behind a number of promises.

The Republic of Korea still had the control of the air. The servant, who was given the land, came to the landowner to ask for advice. The North Korean People's Army soldiers sleeping in the air-raid shelter with the policeman's wife, who subsisted on the porridge she bought from selling the watch she stole from the corpse of a South Korean soldier, were both buried alive when the shelter collapsed from the bombing raid. The partisans were taking vengeance to their heart's content. They killed people in accordance with their mood. They speared someone's eyeball and displayed it on the roadside. They dragged away those who were fishing at night, accusing them of secretly contacting a submarine.

The Waikato River receives clear water from Mount Egmont to Mount Ruapehu and Mount Tongariro to the White Island in the Bay of Plenty and the volcanic island that stretches from the southwest to northeast, thereby cleansing the fields and the mountains of New Zealand and then heads to the Pacific Ocean. When white blood flowed from this long artery where the red volcano is lined up, in order for the Kauri and the conifer trees and the tree fungi to shield the sky, the Waikato River supplies water to the field where tangerines, barley, lemon, and Indian mallow grow in abundance. God had created countless lakes and mountains in New Zealand but none of them came close to being as beautiful as Lake Rotorua. One wondered, how the mountain and the field and the lake could be in such perfect harmony. When traveling from Hamilton to Tuakau by van, one could see afar in the milky sky that there is not a cloud or fog. Going farther from Tuakau, Poenua appears like a perfect dream, with her flushed face in August sunlight and the violet cloud draped around her waist reaching down to her feet. Has she just finished her bath in Lake Rotorua? With a movement as light as a feather, she was looking for her angel's cloud robe. Lake Rotorua, where not a fish could leave a trace on the surface, could be a bathtub for angels, filled up with morning dew. The pink and white land, the remnant of nature from the explosion of Mount Charawera hundreds of years ago, is looking at its own face on the lake surface. The armored robe around Poenua slid down of its accord and brushed against Lake Rotorua. Its silk robe is not made of heavenly clouds but created through the mist from Mount Rotorua that froze on the flesh of the lake. Somewhere, the sound of the drum of the Maori tribe resonates like an accompaniment to the crowing of the kakapo birds. The drumbeat collides in the air and rebounds like an echo.

A van zooms past the Kauri trees. It brakes when the lake comes into view. Gu Rin helps Sosia to get down from the van. Sosia had the appearance of an Asian woman, that is, simple and elegant. Except for her blue eyes and silky brown hair, any Asian woman could've looked like her. Unlike a typical English woman with her blotches of red, she was shapely and well proportioned, as though she'd been molded by hand. Her fair complexion radiated a glow. Her face, albeit slightly round-shaped, was fortunately offset by her slender chin. Her intelligent-looking eyes were slightly sunken and her thick eyelashes were long like the afternoon sunlight. Her eyebrows were quite dark. The tiny mole on the spot where her cheek met the chin was terribly attractive. Underneath her thin, purplish coat, a green skirt was visible. She was wearing flat-heeled sneaker-like shoes that one would wear on a picnic.

Sosia gazed at the dazzling lake and then turned toward Gu Rin. Instead of saying anything, he nodded and offered an unimpressed look. They walked in step. Sosia pulled her hand out of her coat pocket and she crossed her fingers with his, leaning against Gu Rin, like she was almost in his arms. Gu Rin, captivated by the scenery, viewed the lake in silence. The place seemed like it had been preserved in its original state as God had created it. Perhaps Rotorua was where Adam and Eve resided during the time of *Genesis*. With a gentle smile, Sosia was asking with her eyes, this is your first time here, isn't it?

"What a shame that I didn't come here until now, although I've been in New Zealand for over half a year…"

"What did I tell you? Aren't you glad we came today?"

They were on a weekend trip to Wellington. They had discussed a sightseeing tour to Rotorua with its beautiful scenery and many Maori residents but they had been too busy with their studies until now. Gu Rin had come to do library studies for a year on UNESCO funding. He arrived before the outbreak of the Korean War.

They strolled around the lake where the grass was endlessly spread before them. Although it was winter, the golden turf had gloss to it.

There was not a person in sight at the lake. Gu Rin had this sudden impulse to fracture the surface of the lake. He looked for a pebble but couldn't find any. He ran back and forth but to no avail. Sosia ran after him. It was like hide-and-seek. They barely managed to find a stone. It was like breaking a mirror as he was about to toss it on the lake. The lake cracked. The scenery that had descended low to the surface of the lake shook in surprise. It didn't feel like winter. Not a wind was blowing in the air.

"Shall we go for a boat ride?"

"No, let's go for the canoe. You know, the one that looks like a goose."

"Either one is all right. You know how to row, right, Sosia?"

"Of course. I've lived here for four years already." Sosia assured him that she could row.

They wrapped their arms around each other and walked to the shore where the log cabin was.

They rowed the canoe along the bank. Sosia sang Polish folk songs. Her lovely crystal voice resonated far and wide. It seemed to reach even the heights of the heaven. The lake echoed like a resonator. Gu Rin rose on his feet and took control of the oar.

"You must continue your music studies," he said with a rapturous look on his face.

"What music studies?"

"In the USA."

"Oh, darling, you are so bent on sending me to America. But I don't want to go. Would you like for me to go?"

"No, but I don't want you to wreck your life."

"Wreck my life? But you are my life."

"But…is it possible for you to come to Korea with me? And your brother is getting you a scholarship, so if you don't go, it would make me feel regretful."

"Don't worry. I'll be with you no matter what."

Sosia put down the oar and snuggled to Gu Rin.

"Yes, you must comfort your brother, Sosia."

Covering her face with his palms, Gu Rin gave her a gaze that spoke this wish. In a quick gesture, Sosia kissed his lips. The two were wrapped in each other like that for a long time.

"Shall we go for a stroll in the forest?"

They turned their canoe. The ridges surged upward as if they would bump into them. The thin roots of a ponga tree spread over the rock and its branches were dangling over the water. Dark shadows from the trees invaded the edge of the lake. The cacti were looking down at the water, as though they were curious to see what their shadows looked like. A wild rabbit with very round and alert eyes was sniffing the leaf of a cactus that had a human smell. It quickly spotted the two of them and to avert their eyes, it pulled its head down but then got caught when it tried to get a quick glance at them. The rabbit gave them a slow and awkward look, and then clawed the ground with its hind paws.

They returned the canoe and headed for the wooded area with the golden turf. The sunlight spread through the kauri trees. Gu Rin lay down, stretching all his four limbs. His Pakistani cap dropped from his head and fell on the ground upside down. His still clean new cap was saturated with a slight sweat around the edge. Standing straight, Sosia gazed down at his face. Gu Rin opened his arms, as though he was about to embrace a child. Placing her two fingers on her forehead, she inspected their surrounding then dropped down by his side. He stretched out his left arm for Sosia to rest her head. The air was permeated with the vigor of the tree fern and Indian mallow. The shadow of the ponga tickled their faces. The sky was too high and deep. In no time, purple and white clouds spread out like flags. Both Gu Rin and Sosia could sense their eyes reaching above those clouds. They could also feel the wind high up above the sky. The wind would drive those clouds only to dispel them into different patterns on the vast canvas. The sky seemed to be made of dreams. The wind drew the dimples, flying across the ocean. They then requested for a Maori tattoo. The sky now looked as lovely as a finely sculpted ceramic. The wind swished past. From afar, the sound of the kakapo birds intermingled with the drumbeat of the Maori tribe could be heard. The two sensed a movement above their head. A flock of sheep was passing by and paused to look at them. One of them stuck its nose into the Pakistani cap and sniffed it. The drumbeat was becoming more intense. The wind was painting a dark palette across the sky.

Gu Rin got up abruptly, and clutched Sosia's hand.

"Let us now go visit the Maori Village."

Almost dragging her, he ran away from the damp field that vanished from their sight as the forest deepened. The Maori Village was playing peekaboo with them. Mist was rising from the hot spring. The Maoris must be preparing their dinner. Some young women were crouching near the hot spring and heating meat. The Maoris cooked their food in the hot spring. They were also well known for their tattoo but these women must be more "civilized" ones for none could be seen on their face.

"The tattooing has almost all disappeared, I hear. It's only the old people or the nobility who still do it. Oh, it's raining."

The rain swished down with the wind. The two raced to the village. They entered the biggest house. The entrance pillar showed many sculptural reliefs that expressed great harmony in engraving. They became engrossed with them. When they opened the door and looked inside, they didn't see anything. With wonder, they looked up at the ceiling to see variegated shapes and patterns, such as different leaves of fern and pine trees and shapes modeled after animals like a kiwi, kakapo, and moa.

Like a tour guide, Sosia explained them to Gu Rin, pointing each one out, "The Maori tribe likes wooden sculpture. They must really like drawing because they like to draw everywhere, including on their faces. Ha, ha. Look over there, at the yard. It's a bird called the moa that used to be around a lot but are now almost extinct."

The village lay low, like a turtle, in the rain. From somewhere, they heard the song of the Maoris. Close by, they also heard a responsorial song like an echo. It sounded as poignant and fervent as the sound of a downpour. The Maoris were known to love to sing and dance. Sosia asked Gu Rin if he knew what "yodel" was. He shook his head. She then explained it was a form of singing by the people, who lived in the Swiss mountainous region, and it had no words but is a purely vocal sound sung that was an exchange between the people and the mountain. She said the Maori's song reminded her of it.

"Poland, too, must be a country of mountains?"

"Yes, of course. New Zealand reminds me of my home country."

When the rain stopped, they returned to Rotorua. They stayed at the Tarawera Hotel.

In the evening, they attended a Maori concert at Kawhali Flowers Theater. It was a heartrending musical performance. The melody, filled with pathos, was an elegy to an ethnic culture that was being annihilated. The only remaining remnant of a primitive age was vanishing.

Instead of just one day, their break lasted four days. Their absence from school could get troublesome. They did not arrive back in Wellington until night. All tension evaporated and fatigue overcame them when they returned to their apartment on Sydney Street and they crashed. It had only been about a month that he'd moved into this apartment that UNESCO had rented for him. Until then, he was staying at a UNESCO-designated hotel where he was spending thirty dollars of his fifty-dollar stipend for lodging—after which there was hardly enough money left for transportation. His initial plan was to diligently save the money so that he could bring his wife an armful of gifts and possibly spend a month or two in Tokyo, doing research work. He considered moving to a cheaper place to economize but UNESCO deterred him, claiming it had to do with the dignity of the organization. He hadn't yet given up on studying in Tokyo. Just the other day, he had inquired about it with Hayashi at Ueno Library in Tokyo and Ariyama, the secretary general of the Association of Libraries. Meanwhile,

188

he found out coincidentally that Hendryk Skawinsky, who was also in library studies with him, lived in a flat with his sister and he decided to move into the same apartment building. Hendryk Skawinsky, who was from Poland and had studied at Cracow University, was managing some factory, but after the war he decided to defect to New Zealand with his wife, their four children, and his sister. Some English man seduced his wife, who left with their children, and he now lived with his sister only.

Gu Rin was sleeping like a log when Sosia awoke him with a glass of milk. He could barely open his eyes to see a newspaper in front of him.

"Your brother isn't back yet?"

"No."

He turned his eyes toward the paper. It was a Korean newspaper. It had been exactly a month. Suddenly his family came to mind. He felt like he'd been in a dream until now. He had no news of his family since July. He'd had a nightmarish time, worrying about his pregnant wife, wondering if she had a safe delivery. His body shook, making him dizzy.

He wasn't sure how long it lasted but a loud commotion outside woke him up and he saw Skawinsky who was completely drunk swaggering toward him.

"You two are living the life of Riley, going off for four days," he jabbered in Polish. Sosia looked at them alternately with tearful eyes. Gu Rin decided to remain quiet, for saying anything could provoke him more.

"Hey, Gu Rin. Look here don't make me sad, please. Don't take Sosia away from me. She's the only family I have left."

Skawinsky, who had intended to strike him, was overcome with his own sorrow and instead let himself be led away by his sister.

The Republic of Korea recovered from its death throes. The retaliatory counteroffensive by the UN happened like a bolt of lightning. A cup of water from the Aprok River was presented to President Syngman Rhee. But the war became more complicated. With the Chinese intervention, the war took on a new turn. Seoul was reinvaded for the second time. Gu Rin's family became separated. Neither his brother nor his wife could be found among the refugees.

Gu Rin couldn't claim he loved his wife very much; nonetheless, he loved her as any husband would his wife. It wasn't a marriage of love but matchmaking by his brother. When he was in Korea, he was too busy going around for the consummation of their love. He'd only heard that his wife had a son who died at birth.

It was his graduation day. Twelve students, which included seven women and five men, were graduating. Skawinsky asked Gu Rin that they go back home early, as Sosia wanted to celebrate with them by preparing dinner. Could she truly celebrate knowing he'd be leaving for Korea any day now? He had made a promise with her, though. He had vowed he would not abandon Sosia under any circumstances. But it was questionable whether a Polish national could enter Korea.

As it was still early, Gu Rin persuaded Skawinsky to go for a drink. Skawinsky, too, had wanted to have a private talk with him, feeling apologetic over his drunken misbehavior, and to congratulate him on his graduation. He took Gu Rin to a pub called "Cook," where they ran into Romerei from Indonesia and Hayashi from Japan.

Skawinsky ordered whisky at the counter and requested a Scottish folk song, "Auld Lang Syne," to be played. Gu Rin hummed along with "Should Old Acquaintance Be Forgot and Never…"

Offering a glass of whisky to Gu Rin, he said, "Good, good."

They raised their glass but weren't sure what they should toast to.

If things went well, he could be hired by the Wellington Library, if not, the university library. What a fool to have his wife seduced by another man. How pitiful. Like your home country, Poland, which Hitler got indigestion from indulging on it, only to have the Soviet

Union gorging it. Like Korea, it was a country subject to so much turmoil. A solitary citizen of a forlorn country. A pathetic single man. Why don't you just get remarried? Thrusting a fist at me, saying how I tried to steal his sister… A truly lonely fellow.

(The music shifted to Chopin's Études Op. 10.)

The irrational people, who divided their country into two parts and are fighting against one another, and the idiotic people who have inexcusably attached themselves to the Soviet Union. You can't avoid being a fugitive when you return to your country. At best, you'll become the head librarian of Poland's National Library. Going back to your country at a time when the Chinese army is invading Seoul is no different from throwing yourself into gunfire. How dare you play around with my sister? Just pray your home is sound and hope everyone is still alive.

They clinked their glasses.

"Let's toast for the safety of your family."

"You fool, get yourself a good woman."

They roared into laughter and drank to no end, thinking they should both speak their mind, before they passed out or fell asleep.

"Skawinsky, are you drunk? Can you understand what I'm saying?" Gu Rin thought it easier to say what was on his mind when they were both inebriated. Skawinsky was interested only in drinking and poured another glass for himself.

"What is it? Say it," he shouted at his glass.

"Now that we've graduated, it's time for me to leave. But then, I'd like to take Sosia with me."

"What? You want to take my sister to a country where there's a war going on? Is that what you're saying?" he asked, glaring at Gu Rin.

"Here, Skawinsky, have one more glass."

Gu Rin quickly realized it was a mistake to broach it so soon and quickly shifted the topic.

"You're so lonely. Or rather, it is all of Poland that is lonely."

Skawinsky leaned over the table.

"You dare to pity me? A dog is better off than us. Take a look at yourself first. At least we are a people that don't direct guns at each other. Korea needs to stay enslaved to Japan longer. You need to learn what freedom and independence really mean. Even though Poland is permanently subject to the Soviet Union, we'll gain our independence in the end as long as the spirit of Kosciusko and Henryk Sienkiewicz lives on."

"Of course, I feel alone too for all I know, my whole family could've been slaughtered. It feels like I am going back to Korea for the funeral of my mother, brother…"

He almost said, wife, aloud. He had kept quiet about his already being married to Skawinsky and Sosia. The thought of his wife never entered his mind whenever he was with her. He completely forgot about his wife after meeting Sosia. He had no idea what he was going to do if he were to bring her to Korea. It was more like he didn't want to think about it.

"That's right, Mr. Lonely. The colonialists are rapacious plunderers. The evil English bastards don't just steal your land but your wife and children. The Soviets can't be any different. The Communists are merely political colonialists. They're sure to steal your family, too. Including your wife."

"My wife?"

"Ah, that is to say. To think the place I flee to with all my effort turns out to be a colonized country! Do you know what Sienkiewicz's first name is?"

"Nope."

"You stupid. It's Henryk, just like my name. I've become the lighthouse keeper of Aspinwall."

"I remember now. It's the title of Sienkiewicz's short story."

"That's all you know about it? You idiot. Don't you know Skawinsky, the lighthouse keeper?"

"That's right. Here's to Skawinsky."

Gu Rin forced another drink upon him and brought up the subject again. "I love Sosia. I am being utterly honest. And you can't stop me. Let me take her with me." He pleaded, gripping Skawinsky's hand.

"What? Let my precious Sosia go with a coward like you?"

Skawinsky, whom Gu Rin thought was completely drunk, was enraged at the mention of Sosia. He got up suddenly from his chair and mercilessly slapped Gu Rin. Taken aback by the unexpected turn of events, Gu Rin remained stupefied, bearing the blows. People gathered around them. Something warm streamed down from his nose and dripped on his clothes.

Skawinsky recklessly struck his fists at everyone who tried to intervene. He then collapsed onto the table and broke into sobs.

"Just pick up a gun and go fight. You are not in a position to have a romance here. Your home country is being vanquished and here you are, idly having an affair with someone else's girl."

He kept rambling on, beating the table with both his fists, and wailing only to become quiet momentarily, and then talking gibberish again.

"Mr. Gu, I am sorry but don't you think it's too cruel of you to deprive me of my one and only remaining source of happiness? I've been robbed of my wife, my children, and now you want to take away my sister who's the only person left for me?"

Like a child, he sniffled. Then raising his head, he looked all around him, searching for something. He quickly got on his feet and walked over to where there was a group of people and helped Gu Rin up, who was lying down to stop his nosebleed, and took him outside. Someone tried to divert him by pulling him, saying he should be taken to a hospital. But like a completely different person from a few minutes ago, he assured them not to worry and walked out with his arm around Gu Rin's shoulder.

"Why don't two lonely people walk together?"

Gu Rin collapsed on his bed with his clothes on. He barely could sense someone taking off his clothes and wiping his nose as he fell asleep. It was definitely Sosia. He wanted to caress her hand but couldn't for the life of him reach it.

With an apron around her, Sosia showed Gu Rin his room. He was astonished upon seeing her the first time. She had a face of some-one he had dreamt of even before she was born, and for more than twenty years. She looked terribly lonely. She was also searching for something.

Nauseated, Gu Rin wanted to throw up. He didn't want to vomit on the bed and tried to move his face but couldn't. He somehow man-aged to get up and walk over to where he thought was the window. But it was his blanket that got all damp after he vomited, thinking it was by the window. Feeling strange, he opened his eyes, as if they were metal doors, to see Sosia wrapped radiantly in red light. The red light dimmed and gradually turned yellow. She was bending over, probably wiping up his vomit.

Sosia always liked to go for a walk. They took a walk whenever they could find time. They always came back all wet from the rain. Sosia said that's what she liked.

Gu Rin could smell the disinfectant. Someone was spraying it to get rid of the smell of the vomit. He tried to open his eyes to see who it was but couldn't. He could sense Sosia's white hand in motion.

Sosia had studied violin at a university in Auckland. Her brother tried to send her off to America. But Sosia gave up on it because she didn't want to leave Gu Rin, who in turn wanted her to go. She lied to her brother that she didn't want to go because she didn't like America. Skawinsky also didn't want to separate from her. Consequently, he was comforted.

Gu Rin wanted to drink water. He said "water" aloud several times. He could feel Sosia's hand. He turned over and drank the water. Suddenly sleep went away. Nervous, Sosia was hesitant to come near him. He opened his arms wide and motioned her to come. Sosia came running to him, buried her face in his chest, and rubbed against it. He could feel her nose on his chest. His lips felt ticklish against the nape of her neck.

"My brother is sorry."

"About what?"

"For striking you."

"Is that all?"

"I shall come with you to Korea."

"Whose idea is it? Yes, you must come with me. After I got beat up by your brother, my desire to take you with me has gotten greater. Either you come with me, or I remain here."

Cupping her face with his hands, he gazed at her. "Play some music."

"It's late."

"I just want to be sure of your presence."

(Sosia played Tchaikovsky's Violin Concerto D. The room was filled with its melody.)

Gu Rin did not leave New Zealand even after his yearlong lawful stay expired. UNESCO suspended the monthly stipend of fifty francs to him. He went to the harbor today and saw Hayashi and Ariyama off to Japan. Hayashi told him if Gu Rin didn't want to go straight back to Korea, then he should come to Japan to study until the war came to an end. They were surprised when Gu Rin turned down the offer. He lied, saying it was useless to go back. They wondered how he could not think of his family in the middle of a war. Gu Rin was actually curious about his family. He wanted to see them as soon as possible. But, the thought of meeting his wife frightened him. He wished her dead. At the same time, he wanted to find out for himself if his whole family had died. The Communists were known to slaughter the landowners, so there was very little chance that they were still alive. He made such assumptions, scaring himself at the same time. Hayashi suggested that he stay in Japan until the war was over. At first, he was almost prepared to go with them if Sosia could accompany him. But what would he do with her in Japan? He thought he might be comforted if he could bring Sosia close to Korea at least, regardless of the war situation. Thus, he inquired at the Japanese diplomatic office about it, however, the prospects were not good, for even if her entry was permitted, she would have to return to New Zealand once her student status expired. He told them that would be okay but was told again that they couldn't issue a visa to a Polish national with potential problems. So, he gave up on Japan. Moreover, if he couldn't go with her, then there was only one solution, that is, for him not to leave.

Like an alien who has been deprived of his nationality, he felt horrifically alone. On his way home, he stopped off at the "Cook" bar to drink. All he seemed to be doing was drinking and he was running out of money. If he didn't earn money soon, then he would have to starve. Furthermore, the government of New Zealand would deport him. In addition, Hayashi had left as well as Romerei. He kept on drinking. This is where I got beat up. You are a coward—Skawinsky's words pounded his heart.

He staggered his way back to his apartment.

Sosia came running to support him. He leaned his body against her then collapsed. His necktie came undone and fluttered in the wind.

Skawinsky was surprised. What did it mean if Gu Rin wasn't even going to go to Japan? It was going to be a big headache for him. He must love Sosia very much. But what was he going to do then? He was greatly worried about him. At this rate, he would become stateless.

"Hey, Mr. Gu. Be reasonable. What you're doing is not rational. Try to look at things in a more cool-headed way."

"It's none of your business. You called me a coward. Well, you were right. I am not going back to my country because I am scared of the war because I am not a patriot like you. But most of all, how could I leave Sosia behind? I'd rather we both die here."

"How could you call yourself a man? You depraved jerk!"

"You call me depraved now? So what if I am? But why are you so possessive of Sosia? Because you miss your wife? Are you trying to cover up your loneliness through her? Why can't you overcome your loneliness on your own? Why can't you live alone?"

"What? My loneliness is incomparable to yours. Get lost. You loser."

"All right, I'm out of here."

Bursting into tears, Sosia held on to Gu Rin. Nearly dragging him, she laid him down on the bed. (Richard Strauss's "Death and Transfiguration" was playing on the radio.) Sosia undressed Gu Rin. The *Wellington News* fell out of his pocket.

"The Armistice to be signed in Korea…talk of establishing a demarcation line along the 38th parallel line is in process. For the Neutral Nations Supervisory Commission, Poland, Czechoslovakia, and India were recommended by the Communist side and Switzerland and Sweden by the UN."

Once a provisional peace was in place, newspapers and letters would be delivered for the first time. Gu Rin also got a letter from his older brother.

"Korea is at the moment taking care of the remnants of the war. We too have inherited a sad portion. We have received the corpses of our mother, your wife, and your second oldest son. I wish for you to come back and bury your poor wife."

Gu Rin stopped himself short as he was about to open Sosia's room, for he heard the sound of the violin. He was just coming back from selling the *Legend of Rotorua* by John Gashrin, a New Zealand author still alive, which he had meant to bring as a gift to his older brother. It was his very last asset.

Sosia was playing "Solveig's Song." He opened the door very quietly and waited until she finished the song.

"Sosia, let's take a weekend trip to Rotorua for a change of scenery. Quick, get dressed."

With mixed feelings of joy and fear, Sosia stood still for a while looking at Gu Rin, who seemed unusually upbeat.

Going from Hamilton in a van, they looked around Cambridge and Taukau then headed for Rotorua. Spring in Rotorua was resplendent. The October spring breeze created beautiful dimples in the sky.

They got on the boat. Gu Rin rowed and Sosia sat in the front and played her violin, a solo piece called "Nymph of Zurich Lake."

For a brief while, Gu Rin stopped rowing and gazed at Sosia, as though mesmerized. Frightened by his scrutinizing look at her, Sosia stopped playing and fell in his arms.

"How come you're looking at me like that?" she asked coyly. The boat lost balance and shook as Sosia fell. Couldn't it just capsize right here and then? As though that was what he wanted, Gu Rin closed his eyes and counted one, two, three. The boat regained its balance.

"You are like the heroine of Rotorua, the one from Gashrin's novel," he said, stroking her brown hair.

"But there is a part I couldn't understand. Why did the two people who were so happy together commit a double suicide? Gashrin failed to explain that."

"It wasn't a double suicide. They died because the boat capsized."

"Is that right? What could have caused such a fury on a placid lake like this?"

All of a sudden, Sosia was trembling as she looked at him. Then she let out a short scream, burying her face in his chest. She caught a flick of madness in his eyes.

"Don't be scared. We can be forever happy, sitting here like this."

(Falling from the Malcom Bridge after a drinking spree. Pawning his books, overcoat, and even his shirts. Pleading with Sosia not to become debauched. The Korean government office in Sydney refusing to acknowledge him. Hearing the boat whistle and gazing at the sea all day long after he lost his Korean nationality. The news of death, like a spell, from his older brother. Crying and hugging each other with Skawinsky at a pub. Wandering around the shore like a mad man every day in a white shirt.)

Holding Sosia tightly in his arms, he shook the boat as vigorously as he could. The Rotorua Lake quivered, creating a water pattern as fine as a dream. The scenery on the surface of the lake recovered their form after a while. From somewhere in the distance, the kakapo bird was crowing.

The Forest Protection Act,
the Old Woman and Special News

Verdict
Birthplace: Heungnam, South Hamgyeong Province
Address: Miari, Songji sect, X district, X province
Name: Bogeumi (50 years old)
Court Order: The defendant must pay 5,000 *hwan*
    and serve 4 months of prison labor

In a sonorous voice Judge Kong read out the verdict.

As he rose from his chair, he threw a quick glance at the defendant. He couldn't take his eye off the transfixed body buried in the old rags looking frozen stiff, and paused in front of her, and gave a long pensive look. He reflected on the defendant's interrogatory.

He entered his office, thinking he should perhaps go see the defendant as he looked up at the wall clock. He juggled his home, friends, and the government office in search of diversion; however, he kept being interrupted by the thought of the defendant. He gave up on going out and opened the door to his office to spot the reporter of law from the S Newspaper, sitting on his revolving chair with a hat on the back of his rear head. His legs stretched out, he was searching through a pile of documents. This fellow who had a four-character name, Park Yi Su Eok, like that of a Japanese, didn't bother to look up even after he heard Judge Kong enter.

"Herr Kong, Wie befinden Sie sich. Setze Sie sich," he greeted Judge Kong and pointed at the chair in front of the stove. His over-the-top manners vexed Judge Kong but he was also enthralled by the fellow's eloquence that almost always curtailed his resolve to let him have it. Judge Kong came to respect Park Yi Su Eok after finding out that his recklessly frivolous and down-to-earth tendency to unmask the officialism was not derived from an inherently uncouth personality or lack of education or refinement but instead was rooted in some insight he had gained from his own life experience.

"How was the case today?"

"Not worth reporting."

"How do you know?"

"Hmm, what do you take me for?"

"Although she's guilty of taking a bribe?"

"What're you talking about?"

"You don't think there was a censorship? And the patent was authorized?"

"What do you mean?"

"I'm saying, maybe it was sold to another company."

"Sold to a company?"

"So how come it is such a news crisis?"

Like a judge interrogating the defendant, his friend banged the desk with the pile of documents and put on a somber face.

"Ha, ha, truth be told, you are useless as a reporter."

"What the hell are you talking about?"

"The era when one sought a top news in the court dates back to the stone age."

"Don't you know the goldmine for news is long gone from here? This is like a mine shut down a long time ago. So, if you want to come into sudden fortune, look for a different mine."

"Who says that? Look into the cases of rape, murder of children, kidnapping, and murder. You think the ruling is an end to these cases? It's a reporter's duty to investigate the root of the case that the law has failed to detect." His friend raised his voice, going as far as tapping his heart with his lean finger.

In amusement, Judge Kong listened to his friend's admonishment, as though he was the first to point it out in the same old words of reporters. He was piqued for being deprived of his rights to lead the conversation. Judge Kong quickly changed the topic.

"But why are you early today?"

Without replying his reporter friend, he snatched the documents and said, "The Interim Protection of the Forest Act... Concerning the Forest Protection Law, besides the ban on the cutting down a tree, the collecting or mining of soil and rock, or cultivating or grazing concerning the roots, bark of a tree, pine resin...in other words, don't even eat herb roots or tree barks but simply starve."

The sallow face of the defendant—from malnutrition, poverty, and ascariasis—came to Judge Kong's mind. With her twelve-year-old son, the old woman wanted to come to the south but somehow landed here where she didn't know a single soul. Begging for food was possible but she needed the money to get clothes, unless she was going to steal; hence, she made a shoeshine box for her kin while she herself looked for work but the world was too miserly for even just two people to survive. She had lost all her family members except for her twelve-year-old son and wanting to cross over to the south, she somehow ended up at this place. Granted, there was a saying how one could be so impoverished as to have just nine meals in thirty days. She was unable to find blighted barley to eat, let alone food for a dog, compelling her to dig through the garbage in the dark, and was mistaken for a dog by some idiot who threw her a stone at her, thereby injuring her back. When her body, her last resort, was all used up, she lay underneath the bridge, like a living corpse, and waited to die. She found out it was a complete lie that a living person could never die of starvation. So, instead of waiting to die and not wanting to freeze to death, she climbed up the hill while her son was out desperately picking pine twigs, only to be captured by a policeman.

Because Judge Kong was preoccupied with the defendant, he was not listening. When he came to his senses, his friend seemed to have nearly completed the story and was pondering about some conclusion.

"Could there be some earthshattering scoop? One that would bankrupt Geumsung Airlines in an instant?"

"What can you get out of that? Be careful not to wreck your career by attacking in a foolhardy way. Do you know who the patron of that company is?"

"That's why I am making an advance. Eh, Herr Kong. It is a leading Korean monopolistic corporation, a de facto labyrinth behind an impenetrable veil …how about it? It is an important matter. Wouldn't you like to take an active stance in this? For example…"

"For example, behead someone without even a drop of blood; is that what you're saying? In short, fabricate a crime of subversion of the national Constitution, instigation of rebellion? How? Koreans have succeeded in conjuring up a play that even Shakespeare would've been hard pressed to come up with. We live in an era where news is created, so by all means, try it. But in any event, how do you expect to make a fortune amidst the ashes? How can you make money from it?"

"There is a way. You are proving yourself an ignoramus in politics and economics. A smart fool, so to speak."

"I wish I were one, rather. As a smart fool, here's how I'll imagine it. Replace one monopolistic corporation and build another monopolistic corporation in which you have the rights. In addition, how about this? Through anonymous blackmailing and bribery, obtain the rights and fees. It is an ingenious manipulation of law by way of applying the methods of blackmailing and threats to undermine the benefit and protection of laws about bribery. Can it turn into a goldmine or provide political funds for the next ruling party?

"It's that and more. Isn't there a criminal case about Geumsung Company? It doesn't matter how small as long as it can elicit hatred among the people. As long as the people don't get burned."

"I am sure there could be."

"Do you mean one could be fabricated?"

"That's right. You just have to believe it's real. For example…"

"For example?"

The defendant's face came to Judge Kong's mind.

"How about a clever fool who can't attack a big thief but only picks on a beggar and fines them for finding food? Why don't you look up 'news value'?"

"What are you talking about? Stop saying nonsense."

Park Yi Su Eok was all anxious, unlike his usual demeanor.

"How about claiming an old woman refugee was killed by a Geumsung-owned vehicle? And they didn't do anything about it?"

"What's worse, they didn't even provide the funeral fee. And…"

"Yes. You are indeed a reporter all right. So then what happened?'

Judge Kong felt as though the story that Park had just made up was for real. He looked like a judge who was listening to the prosecutor's argument.

"And what is abominable is that the murderous driver is still driving the same car. He happens to be a relative of the owner of the company and even though he falls under the category of one who should be conscripted, he received draft deferment by some authority."

"Can a human life be killed off like this from the world without anyone knowing?"

"Yes, readers, boycott Geumsung Transportation!"

His reporter friend gave out a gleeful scream and ran out the door.

"Where could he be going to?" Judge Kong murmured to himself as he put on his coat and headed for the parking lot. He told the defendant that he had paid the penalty for her; hence, she could go home with a clean conscience. He had to brush past the defendant, who gripped his sleeve wailing in gratitude, in order to complete the document for her release.

"Fraudulent philanthropist, elusive political strategist, a "savior" who builds a nation is busy, working on a mask to hide his identity.

Who is the last man of conscience?" That evening, Judge Kong murmured the headlines of a front page of a daily evening paper and as though he felt dizzy with them all, he covered them with his palm and looked out the window instead.

The next day, an article in the evening newspaper startled him. The article is as follows.

"Geumsung Transportation Kills a Person for Ten Hwan. An old woman, who boarded the bus without a ticket, was run over when she was forced to disembark from the vehicle. Bogeumi (age 50) from Miari, Songji Sect., X District, was released from the Provincial Court of Gwangju and secretly boarded a bus without a ticket. Feeling anxious about not purchasing a ticket, she explained her situation to the driver assistant (Kim Saeng-su [pseudonym]) and begged for clemency but was asked to pay in cash instead. Bogeumi told him she did not have any money and was eager to return home, she got on the bus anyway, pleading for forgiveness. The driver assistant demanded that she pay ten *hwan* or get off the bus instantly if she couldn't. He then asked the driver to bring the bus to a halt and pushed her off the vehicle. The old woman fell when her skirt became caught in the slowly moving bus. The bus suddenly accelerated and she was killed when the front wheel of the bus ran over her."

Judge Kong wanted to believe this was an article made up by Park Su Yi Eok. But no matter how many times he checked, the news was printed in the *R Daily*, and not the *S Daily*.

The Law of Cause and Effect
–The Realm of Ethics

"If you want to see me dead, take care of it cleanly."

If it weren't for other people, Gyeong-jik would've liked to spend the nights at the office. But since everyone knew he was married and owned a house to boot, he got up briskly, too embarrassed to deal with the errand boy who with a blatant politeness was waiting for him to leave first. But it was still early evening when he took the commuter bus into town. He stood on the street with his hands shoved in his trouser pocket, trying to figure out how he could kill the damn time; when his legs got tired, like he'd been waiting for someone, he swaggered into the theater, only to come out after seeing it was all empty. Then he would follow the others into a teahouse but again, he saw the serving girl leave work. The streets were awake and completely drained and he entered the bar, only to be kicked out again for it was closing time. He was left to drag his shadow through the night, strolling the streets where the sound of the policemen's steps could be heard, searching for Orion and counting the stars in the sky; it was when his clothes were all damp with dew that he found himself in front of his house. He would open the door to see his wife knitting under the lamplight. She would lift her head and with her eyes, quietly point at the room across where he could hear the groaning of his father, whose coughing and hemoptysis were getting more severe after a long, tiring bout of illness. But for his part, his nerves were frayed and he had a perverse feeling that what should've happened had been delayed too long.

His father, who failed to have another son, was bedridden with a lung disease on the day of Gyeong-jik's wedding, and his new daughter-in-law was forced to become his nurse and had to prepare his herbal medicine, always on standby. This hopeless situation nauseated and dispirited him to no end.

Unless Gyeong-jik's father and his daughter-in-law had been mortal enemies, it was improbable that he would set out to wreck their lives the day she became part of their family; and hence, Jeong-mi, who had married into a family where it was a given that she look after her in-laws, could not claim to be a modern woman and refuse to obey her in-laws, let alone move out to live independently. All she could do was accept her fate and resign herself to her misfortune, possibly mandated from her previous life.

But, as unfortunate as it was, his father's condition became worse after Jeong-mi became part of the family, and whenever his mother suspected his wife by saying that she might be the cause of a curse or if they had held their wedding on an inauspicious day, he could not help but give his ignorant mother an incredulous look, while his wife, in disbelief, burst into tears. His wife's bitter lament about his father ruining their life by becoming bedridden shortly after they got married was not unfounded. In the beginning, he had gotten the best herbal medicine, newly introduced Western drugs, if not all types of well-known prescriptions, not to mention giving in to his mother's wish to have a shamanistic ritual performed for his father; he went as far as relying on his grandmother's faith and offered a prayer to Buddha and alms to the temple, however, his father's condition did not improve or become worse—even if he were made of iron, he could but waste away when his hipbone was glued to the floor every day of the year. Meanwhile, some wise old man advised them there could be a hundred remedies for an ailment, depending on how prudently it was applied, and an uncle told them about a secret cure that worked for another person, thereby getting the patient's hopes high. Then his mother heard from somewhere that water prepared in a bottle seeped with freshly cut pieces of bamboo after several days was highly effective, then again bothering him with an order of steamed mugwort only to importune him the next day for the new special drug. Of course, Gyeong-jik went out of his way to get hold of whatever medicine that was known to be effective, while his wife, Jeong-mi, trying to come up with all the money for the treatment, failed to become cognizant of her pregnancy with their first child.

The so-called modern women viewed honoring the parents of their husband as a hindrance or the cause of a break-up of a family, if not a thief of their youth, prepared to give up on their love altogether, or doing so in actuality, however, here was his wife, who had to tend to an ailing person from morning to night, having to put up with his caprice. It was a truly pitiful situation. At first when his father fell ill, his relatives at least paid a visit, bringing with them expensive drugs like TB 101 or the new medication like Niazid, but as years passed, they seemed to have gotten tired out and their visits ceased altogether. When Gyeong-jik happened to run into one on the street, he would make a quick inquiry about his father but did not bother to wait for his response. His wife would take on his mother's responsibility so as not to upset his father. There was always leftover cooked rice that they couldn't feed the pigs, and Jeong-mi would finish it out of consideration for his overly sensitive father, as well as not expressing the least reluctance to wash the bowl full of phlegm herself. As the only son, Gyeong-jik had not been doted on by his father when he was growing up, however, thanks to his manual dexterity, he was able to eke out a living with work in printing; and he dropped out of school willingly and took a job as a civil servant not because of the Korean War but for his father's sake.

He flopped down flat on the mattress without changing clothes. His baby was awakened in surprise before she fell asleep again. Gyeong-jik edged closer under the light to Jeong-mi, who was busy at work with a vacant expression. He looked at her from under her chin. Her lips showed a faint contour but no gloss. She seemed bent on completing the spring sweater in just a day for her customer. Gyeong-jik had long ago lost all interest in what Jeong-mi was up to. And it bored him to have to say anything, for not only was he unable to find any topic to talk about but he also lacked desire. He did not want to be coerced into saying anything.

"Just finish me off. What have I done wrong in my previous life to have to die in such a torturous manner?"

"Come, come, don't get so upset. It's harder on your body. Don't move your back."

"Go away. All of you, drop dead. Argh…"

"My dear husband…"

Gyeong-jik was listening to the sound of the cry from the adjacent room like he was hearing ghosts. He stretched and closed his eyes. He felt the shadow fleet across his face as Jeong-mi got up. He knew well he should go over to his parents' room or at least bring his father some candy to placate him but he really did not feel up to it today. He wished he could just vanish or be buried right there and then. Half-asleep and half-awake, he was pondering over a nebulous thought when the door opened and he felt his mother's glare on him, who was lying, crumpled on the mat. Tossing, turning, and snoring loudly, he pretended to be heavily drunk. If there was a way to taunt his mother in any way, he would have liked to bring her to tears. But then his mother just stood in front of the door and let out a long sigh, saying, "I don't know what I can do." Then in great sorrow, she turned away.

Jeong-mi woke him up again. He quickly got up and groped for the baby's hand, which was so small that it could disappear in his hand. The child had slept in the bosom of her grandfather up until his condition became worse. Gyeong-jik paid hardly any attention to her but Jeong-mi, who was terribly worried about her, would react with anger when he expressed any concern for the child. He had also turned away in deep sorrow after telling her how she should just let her die, upon seeing how she didn't feed her the whole day, ignoring her cry and neglecting her until late evening.

Jeong-mi was glaring at Gyeong-jik, who all of a sudden was looking at the child with much love. She sat down next to him and said, "Mother would like father to be hospitalized. And she wants another wild pigeon. Father said he enjoyed eating it."

When Gyeong-jik heard that, he was reminded of the money as proof of evidence while interrogating a soldier a few days earlier, and demanded it, saying the trial was going to be the next day.

"I spent it for the loan money." Jeong-mi explained in a frightened voice, averting her eyes, as though she'd committed a big crime.

"How could you think of spending public money? Do you want to see me in jail so that you can live by yourself?"

"I didn't know about it…"

"I don't care. Get it back to me by tomorrow, even if you have to steal or embezzle it. It's so ignorant of you to…" Gyeong-jik did not dare finish his sentence for he was afraid she'd attack him by saying when she did ever have time to study anything. Whenever she could find time, Jeong-mi would try to read the magazine or a newspaper in the kitchen when they first got married, and he had been a staunch supporter of women's rights and encouraged her by saying, there was no law that forbade women from reading Kant in the kitchen, and not forgetting to bring home a magazine every month. But it'd been a while since he became fed up with anything modern or anything, period.

"Whose idea is it?" Gyeong-jik changed the topic and asked, putting on a friendly face. He wanted to find out if it were his father who asked himself or if it were his mother's wish to get him hospitalized.

"It's father's wish." He remembered what his father-in-law had said a while back.

"If only he would go to a seashore instead of a hospital?" he mumbled to himself in a derisive tone. He argued a hundred years would not be enough time to recover in a house with bad air, whereas if his father, accompanied by his mother, were to go to a place like Noa Island where it was renowned for clean water and good seafood for convalescence, he would have no need for the new drugs. His mother, who did not fail to glean in Gyeong-jik's words his intent to free Jeong-mi from the burden of looking after his parents without a day's rest from the day she got married, lamented how their son couldn't wait to throw his aging and ailing parents out on the street while his father vowed he would do as he wished, embittered his son might really kick them out.

But then his father threw a fit about a withered apple that hadn't been thrown away, changed his clothes all too frequently, even though he never left the house, tenaciously clung to the hand of a guest who wanted to leave after a short visit for the acidic smell was too much to bear, and held him back by straining to get up and grabbing both hands of the visitor; all these peculiar tendencies of his father made shivers run through Gyeong-jik, who thought perhaps his father was indeed going out of his mind. Meanwhile, he couldn't stand to see his father, whose flesh had worn away after several years of being bedridden, groan with great pain as his bones scraped against the floor when he tossed and turned. Sometimes though, his father sitting out in the sun, feeling the blades of grass, would see Jeong-mi come out with his spittoon and ask, in surprise why his mother wasn't cleaning it instead, and seeing how he tried to distance himself from his grandchild, who had grown attached to him while not forgetting to put on a gauze mask, elicited from Gyeong-jik pity and compassion at the same time, tearful joy upon seeing his father's true character.

"There's a charity hospital run by an American missionary that's not too costly and many patients got cured there."

"Who told you that?"

"Mother did. It is 9,000 *hwan* a month."

"That isn't cheap. Why don't we sell my body? My heart has been run down long ago."

"What're you saying? My body has long been completely consumed, too."

"I am not sure of anything anymore. I feel drained in every way. Utterly sapped. I have no interest in anything. That doesn't mean I want to die, though. What in the world is ethics anyway? I've gorged on it to the point of being sick of it. It's got to have at least a slight taste for me to indulge in it."

Gyeong-jik lamented, twisting and writhing like a drunken man, and Jeong-mi just stood there, unable to wipe off the welling tears.

"I stopped Sun-a from going into their room." Jeong-mi said, pointing at the child with her eyes. Suddenly, Gyeong-jik was reminded of the partisan fighter woman who had her infant wrapped in the skirt in the prison cell this afternoon. The baby burst into sudden tears on seeing a man in uniform. Offering his hand through the metal bars, he queried as to why.

"The baby was born in here."

The child must be unaware of the blue sky or a beast called man. Gyeong-jik couldn't help a bitter smile as he thought of how his world was confined to his mother, who spent all her day looking out through the black window, and the iron bars of the prison, yet to become aware of how the world was a meaningless place.

Gyeong-jik left home as soon as dawn arrived without seeing his father. He had never done this. It was Saturday and he didn't feel comfortable staying in his office where everyone had already left. It was still light and he had no inclination to go home in a sober state. He stood absently alongside the street and mulled over a number of places and people he could visit but soon realized there was nowhere he wanted to go. He let his footsteps lead him and in the end, he found himself, standing on his shadow in front of his own house. He was about to enter when he heard the voice of his father-in-law. He paused for a few seconds before going in.

His father-in-law was in the middle of talking and he kept on.

"I'll consider my daughter part of this house but you're the one I feel sorry for, wasting away the prime of your life when all you've ever gotten from your parents are some raggedy clothes, and yet having to pay so much back."

Gyeong-jik threw a cautious glance at his father and caught him, half lying down, with his back on a folded blanket, trying to hold back the phlegm by inhaling deeply and averted his eyes.

"We brought up our daughter in the most caring way possible and married her off, dressed in fine silk but we didn't get even a pair of socks or underwear in return. As a matter of fact, I didn't pay a visit of my own volition. My daughter implored me and as a father, I couldn't turn her down."

Gyeong-jik went out of the room and peeked in the adjacent room that was left ajar but there was no one there. He lay down on the floor. He could hear a thick voice interspersed with a thin and sharp voice from the other room. He opened his eyes to the sound of thump on the floor. His wife, who had returned, put down their child on the floor and dropped a bundle wrapped up in some cloth. Her pale, fatigued face was floating in the darkness.

"Where did you go?"

"To borrow some money."

"What for?"

"You said you needed it by tomorrow."

"Why did you loan money only to borrow again?"

"I couldn't get the loan money back so I took a loan for fifteen percent interest."

"Quite shrewd, aren't you? I am tired." He was ready to go to sleep when Jeong-mi plopped down by his head.

"I'm thinking of starting a money loan group," she said, hoping to peak his interest somehow. "Father needs to be hospitalized as soon as possible…"

"Of course, we'll need money right away then."

"If I start a group for 10,000 *hwan*, then that'll take care of the hospital cost."

"But is father going to live just a month?" was on Gyeong-jik's mind; however he felt too sorrowful to say anything.

They say, a lung disease can be overcome after several years but his father, who became afflicted with it at the age of past fifty, got a little better for him to go out but come winter, he got worse again. This pattern was repeated and as it appeared no medication seemed to work, he had himself examined a number of times, as well as getting x-rays taken, thinking perhaps he had been misdiagnosed. Although Gyeong-jik knew one of his father's lungs was dysfunctional and it was some kind of a respiratory disease, he still clung to a blissful hope that his father would live longer, seeing that his condition remained unchanged. For it was terrifying to suddenly be deprived of someone in life who had kept the family under control. They had lived this way and he thought to go on living, like this could be quite blissful. It was infinitely possible for him to be content with a life in which he and his wife would be filial to his parents, who will dote on their child while he went to work every day in a peaceful frame of mind, and even if Jeong-mi and he couldn't go out for a walk in the moonlight, they could still delight in it from their open door.

"Do as you wish. It's your father's wish also."

It rang clearly in his ears that he was wasting the prime of his life, and the feeling shook something unknown inside of him. His mother opened the door and with an awkward look, she told them his father wanted to see them.

"I am here, father."

"What for? Send me to a hospital. I'm afraid I'm going to die. And I can't trust you. I won't get better here, lying around in this room."

Gyeong-jik's mother followed him out the room and whispered in his ear, "Please do something. It could very well be his last wish."

He felt like sobbing. If only he could get his father hospitalized this instant, it would be so convenient but putting aside the money, he thought he couldn't bear his absence.

It wouldn't be too difficult to come up with the money if he were determined. A matter of life and death could depend on one word in a court-martial. Gyeong-jik was busy taking care of the partisan captives these days. The order came down for the execution of the prison inmates sentenced to death. The death-row convicts were originally imprisoned in a private cell, however, a sudden influx of prisoners on trial made putting them in a group unavoidable. Gyeong-jik took a ride in the military police vehicle to the prison for the midnight execution and went into the long, dim corridor, dragging his shadow along. He was happy that he did not have to go home early today. The military police were lined up in front of the prison gate with the car and they unlocked the iron door when they arrived. Gyeong-jik perused his list and called for prisoner number 1003. There was no answer.

"Is 1003 here?"

"Yes sir."

"You are going to Daegu on the ten o'clock train."

He motioned for the prison guard to shut the gate and unlock the opposite one. He could sense the floating black eyes glaring at him in the darkness.

"Prisoners 360, 396, and 841."

"Yes. Yes."

"You are going to Daegu on the ten o'clock train."

He repeated the words and looked at the guard. Prisoner number 360, with an expressionless face whose head was bent down, pulled up his trousers without a belt and was the last to follow. Suddenly Gyeong-jik thought something was strange and turned around to face the iron door from where 360 had walked out. He scrutinized the faces in the soft light. A few days earlier, when he was walking past this very spot, an inmate gently banged the iron bar to get his attention. When he came closer to him, the man held out to him a piece of paper in his hand. He was asking for an execution of a substitute. He did not identify who it would be from 360, 391, or 864; however, he was asking Gyeong-jik to remain silent about the matter. He left without saying anything but could not be astonished at this terrifying fact. He had fled after throwing back to him the bank note for 150,000 *hwan* inside the folded paper but he was now staring at the man with a different intent. Sure enough, the same inmate crawled his way to the iron bar and tearfully gave the paper to Gyeong-jik and bowed. He snatched it. But he felt dizzy as he was leaving and had to stop to take a deep breath under a starry night. The army doctor and the executioner had already arrived at the site, and several pits, which were newly dug up, were agape by the white post. They removed the masks from the faces and asked for their final words. They also received a cigarette but just stood there, with their hands trembling. No word came out of their open mouths.

Number 360 took a cigarette and after a deep puff, he said squatting down, "Please contact my home at this address and let them know about me. Tell them they can get a payment for a debt for 500,000 *hwan* from such and such address. Also all my assets and property in my name will be transferred to my wife."

Of course, the debt implied the compensation for his execution as a substitute. Gyeong-jik found out from his directory that this man had been sentenced to twenty years in prison; however, he was afraid to know as to why he was paying the debt with his life. Who can say twenty years and life itself were worth simply 500,000 *hwan*? Even if it were stipulated under the debtor-creditor law, could life or worse, yet, could humanity be calculated in terms of a monetary figure?

Late at home that night, his head spun as he recalled the shreds of clothes that were blown away by the bullet. The face, which had been depleted of all light in the darkness, overlapped with his father's face and a great terror swept through him. He couldn't live on with a lucid mind. Like a thirsty person, he drank a whole bottle of liquor and staggered onto the street. He decided to take Jeong-mi to see a movie tomorrow and also go hiking in the mountain with her while regretting not buying her a fashionable velvet skirt that all women wore these days, and as it was too late, he would ask her to get the fabric first thing next morning. With these thoughts, Gyeong-jik was spitting out what sounded like neither laughter nor a cry into the space. I can be perfectly happy as I am, he was telling himself. In the American novel, "The Happiest Man in the World," the protagonist, an unemployed worker during the economic depression after the World War II, got a most perilous delivery job through the risky underground market but viewed himself as the happiest man as he swaggered home after dark. Gyeong-jik couldn't help smiling bitterly as he likened himself to him.

Jeong-mi was still knitting the sweater by the lamp when he came home.

"How I envy you," she said, looking like she would burst into tears any second.

"What?"

"You seem quite happy. Go see how father is. Mother says."

"Mother was wondering if it doesn't upset us not to see father dead," Jeong-mi collapsed on the floor and cried.

"What is the problem? Why is everyone bent on driving me insane, including you?"

His world was collapsing and he was about to run to his parents' room, screaming. Jeong-mi became startled and blocked him.

"I'm sorry. You can't go there. Please go to sleep, now" she begged him.

"Ahhhh, this is how I'm left speechless. Speechless. All I feel is bottomless abyss in my heart."

She then explained how she'd been out all day, trying to organize a money loan group but everyone was already part of one or the other, if not lacked the money, hence she returned home with all her effort in vain, only to have mother unfairly torment her by saying if she was going to allow father to die without doing anything. She protested in sorrow how she was not an unfeeling object, and thus could but vent her pent-up anger and frustration. She added how she felt pity for mother who did not show any indication of fatigue, even after staying up all night, nursing father.

"She must love her husband, still," he said cautiously. "I don't understand how."

The faint smile on her face put Gyeong-jik in a good mood.

The thought that he could be happy in their own room was enough to induce him to fall asleep in a most gleeful state. Something fluttered by his neck and he felt a bird's claws land on his chest. Startled, he woke up to see a white pigeon on its bloody foot and its black goggling eyes. Gyeong-jik instantly recovered his clear-mindedness and felt an impulse to crush the pulsating heart.

"I got this one instead because I couldn't find a wild pigeon."

"Why did you have to break its leg?"

"It will die anyway."

"What do you mean? Let it free. Father won't die from not eating it."

Gyeong-jik truly felt blissful. He was reassured that the world can indeed be beautiful. He got up late in the morning and as he got dressed, he told Jeong-mi, "Get ready to have father hospitalized."

Out on the street, he stroked the bank note in his pocket. He stroked it like a live animal, then crumpling it up and shoved it into his pocket. There were too many ten *hwan* bills to put them all in his pocket. He bought a cloth sheet in the store and wrapped them in it. The day was too bright and he felt too dizzy to keep on walking.

He went into a department store for he didn't feel like walking with a large bundle of money. He got a strong urge to lighten his load a little. He asked for the most expensive cloth for women and was presented with a silky black velvet fabric. He paid for the sky blue nylon outfit for spring and the exquisite velvet cloth for the outerwear. Afterward, he felt like spending more money and looked for clothes for two-year olds.

On the way back home, he recalled his father in-law's statement of how he was wasting the prime of his life and cast an angry glare at no place in particular, with a thought that it should placate him a bit at last.

Jeong-mi, who was taken aback by Gyeong-jik coming back home, was about to ask him something when she caught a sight of a large bundle and gave him a questioning look. Gyeong-jik unwrapped the bundle and asked, "Did you go to the hospital?"

With a look of awe at the sight of scattered money on the floor, Jeong-mi said evasively, "I was going to." She thought Gyeong-jik was mocking her this morning when he talked to her. Therefore, if she weren't able to come up with a loan group, she was going to take a loan with interest but to see the money, scattered on the floor like fallen leaves, she could only be dumbfounded. For fear of being rebuked, she couldn't bring herself to ask him where the money came from, and at the same time, she was in awe of Gyeong-jik who could provide them with this money just overnight.

Jeong-mi left hurriedly to go to the hospital. When Gyeong-jik entered the room, his mother probed him in silence as she pushed the chamber pot to the edge of the room.

"Sit down, Gyeong-jik. Uhhhhh. What're you going to do about me? Though I made your lives difficult, I can't die like this. If I were to die, you will be the one to suffer and be sad. Wait till I'm gone. You won't be able to survive," his father said, with cold sweat running down, trying to hold back his cough in agitation. Gyeong-jik was at a loss as to what to do, for he had not considered putting his father in the hospital because he did not want to be blamed for doing something against his will and in addition, he did not know where he could come up with 9,000 *hwan* every month.

"I want to get treated in the hospital, but I don't want you to see me die yet. I'd like to die in this very room if I have to. Get me to the hospital. I'm going to die. Won't you let me live? I feel pity for you. I've committed a great sin against you. That's why I want to see it end."

Gyeong-jik wasn't sure how he should construe his words, whether or not he should take his father to the hospital or let him die. It looked like his father wasn't going to live more than a few days but if he were to die at home, he was afraid that not having taken him to the hospital would be the regret of his life, and even if he were blamed for his death, he couldn't say anything; and most of all, it would be most painful for him.

The hardest task, as the son, was to remain by his father's side until his death. Did a sick person of his father's kind have to be completely cremated, including his bones? Wasn't a sack made with the blanket of his deathbed used to cover the body from the head to the toes? Since it was out of question for him not to be by his father until the last minute, should he just disregard it all and get him hospitalized?

Gyeong-jik remained undecided as Jeong-mi called him from outside.

"There are no beds available at the moment. We have to wait a few days. What should we do?" she asked.

"I am not sure. If there are no available beds, that could only mean he should just die here. That puts my mind to rest."

"Please ask mother what she thinks."

"What can she do when we can't get a bed? We'll just have to wait and see."

But then, he thought it might still be a good idea to ask his mother what she thought, and explained the situation to her.

"It looks like we'll have to prepare. Do as you like," she said, with a blank look.

Gyeong-jik was nervous about watching his father die. It was too excruciating. He made up his mind to let things be and came into the room. He became dazed at the sight of the paper bills scattered on the floor. The images on the paper looked like they were crawling around like bugs and transformed themselves into the face of prisoner 360 who was tied to the tree, with his head hung loose.

His father's condition improved somewhat but deteriorated again within four days. It now seemed hopeless and everyone stayed up, waiting for the sick man to take his last breath. His father allowed only his wife to be by him and forbade Gyeong-jik and Jeong-mi to come even close to the door. Gyeong-jik couldn't help feeling sympathetic toward him, yet his father's refusal to have him near was a valid excuse for him not to witness his death.

When his father died at dawn, Gyeong-jik told Jeong-mi to fetch a rickshaw on her way back from reserving a bed at the hospital, and he, with a light heart, dressed up his two-year old daughter, Sun-a, in the new baby clothes. His mother and his wife, who were too stupefied with his odd behavior, couldn't bring themselves to say anything. It was Gyeong-jik and the worker who tied the corpse, wrapped in white cotton, to the rickshaw.

Gyeong-jik closed the rickshaw door and told Jeong-mi in a menacing voice to get dressed in her new nylon outfit for an outing.

His mother was wailing in the room but Gyeong-jik was oblivious. Instead, he left the house, holding Sun-a in his arms and led ahead by Jeong-mi and the rickshaw, like he was going for a walk. He did not forget to bring the money he received from prisoner 360, for he was going to make sure to get his father hospitalized today, even if he were going to be rejected. In any event, he was going to go for a long walk with Jeong-mi this evening. Gyeong-jik, who had stayed up all night, was turning paler in the bright sunlight.

The Pillar

1.

Clerk Wu was very busy from early this morning. His hours were filled with important chores that he had to do. Today was Sunday and he left his house with a strong resolve to complete the tasks he'd been mulling over all night. His workplace, which was on the outskirts of the county, took thirty minutes by bus, a rather long distance to commute. If he were a student, it would be apt and convenient to commute, however, for a civil servant who was in charge of office work for middle and high schools, it couldn't be helped that he stayed at the premises. But the truth be told, he would've liked to walk away from his job for another position without hesitation. Some of his friends mocked him for working as a clerk in a middle school, of all things. They weren't entirely wrong. For one would be hard pressed to find a resume like his. His education consisted of only several years of studies at a Chinese Classics institute and three years of regular school followed by countless different jobs and affiliated titles, which almost constituted his autobiography. After going through all the numerous jobs to the point of making him dizzy, and ending up working as a clerk at a middle school in his later years made it deplorable and unbearable. It would be at least comforting to think it was just his fate but such was not his thought. More than anything, he was convinced he was most capable in what he did and furthermore, he thought he'd been shunted off by the former county chief of industry, purely on the ground of a false charge.

There is a saying that an innocent bystander suffers a side blow in a fight and Clerk Park thought he was the only man who suffered a great loss in the conflict between the old and new governor. The new governor fired him just on the ground that the old governor and he had the same last name. He had no idea why the two became mortal enemies but to be relegated from the army to a school was a great blow for him. Putting aside his pride, his livelihood was going to be imperiled. Since household furnishings were the first to be sacrificed to the Communists, he had only a number of boxes to move; however, he received the transfer notice when he was unexpectedly bedridden with meningitis, not to mention the incredulous news that the dean was plotting to give the job to his right hand man amidst the power struggle between the dean and the board of trustees. He would've felt completely hopeless if he hadn't had at least a house to his name.

Although it is inevitable to cut the scrubs in order to chop down a big tree, the scrub has no use. But his fate didn't seem like it was doomed. He was initially given a post in the city, perhaps underserved, for he was demoted to a county school, then to an even smaller one— the repeated relegation wearied him completely. As the present governor was like his enemy, he prayed every night for a new governor, thinking that he could regain the managerial position, however, when the new governor took office, there was absolutely no gain for him. His lifelong aspiration to become the county head of his hometown, Haenam, went down the drain. It was now his wish just to be transferred back to the school in the city where he lived.

The reason why he was assiduously making a weekly Sunday trip to the city was to see to it that he find a job in any school in the city before the winter passed. He thought all his problems would be resolved if that were to happen. He had long given up on the hope of reentering county politics for there was nothing he could do, as all the personnel he had known in the past had changed and his one remaining wish was to be transferred to the city. He went through an unspeakable sorrow that he couldn't even confide to anyone before he renounced his lifelong goal. Now, transferring to a job in the city has become an inconceivable dream. To be hired as clerk in a middle school, it was a prerequisite to have a connection with a National Assemblyman or a high-ranking person in the central office.

After attempting twice and failing both times to get himself transferred to the city, he got in the habit of blaming everyone. On top of that list was his children and the secretary of the Minister of Education. His family was an everlasting target for his anger and resentment, as well as the chief secretary, for his failure to get him transferred, and it was a reflection of his indirect animosity toward his son-in-law's family.

When the poverty of his family reached a climax, this is what Wu always said, "It's all because of you. If it weren't for you, your mother and I could've lived a fairly good life."

He thought of how he bought his own father a new hat and an overcoat when he was his children's age and lamented not having children was one's best choice in life. His oldest child was not like this when he was in primary school. He was frighteningly strict about how his children were brought up at home. If his kid did not complete his assignment for the day, he would tie him up in a sack and left him in a snowfield all night. For two years, he traveled from his country hometown to Seoul in order to send his daughter to school in the capital city. But what was the outcome of it all? His older daughter is "happily" married to a man with tuberculosis and his oldest son takes money from his pocket to go out drinking. What a waste… How did his lovable daughter end up marrying a tuberculosis patient—his daughter who was so smart that he wished she could've been born a boy instead? He just couldn't get over how his daughter could be the wife of a pathetic sick man, his daughter who gave all her earnings from her job at the provincial office upon seeing her father traveling miles over the mountains to get wood after the family had to move to this city after the rebellion took place in his hometown, Haenam. In some ways, having a lot of children is like shackles for without them, there'd be no need to stoop low to anyone or hold down a deplorable job. The children of today didn't know what responsibility it entailed to be someone's offspring, nor did they desire to find out. In his case, he had done the utmost for his father, who left nothing for him to inherit except his liquor bills.

He could still remember how he had aspired to achieve fame and prestige to become the best filial son to his parents. But he had to brace himself to support his oldest son who had not once brought home the allowance for rice or given him any pocket money to buy cigarettes. Even if he couldn't provide any help to the family, he'd at least be gratified if his son would show a minimal concern for his parents.

In fact, somehow he had to find a way to bring his son, who had been relegated to a school out in boondocks, for he had lost favor with the principal, back to the city by seizing the chance of major transfers for teachers during the summer vacation. He was also determined to be shifted to a city position during a transfer for some clerks, which was expected. The reason why he thought of moving his son to the city was that he could commute from home, possibly saving the family some expenses, and he wouldn't be so free to go crazy. On the other hand, he felt rancor toward the principal who demoted his son. How dare a mere principal treat my son that way, he thought. He bore a grudge against him and wanted to show him and his own son who he was. And he was going to meet the chief of personnel to take care of the job matters of his son and himself.

It put him in a good mood to hear his son went around, bragging about his father, but then readily got himself into trouble, knowing his father would bail him out. Granted his oldest son did not attend college and his behavior was somewhat comprehensible but his third child had an abominable side to him. Whereas his oldest son was a source of worry, his younger son made no secret of looking down at him. When he told him not to apply to college for they were too poor, he went out of his way to go all the way to Seoul to take the entrance exam. His oldest son had taken a year break in primary school; hence, the two of them graduated from high school the same year. He tried to persuade his younger son to allow his older brother, a militia soldier, to go to college first, and then he could attend once their finances got better, however, he was heedless and went ahead to secretly take the exam. His son seemed to regard himself as a genius but when he read what he called a novel that he wrote, he couldn't help thinking otherwise, for it read like an incomprehensible childish gibberish. But people talked about his son a lot and it was only his third child who made him proud and quite happy. He couldn't go to sleep, feeling sorry for his son who couldn't go to college in Seoul even after being admitted, for there was no money. But then he felt angry toward him for not showing any consideration for his father, who couldn't even afford a tonic for his frail health because he had to support his family. Because his son was so smart, he had recommended to him that he take the general civil service examination, which he himself had attempted five times but never passed; that was his lifelong aspiration and he wished one of his children would fulfill his dream. Yet his son was aghast and protested that it was beneath him to become a civil servant at level four. He was shocked. A fourth-level civil servant was beneath his son—when it took him over twenty years to reach that level. He thought what a remarkable person his son could become if such a thing didn't mean anything. Of course, it wasn't like he couldn't understand the great ambition of a young man, however, he had seen many college graduates with impressive aspirations end up as a bum. Reality by no means served men. It seemed to exist solely to harangue him.

But then his younger son took the exam in secret and passed it. He then played a prank on him by visiting his office, presenting himself as Clerk Wu.

It was since then he had stealthily respected his son, who was now studying in Seoul, working on the side as a private tutor. He chose to study English and not law like he had wanted him to. Assured of his son's capability, he pestered him to take the higher civil servant examination.

He was infinitely pleased to discover, not his oldest son but the younger one surpassing him, yet at the same time, he also couldn't help feel his dignity being somewhat undermined. He had just sent a letter

226

to him, pressing him to get ready for the higher civil servant exam next July.

The chief secretary was another person he begrudged because of his employment. He found out the master of ceremony at her wedding was the uncle of his son-in-law, also the chief secretary of the Minister of Education. He importuned his daughter to get a letter of recommendation from the Minister by way of her husband's uncle. If it wasn't possible to get the Minister's signature, then one from his chief secretary would be fine, he told her, adding that it was a sure bet that a referral from not any minister but one from the Ministry of Education would sway the Director of Education here, if not, the governor. If the director were to be transferred to Seoul, he'd become part of the Ministry of Education; therefore, one word from the chief secretary would assure him of a promotion. That is why he had asked his daughter to implore her tuberculosis-ridden husband to write a letter. After that, he thought there would be a welcome result in the last reshuffle but nothing happened. He had boasted to the deputy director of personnel that the chief secretary was a close relative of his daughter, and was advised to recover his former position, as a referral from the chief secretary alone would be enough. The personnel chief director was on his staff when he used to work at the city hall; hence, he was in no position to behave arrogantly toward him. In addition, whether he meant it or not, he promised to help him in any way possible. While he was waiting for the letter of recommendation, he turned down other prospective positions.

He wrote to his son in Seoul many times to find out from his son-in-law whether he'd written the letter. But his younger son, who did not have an iota of affability, was dead set against it. He said, first, he didn't want to see him, let alone broach the topic. What was the use of supporting a son all the way to college when he wouldn't even go on an errand for him? It was after all on account of his children that he was desperately trying to hang on to his job. He was fuming how his son couldn't care less, even though he was most anxiously waiting for the letter. It turned out not only did his son-in-law not write the letter, it didn't even seem to be on his mind. Because he had let everyone know that he knew a relative of the chief secretary of the Minister of Education, the deputy director of personnel didn't hesitate to gall him by saying why he didn't ask the secretary himself, while the others to whom he would ask for a favor politely demurred, with a seemingly plausible excuse that they were only low-ranking civil servants.

He even found his son-in-law with such an uncle distasteful and his daughter who married into his family aggravating. But he decided to put it out of his mind and look for a new solution—that was to deal directly with the Director of Educational Affairs. But then he found out the director was the former Chief of Accounting at the provincial office when his daughter used to work there. He then thought that perhaps it was best to involve his daughter. He wavered somewhat but he decided to ask her for a hand, as it was imperative that he be re-posted.

Wu checked the resume in his inner pocket. The envelope of money in the same pocket made a rustling sound. He was going to send a box of apples by way of his daughter. He had gone through much toil to get that money. Fifteen hundred *hwan* for the box of apples was not quite costly; however, in view of how he made only eight thousand *hwan*, including the food ration and bonus, to manage an eight-member household, it was beyond him to come up with the bribe money. It was a big risk for him to spend on any extra expenditure from his salary. Come to think of it, he had to go through great trouble to come up with this money. He was able to save all the travel money since he stayed in downtown, not to mention the extra stipend he received for going home once or twice a month. Some government clerks were shameless about accepting a huge bribe; however, he was extra careful about dealing with even the smallest sum, lest word got out. He was so meticulous that he was mocked as being mulish during the Colonial period.

He gave two false coughs at the door of his daughter's house. Although they lived not too far from each other, he rarely took out time to visit her. Not only was he reluctant to see his son-in-law, he also abhorred the idea of having to greet him in his bedridden room. Because Clerk Wu was himself a frail man, he was frighteningly irascible about illness.

He mulled over how he could bring his daughter out of the house and lied instead, landing himself in a predicament.

"Your uncle is visiting and he wants to see you."

"He is?" His daughter seemed much taken aback. She remained speechless for a while then cast a suspicious sideway glance at him.

"Is that the reason you came all the way here?"

He suddenly felt a pang of conscience and struggled to support his lie.

"I had to stop by the provincial office and also find out how Wonshik is doing…it's been a while since I saw your in-laws, as well…"

As he put on his shoes, he mumbled, "You come with me."

"I'll come by tomorrow," she retorted, like she had no interest in her parents, as a way of getting back at her father who seemed to lack any concern for her and her husband. He advertently took time to put on his shoes to figure out a way to induce his daughter outside. The saying that once your daughter was married, she was no longer your family was no exaggeration. How despicable. Why did she not know that his success would benefit her greatly?

"Your uncle's leaving tomorrow morning. And there's something I must tell you," he said, straightening his back.

This time, he spoke with more authority to make sure he could get her out of the house. He left her house, without turning back, and took slow steps in anticipation of her catching up with him. When she showed no sign of showing up, he thought perhaps she was getting dressed and stopped off at the small store in the alley to bargain for the box of apples, just for the heck of it. Quite a while later, he waved at his daughter, who finally came out and was looking for him.

"Is that the only dress you have?" As they walked side by side, he antagonistically asked his daughter, who hadn't bothered to look presentable.

She, in turn, rebuked him, "Why, you want to marry me off again?"

"Actually, I need to send you on an errand," he spoke cautiously, so as not to antagonize her further.

"I won't go into detail, as you know about it already but wasn't the Director of Educational Affairs the former Chief of Accounting when you were working there? I can't think of any other connection besides him for me to be assured of a transfer to the city this time. Putting any stock in Won-shik's uncle, the chief secretary, will get me nowhere. I was a fool to think he could help us…Maybe when it's too late"

He stopped himself short, as it didn't feel proper to disrespect the relative of his son-in-law before his daughter. It was wise not to incense his daughter, whose nerves were probably already shot from caring for her husband with a lung disease.

"I heard the Director was very fond of you so maybe you can ask him for a favor. The reason why I lied earlier is that I didn't want you to get overly upset about visiting home, when you have enough concern with your husband and your own household. I want to send him a box of apples, although he's of course not there at present. I don't know if he has moved to an official residence but it's best to show your face to his wife during the day, and grab the chance to mention my name. There's no one else I can think of who can do this. He won't be able to turn you down. What's the address? How about if you come with me? I'll just show you where…What, you want to go by yourself? Suit yourself. He's at Sansu-dong, where the old residence for the provincial chief used to be. It's right there. Yes, that's how it is. Ha, I find it unbelievable that I have to try desperately to hold on to this job. What a fate. When could I stop living month-to-month? What's the point of rehashing the past—but with a letter of recommendation from the chief secretary, he could go back to the county job...What, a letter from his youngest son?

He stopped at the fruit and vegetable store. Bargaining for a box of apples nearly did him in. His daughter, who was used to her father's squabbling for a good price, stood by him and calmly advised him. The two of them were haggling for hundred *hwan* less or fifty *hwan* more.

"A gentleman like yourself quibbling for so little..." said the owner, spitting contemptuously.

"Who's talking? How can you hope to run good business with such an obstinate mind?" Clerk Wu frowned. He wanted to go to another store but his daughter stopped him, saying she would take care of it. He thought it over briefly and gave her the money, adding that they could easily get it for 1,500 *hwan* anywhere.

"I received a letter from Gyun. And guess what? He's asking me for the same favor as you, Father."

He read the letter she handed him, standing up in front of the store, and frowned deeply.

"What a thoughtless rascal he is. He wants to go to America to study? He doesn't want to see his father passing away? I told him to study for the higher civil servant exam and instead he has a preposterous plan in mind? He's asking your husband to get a letter of recommendation from the Minister of Education by way of the chief secretary Bae, right? It was only a short while ago that I asked you to visit the Ministry of Education, to get me a letter from the Minister. It doesn't matter to him that his father will become a pauper as long as he can go to America. I've taken care of him for twenty years and now he wants to get away. Even the crows will pay back its parents...Here I am, paying the price for providing him with a college education...Who does he think I am doing this for, arguing with contemptuous shopkeepers, to pinch pennies! It's all because of my children! How I have sweated blood to make sure my children can dress as well as others, to be sure to pay the tuition on time...when the others of his age are already making a living."

He railed against his son as though he had already left for America. According to what he'd heard, there was hardly an offspring of a high and distinguished official who did not go to America to study. He'd heard unless one has been to America, there was very little chance of having a successful career. It was something he, a low-ranking civil servant, couldn't even dream of. You either had to have money or power, neither of which he had, furthermore, he thought it was impossible to send his son abroad. Of course, he found out about this through his children, who came home over the vacation and talked about it endlessly, for he himself would have had no idea what it meant to go to America to study. He went beyond his means to send his children to college. Although he was openly rebuking his younger son before his daughter, he was stealthily very proud of him. The thought of his son going to America to make it easier to achieve success—was by no means a cause for his intervention, especially if he couldn't assist him. He felt inept as a parent. What a pity that his son had such an incapable parent…he thought and made a great resolve to make money. Wasn't there a way of having money drop from the heaven? Did he have to live a life, perennially athirst for money? What provoked him was that his son resorted to the same means of getting a letter of recommendation from the Minister of Education, saying that it was very useful for getting a scholarship to America, and taking care of the paperwork in South Korea. He told his daughter to take the box of apples to the director herself; meanwhile, he was going to stop off at the Provincial Office to meet the chief of personnel to request for the transfer of his eldest son. He asked her either to meet him at a coffee shop called "Academy" after dinner, or to come home right after her visit to let him know the result.

It was lunchtime and the chief of personnel could be out to lunch, and if not, since Clerk Wu didn't want to take him out, he went home and left at three. There were too many chores he had to take care of, for he hadn't been home in two weeks. He had to fix the gate, clean the pigsty, and repair the *ondol* underfloor heating in the room.

232

He spotted the chief of personnel walking toward him on his way to the Provincial Office.

"It's been a long time, sir." The chief greeted Clerk Wu first. Even though he was on his way to meet him, he pretended to be taken aback, so as not to lose his dignity before a man who used to be his underling, and to whom he had to importune a favor.

"So glad to run into you. I was going to pay you a visit one of these days. Do you have some time, Chief Park?"

"Why don't we talk as we walk?"

Then they simultaneously spotted the Director. Clerk Wu ran after the Director of the Education Committee. As though he'd completely forgotten about Chief Park, he stuck by him for a long time, trying to make conversation with a man who just kept walking. Clerk Wu barely managed to ask him whether he'd moved, and turned away with an empty heart. But he was not in the least slighted by the haughty manner of the man. He was simply proud to be acquainted with a man of such high ranking. In addition, he didn't know why. Even though he felt gratified with his humble status, he was completely different at home, belittling the Director, calling him a Commie, thus revealing his true nature. He had offered his hand, with a smile so big that he thought it might tear his jaw, when he brought him a truck full of logs on behalf of the Parent Teacher Association, however, he must've since then completely forgotten him.

Clerk Wu invited Chief Park to lunch, expecting him to turn it down and not much to his surprise, he had already eaten.

"Then let's have a cup of tea."

They went to "Academy" Coffee shop and he asked for an especially well prepared tea at the counter.

He broached the topic of his eldest son. Chief Park assured him that he himself would put in the request to the school commissioner. Clerk Wu said any school in the city would work, apologizing for asking such a burdensome favor without taking out the time to treat him to a cup of wine.

The waitress brought them two glasses of lemon juice. He tossed the straw and gulped down the juice, thinking of his youngest son, who naturally reminded him of his entire family, who choked him with worry about their livelihood. Although he cursed his youngest son as being the most worthless person in the world, he often bragged about him to others. It wasn't about how well he did in school or what a good boy he was but that he was going to be a lawyer or go to America and become successful—hence, letting them know that they should try to be nice to him and not power trip over him. Then again, he lamented over how he was unable to provide a better education for his children. In short, it was a prelude to his scheme to get his appeal through.

"You live off a salary like me, so you must know how difficult it is to support a family of six with fifteen thousand *hwan* a month. I can't steal like others or have an exceptional skill…I barely eke out a month-to-month living, yet I sent my children to college and one of them wants to go to America, and another is conscripted into the national army…It seems like I am here for lifelong hardship and then die. I have no enjoyment whatsoever in life…I am not a wealthy or powerful man, yet I am subject to all the pitfalls…I'm weak, so I can't work as a menial laborer. Nor can I go around begging, for my pride and dignity won't let me. I can't do sales because I'm not clever enough or have the capital. Chief Park, for whom do we live our life? We do all the dirty work for our superiors but instead of being rewarded, we are the ones who have to bear the burden when a new person takes office, unless we hang on to our job for dear life, we'll be thrown on the street, not to mention how we have to shamelessly kiss their ass. Even if we have to starve for a day, we must give them a present. That's not all. We have to wear a different suit for each season with our shirt collar kept white at all times…Chief Park, I should've resigned long before when I was demoted from my job at the Provincial Office to the school. I'm sure that's what they had in mind. But what do you think is the reason I'm doggedly holding on to this job? We don't have the strength to become a porter, nor do we own land to do farming. We're simply fated to go back and forth between schools. Ha, ha, ha. What else could it be but a school since I leave home with a lunchbox with my children and come home in the evening?"

"What a great pity that I have to work and live at a separate residence at an age that most people are spending their leisurely time with their grandchildren. Chief Park, I'm renting a small room because I can't afford a lodging house and for me to commute would affect my work quality, not to mention, how my body cannot bear it. So, to save even a little, I'm staying at a public employee housing. I don't have any other choice. Others must be impressed with me—that I'm supporting two of my children in college, one in high school, my second youngest daughter in Girls' School, and my youngest in primary school. They must think I'm leeching off the provincial government money with all the tuition and a decent life but they have no idea. Have they ever put rationed petroleum on their wife's head, and gone around the village bartering for rice or pepper in the dead of winter? Have they ploughed the land, sold the manure they made, or raised pigs and bred them? In addition, to save on delivery fees, have they ever carried a heavy load themselves or rolled plain grass on a piece of paper, and then stuck it in the "Legend" cigarette pack out of embarrassment? Still, there are rats who accuse me of stealing the government money, that I am pro-Japanese, and spreading slander that I belong to another party. Honestly, I don't have time to worry about all these things."

It was only after Chief Park excused himself that Clerk Wu stopped talking. As they left, he secretly hoped that Park would be quick enough to pay for the tea and walked behind him, who quietly left two hundred *hwan* on the counter and walked out. Surprised, he quickly groped in his pocket for the money.

"What? Two hundred *hwan!*"

He was too embarrassed to check the price again and hurriedly counted the ten-*hwan* bills, while it occurred to him he should return the two hundred *hwan* he snatched from the counter back to Chief Park.

But then he decided it wasn't proper to call out someone in the middle of the street to give him money. He was thinking perhaps he could invite him out to dinner, instead Chief Park, who was walking ahead of him, stopped to greet someone courteously. It was his daughter. He looked at both of them in surprise.

"Won-Shik and I are childhood friends," Park explained.

"Ah, I see. How remarkable that you and I worked at the same office and you're also old friends with my son-in-law. How about celebrating tonight? That way I can pay you back for earlier as well."

He turned to look at his daughter for her consent, as Chief Park declined the invitation, freeing his hand from Clerk Wu's grasp.

"How about a big one, next time?" He said with a grin and took off.

He was quiet dismayed that it seemed unclear as to who was going to benefit whom. In the end, it turned out to be an exchange of two hundred *hwan* with several ten *hwan*. Once, when he had lamented about his needy circumstances to a friend, he gave him some money.

He went back to the coffee shop with his daughter. She looked around the place in bewilderment, as though she'd never been to a place like it.

"So what happened?"

Before she could bring herself to say anything, he blurted out the question as soon as they were seated.

Instead of saying anything, she took out a business card.

"It's clearly his name on the card, but what does it say on the back?"

Clerk Wu quickly turned over the business card, worried that she might have delivered the box of apples to the wrong place. The business card did belong to the director, however, something strange was written on the back.

"Raju Middle School. XXX Vice-Principal. Would like to be promoted to Principal."

He smiled bitterly. He pensively gazed at his daughter, and then burst into laughter, as though he remembered something funny.

"It's quite possible that he gave you the business card intended for someone else. I've done that myself. But who gave you this? Some girl, you were told? You mean, you didn't go there yourself? Goodness. Are you sure it was the right house?"

He checked the business card once more.

"It's obviously the Director's card with his stamp on it. What did I tell you? What's so bothersome about going there yourself? You didn't want to see the old Chief of Accounting? Are you embarrassed? Ashamed that you don't have the right clothes?"

He furtively examined her attire and was much taken aback. She was dressed in shabby, dull clothes, and her expressionless pallid face went frighteningly hand in hand. But he thought now was not the time to ask her about it. First and foremost, he had to find out the result of her visit before being concerned about her wellbeing.

"Who did you ask?" He asked in a loud voice, as though to shake off his other thought.

"Ah, you ordered the store errand boy? The Director's wife was not home? So they haven't moved yet?"

"You must go tonight. Come home with me now. I have a roll of fine quality ramie cloth that you could bring to them. If you know his size, it might be a good idea to tailor it for him even. It's actually something I shouldn't give away as a present. A relative of a governor begged to work in the general affairs office and I really didn't want to, in light of how I contemned the old governor, but because he seemed so desperate, I went out of my way to hire him and he presented it to me with profuse gratitude. It doesn't look good to give away a gift as a gift but what can I do? We don't have the money."

"Do you think something like that will be effective?"

"I wouldn't know. It's up to them. In any event, we're showing our earnest effort. You say, it's meager but for me, I'm giving away something dear to me."

He had presented a gift worth twenty thousand *hwan* in the past for a job in the Department of Education but nothing had materialized.

He had never spent that big a sum in his life. Since then, he became fearful about bribing someone.

"Why did the Chief of Personnel ask me for such a favor if he is friends with your husband?"

His daughter gave him a blank look.

"He asked me to put in a good word for him to the chief secretary."

"He probably didn't know you're his father-in-law."

"That must be it. Because I never took note of it when you mentioned that your husband knew the Chief of Accounting or someone at the Provincial Office. If he pays a visit, put in a good word for me. You just wait and see. If things go well for me, that will benefit all of you. Do you know why I'm trying to get a transfer to the city? It's to save money. I'm telling only you but you'll find out what I mean when you become a parent yourself. Children today are completely forgetful of how they're someone's offspring. As for me, I realized it too early in my life, hence all my hardship. I've aged quickly, trying to fulfill all the obligations of a son, and now I'm trying my best to be a responsible father. Wait until you are a parent. You'll find out how difficult it is to be a dutiful mother."

He stopped talking only when they reached his house. He brought out the roll of ramie cloth and wrapped it with leftover wallpaper. His daughter watched him write down on the paper the name of the Director of the Education Department.

"I wish you'd ask my younger siblings," she said.

Startled, he put down the brush.

"If it weren't for you, I wouldn't think of giving this. As you said, you think he'll bat an eye with something like this? But because you worked for him and he was fond of you, he might find it difficult to turn you down."

He then muttered to himself, "He might listen to a woman he liked…"

His daughter's face turned pale and she glared at him.

"You're so base, father. I never knew how corrupt you could be. You are plotting to take advantage of me." She turned around and covered her face.

Clerk Wu gazed at his daughter in silence for a while and said, "Yes, I'm plotting to take advantage of you. Plotting? That's right! What're you going to do about it? It is a sin for a father to put his daughter to some use? It's too unjust if a father—who has supported his daughter for twenty years—cannot use his daughter even once. As you said, I might be corrupt. But I don't think so. How can I be corrupt when I'm not doing anything against my conscience? Well then, should I just sit back and do nothing? Then who's going to support the family?"

He abruptly stopped himself, as he didn't want to wreck his plan tonight. He picked up the wrapped ramie cloth and walked out. It wasn't difficult to understand his daughter. But his eyes welled up as he thought of his pitiful life and his daughter's fatigued face. Why is my life so wearisome? It was so cruel that both he and his children were subject to an unfortunate life. He didn't believe in God, however, in the course of experiencing a great deal of chaos, he adapted a conviction that was like his faith—that as long as he didn't harass anyone or did anything against his conscience, things would go all right. But that didn't mean he lived a good life. In fact, following his conscience didn't warrant a decent life. Not obeying his conscience and becoming wealthy were entirely different matters. But then, his daughter told him how debauched he was. He was shaking as he felt a part of him breaking down.

Then he heard his daughter dragging her shoes behind him, and somehow felt better. Although she told him to go home, he went with her to the Director's house, afraid that she might ask someone else, like earlier in the day. He also wanted to know the outcome as soon as possible. From afar, he watched his daughter enter and took out a cigarette. He walked to and from in the dim and grey moonlight. The smoke from his cigarette vanished into the misty shade of the moon.

239

The Director must have been in office when his daughter worked in the accounting department. Was he a little over forty years old? He was only ten years younger than him. Was I inept? Not personable enough? Was he enamored with his daughter? It's possible. Was that why she resisted going to him? It seemed obvious. No use thinking about it. He tried to think of a place to rest while he waited for his daughter, and came up with Suncheon House, which hadn't been on his mind for a long time. He was against drinking. As a young man, he drank heavily but he quit to save money. The Suncheon House was a meaningful place for him in that he met his first mistress there. The proprietress happened to be a widower. He felt burdened enough with his own family, and didn't dream of keeping a mistress. But he had seen many of his friends in relationships with widowers running a pub, and since the proprietress of the Suncheon House liked him, he decided, why not save some money? His wife, instead of protesting or being jealous, encouraged him if it meant making some extra money. But she had a son who was unbelievably tyrannical and he was lucky not to get beaten to a pulp by him.

He entered the Suncheon House to see only new faces. He ordered a cheap drink, as he couldn't just walk out. His conscience, which was wavering earlier, no longer shook, instead his body trembled. He saw his daughter walking toward him. He wanted to yell out to her with gladness.

"So how did it go?"

She seemed taken aback that he was still there, waiting for her. He was happy to see she looked a little more cheerful than before.

"He was surprised to see me. He told me I was a good daughter to pay him a visit on your behalf."

"I'm sure he was taken aback I had a daughter like you."

The Director told her that he'd make a good effort to get him a transfer to the city, and invited her to visit him again. He lost his wife during the Korean War and now lived with his daughter and the housemaid.

"Do that. It's a good idea to go see him in your free time."

"He asked me if I'm still unmarried." She told him, looking affronted. He gave no response, as he had to make sure not to get her unnerved.

He groped his way back in the dark after he sent his daughter back home.

His eldest son was snoring away in the middle of the room, reeking of alcohol. He was so upset that he could've thrown up the wine he drank earlier. He was all prepared to brag about himself at home. But how could he talk to a drunken brat who was dozing away in the middle of the room? He was going to show off how just a few words by him was going to get his son a transfer to the city by those who would only pay attention to the likes of an assemblyman or if not scoff at you unless you offered a bundle of money. He wanted to show his son how he was not just an ordinary man, and that his children couldn't dream of seeking that kind of person out at the Department of Education. Some people created brouhaha over how they spent over tens of thousands, if not several sacks of rice, to shift to a downtown job, and they still couldn't.

He was all prepared to gloat but there was no one with whom he could share his glory. He felt his heart sinking to the bottomless pit. His attempt to obliterate the agony on account of his daughter, and the insult he suffered from the director were for naught. How was he going to bear this feeling of desolation?

"I must be out of my mind to request for a transfer on your behalf." He groaned and kicked his son's shoulder.

"Father, can I come back to the city? Father, I punched the principal today. He claimed, I was corrupting the public morale, dating a female teacher. Father, I'm not worrying about a thing since you'll take care of everything."

"You punched the principal? You'll be fired in no time for striking your superior. You bastard! Who're you trying to drive nuts? If you're kicked out of school, that's the end of your job."

"Don't worry. I'm going to be promoted to a principal for hitting him."

"You've gone completely crazy. I was wondering why you were home so early but you crawled back after getting fired. What? You'll be sent to a branch school? Ha, since you'll be the only one there, you can be the principal and the clerk."

Clerk Wu was greatly worried. He came out of house, not wanting to be with his son. He went to the pigsty and mixed the chaff with water to feed the pigs, and then he was going to chop the wood, however, it was already getting dark. Instead, he decided to plough the tiny plot in the back of the house with a small shovel. He thought children were like spider babies that feed on the mother spider. He ploughed the earth with the spider on his mind.

2.

Although he had a busy workload for the weekend, Clerk Wu was eager to find out about his transfer and his son's status, and hurriedly took the bus home as soon as he finished work on Saturday. His younger son, who was noisily reading the newspaper with a Chinese character dictionary at hand, muttered to himself, "Reduction of Civil Servants."

It instantly alarmed him, as he was undressing. He asked his son to read aloud the article, however, his son complained that there were too many Chinese characters. He angrily snatched the paper from him and straightened his glasses.

"The reduction of public staff members, which was discussed as a solution for the streamlining of the government administrative system and the improvement of working conditions for the civil servants, will finally take place. Yet, there is a big controversy over how the government will resolve the problem of the livelihoods of the 30,000 laid-off people and their families. Meanwhile, the government has instructed the affiliated institutes to consider carefully the age factor and the delinquent workers as candidates for the layoff."

He was reminded of his age and he was sure he'd be one of the staff to be laid off, for there was no need for someone who was old and frail like him.

He summoned his wife and asked her if she'd heard anything from their daughter. He wanted to find out if she had met the Director again in the interim. His wife had no news for him. His despicable daughter had not visited the Director again. He ate quickly and went to her.

She had no idea how much he wanted her to seek out the Director again. Wasn't he all by himself after he was widowed? He might even try to become intimate with his daughter, believing she was unmarried. But then, what should they do if he ended up proposing to her? I'll remain oblivious until I am transferred to the city. But the thought frightened him all of a sudden. If the Director had any decency, he would not harbor such a wanton thought and his daughter was anything but an immoral woman; if anything, she was an overly devoted wife—it was clear he was the frivolous and brazen one, and he felt comforted thinking this way. But then, reading about the layoff in the evening newspaper and no news from his daughter made him feel nauseated at God knows what.

He rushed to his daughter's house and dragged her out. She followed without saying anything. He took her to the Academy coffee shop, even though she wanted to go elsewhere.

"You read the paper?" he asked as soon as they were seated. She instead gave him an inquiring look.

"I'll most likely have to give up even my current post."

He asked the waitress for the newspaper and shoved it in front of his daughter. She began reading, showing no emotion.

"How many times have you visited the Director?" He asked with a sneering tone.

"Not once? I didn't want to say this but you must think you're not part of the family anymore now that you're married? Is it so difficult to go see him once? You'd rather see me demoted?"

He checked her mood, as his words were a bit too harsh. She took her eyes off the newspaper and turned to her father.

"I don't want to," she retorted without flinching.

"I understand why you wouldn't want to but you must bear it and do this for me."

"I still don't want to. And I think you're callous to ask me when you know why I don't want to."

"Callous? I don't think I am callous or shameless. Just do as I say. I am ordering you. I don't need to hear any excuse. What will happen to our family of eight if I get laid off?"

"I did go see him. But I don't want to go again."

"You did? What do you mean you saw him but you don't want to anymore? He's lewd? He is lustful toward you? Is there an indication?"

It was incredulous how his misgivings turned out to be reality.

"You can't blame him. He believes you're unmarried so doesn't give a damn—although it's a shame he actually considers you as his second wife."

"Father, you've become so cowardly."

"Be quiet and pay him another visit tomorrow. He's my only hope and I can't let go of it."

Clerk Wu didn't want to say anything more. He was afraid of what his daughter might tell him, not to mention, how his heart felt unsettled. He thought he wouldn't be able to do anything if he tried to think about it too deeply.

As he was about to get up, he asked her, "How many times did you go see him?"

His daughter did not bother to conceal her annoyance.

"I'm meeting him here today."

"Ah, that's why you didn't want to come here."

"He's ordered me to come."

It was fortuitous that he brought her to the coffee shop. He was debating whether or not he should tell her to pretend she was unmarried for a few days when she suddenly got up to leave. The words were on the tip of his tongue; however, he couldn't bring himself to say it. He was going to order tea to detain his daughter for a meeting with the Director who came walking toward them after seeing her rise. Surprised, he got up and took a few steps, and with utmost politeness, extended his hand to him. The Director, who was all smiles, motioned for them to sit down.

Clerk Wu looked at the smiley face of the Director with wonder and when it dawned on him he was mirroring his own smiling face, he closed his eyes. His heart was shaking and he felt dizzy. He was afraid to look at his daughter. He left the coffee shop like a fugitive. The chilly air of the night cooled down his sweaty face. The shadow that was dragged around his feet grew bigger and bigger like a goblin. He did not want to look back.

3.

The Chief of Personnel had called him. Like a nervous student awaiting the score of an entrance exam, he asked the clerk, hoping it was about his transfer but was just told there would be an important announcement and that he should come in. An important announcement could only be about his transfer and he was on edge to find out. He couldn't sit still for the anxiety of knowing how a major layoff was going on at the moment. But now was the right time to seize the opportunity for a desirable position. However, the Chief of Personnel was by no means a trustworthy man. He could tell by how he handled his eldest son's transfer. He had asked for a post in the urban area, but he was assigned to a place fifteen kilometers from downtown where neither commuting nor lodging was ideal. He received the call in the midst of his displeasure. But he couldn't blame him only because if they hear about his son's misbehavior, he'd have been hard pressed to keep his current position. In this context, he was enormously grateful to the Chief of Personnel. In any event, it was not easy for him to cut out of work early on a Thursday. He gave the seal to the clerk and instructed him to take care of any urgent documents during his absence, and hurriedly took off.

He was told the letter of recommendation was sent from Seoul. He felt like leaping with joy. That's the reason the Chief of Personnel called me, he thought. He'll ask what position I have in mind and I'll sit back and be picky this time. He told his wife he'd eat dinner when he returned and went straight to his daughter's house. Since it wasn't yet five o'clock, he could see the Chief of Personnel if he went to the Provincial Office. He stopped off at the office first, arranged to meet at Academy Coffee Shop at six o'clock, and headed to his daughter's house.

"How did he get the urge to write the letter? What? You asked him? You'd rather do that than meet the Director? In any case, how fortunate. We'll see what happens now. You are gratified to know how the Director will react to the insignia of the Minister of Education?"

His conscience pricked at what his daughter said. He had been outwitted by her. But it pleased him greatly. As she did not want to see the Director and disdained his authority, she decided to take it in her own hands and write the secretary general.

"I know it benefits me too, to reach a compromise with you, Father," she said with a meaningful smile.

"Are you sneering? But of course, of course. As a matter of fact, it will be of great benefit to you. If I do well, you'll all do well."

He asked her to accompany him but she declined, saying it might be problematic to see the Chief of Personnel.

He was already seated when Clerk Wu walked into the coffee shop.

"I asked to see you because of an important matter relevant to you."

He was about to tell him about the letter of recommendation but stopped short for he didn't want the Chief of Personnel to inquire about his own favor.

"What? I'm on the list of the layoff? You mean anyone over the age of fifty will be sacked?"

His mind turned blank.

"That means I'll be discharged… You wanted to let me know in advance? Thank you."

He was praying that it was untrue. What will happen to him if he is deprived of even his current position? He hadn't heard he was going to be laid off until now. His last hope was the letter from the Minister of Education. What would the Chief of Personnel say if finds out about the letter of recommendation? If he were to triumphantly proclaim it, then he would surely be astounded. But what if he were unimpressed by it? The thought scared him.

He straightened up and said, leaning his head against the corner of the chair, "But they couldn't possibly kick…" He closed his eyes, with a scornful smile that remained on the edge of his lips.

"…me out, I earnestly hope." He finished the sentence.

The Chief of Personnel looked at him with a sudden burst of cheerfulness.

"How about a letter of recommendation from the Minister of Education?" Clerk Wu said, opening his eyes.

"In fact, the Director must've got it by now."

"He showed no sign of it. Anyway, it's of no use now."

He trembled as though he'd been given a sentence.

"It's not?"

"Yes, it's too late."

"There is a position available? In the District of Education?"

The Chief of Personnel advised him to spend fifty thousand *hwan* for a managerial administrative position at the District of Education, that is, to give that money to the school commissioner, adding that was the last thing he could help him with. The District of Education was an unreliable place that was in danger of being abolished. It was also preposterous for him to suggest that he give that much money to someone he didn't even know. It was also not an easy thing to come with fifty thousand *hwan*.

The Chief of Personnel asked Wu, who looked pensive, what happened to his request, that he, too, was likely to be sacked in the layoff, and that he should find a solution as soon as possible.

"Is he in the same boat as me?" Wu muttered to himself and was convinced that the letter would resolve his problem. That is, he thought, why the Chief of Personnel was being magnanimous toward him. After all, wasn't he appealing to him for a favor also? He told him that he would try his best to help him but pondered about his choices.

Wu was walking aimlessly. What would he do if he had no job? He would be at a complete loss as to what to do. He thought of other things he could do. There didn't seem to be any. If he had a special skill like other people, that would be one thing, however, he had been doing only clerical work for thirty years. How about working at a scrivener's office? He had originally wanted to study law and as this was the only place where he would use his skill, it seemed the most appropriate place for him. But didn't he need a license right away? Moreover, it wasn't profitable work unless one passed the exam.

He found himself exhausted when he got home. As he was about to eat, his younger son told him that the appointment of the Clerk had been announced. He was terribly startled.

"Bring me the newspaper quickly. Do you see my name? What, it's not on the list? What do you mean? Bring me the paper. Which newspaper is it? *Dong-a Daily*? What did I tell you? You have to look at the local newspaper if you want the news of this town. Was it your older brother who changed our subscription when he came home on a break, saying how we should learn about world affairs and culture? Anyway, where did you see it? Go borrow the paper? There isn't a family who reads the newspaper around here? Ha. How frustrating. Go get it no matter how far you have to go. So that's what the Chief of Personnel was getting at."

He lamented over how he had been clueless to it. The whole family was going around getting a newspaper when his eldest son sauntered in. He felt like smothering him.

"The spider babies. The spider babies," he was chanting it like a prayer.

"It's always only me who is the victim. What to make of it? The son of a mason has become too successful for his means."

He read aloud the borrowed newspaper by the candlelight like a funeral oration and sobbed.

It was now out of question for his third son going abroad to study. His eldest son getting a transfer to downtown was also not going to happen. Furthermore, if he were to get into trouble again, that would be the end of it because there'd be no one to help. It was best to marry your daughter off to a wealthy family. He wished wistfully that he should've had her marry the Director. I must survive to the best of my ability—even it meant sacrificing all that I have.

The Evader

With a poncho over them, the recruits were charging like a herd of animals until their steps came to a halt by a statue of "the unknown soldier" that caught their vision. The summer rain was pouring on the torso of the statue that was standing at the plaza in front of the army boot camp gate. Its chest was bare and it was holding a torch high up. As though the rain signified the sweat these seven hundred recruits had to shed in the following six weeks, Dong-weon, amidst the rain drizzling down his poncho, was reminded of the Statue of Liberty at the misty New York City harbor. At the same time, the seven years he spent at Columbia University—where he had deemed this goddess of liberty as an academic symbol and religious faith—flashed across his mind. But the command of the senior sergeant in charge at that moment, to march in step while calling out "one, two, one, two," sucked him back into the group along the road that was impeccably lined with poplar trees that had grown just tall enough to cast a shade.

The ID card, which was muddied when he dropped it while peeing, remained sweaty in his hand during his trip from the boot camp to this place. As he marched to the count, he was wondering if there were as much of a difference between him of the past and the present as there was between the Statue of Liberty and the statue of the Unknown Soldier. To the right, where there was a wide and flat field sunken in water, and to the left where the regiment CP barrack that was more uniformly sized and aligned than the housing for the poor built by the government, the path extended for several hundred yards to the traffic circle where the memorial stone was. A couple of hundred robust young men, who were screened out from the boot camp, were

250

led out of the gate by a thin and sharp-looking captain whose glasses covered most of his face to the second compound, which was XX regiment, Y squadron.

After the completion of the general background check in the rain, the organizing of the platoons took place. Three groups were formed in accordance with the level of education, college and beyond, middle school and beyond, primary school and below, and then placed proportionately to the four platoons. Since there were four people who had graduate degrees, each one was allocated to a platoon. The senior sergeant from each platoon stood a certain distance apart from each other and Lieutenant Choi, the aide-de-camp of the squadron, had the four men go stand before one of the senior sergeants. Next, like he was cutting up paper, he divided up the rows of men into four with his baton. Since Dong-weon had a graduate degree, he was allowed several seconds to freely choose a senior sergeant. He took a quick glance at the four men and stood before a man with a yellow and expressionless face. He was not wearing a raincoat and just gazed up at the sky, as though he had no interest in the recruits. Dong-weon had no idea why this guy appealed to him. Was it because of a vague hope that he could elicit some sort of empathy from the man who looked like he had freed himself from worldly matters? But when he actually saw the name on his tag, he felt shivers run through his whole body. Coupled with a commonplace but brutal sounding name of Eok-su, his fearsome and wretched service number "03" perhaps elicited some kind of terror in him. In any event, his choice settled the fate of the fifty members of the third platoon for the next six weeks.

When the platoons were all formed, the senior sergeant with his expressionless face led the group into the barracks. Once again, four squads were made according to the educational level. They were then given a service number. Dong-weon was given number 112. Then the uniforms, imbued with the toil and sweat that had belonged to previous recruits, were distributed to them—the raggedy work and military uniforms that must have been worn by many bodies and the spoons that must have been in several hundred mouths. The senior sergeant ordered everyone to toss everything that they wanted saved to ship home in the aisle. He then told them to wrap their personal belongings and the remaining clothes in the way he prescribed. Dong-weon discarded all but his belt and stalled, as he didn't want to send his paraphernalia home.

The senior sergeant came toward him and mercilessly whacked his shaved head with the baton. Rather than being in pain, Dong-weon was dazed. He crashed into the basin where his things were. He heard the aspirin, guanidine, and stomachic pills crack in the basin. The senior sergeant ordered him to show what was in the basin. He took an absent look at the pills and the shaving kit, and then shoved them to the aisle with his baton. Propelled by his action, Dong-weon tossed the belt he had left on the floor to the aisle. But then the senior sergeant ordered him to save it for the homebound pack. He couldn't know that the belt was a gift from Hwa-yeung when she visited him in Geneva where he was studying. He sent the belt to her. Fifty some recruits, with their very short army haircut, gazed down at the discarded clothes, the shell of their past with their many life stories.

When they were done putting away their army stuff in the stand, the senior sergeant lined up the members of the platoon and gave the following greeting.

"I am Sergeant Yi Eok-su of the Third Platoon. With my deputy, Corporal Kim, we will go through together six weeks of life and death. From this point on, you are a soldier. You must not forget that. In the course of training several thousand recruits right here in the barracks for the past three years, I have mastered the way of dealing with men. That is to say, I have acquired an eye to see through even a man's innards. I like no one. That is how I treat men. That's all."

In the afternoon, the rifle-receiving ceremony from the commander himself took place before the company unit. The rifle was to be deemed like a girlfriend. The recruits gingerly positioned the rifle in the stand and strove to memorize their girlfriend's name, the number of the rifle. The training program chart on the wall showed how rigorous and tiring this romance was going to be.

It rained all week. After two four-hour long close order drills in the morning and afternoon for a group of two hundred in the barracks, everyone ended up dog-tired, with their nerves completely shot having to cope with sleepiness and a mix-up of boots.

During the mealtime, each person had to go out and capture twenty flies. But it was rainy season and even if one sat on the poop container with a fly swatter, the mission was difficult. Dong-weon, who was the squad leader, couldn't help but buy a couple bottles of soda pop and set out on the adventure of taking the empty bottles to a civilian over the fence to buy the flies, while avoiding the watchful guard. But he lacked the courage to do it himself and ordered Yeom, a thug from Majang-dong, Seoul. That evening, the senior sergeant required the squad leaders to collect all the flies and bring them to him. Dong-weon presented more than hundred flies that he purchased to the senior and deputy sergeants.

But the senior sergeant let out a scream, scattering the flies on Dong-weon's face and demanded that he go out and catch them within ten minutes. How was he to capture them on a dark rainy night? But his squad had to go out no matter what. They came back, after loitering and being rained on outside. Of course, they had not caught a single fly.

The senior sergeant gave a command to the lined-up squad members to do push-up on their fists and said, "I ordered you to go and catch flies, not pay money to get them. That might work elsewhere but here. If I say, catch them, that is what you must do. The flies are of no importance to me. It is the means by which you capture them. If there are no flies, then you must create them, even if you have to use matchsticks to make it. But the flies you bought are not from here. They are from outside."

Although he was provoked, his voice remained even-toned, chilly, and resonant throughout.

The first week passed in a flash. The week in Dong-weon's pocket diary remained blank and sweat-ridden. He did not see Hwa-yeung in his dreams; perhaps she sensed he did not have the leisure to see her even in a dream. Come to think it, it was peculiar that he had not heard from her. Did her father's work get complicated? As a member of the Liberal Party, he did not take up an important position but since the Jang Myeon administration and until the revolutionary government took shape, his name was always on the list of corrupt politicians for he had accrued wealth after taking over a number of large companies. Dong-weon could not help being worried; however, there was no way of finding out for he had no access to any newspaper.

In the second week of training, the first stage of the Preliminary Rifle Instruction began, also known as the time of the illicit romance with the rifle. The monsoon was over and the sultry days with the temperature rising above 30 degrees Celsius continued. It was over two kilometers from the barracks to the first stage Preliminary Rifle Instruction (PRI) site. Sergeant Yi was the man in charge today. After lunch, during an hour-long break they were panting away in the tiny shade of the mulberry tree when the warning siren blew. Training had to be suspended when the temperature reached above 33 degrees Celsius. The recruits, who had collapsed in total exhaustion, gave out a joyful scream. Under Sergeant Yi's supervision, the company headed, with their flag, toward the barracks. The line was somewhat disorderly, perhaps because of the weather or the excitement over the siren. Sergeant Yi ordered them to march to the count but when it was in discord, he made them sing the song of the recruits. But their voices were weak and unharmonious. Then he hollered, "Present Arms!" The recruits became more drained. He had them run again. After marching to the count and walking backward a few dozen times in the same spot, the squad was gasping with their tongue hanging loose. It took an hour before they arrived at the company barrack. But they still had to maintain "Present Arms" and run. A recruit, who keeled over holding on to his rifle, was dragged away. Dong-weon, too, felt like he was going to pass out any second. Sergeant Yi smashed his arm with his baton. His rifle rolled on the ground. He felt dizzy. He picked up the rifle with all his might. Right then the senior sergeant ruthlessly kicked his Achilles' tendon and he fell over. But the senior sergeant tramped on his back with even more brute force.

"You SOB shirkers! Can't you hold your rifle straight! I can tell how deranged your mind is by the way you hold your rifle. I shall straighten you out."

It wasn't until around sunset that Dong-weon found himself lying in the barracks with a cold towel over his forehead. The senior sergeant entered, and after casting a quick glance around, he directed his gaze at Dong-weon.

"Why is it so disorderly? Which squad is in charge of cleaning?"

In panic, Dong-weon got up, "It's the third squad."

Without turning back, and as though relaying someone's message, Sergeant Yi ordered him to clean up and report in ten minutes. Together with the squad members, Dong-weon, enduring the dizziness, mopped the floor, messy from dinner. The senior sergeant, who was inspecting the clean-up job, picked out pieces of bone and kernels of rice between the planks of the floor near Dong-weon's spot.

"Is this how you clean? All of you, line up. You have disobeyed my order to clean."

Dong-weon lined up the squad members. The senior sergeant ordered them each to lick up the garbage, one by one.

That night, the squad leaders called a meeting. According to Hwang, who enlisted after he was sacked from a bank for not having fulfilled his military duty, it was for money that the senior sergeant was treating them so brutally. The other leaders were in agreement. Dong-weon could only but agree, for he lacked the criteria with which to judge him. If it had to do with money, then by all means, they should just give it to him. They all pitched in 2,500 *hwan* and put ten-thousand *hwan* in the pocket of the senior sergeant who was asleep. Hwang asserted since he was a clever guy, the senior sergeant would instantly figure out where the money came from and as a morphine shot would for an addict, he would be pacified. Dong-weon prayed that is what would happen.

The next day was Sunday. But the senior sergeant did not go out. A several hour-long break was given after the mopping and weapon cleaning. This was when he mobilized them in the barracks. For the first time, he had on what looked like a cynical smile on his face. Hwang, who was standing before him, looked assured.

He gave an alternate glance at Hwang and Dong-weon and spoke as though he was delivering someone else's words.

"Soldier No. 111 has a doctoral degree in political science, I hear? In any event, he's a doctor corporal."

Dong-weon was completely taken aback. How did the news spread? But then, how could he be astonished and thrilled at the same time? Rather than being glad that your secret source of pride has been undisclosed, it was more like being elated that it has become known to the other but not in a base way, and hence anticipating slightly better treatment to be forthcoming. But who could warrant that it wasn't like exposing the secret place of a treasure to a thief or the puerility of bragging about one's expensive clothes to your friends? Dong-weon almost asked him how he had found out when the senior sergeant spoke first.

"The entire company knows about it. In addition, No. 96, Hwang, you have influential connections, I see. The personnel director seems to know you."

Hwang could not help but put on a triumphant smile, as though he was thinking, "Be careful with who you're dealing with."

"Although it was not Christmas, someone left me a present last night. I know well it is your deed. Could someone with a doctoral degree be so childish? You might be well versed in the academics but you have much to learn about a man. You are all like immature children. Do you remember what I said when we first met? I don't like people. Absolutely. I despise the likes of you. Do you know why I view the army as my calling? That's because the military is an organization to my appealing. It is an ideal place where you can torment people to the extreme. This is a place where you can punish the innocent, where you can live in disregard of money."

The senior sergeant muttered on like a soliloquy, and then took out the sheaf of bills totaling ten thousand *hwan*, shredding them to pieces. Dong-weon, ashen-faced, gazed at the fragments of money scattering in the air. It created the illusion of the pages from his cherished book, *Politics Among Nations* by Hans Morgenthau being torn up. Could Harold J. Laski's *The State in Theory* have embraced this anonymous sergeant's malicious invective?

A day before the sixth stage PRI Test, the recruits were reviewing the entire stages from PRI 1 to 5 by the poplar trees in the old visitation place. While practicing the rifle site adjustment as he was being taught by Choi, the first lieutenant, Dong-weon's mind was wandering. Why haven't I heard from Hwa-yeung? I've written her five times already but why has she not responded? They must undergo censorship. Or perhaps the term soldiers snatched them to read among themselves, for the letters were from a woman.

It was amidst these thoughts that he saw a jeep, stirring dust, driving toward the main building of the platoon. But inside the jeep was a girl in a bright dress with her permed hair blowing in the wind. Doubting what he saw, Dong-weon was about to rise when he was brought to his senses by Lieutenant's Choi.

"Number 121, what are the specifications of a rifle?"

"Yes, Recruit. Park Dong-weon. The specifications of a rifle are the…mark which…" He couldn't quite remember the right word and Lieutenant Choi retorted in a derisive tone, "I'm sure you know it in English."

"Yes, I do. It's scale. Scale." Dong-weon repeated to himself, while thinking of the girl earlier. Who could be the girl coming to this region forbidden to women? He was engrossed in these thoughts when the personnel chief approached Lieutenant Choi and exchanged some words. He then asked the recruits if there was anyone who whistled at the young woman in the jeep that drove past them earlier.

"We didn't even see the jeep," said one of them.

Right away, Lieutenant Choi took the cue and asked, "Did anyone see the jeep at all?" Before anyone could say anything, he turned to the personnel chief and replied himself. "There isn't anyone from our platoon who saw the jeep, let alone who whistled."

In a loud voice that everyone could hear, the personnel chief informed Lieutenant Choi that the major-general and his daughter drove past their way in a jeep, that he heard a recruit whistling from the nearby and consequently made a personal call to the colonel of the regiment and instructed him to impose proper discipline, which enraged the colonel who ordered the training of all recruits in the regiment and to mobilize everyone at the training ground.

With a sour smile, Lieutenant Choi argued that his platoon was in the middle of training when the jeep drove past, and hence there couldn't be anyone who could've whistled then, while giving a logical explanation that his training time ran over to the break time, whereas the other platoons were on a break and hence if anyone blew a whistle, it must be a recruit from the other groups. The personnel chief told him to gather everyone anyway at the training ground immediately, and walked away to the other platoon in training on the other side.

Dong-weon knew he wasn't the only one who saw the jeep. He was sure that Lieutenant Choi saw it also and like he said, it was certain that no one from his platoon whistled. But his cunning to pretend not to have seen the woman to avoid being punished was not surprising but laughable.

The troops from all twelve platoons filled the training ground. The colonel made three squads, who were in training, line up their arms a length apart, while all the regular enlisted men of these squads had to stand in a row before him; then the recruits were ordered to hold their rifle up with both arms and the personnel chief was instructed to beat them with a club ten times.

258

Several minutes passed. Dong-weon's arms felt numb. He felt the pool of sweat in his palms slide down the arm into his sleeve and he twisted his arm. The company leader struck his arm with the baton. The deputy chief of staff's high-pitched voice was heard then.

"Did anyone whistle? There should at least be someone who saw the jeep?"

But there was no response, only the faces that were contorted with pain.

"Anyone who saw the jeep, step forward." Right then, the chief of personnel spoke, adding weight to what the chief of staff said.

Dong-weon stepped forward to the podium in spite of himself. But the recruits were not free or had the leisure to look at him. They were all burdened with their own weight and hence were unable to pay attention to something other than themselves. The chief of staff cast a look of pity on Dong-weon, like he was a sacrificial prey before the altar, and then shouted at the recruits again.

"There has to be more than one person. All of you saw it. And this is an outright act of disrespect for your superior."

Then he turned to Dong-weon and said, "You're lying. Go back."

There was moaning from all sides. About thirty minutes had passed. Then another clown presented himself, one who confessed that he was the one who whistled. But the chief of staff would not condone his sacrifice either.

How did he get entangled in this foolish game, which resembled a drill in a primary school? Did he think it was impossible to act like a grown-up amidst a group of children? But by no means did he feel that his willingness to be a clown was derived from this kind of abstract thinking. Can an abstract move be allowed on this heartless board game of minutiae? He could only conclude his fixation with the undeniable fact he'd seen the jeep, which made obvious the obsession that he could not bear the physical pain. He wanted to include a romantic take in which he was perhaps hallucinating that the girl in the jeep was

259

perhaps Hwa-yeung. This was perfectly valid from the psychoanalytical perspective.

That night there was weapons training. The recruits were in a nerve-racking state before the PR State 6 shooting test the next day. Only those who passed the inspection of the senior sergeant were allowed to have a break. Dong-weon, with a flood of sweat running down his forehead, brought the M1 rifle before the senior sergeant who violently snatched it from him. He took it under the light bulb and looked through the muzzle, after he placed a white piece of paper against the powder chamber.

"Your mental state is filthy," he said and thrust it against Dong-weon's chest. He felt sickeningly dizzy for a moment.

"Your eyes are rotten. That is why you can't see the dust in the muzzle." As though he felt righteous indignation by his own words, the senior sergeant suddenly slapped Dong-weon on the cheek, which set off his agitation even more, for he began to thrash Dong-weon's face and chest. But he did not kick Dong-weon's legs for he knew he wouldn't be able to move from the beating in the afternoon.

"What made you step forward? Did you want to be a hero? What, a humanist? Stop being stupid. Compared to you, the one who claimed to have whistled is a better humanist—his intention was to sacrifice to protect his several thousand fellow soldiers. Rather an impressive sight, it was. You think your sacrifice can undo their suffering? Not at all. The hypocrisy of the so-called the educated makes me nauseated."

How was he to build a bridge of understanding when there was outrush of rage between them? The senior sergeant and Dong-weon were only a finger length apart; however, there was a wide river that seemed impossible to cross. No matter how much Dong-weon cried out from his side of the riverbank that they thought similarly, the sound of the ferocious flow of water swallowed up his voice. What was the make-up of this flow? Was it the stratum of concepts formed by their upbringing and background? If the statue of the Unknown Soldier could represent the senior sergeant, then the Statue of Liberty could perhaps symbolize him.

Dong-weon collapsed on the floor, throwing up a glob of blood.

The bruise on his face was still there in the fourth week of training. Around then, there was an incident of the senior sergeant being attacked in the middle of the night when he was going to the bathroom in his underpants. Yeom from Majangdong, Seoul, under Hwang's directive, hid in the bushes and committed the violent act. Except for the three men involved and Dong-weon, no one else knew about it. No doubt, they must have felt a sense of indignation commonly seen in thugs, after witnessing how Dong-weon was unjustly beaten up but in truth, it was more convincing to view it as an explosion of their pent-up rage. Although the senior sergeant was battered to the point of being unable to walk without the help of a cane, by Yeom who was known to have a black belt in the martial arts, he did not utter a word about it. If anyone asked him how he got so injured, all he said was, "It's the terrorism of the humanists." Dong-weon knew well what that meant.

One day into the fourth week, when they had neared the end, Dong-weon, who was practicing throwing the grenade amidst nasty rain, received out of the blue a summons from the Military Law Society. He was invited to attend a symposium on the hermeneutics of the anti-Communist law. Dong-weon knew who was responsible for this.

Dong-weon was touched to know his friend from high school, Captain Yun, who was at present working as a judicial officer at the Military Law Society, had most likely devised a last resort measure to provide him a day's rest. He was not so obstinate as to turn down the kindness that a judicial officer could bestow on him in violation of the letter of the law from the realm of his authority. Carrying upside down his M1 rifle that was all mud, he followed the regular enlisted soldiers back to the company building, dragging his poncho that was dripping with rain, sweat, and mud. He was told to change his clothes. Although it was sweat-ridden rag, he put on the dry khaki uniform and went to the Military Law Society. When he entered after saluting, Captain Yun quickly got up, as though he'd been waiting and with a faint smile, he quietly led him into a rear room for the overnight staff.

To his great surprise, Dong-weon saw Hwa-yeung crouched on the wooden floor. Their eyes crossed simultaneously—their gaze intertwined with awe, sweetness, and excitement. Her eyes were welling up with tears. Why did the signs of emotion have to show so soon? And not after their feelings toward each other have waned somewhat?

"Why did you not write me at all?"

"Speak for yourself."

"You didn't receive my letters?"

"Mine, either?"

"I got a few with a civilian address but they were meaningless."

"Someone must've played a hoax." Dong-weon couldn't help guessing that it was Sergeant Eok-su. Hwa-yeung took out a Coca-Cola, chocolate, and Charms from a small suitcase and an opener from her purse to open the bottle of Coke. He looked alternately at her chocolate-colored suitcase and her translucent fingers like crystal, and then suddenly asked her, "How was your recital?"

He had bought the suitcase for her in response to the belt she got him in Geneva. Hwa-yeung who spent three years at Juilliard studying piano took out a small scrapbook from her suitcase, like she had anticipated his question. It contained pictures from the recital and newspaper articles. In a splendid dress, she was gratefully acknowledging the audience's applause from the stage, and she shone too bright for him so he closed the book. He had not known that she was so radiant. All of a sudden, he felt they were miles apart. It was a different kind of distance than the one between him and Eok-su, one that was more painful. What was it? He gulped down the Coca-Cola to shake off the thought.

"They still sell this? The soda pop I get at the store here tastes better," he said with a forced smile to avoid a misunderstanding on her part. But she chose to misconstrue him.

"Your revolutionary mind has become more impeccable," she said sarcastically. He found her too somber response amusing.

"That's too great a compliment for someone who's only a corporal and not a politician. It's just my palate of the present. I simply stated a fact of the present."

"Doctor Park, you have changed. The army is truly remarkable. In such a short time, look what the army has done to great Doctor Park..." Hwa-yeung couldn't finish what she was saying and concluded instead with tears in her eyes. Suddenly Dong-weon felt the urge to torment Hwa-yeung, like Eok-su had done to him. What difference did it make whether his desire to ruthlessly trample on something most precious and fragile was derived from a brutal impulse or the dissolution of his philosophy? He desperately longed for the transcendent solitariness that would overcome him after an appalling destruction.

"That's right. I want to see myself changed. Like you said, the army is remarkable. But remarkable means different things for you and I. I've developed an academic interest in it after my experience in the army. I discovered that it's the best laboratory to delve into the fundamental nature of men. Until now, I did not know what humans were about and only dabbled with politics, which is a regulated affair. The military appeals to me. Could there be another place that could be more dismissive of me? Sergeant Eok-su, who feeds off the furor that he elicits by provoking the fundamental instinct of men, imparts a kind of revelation to me."

He was talking vehemently to himself until he realized Hwa-yeung had her face buried in his chest. He gently cupped her face and whispered, "How did you get yourself a visitor's permit?"

Without moving, she replied, "I told them I was going to see the judicial officer for the military law meeting." She shook the visitor's permit on her bosom. He took out a piece of Charms and muttered to himself, "A can of flies would've been more 'Charming."

Hwa-yeung looked up at him with fear.

In the final sixth week, training in simulated combat and infiltration shooting took place. The senior sergeant, still limping, followed them all the way to the combat training site. The so-called "Applied Crawling Obstacle Course," which, he was in charge of, was the most difficult course. Everyone resorted to any means to avoid it. Dong-weon's knees and elbows were severely skinned in the course of going through it three times. It is only after passing through this Onion Route that men in the military come to understand why there are so many shirkers. But why did Dong-weon have no regrets, penetrating the Onion Route?

Hwa-yeung implored Dong-weon to get himself hospitalized upon completion of the first half of the training, saying the procedure for him to be discharged from the military for reasons of an ailment was set in motion. But that thought did not occur to him once, even when he was rolling in the mud, tightly clutching the M1 rifle—rather, he was hoping to go through the combat training with an earnest heart and mind, as he would in all phases of his life. With a faraway feeling that once training was over his life too would reach an end, he was spearing the scarecrow with the bayonet in the final charge, under an illusion that his self of the past was being pierced.

The night they came back after the first stage of the simulated combat, the senior sergeant called the names of several men, including Dong-weon. Then before the entire squad, he lined them up in a row and told them to unpack the package he passed out to them. Dong-weon knew that his was from Hwa-yeung. There was a bottle of vitamins in it. The recruit next to him was holding a small jar that reeked of hot pepper paste. The senior sergeant waited until everyone had opened their package and told them to take one last look at their things, and then ordered to dump everything in the trash bin, except a notebook or books. Dong-weon threw out the vitamin bottle after stroking the label once. The recruit with the hot pepper paste dithered for a long time, not wanting to give it up, only to drop it at the shouting of the senior sergeant. The hot paste spread on the ground like congealed blood. One could but be awe-struck with the senior sergeant, who had no compunction to trample on the poignant love of a mother. He kicked the broken fragments of the jar and spat out before walking off, "That is called love." The recruits exchanged an incredulous look as if they had just witnessed a man who appeared from subterranean regions.

That night there was a heavy rainstorm, with intermittent lightning. The desolateness of the field, combined with ominous air, created an odd atmosphere. Dong-weon was awakened by an eerie scream. He looked on all four sides and spotted near the rear gate a shadow of a man being rained on. His visage became sharp with the lightning. It was the senior sergeant, who was standing upright in the heavy rain. He was looking up at the sky, like a pitiful sinner awaiting heavenly punishment or perhaps like a solemn saint athirst for revelation. Dong-weon felt shivers run through his whole body, for he was reminded of a monster who had gone mad after feeding on the cold and heartless grunge of base human instinct. Why was he standing in rain in the middle of the night? The thought kept him awake until the sound of the trumpet in the morning.

Two and half years were in store for Dong-weon, who had changed into a new khaki uniform after cleaning the mud off in the stream upon completion of the last infiltration shooting in the sixth week of training. With an envelope of his personnel record on his side, Dong-weon sang the song of the recruits, in line among seven hundred recruits, as they circled the Statue of the Unknown Soldier and walked away to the second half of the training session.

"The sweaty recruits of today will be the stalwart soldiers of the ROK Army tomorrow."

The Seven Shadows

I dreamt I was a butterfly. I then didn't realize I was indeed Chuang Tzu. I suddenly awoke and came back to being myself. I really did not know whether I was a man dreaming I was a butterfly or a butterfly dreaming of being a man. —*Chuang Tzu*

In 1950, the bell chimed from the north for the outsiders. He thought perhaps the sound of the bell would never cease. He also thought that it might snow. The wind swirled up in the air somewhere and scattered the hail as it vanished with the sound of the bell. He lifted the coat collar up to his ear. He was counting the ringing of the bell. First, second, the gap between them felt too tense. Waiting for the third and fourth made him run out of breath.

"The present and the past are the present of the future and the future embraces the past," someone said. Perhaps I am the one who said it, for I thought of it just now. Because it isn't something I had memorized. The street was too dark. All the shops were shut down and from between the crevices of the plank gate, the light from inside spilled out and cast a dim shadow on the asphalt. He couldn't stop halting his steps when all of a sudden he realized a large shadow approached him from very close. A tall building was blocking his way. He looked for an alternative path. But there was no other way. He had already passed this road twice. He felt like walking around the city all night. But this city did not provide enough streets to walk for that long. The wind crawled above the asphalt. It was also swirling at the dark corner of a deserted building, creating a storm of torn paper and tattered clothes. His awareness affixed on them, glimmering like a firefly.

A piece of paper became a pumpkin lantern that wrapped his consciousness. Suddenly a gust of wind struck the asphalt and swept the
piece of paper into air. His consciousness dimmed and his eyes
searched for the paper. On the other side, there was a bulb with a bluish
swarm of light that hung in the darkness like a moon. Where did the
sky disappear in order to have only the darkness remain? The light bulb
was illuminating on a rectangular signboard that read "Mademoiselle"
for the coffee shop that was at the end of a dead alley. He entered the
alley. He wanted to rest a little. He had walked too long. He wanted
to take a break somewhere bright and cozy. This was what he was
thinking. The gate was antique and quaint, as though it was brought
from the ruins of some European royal residence. Is it still open? He
pushed the door open with his side. Because it was bright outside, it
was difficult to tell whether it was lit inside. He turned the doorknob.
It was open. But are guests welcome? As he was about to walk in, a
piece of paper got torn underneath his foot. He almost toppled over
because he had pushed the door with so much force. As a result, the
door made a loud noise as it opened and closed. It seemed almost too
bright inside and it dazzled his eyes. But in contrast to the bright light,
the coffee shop was completely empty. Shielding the light with his left
hand, he looked around, and then paused still. He spotted a woman
who was sitting in the middle of the coffee shop, looking at him. She
was looking at him with a tense and flushed face. Like someone who
was discovered spying on something, I nodded with an awkward smile.
As he approached her, her body turned toward him with her eyes continually scrutinizing him. She seemed like someone he had met once
before or a person he'd been searching for until now. Did she work in
the coffee shop? Perhaps. Or was she a customer? Could be. In any
event, he wasn't sure. He felt like he knew it in the past but he has now
forgotten. Seeing that there was water in the furnace, he implored the
woman in silence if he could sit beside her. Without making a slightest
motion, she kept staring at him. She resembled a small sculptural piece
by a female artist who won a prize at the National Art Competition.

267

He had gone there on the very first day this time. He was the only person at the gallery then. This was what he recalled: a voluptuous face that looked a little plump—leaving quite an impression on him. He looked at the woman's face once more as he groped for the chair with his hand. Her powerful features were outlined against the opposite wall. She was facing the shadow that appeared more pronounced than her relief on the wall that stuck out. He felt the chill and thought he might be coming down with a cold. Quickly, he felt fever running through his body. He was still inebriated. He thought he had gotten over his hangover but he felt tipsy again. I must've drunk a bit too much today. He rested his neck against the back of the chair and examined the shadow on the wall once more. He recalled how he'd seen the catalog of Michelangelo's sculpture yesterday. Ah yes, the statue of Daphne had looked exactly like that. It's indisputable. A powerful blue light is radiating from the wall. Where is it coming from? He bent his neck against the chair and looked up at the ceiling. Two blue florescent light bulbs with a white bulb in-between them were emitting light. The ceiling gave off a blue glow. Soon after, the color turned royal blue. Seven pristine white walls with not a hint of shadow gingerly enveloped him. At the south end, a crystal glass covered the wall like a folding screen. What is behind the crystal glass? His thought was abruptly interrupted by music that diverted his attention and rang through his ear. When he opened his eyes, he could no longer see the shadow of the woman. He turned his head toward the counter. She was carrying two cups on a tray and walking toward him. The name of the music was "Autumn Leaf." It occurred to him for the first time that the woman was dressed in white clothes. Why was she wearing white in the winter? Was it the white bulb and the white wall that made it look that way? Suddenly he realized who this woman was. I know that woman. It is for sure a woman I already know. I think I can remember her name also. He made an effort to remember her name. I must recall her name before she finishes pouring the tea. It is a woman I know too well. This woman must feel resentful toward me. She could be enraged at my feigning not to know her. She is about to add Carnation coffee creamer. I don't favor putting Carnation or sugar in my coffee but the woman, who was about to put Carnation in, stopped short and put the teapot on the tray instead. This woman even knows my personal taste. But as for me, I can't even recall her name. He tried to bring to his mind all the women's names he knew. The music had switched to Richard Strauss's "Death and Transfiguration." Could she be the epileptic woman, brought by the novelist Kim, who joined the Underground Troop Orientation and Training? Was he in the end able to love this woman? Since he captivated his readers with powerful humanism, he could present this woman as a living proof of his art? But is this woman indeed the same woman? Has she gotten over the epilepsy? He couldn't possibly let her be a waitress in a coffee shop. (See "Evacuation of Heungnam" by Kim Dong-ri.)

The woman put the tray back and returned to the table, sitting down where she could see him face-to-face. There was a scoundrel who cavorted around with the money his mentor's daughter earned through prostitution. Come to think of it, I have met him once. I remember the story I'd heard then. The college coed prostitute had to switch her job for not being licensed, and it seems certain that she is working at a coffee shop. So then, could this woman be the novelist's lover? (See "The Incomplete Scene" by Son Chang-seop.) Ah, I feel tipsy. This is like warming liquor at a temple. I must drink the coffee before it gets cold. In conclusion, this is the same person as the woman I know very well. This is a fact. But then why on earth did the woman pretend not to know me when she knows me very well? He bent over to get close to the cup of coffee that was on the far edge. He was about to bend a little farther to reach for the cup when the woman awoke from her reverie and quietly pushed the cup toward him.

"Mr. Shin," she said his name in a dreamy voice.

He couldn't quite hear what the woman said, as his mind was on her hand but he could tell she was saying someone's name. Her hand is as seductive as her face. Her finger engrained with a rice grain form around the round inner edge had on a shiny diamond ring that was perhaps a fossil of her soul. His eyes prodded her to continue. The woman's cheeks were flushed as she was sitting by the furnace. He gave her a wondrous gaze as though she was a statue with the most natural color.

"Chun-ho wouldn't fail to recognize me?"

He was dumbfounded.

"Have you mistaken me for someone else? Miss…"

He raised his head so that the woman could examine him closely. The woman's face instantly turned stiff. Without batting an eyelash, the woman glared at him. But her eyes were too beautiful to contain rage.

"I've lost everything. I am at the moment losing the last bit of everything I have. Please tell me that you're not Chun-ho, at least." Tears welled up in her eyes. The woman was addressing me as Chun-ho. It may be that I am Chun-ho. I do not want to cast a stone at this woman's beautiful heart.

"I am defeated. I've lost to others until now but today I have lost to myself," the woman said. She said, she has lost to someone. You adulterous Mary! What do you mean by that? The tiny ripples of sound, which spread through the room then colliding against the crystal glass, felt soft as the bird feather. The moment when music makes its pause is in the fourth dimension where time and space are one. The hail striking against the window makes the heated flesh quite cold. The woman rose silently and turned on the record player by the counter. Has the woman who turned this way transformed herself into an elf even before "Tales of Vienna Woods" resounded through the room? The long skirt, swaying like the spirit of the wind, is pushed this way by the music. Ah, sacred whore. He raised his head to observe the fluttering of the long skirt against the floor. I must have loved that woman. At least, I would love her. Opening her arms slightly, she came toward him. The dew vanished and a smile glided across her face.

270

"Mr. Shin, what did you call me while teaching me the skating waltz?"

"What do you mean?" He asked, as he rose from the chair.

"You called me Madame Freedom."

"Madame Freedom? Ah, Madame."

Grabbing hold of her hand, he brought it to his lips.

"Madame…"

"What're you doing?"

"Madame."

Yes, that's what I had called her. Or at least say this. This woman was Mrs. Oh Seon-yeung, wife of Professor Jang Tae-yeon. I was the playboy Shin Chun-ho to Mrs. Oh, who had come back from America after completing a degree. I already knew this woman. I am now Shin Chun-ho. I am at present somebody else's me. Tightly embracing Mrs. Oh by her waist, Chun-ho showered kisses on her, scratching her earlobe, as though he wanted to make up for all the hugs he hadn't been able to give her. Shin Chun-ho had learned to kiss in America. They held each other, as though they were tied together, and danced between the chairs.

"I am the victor. Because I couldn't be happier than this."

"Are you happy? Are you happy?"

They reached the counter. Above it read, "Happiest New Year," as written on a red paper. Next to it, like a fish spewing water out of its mouth red-colored water, and foaming, and a Christmas tree with tiny shiny bulbs, silver stars, flowers, and cotton cast a shadow. The dance felt as light as the wind. The shadow with two heads was delineating silent music on the seven walls. He looked at the shadow and turned around. I am Yi Du-shin's monster. But this adulterous fairy appears so happy. Let's spin. Spin. Spin like the record. Then become the wind afterward. Become sound afterward. Become a shadow afterward. My body is melting. His eyes felt dizzy. Countless circles splashed like water and vanished into the ceiling. I feel dazed. Madame is excited. Pitifully. I am also excited. Her breasts are palpitating against my chest. I can't stand it anymore. I must lie down. Lie down. Lie down.

The woman was released from his embrace. She was sitting down on a chair, smoking. He saw how his thoughts were crawling like a spider. Right then, a gate, like the one in a medieval monastery, opened and a brash young man with ungreased hair and with no hat walked in. Other than that he was tall with an aquiline nose, he was someone that could be seen anywhere, anytime. He was wearing a camel hair coat that was quite raggedy, and therefore appeared to be more than thirty years old. His eyes looked tearful. He is walking toward me. We sit side by side.

"Do you have a cigarette?"

"You're smoking one now"

"What? Who's smoking?"

"We're both smoking now. You must be drunk. You want to see how far we can go since there's no curfew?"

"I'm sober now. Anyway, can you find me a position?"

"So you ended up having a row with the principal?"

"Stop talking nonsense. How about a place for me? You think you can do it?"

"Here we are in our place. We'll make our way through pitch dark again tonight."

"Then our stomachs will stop working."

"All that we can keep on doing is walk in the dark. Like that shadow over there."

(See "Nocturnal Path In the Dark" By Kim Seong-han.)

They both turned to look at the wall but were startled by just a single shadow. This person was me. Everyone who comes to me ends up being me. He shuddered, as though the hail outside the window was spreading through his skin. Abruptly, there was a person's voice coming from below the Christmas tree. It was Kim, the novelist, with his coat collar up to his ears, who was talking discreetly with the woman. When he cast an askance glance at the woman who shyly lifted her head, he could tell for certain even from afar that it was the young woman he had brought from Heungnam with her frail body and girly cheeks. He happened to be acquainted with her; hence, he unhesitatingly walked over to sit next to her.

"Hmm, what're you doing here, Han-bin when it's quite late?"

"It's all the same for me wherever it is. These days, I am predisposed toward a bright, cozy, quiet, clean, and spacious place like this. As for yourself, who doesn't sleep but just sits around here at night."

"You've become quite a poet since you lost your job."

"Are you worried about less competition? I dream a lot more as I am nearly starving these days. When I am sitting, gazing at the white wall, I soon become the shadow. The shadow does not have to eat but can live on a dream."

Han-bin gazed at the woman. With a Mona Lisa-like smile, she had on a sad expression, like a clay figure, Niobe. How did William Shakespeare express it?

"Like Niobe, all tears" is what he wrote. The woman was looking at me, with a face of someone who was about to throw a complete fit. I had earlier thought this woman was Madame Freedom. If the novelist Kim finds out, he would be terribly let down. There is a rumor that he is going to divorce his wife and marry this woman. That is something I would like to see happen. Beautiful pagan, Silva, I am enamored with you. (See "The Cross of Savanne" by Kim Dong-ri.) He traced the silhouette of the woman with his dazed eyes only to realize Madame Oh's face overlapped with it and turned his eyes toward the counter, however, the woman was not there, and instead the music played around and around like a wandering spirit. Under the wall on the west side, the coed prostitute's lover, who I did not notice coming in, was scrunched in the chair, lost in either thought or asleep. The vagrant had perhaps been sitting there even before he came. He momentarily thought of getting up to go to him but he didn't want to awaken him; he therefore just watched him from where he was. He was on my mind earlier and here he is. This was what he was thinking as he gazed at his shadow on the wall. Maybe he came to ask for money from his girl-friend. Was she here? He thought of Madame Freedom. He had never seen his girlfriend but he thought Madame Oh might look just like her. That's how you should think. Indeed. This is how something kept pressuring him. Most likely, the girlfriend has returned home. But he is waiting. Next to him, Kim, the novelist's story is flowing like a stream. His voice is clear and like chilly water. The neck surged from the black camel hair coat. He started smoking a cigarette like me. He is not yet aware of me. I will pretend to know him. As he raised himself, the main door opened and a disabled veteran came in, dragging his wooden leg. He walked up to the counter, and after realizing no one was there, he turned around in our direction. Ah, he's become so hag-gard. The blockhead had finally ended up a beggar, having fled the house after getting into a quarrel over a crippled epileptic girl he im-pregnated at the lodging house where three other people leeched off him who wrote grotesque and absurd poetry. It was inevitable. He had been correct to the end. And he would be contemptuous of the poet of bloody poems to the very end. Kim, who was sitting next to me, seemed to recognize him. But then, he is the one who introduced me to him. He must know him better than me. One summer day, I met him for the first time at Hyundae Literature Publishing Company. He had just moved out of the poet's place. He walked toward the bum on the west side. Both of us followed him with our eyes. Standing with his back toward us, he was begging from the bum. He was bending over. His old camel hair coat was as wrinkly as a rag.

Gazing toward the west, he told Kim, "Don't you know the man, sitting over there?"

"No, I don't know him."

"You only seem to know the people you work with. Try to read a lot of books."

"Read a lot of books?"

"He was published in a magazine called *Literature and Art*."

"He's a writer?" (See "The Incomplete Scene" by Son Chang-seop.)

"I'm not sure. All I know is that he's a prostitute's lover."

The two were still looking in his direction.

"Not giving it to you." A whisper like a moan was heard from a woman who was sitting quietly next to them.

They suddenly realized they'd completely forgotten about the woman and turned to look at her who spoke. Word came out of the goldfish-like mouth of the woman. It was amazing and mysterious to see plaster transform itself into a human being. Could this woman's face be like that of the young woman who is afflicted with epilepsy? This woman is suffering from epilepsy. Is this a woman who is pregnant? That could be. This woman has gained vigor now because of the injured veteran. Once he leaves, she'll turn into a plaster statue again. Should we call him and give him money? But then we don't have any money. He's purposely pretending not to know us. He looked at the wall on the west side. There is only one shadow. Someone must've left. One of the two people is gone. A sliver of light collides against the crystal glass. The flesh of wind feels chilly against the body. Music circulates the space like floating heat. It flutters like a flock of sparrows on the ceiling. It was Hector Berlioz's "Symphonie Fantastique." He was looking at the shadow. Suddenly it became all dark. There was a power shortage. He could see nothing. He closed his eyes. He was becoming sober. I drank too much today. Drank too much. Ah, my head aches. With his eyes closed, he yawned, waving his arms. It was all bright. The light from the bulb filled the coffee shop. It was so quiet all around that his ears heard the sound of a conch. There was no one. Everyone had left. Umm, his friends did not even bother to say goodbye. How senseless. Maybe, I was too drunk for them to say anything to me. He got up. His legs felt too weak to walk. His shadow is on the wall. That shadow is me. Who had said, "A shadow is a transparency of much more brilliant light"? It was the painter, Edward Hopper who said it. I am going to like Hopper. His "Nighthawks" is terribly impressive. I am going to hang that painting on this wall. He looked all around, like he was searching for someone to serve him. He sees on the wall a shadow much bigger than his, who is straightening his coat collar. He could see the woman's white clothes on top of the middle table. Madame Oh is scrunched over. She'd been there the whole time. The poor woman. He walked over to Madame Oh Seon-yeong and looks down at her waist. She was feeling terribly vertiginous. Madame Freedom got too excited. Let her rest for a while. He walked to the entrance. The light bulbs were swimming around like goldfish on the Christmas tree. Above the "Happiest New Year," snow had fallen. It's saying one should be the happiest. If I am not very happy this year, then I will not be happy for the rest of the year. It's telling me to be happy. It's snowing on the "Happiest New Year." It must be snowing outside. He walked into the alley, as though blown by the wind. A white piece of paper is flying like a snowflake. Tickling his foot, it was following his footstep. It could be the same paper from earlier. Is it getting back at me for my tromping on it before I entered the coffee shop? He picked up his pace, walking away from the light bulb that seems to be floating in the dark air without any sky. His feet miss a step, as if they belong to someone else. He takes a left step first, and then stands still. He almost fell over when he took two right steps at the same time. Ah, my feet are not in sync. He hears footsteps somewhere on the asphalt. Darkness crawls over the asphalt like a rat. T.S. Eliot wrote, so the darkness shall be light, and the stillness the dancing. He was walking through silence and darkness. A big building had a light on. He raised his coat collar. He heard footsteps from behind him. He turned around. There was no one but his long, elongated shadow. I have left behind my footsteps. There is no one; however, I am not afraid at all. I am approached by a two-story building on both sides that look like they're going to collapse. There was no sign of anyone and he was walking through this dense civilization of forest filled with only buildings built by men. With no one coming after him, he was headed for somewhere, dragging his shadow of destiny. With a sign of being alive, he was carrying this cruel punishment, like a cross, and walking through the street of Golgotha.

This short story is an homage to a select few writers whom I deeply respect. I want to express my gratitude to the following authors for inspiring the characters in my work.

1. Kim Dong-ri, "Evacuation from Heungnam"
2. Kim Seong-han, "Journey in the Dark"
3. Son Chang-seop, Letter written with blood, "The Incomplete Scene"
4. Jeong Bi-seok, "Madame Butterfly"

A Dream of the Gray Zone

Inevitably, the sun rose today. The sunlight seeped mercilessly through the cracks of the manger. Gyeong struggled to get himself out from under the blanket. Like a bug peeling its shell after hibernation, he shook off the blanket and looked around the unfamiliar manger. Everything was precisely in its place. Tooso was still lying in bed, alive, and the statue of Heracles was standing in the bush of hay. It would take some time to get ready to sell it. It is bothersome to ponder over something! He made a tentative decision to sell it no matter what, and then turned his gaze toward where the sunlight fell. There was clay plaster where the bright sunlight shone through the gap between the wooden gate. Suddenly he couldn't control his joy. He crawled on the thicket of hay on the floor, as though he was swimming, and smoothed over the distorted part. He found the bust, particularly troublesome. His long and white fingers trembled as he groped the clay. After totally being absorbed in it for a long time, his eyes got tired and he felt dizzy, and he lay flat on the ground with his arms and legs stretched out. The clay piece, seen from where he was lying, appealed to him to no end. He was dying to show it to someone else.

Still lying down, he shouted, "Hey Tooso, take a look at this!"

It must be Tooso, who awoke and was staring at the clay work of a woman from the bed. Gyeong murmured audibly as he sensed Tooso's eye on the object, "The image of a woman with a potent appeal from a mere chunk of clay. The dialogue of silence between the creator and the created. Ah, it is the merger of God and the universe…" He is so excited that he punches the ground with his fists.

278

"Tooso, why aren't you saying anything? Who's going to celebrate the birth of a god? God has created the universe and hid himself."

"Hey Gyeong, you're too loud for me not to respond. Your problem is exploiting the body with your mind. Do you know why people are left only with a head? That's because they abuse and maltreat their body. It isn't a bug that gnaws at the lung but the mind. Men should all be sued for self-abuse. What's so great about ailing from a lung disease that you have to get so irritable? Irritability is just another term for narcissism and pride. If narcissism is an artistic terminology for irritability, then irritability is a clinical term for narcissism. Ah, I said too much. Let's try to live in quietude."

"Ah, I am speechless. Let's just say I am ill because I am a colonialist who abuses my own body…of course, this colonialist is a tragic figure who exploits his own self…What are you then guilty of, Tooso, for cutting off your neck? You're a bundle of contradictions. If you so value your body then why aren't you nourishing it well? Why are you lying down like Tooso and putting your fine body on strike?"

"What? Say it again."

"Quiet. What will happen to you if I am gone suddenly? I am drained myself. Why don't we go on a joint strike and fast together? You keep deriding art but it is art that has kept our bodies afloat. I might have to sell Heracles, my last remaining piece, today."

"Oh, all right. Stop it. I can't explain it although I could no longer explain myself from the time I joined the People's Army. Why I've become a prisoner of war, how I came to be an anti-Communist prisoner of war, why I am lying here in this bed, like Tooso, the name you gave me. Isn't it faulty to begin with to try to explicate life? We're fated not to reach a conclusion. Why do we need so much learning to live? The modern times are about clarifying ideology. Just think of how many young people have died in the turmoil of this ideology."

"Then let's stop here without reaching a conclusion. What's certain is we live on. I need to go buy some energy for both of us. The first thing is we need to survive. Right? That is the tentative conclusion

I've arrived at here in South Korea. Ha, ha, an interim conclusion, get it?"

Gyeong let out a desperate laughter and put on his jacket to wrap Tooso. The contour of the female figure, which was floating in the sunlight, seemed to almost reach the bed. Tooso felt as though the woman had been with him since a long time ago. He thought it resembled Jeong-mi but was afraid to say anything to Gyeong, who was her brother. He recalled the face of Jeong-mi as he looked at the figure when he heard Gyeong's sonorous voice.

"Tooso, I am taking Tooso that I created out of clay. If Tooso of Heracles was a lifeless human, then are you Tooso full of life? If Heracles is Tooso who nurtures me, then are you Tooso whom I nurture? Is poetry a first-dimensional art; sculpture, second-dimensional; and human beings, third-dimensional? This piece is God's failed work, Myeong-wu, ha, ha, ha. It is a rendezvous with an incomplete work of a human being."

Gyeong took a cheerful step out the door but returned to lightly kiss the clay figure on the forehead.

Myeong-wu lay motionless in bed. He seemed to exist for the hours when he didn't have to think. That could perhaps explain why he was lying there in a manger, like a failed Tooso by a sculptor. One cannot help but think in order to coexist with another person, at least for his time and to think in order to co-inhabit, most likely meant harming someone else. A brand name of "theory" is concocted to cover the avaricious production. The modern times resorts to all kinds of scholarship for self-rationalization. Why does it do that? What is the reason for their claim for justice, as though it were a magic pearl? Satan likes to play an imposter of God. The cruelest criminal will insist on his innocence. It's much quicker and easier to seduce a beautiful thing with a beautiful thing. I grew up amidst the most paradoxical ideologies. Imperialism, colonialism, toadyism—all these different ideologies were disseminated in a microcosmic universe called my mind and gave rise to a cluster of hardened rocks. The growth period of my sensibility

280

happened during the militarist time; my reason was developed under imperialism; the development of my ideology took place during the Communist era. My limbs belong to Hitler and my body to the Wall Street and my mind to Marx. I am like a snake with eight heads. Unless eight of them are cut off all at once, they grow back. Although my legs have been severed, Hitler's ideology will return. The modern times have bequeathed too many ideologies to the young people. There couldn't be another lot who is caught in a greater chaos of ideologies than us. Our bodies have been subject to more than enough abuse by our minds. The modern times have to declare an urgent martial law to prevent an enormous deluge of ideologies. If this state of emergency continues, we cannot make an ordinary decision. I abhor thinking itself. I do not just dislike it; I contemn it. I don't want to see the predicament of theories when I go out today. How would I be able to carry my annihilated body through the street that's inundated with theories on placards in the name of justice? First, let me take this opportunity to get rid of it all. I have left behind too many graves in my past. It is time to pay my respect to them. I have sensed a powerful smell of nuclear fission that seemed like a harbinger to Armageddon, suffered nausea in Heungnam from the odor of the flesh of war, foretelling the end of humanism, and was left bereft of all reason in Geoje Island at the vast human artificiality of Communism. I have always loved poetry and novels. But how I despaired after discovering that literature was but an undernourished cripple in the world of suffocating minds. I cannot forget how Hegel extolled at the drumbeat of Napoleon's March, saying "Weltgeist, Weltgeist." He was gazing, as in a dream, at the clay plaster with sleepy eyes. "Jeong-mi," he called out her name quietly. He loved her. Gyeong became furious at the mention of her name. If it were better not to know, he would not ask him anymore about her. He did not harbor a hope the misfortune that befell everyone could miss her. Have we encountered anything else but misfortune? There can be no other who is less fortunate. It is admirable if Gyeong wants to remain silent for fear of destroying the beautiful dream of our past.

281

I must admit the biggest reason why I don't want to be repatriated is that I am afraid of seeing Jeong-mi. It was past lunchtime when Gyeong came back. He looked suspicious with something red on his head and sure enough, he plopped on Myeong-wu's bed.

"What happened, Gyeong?"

"It's the terror. A lot like yourself!"

Myeong-wu did not want to hear more and closed his eyes. Thinking it was fortunate that he didn't get more seriously hurt, Myeong-wu groped for the injury on Gyeong's head against his chest.

"Tooso, why won't you ask me what happened? I am completely worn-out. Go out and beg for food if you're hungry. You're hungry, right? Why won't you answer?"

"I am. Give me something to eat."

"Yes. A few words will get you something. I want to see you, pleading for food at my knee. Do you think there are freebies in life?"

"I think you need to calm your mind."

"How worthless. Please at least ask where I stashed away Tooso, who I got struck by, ask me anything at the least."

Gyeong must've fallen right asleep.

It was close to evening when he awoke. He took out bread from his jacket for Myeong-wu, and smiled bitterly when he told him he'd already eaten. He let out a dry cough. He had left Tooso in Cha's care and asked Myeong-wu to go out and sell it for him instead. Cha was an art student who had studied with Gyeong in North Korea. Myeong-wu said he would.

"Hey Tooso, looks like we might both end up dying at this rate, so why don't you try going out? After all, you're a disabled veteran and anti-communist prisoner of war, so why don't you take advantage of it? What kind of a world is this where I have to pay a hundred *hwan* for a pencil?"

"You're asking me to go and commit violence?"

"So what of it? They shouldn't be battering a patient of lung disease like myself but criminals who are above the law. Come to think of it, they had to suffer a dismal death."

"Who are you talking about?"

"Didn't you know two anti-communist prisoners of war were shot to death last night? The American soldiers killed these two who were stealing something."

Myeong-wu was igniting a portable cooking stove to cook rice. How absurd, those anti-communist prisoners of war got killed for stealing?

He couldn't help laughing. He had a habit of laughing when he found something hateful. With a smile on his face, he turned his eyes toward the clay plaster of a woman. He could sense his smile on her face as well. Myeong-wu could tell his mind was affixed on the clay piece.

"Gyeong, who does that woman belong to?"

"It's mine. Whose else could it be?"

"Right. Since it's your sister, it must be yours."

"What? If you're going to say rubbish like that, get lost. You're slandering art!"

"What are you talking about? Me, slander art? Jeong-mi cannot be an object of art?"

"What insanity. It's the statue of Antigone that I created out of my own imagination. Do you even know who that is?"

"Your sister must've inspired you greatly in your creation of Antigone. In fact, too much so because it's become a duplicate of your sister."

"Shut up. How dare you talk about her! You've no right."

"Well yes, but why do you despise her when you should be terribly fond of your own sister?"

"Stop it. If you mention her again I'm going to throttle you."

If it were possible, Myeong-wu wanted to cherish their past as it was. He didn't ask anything more.

Next day, Myeong-wu paid Cha a visit. Gyeong told him to take Tooso to a big store or school and forced it upon them. Myeong-wu felt like he was walking much faster on his wooden legs than most people. Gyeong lay in bed, listening to the wooden steps of Myeong-wu walking out the wooden gate, and gave a blank look at the clay plaster.

His head seemed to be making some noise. Myeong-wu felt like he would never be able to rise from the bed. The mind has not just merely exploited the body, but wrecked it. Even if the body like a candle melted away from the bed, the mind would remain alert and forever gaze at the clay plaster. He had left behind much happiness in the north. When the future does not seem to compare with the past, then the past becomes a much more valuable prize. The bleaker the future appears, the more glorious the past becomes. It is evidence of old age if a person thinks he has a glorious past. The weak nations in the present were for the most part countries with a resplendent past. Gyeong regards himself like a migratory bird who has come to the south for the winter. When summer arrives, he'll be heading north. But that can't be the real story. The reason must lie in something more depressing. He must have come to south for the funeral of his rotten body.

He would feel better if he could confess that he loved Jeong-mi. If loving something beautiful is a sin, then is loving something repulsive a good deed? If the unwritten code of ethics defines the realm of what can be loved, then it isn't like he doesn't have some excuse. They were born of different fathers. But this is completely different from his feelings for Jeong-mi. What is wrong with feeling love for something that is beautiful? That's all. There's nothing more to be said if it isn't vulgar to feel jealous of Myeong-wu. An aesthetic concept is always accompanied by a desire to monopolize. He felt his whole body relaxing and tried to fall asleep. He heard the gate open and the wooden legs sliding against the floor. Gyeong instinctively held out his hand, waiting for anything to fall in his hand, but there was nothing. He opened his eyes to see Tooso standing over him.

He demanded with his eyes.

"I broke it."

"What? You broke what?"

"Yes, it was too cramped in the tram."

Myeong-wu seemed terribly let down. Gyeong did not have the heart to admonish him for his face looked pallid.

After a long silence, he said, "Putting that aside, it's a shame to waste my artwork, how're we going to survive now? Should I just die? Not even before trying some medicine? Was I born for the sake of the others? Get me the medicine, you bum! Let me have it. Don't you feel sorry for me? You must feel pity for me. I was going to get 10,000 *hwan* medication to see if I can get better. I desperately want to live. You couldn't care less if you stay or go to heaven but I intend to live. Imagine your lungs rotting. It would drive you mad!"

"I'm listening to you because you're talking but don't expect anything from me for I won't respond."

Myeong-wu crashed on a straw bag on the floor. Gyeong became quiet after saying it was foolish of him to ask a cripple to do anything for him. The afternoon would pass like that. Myeong-wu wished it would get dark quickly. He starts counting the rafters laid out like ribs. He plays a game with numbers. First, what is the date today? Is the number of the rafters even or odd? Can it be divided by three? Is there a historically significant same number? He thinks he could spend the day in a quite meaningful way, just with the numbers. Could there be a more blissful time than when you're sleeping? And a dreamless sleep tops it by far. It is only when you're asleep then you stop thinking about anything. Who could be evil during sleep?

Gyeong was still ill the next day. His eyes were flushed red. He couldn't move at all from the bed. Myeong-wu even helped him with urination. His coughing got more intense. He talked gibberish from time to time.

"Tooso, you have to be my living Tooso to make up for destroying my Tooso. Thank you for not abandoning me, for who would want to be by a patient with lung disease?"

Spring rose from underground like fermenting wine. The smell of earth filled the grey atelier. Gyeong was crouching before a clay piece and refining its form. Tooso had recovered its shape in just a few days. Neither of them went out.

"Cha has become successful. Why does a fake do well while the real is ignored? They say he created Asia's Number One statue. Drat, he'll be sitting on a pile of money now," Gyeong gave a big sigh.

Then he suddenly got up, screaming, "I am the sculptor! Your Rodin is here!"

His eyes reached for the face of Tooso, who was lying still like an object in the dusk then the light vanished from his eyes.

"I have a good idea, my Tooso. Let us try to correct our lifestyle. I am already as ill as can be. I can't go out anymore. I will draw portraits and you can go out and get orders for me. Since you're a war veteran, you'll be welcome. Seek out the governmental Ministers. How about it? I thought of this idea just now from looking at your face."

"Why don't you try making the world's largest statue instead so that you can be as successful as Cha? Besides will a Minister want to have his portrait done by a no name young artist?"

"Why not? You can bring a sample of your portrait that I did and show it to him and say it's by Cha's teacher."

Gyeong sets up his easel with excitement. He adjusts the canvas on it. Myeong-wu is grateful that he is showing great enthusiasm. How despondent it would be if the pale-faced Gyeong remained immoveable like plaster? His actions are pleasing and gratifying, like watching a piglet grow, however, at the same time it is burdensome and demoralizing for it is so transparent.

"Am I capable of that kind of passion? I am not sure. I feel bad that I can't help you. But how could I when I get no any pleasure out of it? Could Jesus carry out charity with no self-fulfillment? Could the Shakyamuni Buddha live the life of an ascetic without any religious rapture? As for me, I don't have it in me. Anyway, I found it revolting, and that's the reason why I destroyed Tooso the other day. As you said,

I want to be your living Tooso. You can use me as your model if you have to—if you don't mind placing me where I can see the figure of the woman. It's too cruel to deprive me of the one last thing remaining to me, that is my desire to love. I wish you'd allow me at least that discretionary choice, as a token of my being alive."

"All right, all right. Your bed will be the stage. It's just right. Your posture is great, as it is."

Gyeong began his drawing. First, he decides to do a sketch. A fuzzy face shows up in the middle of the paper. That is where he has to start. His eyes, as though he is squinting, can only see the face in front of him and nothing else. And everything else becomes a line— his sketchbook shows a gradation of lines.

"I don't care what you do with the money you get from selling my drawing but I want to be in complete control when I am drawing. Irrespective of the purpose of the drawing, I don't want to sacrifice the means for the final goal. Art is not a manufactured product. It is a creation. It's not the artist's responsibility to pay respect to the artwork. An artist is someone who gives birth to his work. That Millet's "The Angelus" is in the possession of the bourgeoisie, and not a farmer, proves it. Because art is but the creation of beauty."

"Hey Sir, listen to me as I can't hold it in. Sounds just like Oscar Wilde. The purpose of art is in creating art and hiding the artist. He must've come up with that because he was so impecunious. They're all the same. What good is beauty for? Isn't it just for the purpose of a décor for the salon of a busybody? There isn't a theory that can't justify anything. If Gorky were to find out his works were prohibited from publication, he'd be wailing in the underworld. Even if you were to get a small sum for a portrait of a pig-faced man, wouldn't you like to say it was for the sacred purpose of getting your clothes and medicine? According to your own principle, there's nothing more sacred than life itself. That's right. But no one knows what it means to live and how to live." Tooso, who became excited, tried to get up in bed.

"Just bear with it."

"I wasn't going to say anything but I can't bear it. Just three phrases a day will suffice. A greeting and a question on eating and things that change. The change would include the weather since that interests us both greatly. As we don't read a newspaper, we won't know about the changes in the world."

Gyeong had pretty much completed his sketch and was examining it.

He said, getting up, "I don't have the colors. Even for a small business like this, one needs the capital."

After much pondering, he asked pleadingly, "Tooso, can you go out and get me some charcoal?"

"I've no way of doing that."

"You good-for-nothing schmuck, why can't you go for it like a madman? You might just as well pillage somewhere. You're an anti-Communist prisoner of war after all. So why don't you beg people to support heroes opposed to Communism? Under the circumstances, it won't hurt to capitalize on your label."

"Sir, you're former nobility. How repulsive it is to witness a depraved nobleman. I am never going to sell the drawing. Why don't you just beg instead? What's the point of begging with a drawing, of all the crazy things? At the least, it'd be better to try to get something from the monumental Cha!"

"I dislike him. You go to him."

"Why do you dislike him? You're probably jealous of him. The nobility are jealous beings."

"Me, jealous? Shut up, you son of a bitch."

Enraged, Gyeong stomped out the door. But he soon came back and was kissing the forehead of the woman figure."

"Get your mouth off it. Ha, ha, ha. You're jealous!" Startled by Myeong-wu's laughter, Gyeong got up suddenly.

"Are you jealous?"

"You told me once the two clay plaster figures should have a rendezvous? I liked what you said."

288

"Ha, ha, ha, you, too, are losing your mind."

Gyeong burst into an uproarious laughter and left. Myeong-wu muttered to himself, "This is the first time we've laughed together. We've become overly excited in the ambience of the grey zone, deluding ourselves."

Tooso took a good nap. Gyeong, who had come back, was whistling and preparing a meal. Gyeong, who sensed Myeong-wu's gaze on him, turned around and grinned at him. His whistling tune sounded familiar.

It was a theme song called "The Song of Siberian Plains" from a movie, which he had sung together with Jeong-mi. Music had not been on his mind for a long time. Myeong-wu recited the words to the tune of Gyeong's whistling. There were a number of passages he couldn't remember. Suddenly he felt an urge to write poetry. He really had not forgotten this song. With this thought, he was looking up at the ceiling for a long time.

"Tooso, your duty has become quite important. Look here," Gyeong said, tapping his buttocks.

"I've got hold of the material."

"I decided to toss that idea. I shall take care of it myself but you will have a purpose in life, too."

"What, what kind of purpose?"

"Can you believe I found Cha?"

"Well, you didn't have much choice."

"Yes, yes. I had no choice. This Cha is on quite friendly terms with the Ministers. Maybe power is what makes an artist."

"How enviable. Why don't you build a statue for one of them? Get a block of stone and sculpt it for one of those bums. There wasn't a dictator who didn't like a statue of himself."

"Stop your nonsense! I would never sculpt a stone for you!"

"Anyway, what's the new purpose in my life?"

"Cha asked me about you. Apparently, the Ministry of Defense plans to publish a memoir by anti-Communist prisoner-of-war and he can have you write it, and wants to know if you'd be interested. I told him of course you would do it. In fact, I told him you could start it right away. He wanted me to bring you in but I asked him if I could go in your place instead. He then said he and I should go together to let them know. So we went there. We met some director who was quite delighted with our news. He even wanted to shake my hand, mistaking me for the author, saying how difficult it must be, apologizing for not helping people like us more. He said he would appreciate a resume from me. Cha, who was standing next to me, explained how I was forcibly drafted into People's Army while I was still enrolled at Kim Il Sung University, and had to undergo all kinds of ordeal, praising me as a patriot who came down to the South, seeking freedom which impressed the director to no end. So I ended up as an anti-Communist prisoner of war. The director continued to ask me where my family was, how I made my living, what it felt like to have found freedom and all these other questions. I felt uneasy that he mistook me for you, so I told him it's actually my friend who'll be writing the book. He seemed disappointed and gave Cha a probing look. So I explained to him, this friend of mine was an officer in People's Army and so on and so forth. The director's response was rather noteworthy. He said, it's the most exceptional case when an outright Communist converts to an out and out liberal, and asked for detailed recounting of the process of the ideological change—that he would provide all the necessary references, hinting his doubt about your level of intelligence by saying the autobiography of recent refugees to the South have been sub-standard, and therefore can't appeal much to the intelligentsia. And lastly, he asked me to come back with you tomorrow, promising all the amenities. I also can't get over how thoughtful he is, for he said if you have family members who still live in the North, he'll allow you to use a pseudonym if you want since we don't know what atrocities they might commit against them."

Gyeong was chattering away and paused to look at Myeong-wu, who was listening without saying a word, which disturbed him.

"Hey Tooso, it's time for me to pick up my paint brush again after ten years. Even if it weren't for an opportunity like this, isn't it worth writing? You've just been given a chance to write your memoir, and you can take this time to reflect on your ideology and your life." Unlike just a while ago, Gyeong spoke in a solemn manner but with a persuasive tone. But Myeong-wu remained silent.

Gyeong became angry. "They say silence is a token of one's right to remain silent. If we could somehow survive as it is, I might acknowledge your refusal. But I am no longer able to go out and you're just lying there. How're we going to live? Foremost, we must live— even you said, the most sacred thing is to live. And I am in total agreement with that. But then we must be able to provide for us. I need the medicine. If you turn this down, I'm going to force you. I have the right to order you." Gyeong glared at him as though he would strike him.

"I refuse," Myeong-wu finally spoke.

"How can you be so shameless as to say that? You pretend to be an adult but you're nothing but a bug that leeches off me. You were too expensive a model. If you can't help me out…" Agitated, Gyeong couldn't continue.

"Is that what you meant by my new purpose in life? Your story, which is the prologue to it, was interesting enough for me to listen to but your irritability got the better of you and I can't help myself getting angry. I tried very hard until now not to feel sorry for you. But then I can't help feeling sorrowful because that has become impossible. How could I be so shameless? It's regrettable that I am not even aware of leeching off you although that is what I am doing. If you insist, I will write it. But I am not sure what it is that I'll write. That is quite risky, and that's the reason why I refuse in advance. Do as you wish."

Both of them became quiet. They ended the talk without reaching a conclusion. Gyeong left early in the morning and returned a little past lunchtime. He carried some kind of a sack. He looked pitiful, not being able to carry it with just one hand. Gyeong threw the sack on the

291

bed and said, "It's paper for you to write on." He then turned around and left again. Myeong pulled the paper closer and rested his head on it as a pillow, gazing up and down at the statue of Antigone. He thought of a conversation they could share. Can I call you, Jeong-mi? She must now be an adult, so he should treat her like one. What should he say next? He couldn't think of anything nice. He thought about it for a long time then, decided to say this.

"Jeong-mi." Surely, is there nothing else he could say? He smiled apologetically to the statue.

"I'm sorry I don't have anything to say," his eyes said.

Then should he listen to Jeong-mi's story? She must have a lot to tell. What would she say first? "You can't imagine how much I missed you." He savors these words. His whole body is tingling. He is intoxicated by his own statement. Yes. Yes. Let's think of what to say next. With bleary eyes, he observes the look on the female statue. What could an expression like that be saying? "I have never forgotten you. Right? That is what you said." He leaned over to the statue as though he was seeking her consent. All the things of the past come back to him in a clamor. His ears sound as loud as a speaker. It is raining. He splashes through the rain without an umbrella. He hears someone calling out to him. "It's raining on you." Jeong-mi holds an umbrella over his head. "Where are you coming from?" "A movie house." "Me too." "I see." He can't find anything else to say. "Ah, really. I cried." He quickly glances at her eyes. "It's a lie." "A clever girl." Are you inspecting the traces of tears? Jeong-mi tells many more stories. He prefers listening to her. He walks, looking at the arm of Jeong-mi, who is holding the umbrella. The fine soft hair is barely visible. A yellow watchband is tightly wrapped around her round arm. Raindrops spread on it.

Myeong-wu had fallen asleep when Gyeong returned. He is straightening a canvas to prepare to draw. He attaches on it a photograph of a sleazy looking gentleman.

The Pigeon and the Coin

I. One Afternoon

It looks like there'll be no rain again today. It is indeed tiring to see a clear blue sky all the time. Come to think of it, there is no seasonal distinction. It is perennially spring. But the reason I long for some rain is that the days are too repetitive here. Today is no different from yesterday and yesterday feels the same as the day before. The people's life in this city resembles the passing years. In addition, look at my life! For close to twenty years, I have left home at eight in the morning for the Peace Park in the central part of the city, in order to look after the countless statues, the trees, and the pond with the fountain and the pigeons, only to return home at five.

I saw these statues more often than my children, and stayed closer to them than any of my acquaintances. There were way too many statues relative to the size of the park. But you can see why. The park keeps a collection of statues of the politicians from around the world, who have formerly been revered as great men if not heroes but then later branded as a rebel or traitor. These include Adolf Hitler from Germany, Tojo of Japan, and Mussolini from Italy, who are the legacies of World War II; and Qasim of Iraq, Ngo Dinh Diem of Vietnam, and Peron of Argentina, products of political upheavals; and Lloyd George of England, the refuse of colonialism. Certainly, one can call the park a site of historical statues. But then, what was the cause of the abrupt rise in the number of the traitorous leaders in the twentieth century?

Just this year, not a statue, but a politician from a country called South Korea in the Far East, sought asylum. He had been the president before the revolution took place. It looked like the aforementioned old man would show up soon as the church clock was striking twelve. Hmm, I was right. There he comes. He hasn't missed a day and made his appearance at twelve noon, every day. Like a statue, he sat on the chair by the pond and left at sunset. He was like a moving statue. Ha, ha, look at the pigeons. They were already flocking around him, knowing the old man would feed them peas and roasted corn. If you lent your ear to the pigeons that goo-goo like a taut and bouncy tennis ball against the racket, in no time you would see their wings dropping from the clear blue sky like a silk cloth. It was spellbinding to watch the gliding pigeons. It was at such a moment that I felt life was worthwhile, and I would regret dying as I wouldn't be able to see them anymore. Of course, it was grimy work to clean their nests. The pigeons were so cute when they gazed at me with their circled eyes that looked like they were drawn with white paint. Ha, the man, who was always following the old man like his shadow, must be a surveillance guard. The old man surely must know it, too. It seemed to me more foreigners visited the park than the people who lived here. That was because many tourists visited this country. That mob of people must be tourists. They looked like Americans. I've lived here so long that I could tell right away where the visitors came from without even hearing them. But then I also studied at the College of Tourism. After graduating from Matterhorn Tourism College, I worked as a tour guide for about a year before I had to quit when I injured myself while rock-climbing.

They're tossing coins in the pond. I need to clean up after the coins. All the coins I scooped up every year must amount to over a thousand US dollars. Even if it were just a penny that each person threw, a one hundred thousand of them would make a thousand dollars. I need to fetch a net. In any event, I cannot fathom why people would want to throw a coin into this pond. It was particularly true of the Americans whose love of money was well known. If an apple were an intrinsic symbol of sin, then money would be the extrinsic one; one is hard pressed to know what the cause of human alienation is but money is what represents our times. I have a hard time believing that these people are contemptuous of money or the look of it—they must simply enjoy throwing it into the clear water. Perhaps because of the pure nature of water. The old man was still gazing at the water. Why doesn't he turn his eyes toward the cool water shooting up to the clear blue sky from the fountain? The splashing water on the marble statue of Paris with a triangular shaped Phrygian hat and holding an apple in his hand. The water was sprouting from the stem of the apple. Paris was surrounded by three goddesses, Hera, Athena, and Aphrodite, who are extending their arms to take possession of the apple.

Hera with eyes blazing like the midday sun, Athena with a bright and cool look of a winter full moon, and Aphrodite with her dazzling figure, like the morning sun that just rose from the horizon of the sea. They are all flawlessly and completely ravishing while each boast of her beauty in a contrasting manner. According to a legend, the three goddesses each offered to give Paris the best thing in the world if she could have the apple that would be presented to the most beautiful woman. Hera promised power and wealth; Athena proposed glory and honor; and Aphrodite, a beautiful woman. These were the things everyone aspired to attain in life and even if one succeeded in getting one of them, one still wouldn't have complete control—in short, they are an object of great longing and a mirage that represented happiness.

But why did Paris choose beauty over power and wisdom? If he were given another chance, might he pick power without hesitation? Didn't that old man and all the men, represented by the statues, choose power? Here, we have a modern Paris who opted for power, gazing in a self-punitive mood at the statue of Paris who pursued beauty and love. The history of humankind perhaps stretches between these two different Parises. Would they have still chosen power, knowing in the end they would be destroyed by it? What could be the reason for their obsession with power? Isn't the history of humanity about banishing Eros by pursuing their goals through power? Power has ousted Eros and taken over the throne of happiness. Power is but a means to obtain happiness and is not synonymous with happiness. But when power takes on the role of happiness, instead of an instrument to achieve happiness, then it could only become self-destructive. Like that statue, the Garden of Eden must be a place where there is only Eros and no authority. Accordingly, the reason why humans were expelled from the Garden of Eden was not that they picked the apple of Eros but an apple of power. Didn't human alienation begin at the moment the power factor entered human society? But if there were no power factor, then wouldn't human civilization have collapsed overnight? Human beings need to have their freedom forever shackled in order for them to achieve complete freedom. Another person is tossing a coin. Why am I becoming more and more reflective? I've now passed the age of fifty; hence, I've entered the phase of retrospection. Or it could be because I am taking a night course on philosophy and political ideology at Geneva University.

Ah, take a look at this coin. It glows like a colorful shell!

"Bonjour, Mesdames and Messieurs."

Hmm, they don't speak French, judging by their startled and uncomfortable demeanors, as though they've been caught doing something inappropriate.

"Bonjour Messieurs."

Ha, who's speaking French?

It's the young blond girl. A young woman, a sophomore, but looking like she has just reached her teens, is looking in my direction with a dazzling smile.

She exudes the kind of vitality that could perhaps condone any mistake or sin. Her bold smile also hints at a budding sexual passion. She seems more like Aphrodite, and not Athena.

"Why are you collecting coins? Why don't you leave them in the pond?"

Her knowledge of French must extend to only greetings.

"Can you speak French, Miss?"

"Non, my name is Alice. We are from America."

"Well, I am sorry. I can just barely make myself understood in English but I will try to speak in English."

Are the others her family?

She's looking at me with abundant curiosity.

"Do you collect them for your government or for yourself?" The man, who appeared to be her father, asked.

"How much do you collect from the pond a year?" The woman, who seemed like the mother, asked next. How could two people who ask entirely different question on the same matter live together?

Their daughter's question was the most pleasing one.

"Just to keep the pond clean. There is no particular reason for it."

With an awkward look, they were about to walk away, as though they had no more questions to ask.

Wait, I have a question.

It is incomprehensible to me as to why the government is amassing the statues of dictators and why people throw coins in the pond.

Are they all doing it for a different reason? Or are they motivated by the same thing? It is obvious that they do it because the pond is beautiful, for I don't see people tossing money on the street.

Is it because all they can find in their reach is a coin at the moment they get the urge to throw something upon seeing a beautiful pond? Would they throw a pebble if that's what they had in their hand?

But there are copious pebbles around the pond. It is unfathomable. Better to just scoop up the coins.

There are coins from Switzerland, Sweden, the U.S.A., and England—all of them with a different emblem.

But they share one thing—they show the face of men who chose power.

I am not sure if coins existed during the Ancient Greek period, however, if there was, then instead of Zeus or Alexander the Great, representing authority, Aphrodite if not Helen of Troy, the symbol of beauty must've been on it.

The sun must be setting, judging by the pigeons flying in a flock. The old man, too, must be thinking the same thing for he is looking up at the sky.

Today is Saturday and since there is no lecture, I am going to get a glass of beer before I go home. The pigeons are circling above the old man. Fly, fly away, as freely as you can.

II. Another Afternoon

Yikes, the pigeons startled me. I must've dozed off in my office.

Why are the pigeons on the roof so loud? The ongoing controversy over pigeons has turned the birds in question clamorous.

The ruckus began after the janitor, who cleaned the pigeon nests, died of an unidentifiable disease. After a medical professor's research result became public, followed by the statement of the Doctors' Association who gave him their full support, the government submitted legislation to the Assembly for the prevention of breeding, and the annihilation of pigeons. According to the statement, pigeons carry diseases like psittacosis and cryptococcus neoformans. Among these, the fungus cryptococcus neoformans is known to be deadly. One can be infected by inhaling the microscopic fungus from a pigeon dropping. Even though there is a vaccination against it called Amphotericin B, as it isn't completely effective, the Doctors' Association made a strong proposal to the government to exterminate the pigeons.

I got the shots myself; nonetheless, just seeing the pigeons put me in an anxious state. Who would have thought the pigeons I loved would become an object of great fear?

It is truly ridiculous to see the pigeons, which made my life worthwhile, become the angel of death. The people who come to the park now run away in panic when they see pigeons. That is probably why the pigeons are in uproar. The government has purportedly proposed to the Assembly two short- and long-term solutions for getting rid of the pigeons. The long-term way entails putting something in their food that will prevent their propagation and the shorter one is to beat them to death while pretending to feed them.

The pigeon rights people issued a statement, demanding the government to withdraw the legislation, while the news has it that some cities have already put it into practice.

It would be best to return them to nature, however, how does one expel them from the world of humans?

Not too long ago, a diplomat pulled out a pigeon from his chest at the UN Assembly to prove to the participants just how much his was a peace-loving country, and it turned out to be a very effective gesture. If he were to do that now, he would result in the opposite, since the symbol of peace has now changed to that of war!

As for the pigeons, they were trusting of people, not knowing that they were being used as the icon of peace. But then, how did they become the symbol of peace?

It can't be because they are more beautiful than other birds or that they are more agreeable toward people, for there are many more beautiful and congenial birds.

Since humans have to designate all things that are harmful to them as being filthy and evil, it isn't surprising that pigeons have been degraded to the status of a wicked creature.

If it is a convention that induced us to view the pigeon as a symbol of beauty and peace, then could it be that we have until now loved the concept of beauty as bestowed on them by convention, instead of their innate beauty?

Can it be that beauty does not exist in the human mind but just the idea of beauty? Several dozen pigeons are spread like a rug around the old man.

He must be feeding them again. He's still doing it even after I've advised against it a number of times.

Does he not believe my warning? I must talk to him again. I've no idea what this will lead him to. I will chase them away with a stick.

The old man looks at me with an angry face.

The pigeons with a variegated palette, like a colorful shell, instantly soar from the ground. Fluttering their wings wildly, as though in preparation to descend again, they storm away like heavy downpour.

Like a child who had been admonished, the old man looked at me vacantly.

"Do you speak English?"

He just nodded. His hair, which was all white, felt almost ghastly.

"You might not have read or heard about the pigeon diseases. As I have told you, recently, the government has ordered that no person should feed pigeons in public places, because it's been discovered that pigeons are agents of fatal diseases."

A spasm flickers over his pale face. Sadness cannot manifest itself in such severe terror, for even I who am second to none when it comes to love of the pigeons, was not that surprised. Am I misguided in thinking a man who was a former president would indeed obey the government order?

It could be a sign of a psychological panic of someone who can't imagine taking orders from someone.

The pigeons are especially unruly today.

Look at that.

The pigeons have taken over all the statues.

I've never seen something like it.

The pigeons hardly ever perched themselves on the statues.

It would be quite troublesome if they pooped on them.

How will I clean them?

It doesn't rain much these days, either. Ah, I am drowsy.

I can't believe it…when I've already taken a catnap.

Could it be because of the little wine I had for lunch?

I think I'll head back to the office and smoke a pipe. Alas, that old man is giving something to the pigeons again.

How troublesome.

I must be adamant with him.

It's almost the sunset and he should be going home.

Ah, he's risen.

I need to tell him before he leaves.

"Sir."

He's walking in the other direction. He must've not seen me.

What's this? I see coins on the ground. There are more than twenty. He must've dropped them.

And I thought he was feeding the pigeons, instead of throwing coins at them.

Is the old man going senile? Ha, look at these coins. His face is engraved on them.

They're coins from Korea.

What kind of bizarre behavior is it to give coins with the engraving of his face to the pigeons? Something that has now become but a useless piece of metal in his own country….the meaninglessness of it must have controlled the lives of at least twenty million people. When power was an accessory like a medallion, the spirit and ideology of men must've been as trivial as a withered leaf.

Instead of exiting the park, the old man is walking toward the statue of Ngo Dinh Diem.

The old man, who is gazing at the statue supported by his cane, appears as an embodiment of futility.

Ah, today is Saturday.

I wish it would rain.

III. Yet Another Afternoon

The clouds are coming together as though it is going to rain for the first time in a while. According to the weather forecast, there will be some rain in the afternoon.

Since there aren't that many visitors, I think I'll read a newspaper. Has the legislation for the pigeons passed? "After a heated debate in the Assembly, it went through with some modification…"

"… All the members of the Assembly conceded that the pigeons must be exterminated in order to eliminate the risk of any threat to people's lives but there were many who objected to the method proposed by the government. The long-term method could result in the extinction of pigeons, while the short-term is too brutal; hence, the people disapprove of it. But the members of the Assembly are well aware that the current issue would not jeopardize their political career, and therefore there was a low turnout, not to mention those leaving early during the debate. Whether or not they were for or against it, they knew it was a bill that their voters would not take a great interest in…"

I haven't the faintest idea as to what the politicians are up to. The government has misled the public in a most deceptive manner, thus making it possible for them to do anything. Since they've deceived people, pretending like they didn't, the government can do anything. No matter what it is, if they can resolve the problem without besmirching their name, then it will be deemed as a good solution. Hence, the government does not have to take any measure.

Heck, I don't know. But isn't this the old man in the newspaper?

What, he's dead? According to his medical certificate of death, he died of a disease from a pigeon?

Let me see.

"The former president of South Korea, Cheol Su Jeong, who sought political asylum after he was overthrown in a coup at the end of last year, died last night at his residence on Peace Avenue. No one was with him at his death. He was known to have caught a cold. According to a medical diagnosis, he was infected with cryptococcus, which is transmitted by pigeons. The Swiss government is presently consulting on the funeral ceremony with the South Korean government."

The clock tower strikes twelve. It is when the old man should be showing up at the pond. I know now why he hasn't come by. The pigeons are by the pond, as always. Many of them have taken over the bench where he used to sit. Are they waiting for the man who died on account of them? Judging by how the fountain water is dropping in a heavy way, rain must already be in the air.

When the pigeons soared with their fluttering wings, the rain began to fall. There might be one more statue in the park. For in our modern times, only the surplus value means anything.

If only all the statues and the pigeons would vanish from this park, and even if there were no more coins tossed in the pond but the statue of Paris remained, holding the honorable apple. As Heinrich von Kleist said, "Wir mussen wieder von Baum der erkenntnis essen, um in den stand der unschuld zuruckzufallen?" [Would we then have to eat of the fruit of the tree of knowledge again to fall back into the state of innocence?"]

Ah, since it's Saturday I think I'll get myself a drink before I go home. Let me turn on the radio to find out what's going on with the old man.

This world is a park that must be tilled so that the birds, animals, and men may grow together.

I hear a chanson from my younger days.

CPSIA information can be obtained
at www.ICGtesting.com
Printed in the USA
FFOW04n1711040318
45438284-46172FF